Joel Chandler Harris

Sister Jane, her friends and acquaintances; a narrative of certain events and episodes transcribed from the papers of the late William Wornum

Joel Chandler Harris

Sister Jane, her friends and acquaintances; a narrative of certain events and episodes transcribed from the papers of the late William Wornum

ISBN/EAN: 9783337185152

Printed in Europe, USA, Canada, Australia, Japan

Cover: Foto ©Andreas Hilbeck / pixelio.de

More available books at **www.hansebooks.com**

SISTER JANE

HER FRIENDS AND ACQUAINTANCES

A NARRATIVE OF CERTAIN EVENTS AND
EPISODES TRANSCRIBED FROM THE PAPERS
OF THE LATE WILLIAM WORNUM

BY

JOEL CHANDLER HARRIS

BOSTON AND NEW YORK
HOUGHTON, MIFFLIN AND COMPANY
The Riverside Press, Cambridge
1896

CONTENTS

SISTER JANE.

I.

A QUIET PLACE.

A QUIET place and the quietest spot in the quiet
place — these were my delight as soon as I discovered that life had no great honors in store for me.
And this discovery was made early. There was
plenty of ambition to urge me on, but the ends it
aimed at were vague and shadowy. I would be
a noted physician, a great lawyer, or a renowned
statesman; I would be a writer of books, an ex-
plorer, a famous soldier. 'T was all a passing
fancy — a dream to breed pleasant recollections
instead of useless regrets. If opportunity came,
I knew it not; it made no noise at my door; there
was no fluttering of wings at my window. No
matter in what direction vague desires carried my
feet, in the end I always sighed for the quiet little
side porch, shaded by a honeysuckle vine, or for
the snug little room behind the porch where so
many years of my life had been spent. They
were the years of my youth and of my young
manhood, and somehow I could not be brought

to believe they had been wasted, though now, at thirty-five, I was nothing more than a modest practitioner in the Superior courts of the Oconee circuit.

The little porch and the cosy room behind it belonged to a rambling one-story house standing sidewise to one of the two main thoroughfares of the village. The building had been a small cottage of three rooms, in which my father dwelt and carried on the tailoring business; but in times of prosperity he had had the forethought to add four more rooms, so that now the house was in the shape of a big U, its head facing the street and its heels stretching toward a garden that ran behind the house and behind the stores that were ranged along the southern angle of the street. The sign, "William Wornum, Tailoring," hung on the corner, next to the little porch for several years after my father's death, but one windy night it came clattering down, and was stored away among the small stock of family relics.

My sister Jane was the only mother I had ever known. She was the eldest by twelve years, and most nobly and fitly did she fulfil the duties that Providence imposed upon her. Whatever sacrifices she was called on to make — and they were many — she made with an eagerness that went beyond anything of the kind I have ever seen, or ever expect to see, in this world. Our father had had his little weaknesses — weaknesses that are sometimes a sore trial to a sensitive and loving heart, but they were all condoned and freely forgiven. In this way sister Jane became grounded in experience, so far as the demands of an exacting household go, long before she had grown even to young womanhood. It is perhaps due to the doubts, perplexities, and responsibilities that shut her out from the ordinary pleasures and enjoyments that should belong to the life of a young girl, that her tongue and temper were somewhat sharper than they should have been. To those who knew her those characteristics were but the twang and flavor that told of the kindest heart and openest hand that ever woman had.

My father died when both his son and daughter were old enough to face the small world of the village in which they were born and reared. They buried his weaknesses with him, and thanked heaven that his failings had taken no serious turn. For he was faithful to his children, industrious, economical, and, besides the house that he had bought and paid for, and to which he had made additions from time to time, he left a competence, which, though modest, was sufficient to make my sister comfortable the rest of her days. Moreover, he had taken pains at odd hours to teach her how to make men's clothing, and such was her aptitude that, when he died, she might have kept up the tailoring business with as much success as, or even more than, our father had won. But she contented herself with obliging only the best of village customers, or those whom (according to some mysterious rule of her own) she had conceived a liking for; for I have known her to sit late at night over a frock-coat for some one who had no thought of paying even the smallest part of his debts: on the other hand, I have seen her refuse, with a vigor almost impolite, to sew for those who came with money in their hands.

On these occasions I said nothing, for I knew that her reasons, however illogical they might be, were good and sufficient from her point of view. Logic becomes almost impertinent when it begins to strut before the door of views and beliefs that are unchangeable. So far as sister Jane was concerned, the whole village knew of her peculiarities, her strong will, her firm opinions, and the sharp flavor she conveyed into the most ordinary discussions; the whole village knew of these, but only a few knew how thin and frail a partition stood fluttering between the shrewd tongue and the tender heart. None knew as I knew — none could know.

Verging on years of age my sister was still plain Jane Wornum. Her hair was turning gray, but her eye was as bright and her step as firm as ever. Her features were strong, but not coarse. She had the heartiest laugh ever heard, when in the humor, but it was not wasted on everything that came to her ears or fell under her observation. She had a firm chin, and lips that were ready at all times and under all circumstances to frame the decisive word. She never had an affair of the heart, such as we read of in books. I used to say to myself that if she had caught Master Cupid hiding in her rose bed, she would have run him off the place at the point of the broomstick, much as if he were a stray cat. She expressed supreme contempt for men who had no knack of getting along in the world, but secretly pitied them.

As for myself — well, I am not writing my own history. My place is in the background of the events and episodes that are to be mentioned in this chronicle. It may be said of them here that they attracted my attention without seriously disturbing my repose. There is much that is pretentious in the altitude that is called philosophical; but it is a fact well attested that the birds sing as sweetly, the roses flare forth as proudly, and the wind that steals through the honeysuckle vine is as odorous after a moral cataclysm or a physical disturbance as they were before.

My own little porch was my point of view in pleasant weather, and when the rain or the cold season came, there was the window that opened on the porch and looked beyond it. This arrangement did not face the street, but lay sidewise to it. You opened a wicket gate, went forward five paces, mounted three small steps that led to the porch, turned sharply to the right, and there you found yourself at the door of the room, which was always open in pleasant weather until long after

the nine o'clock bell had rung. Beyond the door
was the window I have spoken of, and a few
inches farther the honeysuckle vine hung its fragrant curtain. The porch was so small that there
was room only for a wooden seat that was built
along the side, and for the cushioned rocker in
which I sat. Sometimes during the summer evenings the seat was occupied by my sister Jane,
but for the most part my sole companion was
Tommy Tinkins, the large yellow house cat, who
was either too old or too lazy to waste his nights
in prowling. The only occasion on which he displayed anything like energy was when his domain
was invaded by some strange Tommy. At such
times Tinkins would slip quietly from the wooden
seat and rush into the garden, from which presently would issue a series of blood-curdling yowls.
Then, after escorting the intruder from the premises at race-course speed, Tinkins would return
soberly to his place on the bench and proceed to
celebrate his victory by washing his face. But
as a rule, in spite of this occasional display of
energy, Tommy Tinkins was buried too deep in
his own reflections after nightfall to pay much
attention to passing events.

The old cat, sleek and lazy, was a great favorite with my sister Jane. She had rescued him
from a crowd of negro children when he was
a small and disreputable-looking kitten, and he
repaid the care and attention by an affection that
was as complete and as touching as anything of

the kind I have ever seen. He had a peculiarity which, although it is possessed by some animals, was developed in Tommy Tinkins to a degree that was amazing. He was an infallible reader of human character. He knew instinctively whether a person had mean traits or good ones. Sister Jane found out this gift long before I did. She knew by the action of the cat whether to trust or distrust an acquaintance or a stranger; and it finally came to be a matter of common observation with both of us. Whether we would or no, the Tommy Tinkins test was applied to all who crossed our threshold — to old and young, to familiars as well as strangers. If the cat showed a disposition to run away, or took refuge under sister Jane's chair, the person who was the cause of this disturbance was not to be taken into our confidence or trusted in any way. On the other hand, if Tommy Tinkins made friendly advances and betrayed his satisfaction by walking around, rubbing against chair legs and purring complacently, the person who was the source of the manifestations was entirely worthy of confidence.

In this way, at one time and another, we came to know all our neighbors and acquaintances as well as they knew themselves, and when some one in the village went wrong it was a common thing for sister Jane to exclaim, with an appearance almost of satisfaction: "What did Tommy Tinkins tell you?" One by one the cat's predictions (if they may be so called) came true; but there was one exception which I felt and said must, in the nature of things, remain an exception. It was the case of our good friend, Colonel Cephas Bullard, who, although he lived at the far end of the block, was our nearest neighbor. Our home, as I may have stated before, was next to the stores and shops that ran along the southern side of the square, facing the stuccoed courthouse, and fronting the thoroughfare that ran at right angles with our own. On the northern corner of the square stood Colonel Bullard's fine mansion, and between our humble home and his lay the large garden. The greater part of this garden belonged to Colonel Cephas, but there was no fence or other boundary-mark to show where his land began and ours ended. He knew and we knew that he had so many feet of land; we knew and he knew that we had so many feet; and, as there was no room for contention, so there was no need of a boundary-mark. We planted asparagus and bachelor's buttons on his ground, and he had planted his favorite coleworts and made a bed of violets on ours. It was the hand of his daughter Mary that planted and tended the violets; but no matter; I have mentioned the fact only to show the relations between the two families. When people use each other's land indiscriminately they must be on the best of terms. "Neighborly dealing makes neighborly feeling," as I have heard sister Jane say a hundred times.

But where Colonel Bullard was concerned, neither neighborly feeling nor neighborly dealing had any influence on Tommy Tinkins, the cat. From the days of his innocent kittenhood (when he chased his shadow in the sunshine, or his tail in the shade) to the years of his sober maturity, the appearance of Colonel Bullard in the garden or on the sidewalk was the signal for Tommy Tinkins to disappear under the house or under the bed. And he only ventured forth from his hiding place with extreme caution, looking carefully about in all directions, and holding himself ready to vanish if he heard the colonel's voice.

I had small patience with Tommy Tinkins's panic-stricken behavior in so far as it concerned Colonel Bullard, and I often chided the cat in round terms for running away from so amiable a gentleman and so friendly a neighbor. But sister Jane said nothing, and my chiding had no effect on Tommy Tinkins, who was repose itself until the colonel's measured tread sounded on the graveled garden-walk. When that came to his ears he seemed to be charged with all the energy that fear can give rise to. In spite of this Colonel Cephas Bullard was one of the most affable of men. I have frequently heard sister Jane say that she wouldn't be afraid to meet the colonel's ghost at the dead hour of night. "It couldn't help being polite and nice," she explained.

And, indeed, if actions count for anything, the colonel merited the respect and esteem that he had won in the community and all the praise that his name suggested. It is easy to be affable; society has never invented a thinner mask than the formal politeness it has given currency to; but Colonel Cephas Bullard was something more than affable. His politeness had the old-time flavor of sincerity. If his manner sometimes had the appearance of condescension, it was because of his natural dignity. His benevolence was well known, and his charity was so gentle that his voice always sank to a whisper when he protested against the attacks that anonymous gossip frequently makes on our neighbors and acquaintances. He was deeply religious; he was a class-leader in his church, superintendent of the Sunday-school, and, in that capacity, frequently delivered the most elevated and profitable lectures to the young people. He had a fine baritone voice, which he employed with fine effect in leading the congregational singing; and rumor went that in his young days he was proficient with both the violin and the flute, but these he had laid wholly aside on account of their worldly use and reputation.. I never passed him on the street, nor did I ever know him to go by our door, but he was humming a sacred tune. Even between the pauses of conversation, I have heard him hum a bar or two from some air to be found in the "Golden Harp," and I used to say to myself, "Truly, here is a man who has set his piety to sweet melodies."

The personal appearance of Colonel Cephas Bullard fitted his character like a glove. He was tall and straight as a soldier. His hair, which had been auburn, had turned to what sister Jane called "a pepper and salt" color. He was not portly, neither was he lean. Over his prominent nose he wore spectacles. Behind his glasses (I never saw them otherwise except on one memorable occasion), his eyes were of a cold gray color. His face, which was smooth and round enough to be handsome, wore a complacent smile, as was becoming to a man who was at peace with his Maker and all the world. His title of colonel was not a military one, although, as I have said, he had the stature and carriage of a soldier. It was purely a title of respect, a mark of the esteem in which he was held by his friends and neighbors, a tribute to his moral and business qualities. True, it was a feeble mark of respect, and a very small tribute, but it seemed to please him. He accepted it, and adorned it. And truly he had the appearance of a real colonel as he walked along the street wearing his broadcloth suit, his Marseilles waistcoat, his black satin stock, flourishing his gold-headed cane and bowing kindly to all whom he chanced to meet.

His wife was a pale little woman, who rarely went out of the house. Sometimes, when twilight had taken possession of the garden, she would glide swiftly through the shrubbery, and have a few minutes' friendly chat with sister Jane. But she usually talked in a tone of voice hardly lifted above a whisper, as if she were afraid some one would recognize her voice, and she always seemed to be in a hurry to run home before any one had missed her. One peculiarity she had was that she either laid one hand on sister Jane's arm while talking, or touched it lightly with her forefinger whenever she desired to emphasize a word. She had a beautiful hand and wore some very large and showy jewels on her fingers. She must have been a very beautiful girl, but now there was a weary look in her eyes that told either of invalidism or trouble; and yet there was something about her that suggested friskiness. 'T was either a trick of the month or a turn of the hand. Whether from choice or no, she lived a secluded life; but on rare occasions she was to be seen riding out in the family carriage, and when the Methodists held a meeting, she was to be seen at church, though I have heard it said she was a Presbyterian at heart.

When my reflections ran in the direction of the colonel's wife I invariably found myself wrangling with the problem she presented. The more so as Tommy Tinkins afforded no clew whatever to her character. The cat neither ran away at the sound of her voice, nor made any display of satisfaction when she came. Sister Jane was as much puzzled as I was, for she always called her "That poor creature," and I have noticed that when one woman fails to understand another with whom she is on friendly terms, she ends by pitying her.

There was another member of Colonel Bullard's

family that was more interesting than either the colonel or his wife — their daughter Mary. She was a study for those who love beauty for its own sake, as well as for the more serious-minded who watch with expectant eyes the slow but sure unfolding of the flower of womanhood. I had dandled Mary on my knee when she was a child, and twenty times a day she used to run to me for aid, for advice in her troubles, or for comfort in her childish sorrows. Until she was twelve, and I had turned twenty, we were companions and playmates, and then she went away to reap such advantages as are to be found in a young ladies' seminary. When she returned to spend her first vacation she was still, in a sense, the same girl who had gone away six months before. But she was never the same after that. She was friendly, even cordial, but there was a difference. We had no more romps among the rose bushes; indeed, it would have been unseemly for an old fellow to be seen capering around; nevertheless I felt somewhat hurt at the various manifestations of indifference that the young lady took no pains to conceal. Being sensitive and somewhat diffident where the women are concerned, I drew myself within my shell, took "Urn Burial" from the book case, and mentally bade farewell to the child that had given place to a beautiful young girl.

Then came a year or two at some finishing school in Philadelphia, and, behold! instead of the beautiful young girl who had gone away, there returned to the village and her friends a more beautiful young woman. To me, whose memory had been so steadfastly fixed on the girl, the woman was a dazzling revelation. A miracle had been performed and nature had made no fuss over it. I watched this young woman, who had sprung from the germ of the girl I had known, with emotions impossible to describe. But chief among them all were astonishment and a bewildering sense of loss — a sense of having been cheated out of some precious possession. Strange to say, this young woman, who had returned to dazzle us all, made no show of pride or affectation. She was as simple and as natural as she had been when a little girl; she brought back with her none of those airs that seem to stick, like cockle - burrs on a sheep, to many young ladies who have had the advantages of the finishing schools; and, withal, she had a natural dignity of manner that made a charming foil for her frankness.

Her attitude toward me also underwent a kaleidoscopic change. Where she had been cool and indifferent she was now friendly, and she discovered to me by many pleasant allusions that she had not forgotten the time when she poured all her childish troubles in my ear. But the day had passed when I found myself at ease in her presence, and when she ran in to see sister Jane, which she never failed to do at least once a day, I was happy if I chanced to be in my room or in the

little porch, where, unembarrassed, I might listen
to the clear tones of her voice and picture to
myself each little gesture she might be making;
how she was holding her head, and when she was
smiling. In her presence I felt awkward, old,
and unhappy. She carried with her an atmosphere so entirely different from that in which I
had always moved — she imparted so much light,
and warmth, and color to our dull and prosy surroundings — that I was always glad to return to
the solitude that gave me a world of my own,
where, as the humor chanced to seize me, I might
be president, dictator, or emperor, and where all
the treasures of the world were mine if I might
choose to appropriate them. I was more than
content if, concealed by the porch and the fragrant honeysuckle screen, I might watch her moving about the garden, making the flowers more
precious by her presence, or romping with her
little brother, a toddler of uncertain age — her
movements as graceful as if she were borne along
on wings. Many and many a time I have seen
her press a rose to her lips and blush at some new
thought that blossomed in her innocent breast.

And so the days went by, she radiant and happy
and making all things lovelier by her happiness,
sister Jane busy and critical, and I reasonably
comfortable, but somewhat disturbed by a vague
uneasiness that had never troubled me before.

II.

LET it not be supposed that my sister Jane and myself led a lonely life. We had more company than we sometimes found comfortable, and might easily have enlarged the list of those who seemed to find a pleasure in visiting us. But, for the most part, we were sufficient to ourselves — sister Jane with her sewing and I with my ruminations and reflections. We cared neither for the small gossip of the town nor for the large questions of politics, being content to feel that the gossip was unprofitable, and that the great questions would settle themselves sooner or later. Howbeit, we had one caller who was as persistent as the seasons themselves. This was Mrs. Sally Beshears. Hot or cold, wet or dry, we knew when evening fell and the hands of the old brass time-piece began to turn to eight o'clock, that Mrs. Beshears would come limping along the sidewalk and lift the latch of the gate that opened near the porch.

When the latch clicked on the stroke of eight, sister Jane would say, "There's Sally. I hope she won't want me to give her nigger boy another biscuit to-night." Then a light rap would fall on the outer door, and Mrs. Beshears would come in leaning on her walking-stick, saying, "I believe in my soul you 've all gone to bed." Then as she opened the inner door, "Why, no, you have n't, but it 's a wonder." And in Mrs. Beshears would walk, followed by the small negro boy, who trotted after her wherever she went.

"Come in, Sally, and take off your things and stay a while," sister Jane would say. "Make that nigger fetch you a chair — I 've got this pressboard on my lap, or I 'd fetch it myself."

It was the same thing over and over again evening after evening, and yet somehow we never tired of Mrs. Beshears. She was older than my sister, being above sixty, and but for the fact that there was a halt in her walk, the result of a fall, she was as pert as a woman of forty. She had a keen eye, a resolute mind and sharp tongue, as many people knew. Observation had done for her what the best education fails to do for the great majority of mankind. Her knowledge and her humor gave a spice to her conversation that I can remember and appreciate, but cannot hope to faithfully report. She was a woman of some property, which was held in common by her and two older sisters, — Miss Polly and Miss Becky Pike, — one seventy-five and the other eighty. Their place, indeed, was something of a plantation, covering above five hundred acres of good land, just outside the corporate limits of the village. In addition to this they owned twenty-five or

thirty sleek-looking negroes, who, according to
report, worked when in the humor and played
when they pleased. The dwelling-house and all
the out-houses were relics of the days when the
country round about was a wilderness. They were
substantial, but were built of logs, and the chimneys were made of rough stones and mud. The
hand of time that tumbles all material things
about, had touched these old chimneys with some
severity. The rains had eaten away the mud in
the parts that were exposed to the weather, and
they presented a jagged and grinning front to the
passer-by. All things about the place were of the
most primitive character, so that they gave rise
to solemn thoughts, such as haunt and sometimes
overwhelm us in old graveyards, telling us of the
brevity of life and the mutations of time.

Two Sundays in the year, and sometimes on
the Fourth of July, my sister Jane and myself
were in the habit of spending the day with Mrs.
Beshears and her two sisters, Miss Polly and Miss
Becky. These old ladies were spinsters, but the
energy and individuality of the family were cen-
tered in Mrs. Beshears, and Miss Polly and Miss
Becky remained in such seclusion that their names
and even their existence had been forgotten by
many people to whom they had once been known.
Miss Polly was tall and fat, and Miss Becky was
tall and lean. Their hands trembled so that a
negro boy had to light their pipes for them. But
they were both good-humored and seemed to be

sincerely glad when we went to see them. Their dining-room was apart from the dwelling, and I never had dinner there but the chief feature of the meal was roast goose, over which sister Jane said grace with unction.

Sometimes Mrs. Beshears would ask me to walk with her about the place to look at the fowls, the pigs and the horses. "Folks ask me why I don't have the place fixed up," she would say; "but who on earth shall I fix it up for? Pap started to fix it up, but he took sick and died; and then Uriah," (her husband) "he begun to fix it up, and *he* took sick and died. It's the living truth. Now, whoever wants to fix it up is welcome to try it. I'm old and ugly, but I don't want to be put on my cooling-board on account of driving a new set of nails in the front palings." I could but acknowledge that there was a good deal of truth at the bottom of Mrs. Beshears's remark, leaving the omen altogether out of view. Why should these old people go to the trouble of putting up new fences and new gates? They had no heirs and cared nothing about appearances. Moreover the Cherokee rose was rapidly covering the broken-down fences with its glistening green shield and its fragrant white flowers.

While it was in the nature of a holiday excursion for sister Jane and myself to visit Mrs. Beshears, yet it was not pleasing to sit and listen to the wandering and random talk of the two old women — Miss Polly and Miss Becky — now verging on, if they had not already entered, their second childhood. There is a certain charm to be found in the melancholy that is pressed home upon you in many of the pages of Sir Thomas Browne. To read of the futility of fame and reputation, and to take it home to your reflections in the solitude of your room, are matters that appeal to the imagination. But to be brought face to face with the futility of life itself in the presence of these old ladies left no room or excuse for the performance of the imagination. Here mortality, with its own hands, had torn off the thin mask under which it parades, showing the grim and unseasonable reality. I doubt not the lesson would be wholesome to those who have not the knack of reflection; but, as for me, I preferred to be melancholy in my own way and at my own pleasure.

Sister Jane, who was more practical, perhaps, seemed to take pleasure in talking to Miss Polly and Miss Becky, and the conversation sometimes took such strange terms that I felt in my bones she was experimenting with their faculties, seeing how far they had fallen into decay. Frequently they would fall to laughing at nothing, and continue in the fit until the tears ran from their eyes. On one occasion Miss Polly suddenly remarked: —

"La! have n't you heard? Sally's about to git married."

I expected an explosion from Mrs. Beshears, but she only said, "Yes, Jane, and they are both as jealous as they can be."

"La! no, we ain't neither," exclaimed Miss Becky, bridling. "You may marry who you please, but narry thrip of our money do you git."

"It's as much mine as it is yours," remarked Miss Polly.

"I don't care if 't is," said Miss Becky; "*she* won't git a thrip of it when she comes a-bringin' a young feller around here a-honeyin' and a-huggin'."

"Do you reckon she's really fixing to get married?" Sister Jane asked, pretending to be very serious.

"If she ain't," cried Miss Becky, "what under the sun is she trapsein' and trollopin' up town for every night the Lord sends?"

"Why, she comes to see me," replied sister, as much amazed as amused.

Here Miss Becky transferred her pipe from her mouth to her trembling hands, closed her eyes, and began to nod her head emphatically. "Sally may tell you that," she said, solemnly, "and you may believe it; but she can't fool us, and she won't git narry thrip of our money."

"Much money you've got!" exclaimed Mrs. Beshears, with kindly sarcasm.

"She thinks she's mighty smart," said Miss Becky, reaching over and touching Miss Polly on the knee.

"Don't she, though!" exclaimed Miss Polly.

I was curious to know how Mrs. Beshears would compose this senseless quarrel; but 't was the easiest thing in the world. She placed her hands over her face, sighed deeply, and turned to sister Jane with an air too solemn to be duplicated on the stage.

"Jane," said she, "there's a vacant room at your house. It's not a big room, but it's big enough for me. I'll just send my things up there and come along myself after supper. As I'm not wanted here, I'll go with you. We'll see, then, if money will wake the niggers in the morning, and make Polly's and Becky's coffee and sweeten it. There's too much money here for me."

By this time Miss Polly and Miss Becky were sobbing, and if their tears had meant anything more than the tears of children mean, I should have laid the matter up against Mrs. Beshears in my mind; but she soothed them at once, and in a minute they were laughing as blithely as they had been crying bitterly, and with no more excuse in one case than in the other. So that when sister Jane and myself bade them good-bye on that particular occasion, I carried away a better opinion of Mrs. Beshears than I had ever had before. My first impressions of her, formed long ago, were not of the best. Out of sight and hearing of her two sisters she had a hectoring way, and I think it was her natural way. Her voice was harsh, and she had a way of saying things that left a sting. But, after the incident I have related, I was no longer surprised that Tommy Tinkins, the cat, should be so anxious to run and greet her when she came, his tail carried as erect as a battle-flag, and his back curved upward to meet the hand that was always ready to give him a friendly touch. I knew, too, that when she had put her aged and decrepit children to bed the impulse to escape from her surroundings, by visiting sister Jane, was more than she could resist; and so it happened that her company came to be as agreeable to me at last as it had been to sister Jane from the first.

She always called me William, having known me from a child, and seemed to keep a watchful eye on my moods, for when, as sometimes happened, I remained in the room after she came, instead of going to my own, she would say at precisely the right moment: "Well, William, you can go and do your moping by yourself. Jane and I have some matters that we want to talk about." This took from me the excuse of politeness and sent me off whether or no, for which I was duly grateful. Many a time I have listened and waited for sister Jane and Mrs. Beshears to lower their voices in talking over these confidential "matters." But they kept right on in the old familiar strain, and in this way I found that Mrs. Beshears's confidential "matters" were purely mythical, invented for the purpose of giving me an excuse to return to my books or my reflections, as whim or fancy might lead me.

I could sit in my room or on the little porch and hear every word the two old friends said, and was under no necessity of affecting an interest I did not feel. Howbeit, a great many things they said were sufficiently interesting as well as amusing. On one occasion I heard a conversation between Mrs. Beshears and sister Jane that gave me a feeling of uneasiness I could not account for.

"Mary Bullard hollered ' howdye ' at me as I limped by," remarked Mrs. Beshears. "When is she going to git married? 'T won't be long, I reckon."

"The Lord knows. I hope she 'll get a good husband. You know how it is — good woman, shiftless man; good man, tacky woman. Providence has paired them off that way, I reckon."

"It looks so," said Mrs. Beshears. "Why don't " — if she mentioned a name it never reached my ears; it struck me afterwards that she wrote it in the air with her forefinger. "Why don't — drop his wing and cut the double-shuffle around her? I lay that would fetch her."

There was a long pause during which I imagined that sister Jane was dampening the seams of a trouser leg, preparatory to pressing them, an operation which she always performed in silence. Presently she remarked, in a lower tone of voice than usual: —

"Why, bless your soul, child, he would n't do at all. He has n't got the chink. He don't belong to the big-bugs."

"And what if he don't? What if he don't?" asked Mrs. Beshears with a touch of indignation in her tones. "Ain't he every bit and grain as good as any of the Bullards that the Lord ever let live on the earth?" Sister Jane said nothing; she was probably testing the warmth of her tailor's goose; and Mrs. Beshears went on, her voice becoming more strained and tense: "If you talk and feel that way, Jane Wornum, don't never up and tell me that you know Cephas Bullard, because you don't. But old Sally Beshears knows him through and through, up and down. Why, le' me tell you, Jane Wornum! Cephas Bullard"—

"Sh-sh-h!" whispered sister Jane, loud enough for me to hear. She probably jerked her thumb or waved her hand in my direction.

"I don't care," cried Mrs. Beshears, louder than ever. "I don't care who hears me, not if it's old Cephas himself. The next time you see him jest ask him where his brother is and what has become of his brother's property; and if he wants to know how come you to ask him, jest up and tell him that old Sal Beshears, cross-eyed and crippled, told you to ask him. And if that don't make him flinch, it'll be because the Old Boy's done took possession of him."

Sister Jane made some comment in a tone of voice too low for me to hear, though I was listening with all my ears.

"Oh, I don't doubt that," replied Mrs. Beshears. "Mary'd be an angel if this climate suited angels. She's as good as she's handsome, and that's more 'n you can say for the common

run of gals. Why, she's just as different from
old Cephas as she is from old Jonce Ashfield."

This was putting it pretty strong, for old Jonce
was noted far and wide as an irredeemable toss-
pot. A long silence followed this surprising remark — a silence that was finally broken by Mrs.
Beshears.

"I believe in my soul Mary's in love with him,"
she said.

"With ——?" asked sister Jane. Could it be
possible that she, too, wrote the name in the
empty air with her forefinger? If so much as a
murmur of it had passed her lips it would have
come to my ears.

"Yes," replied Mrs. Beshears. "She came to
my house the other day, with her little brother,
hunting sweet-gum, and I teased her about him.
She blushed might'ly and looked as purty as a
peach. She looked at me much as if she'd say,
'Hey, old lady! how'd you find out my secret?'
And I ups and says, says I, 'Ah, honey, innocence don't know how to hide its heart from eyes
that are old and sharp.'"

"Well, I hope it ain't so," remarked sister
Jane, after a while.

"Why?" asked Mrs. Beshears, plumply.

"Because" — Here sister Jane paused and got
no further in her explanation.

"Fudge! fiddlesticks!" cried Mrs. Beshears.
"A whole quintillion of becauses ain't as big as
a grain of sand in a matter of that kind."

I heard no more of that conversation, for I went out into the garden bare-headed and walked, for an hour up and down trying to get rid of a feeling of strange uneasiness that possessed me, and for which I could not account. It was a feeling as near to fear as any I ever had, and there was a queer buzzing in my head. After walking for an hour, I felt better, and then I went into my room and went to bed, promising myself to be careful of my diet hereafter.

Next morning, the first thing that popped into my mind was the conversation of the night before, and at breakfast I tried to broach the subject.

"Sister Jane," said I, "did n't Mrs. Beshears say last night that Mary Bullard was to be married shortly?"

"If she did, I did n't hear her," replied sister Jane, decisively.

"But I 'm sure," I persisted, "that I heard her say Mary is in love with some one."

"No, Sally did n't say that," sister Jane answered. "She said she thought Mary was in love."

"Who is the happy man?" I asked.

"You, I reckon," said sister Jane, giving Tommy Tinkins a morsel of meat.

I felt the blood mount to my face, and then rise upward to the very roots of my hair. "Nonsense! Why, you must take me for a nincompoop. I 'm no child for you to play with."

At this, sister Jane fell to laughing and continued until she was on the verge of convulsions, and I was painfully conscious that my red face and my efforts to maintain my dignity were the cause of her merriment.

"Don't you know," she remarked when she could control her voice, "that I 'm not going to blab everything Sally Beshears tells me?"

Thereupon, I rose from the table and strode out of the room feeling very much offended. But I paused at the door long enough to hear sister Jane say to Tommy Tinkins.

"Well, well, well! If men ain't fools, I wish somebody 'd show me a sure enough one!"

But all these things passed out of my mind as the season passes, and my thoughts fell back into their old channels, where doubtless they would have remained but for a circumstance that stirred our little household as it had never been stirred before — a circumstance that brought about unexpected complications, and changed the course of more than one life.

III.

WHAT THE STORM LEFT AT OUR DOOR.

ONE night in the winter of 1848 — I think it was the 17th of January — I was sitting in my room ruminating as usual. The fire on the hearth had burned low, the weather having been rainy and warm during the day. Through the closed door, I heard the subdued hum of conversation between Mrs. Beshears and my sister Jane, and it made my solitude more cheerful. Once, hearing the whistle of the rising wind, I looked from the door, and saw that the rain-clouds that had been coming from the west all day were now driving swiftly before a northwest wind. Patches of dark-blue sky showed here and there in the zenith, and in these the stars twinkled as freshly as if they had been washed clean by the white vapors that went whirling through the sky.

By the time the nine o'clock bell had rung, the temperature had fallen considerably, and I was compelled to replenish my fire. The northwest wind increased to a gale, and presently I heard the tinkling spatter of sleet as the wind hurled it against my window-blinds. Sometimes the wind would rise away from the earth and roar in the tops of the trees and chimneys; then it would fall to the ground again, bringing with it a blast of cutting sleet. Mrs. Beshears had stayed longer than usual, and I wondered how she and the negro boy who always accompanied her would manage to get home through the storm. Worried somewhat by this thought, I rose from my rocking-chair and walked nervously about the room. Suddenly I heard the sound of voices on the sidewalk. What they said at first was drowned by the roaring wind, but presently I heard a woman's voice: —

"I ain't goin' narry step, an' you can't make me. I 'll die fust."

Then came the voice of a man: "Ef you don't come, you 'll rue it. You 've come this fur; you might as well go furder. Come on, I tell ye; I 'll call 'em to the door."

"I won't!" exclaimed the woman. "I won't and I shan't!"

There was an ominous pause. The woman cried out again: "Mind now! Ef you hit me, I 'll holler. You can't keep me from hollerin'."

"You slut!" said the man, his voice choked and shaking with rage. "You slut! Don't you never dast to let me see your face ag'in. I 'll murder you ef you do!"

"Hoity-toity!" I said to myself. "What 's all this about at such a time of night?" and I made up my mind, if any more threats were made by the man, to go out and give him a genteel pummel-

ing, dark as it was. I imagined I heard some one
raise the latch of the gate, and I thought, too,
that I heard a shuffling sound on the little porch,
but on a stormy night the mind has ears of its
own, and has a habit of conjuring up every sound
that the physical ears would be unlikely to hear.
So I traced the click of the latch and the shuffling
on the porch to some queer trick of the wind.

And it was an easy matter to account for the
savage dialogue that came to my ears through the
walls. Three miles from the village there was a
cotton factory that had just been put in operation.
It was a small affair, indeed, but it had already
gathered about it a class of population that seemed
to me to be somewhat undesirable. The men
had already begun to straggle into town after factory hours, and the most of them, when they went
straggling back, carried a jug of rum home with
them, besides the drams they had inside their
skins. They were as lanky and as lousy-looking
a set as I had ever seen — pale, cadaverous, and
careworn — veritable "clay eaters," as I have
heard sister Jane call them. What more natural than that one of these men, coming to the
village after a jug of rum, should be followed by
his wife; that both should have taken a dram too
much; and that they were in a somewhat maudlin
condition when they paused under the eaves of
my room to carry on a meaningless quarrel? I
had dismissed the matter from my mind when
I heard Mrs. Beshears coming along the hall-

way, followed by sister Jane (as usual) with a lighted candle.

"Gone to bed, William?" cried Mrs. Beshears, briskly tapping on the inner door.

"Come in," I replied. "I have been waiting to escort you home."

"Me?" exclaimed Mrs. Beshears, in some astonishment. "Oh, my! Think of that, Jane! What a compliment!" She curtsied in a way that I had not thought her capable of. "Do you reely think, Jane, that a young thing like me ought to trust herself alone, or as good as alone, with as gay a beau as William is? No, I thank you, William. I won't pester you to go to-night. Some other night, when the moon is shining, and the wind ain't so high."

"But," I persisted in all seriousness, "there has been a tremendous change in the weather. Sleet is falling, even now. The wind will blow you away."

"And what would you be doin', William? A-hanging on to my frock, and a-squalling, I'll be bound. And folks 'd stick their heads out o' the windows, and say: ' Run here, everybody, and look! Yonder goes the old witch a-flying high, with a young man to help her sweep off the sky.' No, William; I know you mean what you say, but by the time you've faced as many storms as old Sally Beshears, you won't never want anybody to put themselves out for you. Bless your heart, honey! Here's what's faced wind and rain, sleet and hail, these many long years, with abundance of thunder flung in for good measure."

"I 've begged and begged her to stay all night, but she won't listen to that," remarked sister Jane.

"No, no!" exclaimed Mrs. Beshears, shaking her head and rapping on the floor with her cane. "I know I 'm jest as welcome as anybody could be, and I 'd stay, if I could, if only for the sakes of that nigger boy. I 'm a red-eyed tory if I don't believe he 'll have every stitch o' clothes blow'd off of him before he gits to the next corner. And that 'll be more patching and sewing for me — and the Lord knows I have enough of that. No, folks, I can't stay. If them two babies of mine was to wake up in the night and miss me, they 'd git to wandering hither and yon in the dark, and they might fall and hurt themselves, poor old souls!"

Of course there was nothing to be said after that, so I stationed myself at the door ready to open and close it as quickly as possible, while sister Jane, as was her nightly habit, poised the candle so as to hold it above her head, as if by that means to light Mrs. Beshears on her way.

"Come on, little nigger. I 'm mighty sorry for you, but I can't keep the wind from blowing nor the sleet from sleeting."

But she was careful to tie around his neck the big knitted scarf which she had worn over her head, wrapping her cape around her own ears. Then sister Jane came to the rescue with her big striped shawl, and, in a moment, Mrs. Beshears was ready for her homeward journey.

"Good-night, folks," she said once more. "If it keeps on blowing I 'll likely not come to-morrow night, Jane, and if William cries about it, le' me know. Come on, little nigger."

As sister Jane held the candle above her head, I opened the door, and as Mrs. Beshears and the negro slipped out, tried to push it quickly to. But the storm was quicker. The wind swirled in, caught the door and held it against all my strength, blew out the candle, and sent the sparks and ashes flying out of the fireplace all over the room. It was the work of a moment. Sister Jane dropped the candle, gave a little shriek of dismay, and ran about the room, knocking the sparks and coals from the counterpane and curtains, and from the rug. She had hardly begun to do this, when there came a tremendous thumping at the door, which I had managed to close, and we heard Mrs. Beshears screaming so as to make herself heard above the rush and roar of the storm:

"Jane! Jane! William! For God A'mighty's sake come here! William! Jane!"

Then she began to beat frantically on the panels with her walking-cane. I jumped to the door at the sound of her voice, but in my haste and confusion I forgot to turn the key, and stood turning and wrenching the bolt. Mrs. Beshears must have divined the trouble, for she screamed from the other side: —

"Unlock the door! Here's somebody dead or a-dying!"

At last habit, more than presence of mind, came to my assistance. I turned the key mechanically, drew back the bolt, and the wind burst the door open. By this time sister Jane had thrust a handful of fat pine splinters in the fireplace, and now held the flaming torch aloft.

"It's a woman!" gasped Mrs. Beshears. "A woman and a baby. I found out that much!"

It is wonderful how active the mind is in moments of extreme excitement, and how prone the memory is to seize and register the most trifling details. With one glance I saw that sister Jane was pale, but composed, that Mrs. Beshears was white as a ghost, that sister Jane's big tortoise-shell comb had fallen from her head, and that one of Mrs. Beshears's big crescent-shaped ear-rings had been loosed from its fastening. 'T was all as momentary as the lightning's flash. It was fortunate indeed that in the very nick and point of time the little negro boy, who was clinging convulsively to the skirts of his mistress, should suddenly set up a series of shrieks and yells which, being wholly unreasonable, and therefore irritating, served to recall us all to our senses.

"Sally, for the Lord's sake give that imp a cuff that'll take his breath away," said sister Jane.

This timely advice was promptly followed, and the confusion and excitement we had all felt a

moment before were sensibly allayed. I stepped
on the porch, and, by the dim light of the pine-
torch held aloft by sister Jane, saw a woman hud-
dled in one corner. Her feet were stretched out,
and, from having been in a sitting posture, her
head had drooped forward until it touched a bundle she had in her lap. Around this bundle her
arms were twined. I soon found she was not
dead, for she moved and a rigor shook her frame
when I laid my hand on her shoulder.

"Get up and come in the house," I said, shaking her by the arm. "Come! Get up! You'll
freeze out here."

She raised her head, shook back her hair, and
glanced wildly about her.

"I won't go up yonder!" she moaned. "I'll
die fust! Oh, me! Why — why — *why* can't I
die an' be done with it?"

It was the pitifullest cry that had ever come to
my ears. It reached sister Jane's, too, for she
threw her torch in the fire, came forward, and
took command.

"Lift her by that arm, William, and I'll lift
her by this. Get up, and come in the house.
This is no place for you out here. Come, let's
go to the fire."

Sister Jane's voice was so firm, and yet so kind
and sympathetic that the woman looked up in a
dazed way.

"Who are you?" she asked, brushing her hair
back with her finger.

"Nobody, much," replied sister Jane, "and if you keep me standing out here in the cold, I won't be anybody at all."

"Won't you go in 'less I go?" asked the woman.

"No, I won't!" said sister Jane, decisively.

Without another word the woman rose to her feet with our help, and went in the house. I was truly glad when the door was closed, for the weather was bitter cold — the coldest, it was said afterwards, that had ever been experienced by the oldest inhabitant. Sister Jane carried the woman into her own room, where there was a warm fire, followed by Mrs. Beshears, who was moved by both sympathy and curiosity.

The woman was duly installed in the big rocking-chair, and, by the uncertain light of the candle, presented a picture so forlorn, so desolate, and so miserable that I hope never to see its like again. It was not the faded sunbonnet that she tried hard to pull over her eyes, nor the shabby dress, nor the coarse and muddy shoes, nor all these together. They were the merest accessories. The forlornness and misery lay deeper, in some subtile way presenting themselves to the mind rather than to the eye.

"Let me take your bonnet," said sister Jane.

"I don't mind it; it don't bother me," replied the woman.

"It's better off," persisted sister Jane, as she gently and deftly untied the strings.

"I reckon my head's a plum sight," said the woman, true to her sex.

The one glance that I got of her face when her bonnet came off — for she bent her head over the bundle in her arms — showed that she was quite a young woman, not more than twenty at the most. Her hair was as black as a crow's wing and as sheeny. I judged that if she were furnished forth with the tassels and toggery of fashion, she would be strikingly handsome. So far as I could see, Mrs. Beshears had not bestowed a glance on the young woman, but sat gazing steadily into the bed of hickory coals, tapping the andiron gently with the end of her cane. Presently she turned in her chair.

"What have you got in that bundle?"

"Nothing but a little bit of a baby," replied the young woman, hugging it closer to her bosom.

"A baby!" exclaimed sister Jane.

"Yes 'm. An' ef he don't pester me, I don't see how he can pester anybody." Hearing no comment on this, the young woman looked up. I could see despair in her eyes; I could see misery in the flutter of her nostrils, and in the droop of her mouth. Hopelessness, friendlessness — all the misfortunes that go trooping after sin — had set their seal on that face.

How she misread the sympathy that was written in every line of sister Jane's face, I have never been able to understand, for tears were standing in those honest eyes. But the young woman half rose from her chair and began to gather the thin and shabby shawl more closely around the child.

"Gi' me my bonnet, an' I 'll go," she said. "I know 'd in reason I ought not to 'a' come in here. I ain't got no more business in this house than I 've got on the inside of a church, an' that 's the Lord's truth. Show me the door, please, ma'am. The cold ain't no more to me than the heat, an' the night 's lots better than the day. I 've brung mud in your house on my shoes. Where 's my bonnet? Thess gi' me my bonnet. It 's all the head-wear I 've got left."

"Sit down," said sister Jane. "Give me that child. If it ain't frozen, it ain't your fault."

"No 'm! No 'm!" protested the woman. "Le' me go — I must go! I did n't want to come in, but you all took an' drug me. I ain't no more wuth your thought than the four-footed creeturs in the woods. Gi' me my bonnet."

"Sit down! I tell you to sit down! Give me that child." Sister Jane's commands were given in a tone that convinced the woman that 't would be unreasonable as well as useless to resist, so she sank back in the rocking-chair, and surrendered the bundle into arms that had not borne such a burden in thirty-odd years. Holding the bundle first on one arm and then on the other, (to further the process of unwrapping), sister Jane took off the blanket or shawl — whatever it was, it was shabby enough — and in a moment there was disclosed to our curious eyes a fat and rosy, but extremely sleepy infant. The woman had already indicated that it was a boy, and he was certainly a fine one to all outward appearances. As sister Jane held him up to get a good view of his face, his head wabbled about on his shoulders, and he half opened his eyes. Then he smiled, and leaned his head against my sister's bosom. Whereupon she laughed aloud.

"I declare! He's about the cutest thing I ever saw!" she cried. "Look at him, Sally — he's right now as happy as a lord."

"He ain't cold, is he?" asked Mrs. Beshears, going forward to inspect him.

"Why, he's as warm as a toast," said sister Jane, as proudly as if she had been the means of keeping him warm.

"How old is he?" asked Mrs. Beshears, turning to the mother.

But there was no answer from that quarter. The woman's right hand hung limp by her side; the other was caught in the partially open bosom of her dress. Her head had fallen to one side, and all the color had left her face.

"Take this child, William!" exclaimed sister Jane, thrusting the baby into my lap. No doubt I held him awkwardly enough, but I cuddled him up in my arms to the best of my ability, which, in this direction, at least, was poor enough.

With a promptness and decision beyond all praise, sister Jane seized the sponge which she used to dampen cloth before pressing it, dipped it in a pan of cold water that was always within reach, and applied it to the face and wrists of the poor woman, whose fainting-spell was the result of a reaction from the strain that misfortune and exposure had imposed upon her. She was young and robust, but fainting-spells seem to be a part of the equipment of the sex, and are intended, no doubt, to shield them from the most acute forms of mental and physical anguish.

The woman was soon revived, and, after a glass of muscadine wine, which sister Jane had made with her own hands, and which was uncorked only on the rarest occasions — after a glass of this pungent and aromatic wine, the woman was as well as before. Better, in fact, for the forlorn expression slowly died out of her face, the color found its way back into her cheeks, and her eyes grew brighter.

"How old is your baby?" inquired Mrs. Beshears once more. She had not forgotten that her curiosity in this particular had not been satisfied.

"A risin' of five months," replied the mother.

"Where's your husband?" Mrs. Beshears asked.

For answer, the woman placed her hands to her face, leaned back in the chair, and said nothing, but I could see that she was deeply moved.

"Dead, I reckon?" persisted Mrs. Beshears.

The woman, still holding her hands before her face, shook her head with emphasis, and then

began to cry as uncontrollably as a child might.
Mrs. Beshears looked at sister Jane, sister Jane
looked at Mrs. Beshears, then both looked at me,
and I looked at the baby. No word was said,
but all of us knew that the unfortunate creature
who sat there weeping had descended into the
valley where sin and shame have their abiding
place — a valley that is deep, but not far to seek.

I looked at the baby when sister Jane and Mrs.
Beshears looked at me, and I was surprised to
find that it was looking at me. Its bright eyes
were wide open, and when they met mine, the
child smiled and tried to hide its face on my
shoulder. Presently it reached its dimpled hand
to my cheek, and began to pinch it gently. It
was such a pretty and cunning trick that I involuntarily hugged the little one closer in my arms,
and realized for the first time in my life how
sweet and thrilling the glory of motherhood must
be to a woman — even to the poor woman sitting
near me, consumed as she was with shame and
misery.

"I told you as plain as I could talk," she
sobbed, "that I hain't no business to be in this
house. For mercy's sake, gi' me my poor little
baby an' my bonnet, an' le' me go!"

Not knowing what else to do, I rose from my
chair, and was about to comply, when sister Jane
said sternly: —

"What are you doing, William? Give the
child to me."

"He's not asleep," I remarked, with as much austerity of manner as I could at the moment assume.

"Go show your grandmother how to make a goose-yoke," said sister Jane, sarcastically.

"You seem to know a great deal about babies," I suggested, with some show of dignity.

"I ought to, goodness knows," replied sister Jane, "for I've had one on my hands for the better part of my life."

If I said nothing in rejoinder, it was not because of a lack of a disposition to do so, but because there was nothing else to be said. Moreover, I felt that Providence had directed me aright when I rose to place the child in its mother's arms. If I had said, "Woman, stay," the woman would have had to go. But, by an involuntary movement, I had said, "Woman, go!" Therefore she would stay. The perversity which attaches itself to the feminine mind, as the mistletoe to the bough of the crab-apple — sprouting from the under side, if it can find no more convenient footing — was as marked in my sister Jane as in any woman; but I thank heaven that it never hardened her heart nor soured her temper so far as I was concerned.

IV.

THE situation was so interesting that Mrs. Beshears forgot that she was obliged to go home. As for me, though it was long past my bedtime, I had no thought of sleep. Sister Jane held the baby with a deftness that showed her hand had not lost its cunning; and the little thing played the same trick with her that it had with me. It reached forth its dimpled hand and gently pinched her neck.

"Look at him, Sally! He 's pinching my neck, and he keeps on at it," said sister Jane. "And he 's looking right at me!"

She put her face against the baby's and rocked back and forth in her chair, looking at the bed of coals on the hearth. The matter of her thoughts I could not even guess, but I knew she was happy, for her face wore a smile that made her look younger by twenty years.

The mother of the child was far from comfortable, as I could see. She moved restlessly about in her chair, and I felt rather than saw that the inquisitive eyes of Mrs. Beshears were fixed upon her. With her baby in her arms, she could have hid her face, but now all she could do was to change her position by moving about in her chair. The woman could not know, of course, that there was neither scorn nor condemnation in the eyes of Mrs. Beshears, but only a sort of sympathetic curiosity. Suddenly Mrs. Beshears spoke:—

"Child, what is your name?" The question was blunt and sudden, but the woman seemed to be relieved at hearing the sound of a voice. Such composure as she could command she showed now.

"Mandy Satterlee," she replied.

"Well, I thought so. I used to see you when I went to the mill. Jane, don't you mind me telling you what a good-lookin' gal I saw running wild in the bushes?"

But sister Jane evidently failed to hear this appeal to her memory. When she did speak, she said:—

"Sally, I wish you 'd look at Tinkins."

While I had been watching the woman and Mrs. Beshears out of the corner of my eye, Tommy Tinkins had come in from a night's ramble, a rare event in his later life. Seeing sister Jane holding something in her arms, he jumped in her lap to discover what it might be. He looked curiously at the baby's face — it was still awake — put his nose against the chubby arm, and then began to show his satisfaction in a manner more marked than I had ever noticed before. He purred loudly, making a noise like a small flutter-mill, such as the children play with; he

rubbed his sides against the baby; he rubbed his
chin on the baby's arm; and even when he tried
to stand still his forefeet were moving up and
down as a soldier would mark time. Not content
with this, he jumped from sister Jane's lap, and
went to the baby's mother. He was so well satisfied with her that he jumped in her lap and went
through the same performance. At the end of it,
he stretched himself out on her knee, placed his
muzzle on his forepaws, and closed his eyes con-
tentedly. Neither sister Jane nor myself had
ever seen Tommy Tinkins in a stranger's lap
before, and both expressed astonishment.

"I reckon Mandy's got catnip on her clothes,"
said Mrs. Beshears, by way of explanation.

"No," replied Mandy ,"I hain't seen no catnip
— not sence I was a little bit of a gal."

"William," remarked sister Jane in the tone
she always employed when her mind was made
up, "I 'll thank you to light the fire in the next
room."

"If you 're lightin' it for me, Jane, don't do
it," said Mrs. Beshears. "I 'd stay if I could,
but I 'm ableedge to go home. I 've got to go if
I have to fly."

"No, Sally; there 's another room if you make
up your mind to stay," replied sister Jane.
"Light the fire, William."

As I went from the room, I heard her talking
all sorts of foolish talk to the baby, as women will,
while the baby was cooing a pretty reply. The

hearth was fixed ready for an emergency. Pine splinters of the required "fatness" were stuck here and there between the seasoned hickory logs, and it was no trouble at all to make the fire. The draft in the chimney flue, responsive to the wind outside, was very strong, and a warm and cheerful blaze was soon roaring on the hearth.

Standing before it a moment, I noticed that the fury of the tempest outside had abated somewhat, though the wind was still blowing stiffly. I heard, too, a suspicious tinkling sound on the panes of the window that had no blinds. Drawing aside the curtain, I saw that the ground was covered with snow, and that it was still snowing briskly. This was so rare a spectacle in our part of the country that not many children in the village under ten years of age had seen it, and I caught myself wondering what impression it would make on them. Then I heard the clock striking twelve, and, before the sound had died away, there came a knocking at the outer door. Wondering what this might mean, I hastened to respond, and found on the outside a tall negro man.

"Who are you, and what under the canopy of heaven do you want at this time of night?" I asked with some show of irritation.

"'Tain't nobody but Mose, suh. I fotch de buggy atter Miss Sally, ef she's here, en ef she ain't here, de Lord knows whar she is, kaze she ain't at home, ner nowhars nigh dar."

Of course I knew Moses. Mrs. Beshears had

selected him to be the foreman on her place, because he was a little bit less lazy than the rest of
the negroes. So I made Moses come in, and carried him to my own room, where a fire was still
burning. He wiped his feet over and over again,
shook the snow from his clothes, and struck his
hat against the wall several times before he accepted the invitation to come in and warm himself
while Mrs. Beshears was getting ready to go.
There was no light in the room except the dim
one that came from the red glow of the hearth,
and as Moses stood in front of it, changing his
hat from one hand to the other as he warmed
each by turns, his stalwart figure cast an imposing
silhouette on the wall and ceiling.

"I'm name Moses," he said, as if talking to
himself, "en ef dish yer fire ain't de prommus
lan', I ain't never seed no prommus lan'."

"Is the weather very cold?" I asked, as I fastened the door.

"Hit gittin' wuss en wuss, suh," he replied.
"De fros' done got in de sap er de trees, suh, en
ez I wuz driving' long thoo de grove out yan', I
hear one un um pop. Yes, suh, I hear de tree
pop, en she pop so loud, 't wuz much ez I could
do ter hol' dat ole hoss out dar. Little mo' en
he 'd a run'ded away — dat ole hoss would."

I left Moses enjoying the warmth of the fire,
and went to inform Mrs. Beshears that she had
been sent for. I walked along the hallway,
opened the door, and was about to speak to her

when I heard sister Jane's "sh-sh-h!" and saw her raise her hand in warning. In some alarm, I enquired in a whisper what the trouble was. A gesture of her hand told me that the baby was asleep, and I was glad to find that it was nothing worse, for the events of the night had prepared me to fear that some new complications had taken shape during my absence from the room.

Breathing a sigh of relief, I told Mrs. Beshears, in a tone not calculated to disturb the baby, that Moses had come for her. She tiptoed to sister Jane's chair, peeped at the sleeping baby and said good-night. Then she tiptoed to Mandy Satterlee and shook hands with her. This done, a new trouble arose. How was she to arouse the little negro boy, who was one of the seven sleepers? At my suggestion, made in pantomime, she took him by one arm, while I seized him by the other. In this way, we lifted him bodily from the room into the hallway, shut the door, and dragged him along the best we could in the dark to my room, where, after a shake or two from Mrs. Beshears, and a word from Mose, the boy was able to stand on his feet without assistance.

"I reckon we can talk like folks out here," exclaimed Mrs. Beshears. "You hear me say it, William, if Jane Wornum ain't gone daft over that young 'un, I'd like to know the reason. Why, the minnit it shet its eyeleds, nobody could say a word. If you spoke to Jane she'd shake her head and p'int to the baby. At her time of life, too! I declare, it beats all. Is that you, Moses? Well, why n't you wait till mornin' to come after me?"

"Kaze, Mistiss, I knowed mighty well you 'd wanter come fo' mornin'," replied Moses, ignoring the sarcasm.

"Well, I 'd 'a' waited till after sun-up, anyway, if I 'd 'a' been you," remarked Mrs. Beshears. "Did you fetch the wheel-barrer or the ox-cart?"

"I fotch ol' Sam en de buggy, ma'am," answered Moses.

"Well, good Lord! are you going to walk and lead old Sam, or shall I have to walk and lead him? He can't haul us all."

"He mighty gaily ter-night, ma'am. Much ez I kin do ter hol' him whence we 'uz comin' 'long des now. Better wrop yo'se'f up good, Mistiss, kaze dish yer wedder is de kin' what 'll creep under de kiver, I don't keer how much you may pile on."

But Mrs. Beshears was fortified in this respect. When she was ready to go she bade me good-night, Moses bowed, as I held the door open, and in a moment I heard the horse's feet crunching through the snow, which had already formed an outer crust. Then I went back to sister Jane's room to see if I could be of any service before going to bed. Mandy Satterlee was still holding the cat in her lap, gazing into the depths of the fireplace. The color had returned to her face, and though her hair was tossed about, its black masses made a fitting frame for her features; and I saw at a glance that among her other misfortunes she had the dower of beauty. Sister Jane was still holding the baby, humming a low tune. Her warning hand told me that I had forgotten to steal into the room on my tiptoes, perceiving which, the baby's mother intervened.

"You may make all the fuss you want to, now," she said. "He 'd wake ef you drapped 'im on the floor, maybe, but I don't know what else would wake 'im. He hain't no trouble in the wide world." She made this remark with a touch of pride that was unmistakable. "I 'll take 'im, now," she went on. "Oh, the Lord knows I don't want to worry you-all. I know I ought n't to be settin' here. I ain't nothin' ner nobody."

"William," said sister Jane, "turn down the bed-cover in the next room, and warm the pil-lows."

"Le' me do it! Oh, le' me do somethin', so I won't run ravin' crazy. I don't know how to set here holdin' my han's an' a-doin' of no good," said the baby's mother.

"Show her the way, William." Sister Jane's tone was not less imperative because her voice was pitched in a lower key. So I made haste to show Mandy Satterlee where the room was, and while she turned down the cover and smoothed out the snow-white sheets anew, I took occasion to renew the fire, so that the room would remain comfortably warm for the rest of the night. Hav-

ing finished this I stood before the fire, expecting
to see the young woman fetch the pillow to be
warmed. After watching the fire a moment, and
hearing no sound, I turned and saw Mandy leaning on the foot-board of the bed, which was a
high one, silently weeping. So I took the pillow,
placed one end on the floor and leaned it against
a chair. Presently sister Jane came in bringing
the baby.

"If the pillow's warm, William, put it back
on the bed."

I made sure of the warmth, for I knew that
sister Jane would test it by laying her cheek
against it, and placed it on the bed. She gave
it a light blow with her free hand, laid the baby
down, and drew the cover over it with the greatest care. Then she turned to the mother.

"What's the matter, Mandy?" she asked in
her practical way.

"Nothin' in the wide world," replied Mandy,
eagerly, though the tears were streaming down
her cheeks. "Pleas'm don't le' me worry you.
I'm happier right now than I've been sence —
sence I don't know when. It ain't when I cry
that I'm in trouble; it's when I can't cry."

"Then come and sit by me," said sister Jane,
"and cry to your heart's content. It'll do you
a world of good. See to the doors and the fires,
William."

Taking this as a gentle hint, I went out, and
inspected all the outer doors, trying the locks, to

make sure that they were fastened. This was a part of the nightly routine, but it was a useless task to be set for me, for sister Jane was sure to slip around to each door after I had gone to bed, to satisfy herself that it was secure.

What these two women said to each other in that hour — the one strong and self-reliant, but charitable, the other weak and erring, but penitent in heart and mind — I never knew; I never wanted to know. For revelation would have made commonplace a matter over which secrecy had thrown a sacred veil. There are mysteries which divination exalt, and this was one of them. The cry of a penitent is heard with more joy in heaven than the prayer of a saint; it may be misunderstood here, but it is rightly heard there through all the riot and uproar of the spinning worlds.

After I had attended to everything, as usual, I opened the door of the room to bid sister Jane good-night, as had been my habit since childhood. But what I saw made me pause on the threshold. Sister Jane sat in a low chair with her arms around Mandy Satterlee, who was kneeling on the floor at her side. Mandy's hair fell in black coils to the floor; neither one heard or saw me. There was a murmur of conversation, but I did not pause to hear. Closing the door gently, I went to my room, and was soon sound asleep.

V.

SISTER JANE TAKES BOARDERS.

THE next morning the negro boy who was in the habit of making the fires failed to put in an appearance. And no wonder. The snow was piled to such a height in the little porch, having been blown into a drift by the wind, that it reached nearly to the door-knob. But a beautiful sight met my eyes when I looked out. One could almost be tempted to believe that a miracle had been performed in the night. Everywhere the snow lay thick and white, and over the trunks and branches of the trees a thin mantle of ice had been woven. An arbor-vitæ tree standing in the garden was so heavily-laden with this unusual gift of winter that its branches gave forth a queer creaking sound when they swayed in the light breeze; and the honeysuckle vine made a rare show in its garment of mingled sleet and snow — winter's patchwork.

But I had no time to enjoy the scene. I made haste to go to the cook-room, intending to start the fire, and, in this way, help sister Jane as much as possible. But when I got there a fire was roaring on the hearth, and Mandy Satterlee was sitting before it. She rose as I entered.

"I'm mighty glad you're up," she said, with a movement of her lips that was almost a smile. "I slipped out of bed an' come out here to see ef I couldn't he'p aroun' a little. I started the fire an' then had to set down an' wait for somebody. I didn't want to wake her up, 'cause I know in reason she must be teetotally fagged out. Ef you know how to give out things," she went on, "I'll whirl in here an' git breakfast fer you-all in three shakes of a sheep's-tail."

I found the cupboard key, and showed Mandy where the meat, the meal, and the flour were kept, but further I could not go. How much or how little to give out for making a meal and preventing all waste, was a problem I had not mastered. Instead of laughing at my total ignorance Mandy shoved me gently aside and took charge of matters.

Then I made a fire in my own room, after many efforts, and when I went back, sister Jane was up and out and engaged in a friendly quarrel with Mandy Satterlee.

"Why, what in the world do you mean by not waking me?" sister Jane was saying. "Where's William? William, why didn't you wake me and let this poor thing rest?"

"For the best reason in the world," I answered. "I was sound asleep myself, and when I did wake, I found a fire roaring in the chimney here."

"Well, this beats all," remarked sister Jane. "I'm no chicken, and this is the first time I've ever overslept myself since I 've been a woman grown.''

"That 's because you 've never had to retch out an' pick up a poor stray creetur before," said Mandy Satterlee.

"'T ain't that," explained sister Jane. "I 've been up just as late, and I 've been through just as much and more, too, for that matter; but sun-up never caught me in bed before, not since I was a slip of a gal."

"Well, once in a way won't hurt," remarked Mandy. "By the time you turn 'roun' once or twice breakfus 'll be ready."

Sister Jane opened her eyes wide and made an exclamation, which, plainly enough, was not the result of surprise alone. For, though particular about many things, she was most particular about the preparation of her food. She would never tolerate a negro cook. Cleanliness was a part of her religious creed, and she practiced it unceasingly and (I sometimes thought, especially on scouring days) unsparingly. I am sure she winced inwardly when Mandy Satterlee said that breakfast was nearly ready.

"I reckon I done wrong," said Mandy; "I 'm good at that. But I jest had to do somethin'. Ef you hain't never had the feelin' I hope you never will. When I git that a-way, I 'm jest ableeged to do somethin'. But ever'body says I 'm a good cook. I begun it when I wuz a little gal, an' I 've been a-doin' of it off an' on ev'ry sence.

I do hope you'll jest taste of the vittles anyhow."

"Well, my appetite ain't so mighty good this morning, and I don't care what I eat," replied sister Jane, with characteristic bluntness. Then she went into the room where the baby was still asleep. When she came out, her face wore a pleasanter expression. "He's sleeping like a log," she said.

By that time breakfast was ready and the table set. It was surprising with what deftness Mandy handled the crockery-ware, and how apt she was in discovering where everything was kept. Presently she said, with a somewhat embarrassed air, "Well, I reckon ever'thing's ready. Set down an' eat it while it's warm."

"What are you going to do?" asked sister Jane, seeing that plates had been laid for two only. "Fix a place for yourself."

"Oh, no 'm! I'll hand the things around. I never eat with any heart right after I've been cookin'. It'll rest me to help you."

Sister Jane placed a chair and plate for Mandy and insisted that she should sit down with us. But neither persuasion nor insistence had any effect on her. She only shook her head, and, finally, closed sister Jane's mouth by placing a plate of smoking waffles under her nose.

Now, if there was anything my sister was fond of it was hot waffles. She often tried to make them and as often failed, and finally had placed

the irons out of sight behind the pots, and kettles,
and ovens. A pleased smile fluttered around her
mouth, as she got a whiff of her favorite dish.

"Why, Mandy, where in the world did you
find the waffle-irons?" she exclaimed.

"I know 'd in reason that you ought to have
a pair," replied Mandy, "an' I jest hunted till I
found 'em."

"I hope you cleaned them," said sister Jane.

"The waffles 'll tell you more about that than
I can," was all Mandy would say.

The breakfast was very fine, and I enjoyed it
as much as sister Jane did. The waffles were
delicious, the coffee retained the fresh aroma of
the roasted berry, the ham was broiled to a turn,
and, in fact, everything showed the hand of an
adept. In reply to a question, Mandy said her
mother had taught her how to cook, and then we
remembered that the daughter of a Virginia gentleman, who had emigrated to this region to better
his condition, had outraged her parents and
shocked her friends by eloping with Duncan
Satterlee. Here, then, were my sister Jane and
myself actually enjoying the remote results of a
social dislocation (if I may so term it) which had
caused no little stir when it happened, and which
was still talked of when old people desired to
point a moral for the benefit of their daughters.
It was so curious that I determined to make the
matter a subject for an essay, written after the
manner and in the style of those that still delight

us in Mr. Addison's little paper, "The Spectator."

I have dwelt on these trifles purposely. They were a part of the order of events, and who shall say whether they were not as important in their results as any? Who shall decide whether Mandy Satterlee's own personality, (which was far from displeasing), or that of her baby, or her art of cookery, was most influential in bringing my sister to decide that the unfortunate young woman should thereafter make her home with us? 'T would be a rough and an unsatisfactory way of disposing of an important matter to say that a mere trifle caused my sister Jane to make up her mind to fly in the face of public opinion; but trifles that seem to be light as air are frequently heavy enough to turn the scale.

At any rate, sister Jane decided that Mandy Satterlee should remain with us. I was consulted about it as a matter of form, and (that my individuality might assert itself) I offered some arguments against the proposition and pressed them with a show of heat that I was far from feeling. I foresaw that whatever objection I might put forward would cause sister Jane to make up her mind more firmly, for she was never sure she was right until opposition confirmed her intuitions. We talked the matter over for a good quarter of an hour, and I own that I never heard my sister argue as well as she did when she was pleading the cause of this poor outcast. For my part, I

was glad to see her make so trenchant a display
of the true Christian spirit toward one of her
own sex. The quality of charity is both rare
and noble; it is felt oftener than it is practiced.
Therefore I was glad that our poor house had
been illuminated, as it were, by so large a measure of that virtue.

The upshot of the matter was that, what with
the sympathy and tenderness that were a part of
her nature, the rosy and cunning baby, the waffles
and the coffee, sister Jane decided to give Mandy
Satterlee a home with us until she could find a
better. She was sitting with her baby in her lap,
fondling and cooing over it, when sister Jane told
her. Without a word she placed the youngster
on the floor (where it sprawled, and kicked, and
crowed), whipped out of the room, and, cold as it
was, went into the garden and stood near a peach-
tree, breaking off a twig now and then, and send-
ing its icy covering tinkling along the frozen crust
of the snow. She stood there until sister Jane
called her, and then she came slowly in with
downcast eyes.

"Don't stand out there in the snow, Mandy.
You 'll catch your death of cold."

"There hain't no danger of that," replied
Mandy. "I 'm used to the weather, an' ef I
wa'n't, 't would be all the same. Nobody in the
world can ketch cold when the'r heart 's as warm
as mine is right now."

She spoke in a low voice, and sister Jane was

chattering away at the baby, but I think we both heard what Mandy said. For, after a while, sister Jane touched the young mother on the shoulder and said: —

"You 've no right to fret and worry as long as you 've got that child to look after."

"That 's so," Mandy assented, and then she went about cleaning up the house for the day, displaying a dexterity in this business that was astonishing.

Naturally, in a community as small as ours, the episode that brought Mandy Satterlee to our door was soon bruited about, and I have no doubt the gossips rolled it as a sweet morsel under their tongues. I had no objections to this, though it is possible that sister Jane was somewhat irritated at the thought that her action in the matter would be misconstrued and bandied about from gossip to gossip.

The first of our neighbors to call was Mrs. Roby. She had not visited us for months before, but now she came, helter-skelter (as you may say), to investigate and satisfy her mind. She was sweet as butter sauce. It was, "Why, Jane! how well you 're looking — I reely believe you are getting younger — but look at me how faded and wrinkled I am — I declare I 'm getting old so fast I don't know what kind of clothes to put on — and how is that clever brother of yours? Why, here he is now — how are you, William? It is a shame you should keep yourself shut up so.

Why don't you get married?"—and so on in an
endless stream of questions to which no answers
were expected, and comments that were not intended to attract any attention. Mrs. Roby kept
it up for some time, and then, finally, settled
down to the main business to which we owed the
honor of her visit.

"Jane—I reckon you won't mind me talking
about it before William, because William seems
just like one of my own family, and what I
wouldn't say before him I wouldn't say before
my own brother. I'll tell anybody that, I don't
care who—Jane, what's this great rigmarole I
hear about old Sal Beshears a-going out of your
door yonder and finding a gal and a baby and
a-bringing of 'em in? I don't see how under the
canopy o' heaven old Sal Beshears could 'a' drug
any living human being, or a dead one either for
that matter, out of the blinding snow—I was at
class-meeting that night—and I know mighty well
that if old Sal Beshears could 'a' drug herself in
after she once got out 't would 'a' been as much.
And yet I hear 'em say, up and down, that old
Sal done all this by her own self."

"Well, Maria," remarked sister Jane, when
Mrs. Roby paused to take breath, "what if she
did? What is wrong about it?"

"Nothing, Jane—nothing in the world. It
looked to me like it was past all reason that a
crippled old soul like Sal Beshears could 'a' done
what they say she done."

"Sometimes when folks get excited they can do lots more than they could if they were calm," suggested sister Jane, pleasantly, though my practiced eye could see that she was boiling inwardly — if I may venture to employ the metaphor.

"That's so," replied Mrs. Roby, placidly shifting her ground; "that's certainly so, because I recollect jest as well as if it happened yesterday that one time when I was in my chicken-house nailing on a plank, a settin' hen flew in my face, and it was all done so sudden that it flung me off my balance, and I struck at her with the hammer and missed her, and splintered a scantlin' as big as my leg — please excuse me, William, because I always look on you as one of my own family. I couldn't 'a' done it if I hadn't 'a' been excited to save my life."

"Well, the fact is that Sally Beshears didn't drag the woman in any more than you did," said sister Jane, as she basted the lining in a frock-coat.

"Why, you don't tell me! Well, that outdoes me! And it's the talk of the town. Everybody says that old Sally Beshears took and drug the woman in. And that ain't all — no, ma'am! If you'll believe me, that ain't all by a long sight. They say that the woman and her baby are here right now. Sister Pulliam says that they are jest as much at home here as if they'd 'a' been born and brought up here. I says to her, says I, ' Sister Pulliam, we both belong to the same church, and I don't mind telling you that you ought not to talk that a-way unless you know'd that what you say is so, because,' says I, 'I've been knowing Jane Wornum a mighty long time, and I know mighty well that she's not the woman,' says I, ' to take no risks unless she's got some good reason,' says I."

"Well, I'm glad you told 'em that, Maria," exclaimed sister Jane in a tone suspiciously sweet. "If you'll look over on the sofa there, you'll see the baby, and its mammy ain't so far off but she'd come running in if she heard it holler."

Mrs. Roby sat as if she had been petrified. Her tongue for some moments resigned its office. She could only rub her chin and wag her head. After a while she managed to say: —

"Well, I told 'em you had some good reason."

"The best in the world, Maria," said sister Jane. "If you ain't certain what it is, you'll find it in the Bible, and if you haven't got a Bible, ask your preacher. I'll be bound he can tell you if he knows his business."

"Why, you know I've got a Bible, Jane. It sets right on the centre-table in my parlor in full view. You've not been to my house much, but you've been often enough to see the Bible in my parlor."

"Put it in your living room, then, for the Lord's sake, where you can read it every chance you get." The asperity of sister Jane's tone was ill-concealed by the genial smile that played around her mouth. A woman never smiles more sweetly or sincerely than when she feels or knows she is saying things that are calculated to make a friendly enemy wince.

"I declare, Jane!" exclaimed 'Mrs. Roby, "if anybody that did n't know you was to hear you talking, they 'd think you were mean and fractious. But we know her too well for that, don't we, William?"

I assented to this very heartily, for though Mrs. Roby had made the remark sarcastically, I knew it to be true that my sister had the tenderest heart in the world. Suddenly Mrs. Roby broke forth again: —

"Oh, yes! There 's another thing I like to 'a' forgot. Sister Cosby says that Sister Flewellen told her day before yesterday that the reason you was keeping the gal was because you wanted to take in boarders. But I told Sister Cosby"—

Before Mrs. Roby could ramble off into another of her rigmaroles, sister Jane brought her hand down on the press-board with a resounding thwack.

"Well, I thank Sue Flewellen for that," she cried. "I had n't thought of it before, but it 's the very thing. I never did think Sue was right bright, but I 'll have to change my mind. William, think it over. I don't know how many times the clerks in Harvey's and Wardwell's and Slade's stores have asked me why I did n't take a few boarders, and every time I 've told 'em it was because I had to do my own cooking — and now the Lord has sent me the best cook in the United States, if I do say it myself."

The point of this remark lay in the fact that Mrs. Roby herself kept boarders, and was, at that moment "entertaining" (as she was pleased to call it) the young gentlemen who were clerking in the stores sister Jane had named. It was most interesting to a student of human nature to watch the expression of Mrs. Roby's face as sister Jane spoke. Dismay, disgust, chagrin, doubt, and amazement fluttered over her countenance — a tangled medley of emotions. For once in her life she knew not what to say, and when she did speak, her voice was pitched low.

"All I can say," she remarked, as she rose to go, "is that I hope you'll have better luck and less trouble with your boarders than I've ever had with mine. Well, I must go; I just dropped in to say howdy and let you know that I hadn't forgot you."

"No need to tear yourself away," said sister Jane, hospitably. "Well, good-by, if you will go. When you see Sue Flewellen, tell her I'm mighty much obliged to her for her hint. It's a good one."

Poor Mrs. Roby was neither as voluble nor as gay when she went out as when she came in, and I could but remark, with a vague feeling of regret, that, in proportion as Mrs. Roby's spirits had fallen, my sister's had risen.

"I think Maria put her foot in it this time," said sister Jane, laughing heartily, as she returned from the door. "A nice woman she is to go around telling folks about the slurring remarks that other people have made about them, and all the time a-prying around and nosing about to see what she can find out."

It turned out that sister Jane was more than half serious when she said she intended to take day boarders. The idea dropped by Mrs. Roby grew day by day, until, on the advice of Mandy Satterlee, it developed into a fact. It was not wholly agreeable to me at first thought; but, on reflecting that it would get my sister out of the habit of tailoring, which seemed to grow on her year by year, and bring us both in contact with fairly pleasant people, I decided to offer no objections whatever. Of this I was glad when experience had convinced me that a certain degree of amusement, as well as instruction, is to be derived from listening to the small talk and studying the characters of a parcel of lively young men who regard life as a less serious problem than their elders are wont to do.

VI.

THE young men (as I have hinted) were no bother to me. They came with their light hearts and leaping hopes, enlivened each meal by their chatter, and then were off again. If a time came when I had no desire to hear their small talk, I had but to remain away from the table, knowing that either my sister or Mandy Satterlee would put by something for me.

And so the days went by, winter giving place to the gradual approach of spring. One of the first intimations was the fluttering of a pair of bluebirds around a hollow post in the garden. Then came Miss Jennie Wren and her chosen one peeping about in my honeysuckle vine, and making an extraordinary disturbance for so small a pair when they saw Tommy Tinkins promenading in that neighborhood. Following hard upon their heels (if one may say so) a mocking-bird perched himself in the top of the cedar, and swinging as in a hammock, took it upon himself to show the other birds how they should deliver themselves of the songs that are native to their throats. Then the plum-trees put forth their forward blossoms, followed by the peach-trees, until, presently (in a night, as it were), spring was upon us, and Mary Bullard filled all the garden with her presence, her beauty and innocence comparable only to the first shy flowers of the season.

If her name has not been mentioned more frequently in these pages it is not because she ceased to play a definite part in the scenes, commonplace or otherwise, that were a part of our daily experience. She was in and out of the house constantly, only the severest weather preventing her from paying a daily visit to sister Jane. It may have been my fancy, but it seemed to me that after she had been told the story of the finding of Mandy Satterlee in the snow and sleet on that bitter cold night, her manner was a shade more pensive than before. It was as if she had something more serious to think about, some new and strange problem to unravel. When the weather became really fine, she would wander in the garden with a book, which she only read by snatches. Many a time, as she sat in the latticed summer-house, I have seen the book slip through her fingers and fall to the ground unnoticed, while she gazed into space lost in thought. I used to say to myself with a sigh, as I watched her from my covert of honeysuckle vines, that her thoughts were not my thoughts. She was blossoming into young womanhood, while my star of destiny (if perchance I had one) had already passed the zenith.

Say what you will, there is a wide gap between
twenty and thirty odd when these numbers mark
the years. There is a wider gap still between a
girl of nineteen or twenty, full of life and the joy
of living, and an old man of thirty-five or forty,
who begins to look backward instead of forward,
and who sighs for the days that are gone instead
of fixing expectation on those that are to come.
Sir Thomas Browne says it is the heaviest stone
melancholy can throw at a man to tell him he is
at the end of his nature; but melancholy has
pebbles which, on occasions, she fits to her sling.
She throws a jagged one when, knocking at the
door of a man's heart, she tells him that he has
arrived at the age when love is not for him, that
he has come to the period when youth and beauty
must pass him by. I never looked at Mary Bullard but this jagged pebble came whizzing through
the honeysuckle vines. Sometimes, indeed, it rattled harmless at my feet, but there were other
times when it hit the mark and left a wound.

It seemed to me that pensiveness added a new
charm to Mary's beauty, or it may have been that
her beauty lent a new charm to pensiveness.
Sometimes she would leave her book and her hat
in the summer house, and make our kitchen beautiful by her presence. There she would make
herself agreeable to Mandy Satterlee, and such
was her gift for attracting the love of all who
knew her that Mandy, as she often said herself,
came to worship the ground that Mary walked on.

And Mandy was not without companionship in this; she had her fellow worshippers. By instinct or intuition Mary Bullard seemed to know that here was a woman who stood in sore need of the sympathy of the innocent and pure-minded of her own sex. This sympathy Mary gave to Mandy Satterlee in full measure, and found her reward in a devotion that was beautiful to behold.

I found out long afterwards that sister Jane never told Mary the story of Mandy Satterlee's troubles. Nor did my sister ever tell it to me; I only came to know it gradually, as it is unfolded in these pages. And I thank heaven that all the facts never came to Mary's ears until Providence had robbed the episode of some of the features that had else been such a severe shock to her innocence.

Innocence! Her character, her conversation, every tone of her voice, every gesture of her hands, each glance of her eye, gave a new meaning and illumination to the word. This had been so borne in upon me that when Mrs. Sally Beshears, on an occasion that has already been described, made some sneering remarks about Mary Bullard's father, the colonel, and hinted at some mistreatment of his brother, my surprise was not greater than my indignation, but, besides having a feeling of regard for Mrs. Beshears, I felt that I was no match for her in the bandying of words. Reflecting on the matter afterwards and analyzing the motives that lay behind my indignation, I was soon enabled to discover that Mary Bullard was behind it, and, though the darkness of night enveloped me as a mantle, I could feel that the discovery carried the warm blood to my face. Try as I would, I could find no other motive. In my mind the innocence of Mary Bullard was a cover and protection for her father's good name.

Something or other — I hardly knew what, for self-examination fails to reveal everything — the words of Mrs. Beshears became grounded in my memory, and I rarely saw Colonel Bullard go by in his stately and measured way without defending him in my own mind from the haphazard and flippant attack that Mrs. Beshears had made on him; not an attack either, but merely a reckless hint of what she might say if she had a mind to. Sometimes I felt that the habit of solitary reflection led me to exaggerate the importance of a chance word dropped from the tongue of an old woman who rarely took the trouble to measure the effect of her statements. Once I mentioned the matter to sister Jane, who had good judgment in such matters, but I got small consolation from her.

"For the Lord's sake, William!" she exclaimed, "what have you got to do with Colonel Bullard? He's at one end of the block and you're at the other. He's attending to his business every day and not bothering you; why can't you attend to your business, if you've got any, and not pester him?"

"But you heard what Mrs. Beshears said about him," I persisted.

"I ain't so mighty certain of that, neither," said sister Jane. "As people talk, so I listen. Sally Beshears don't know what she's going to say until the word's out of her mouth, and by the time it's out of her mouth, it's out of her mind. But what have you got to do with Colonel Bullard's ups and downs, I'd like to know?"

"Well, there's Mary," I suggested.

"And what about Mary?"

"She's his daughter."

"Well, you *are* coming on!" cried sister Jane, lifting her eyebrows in a way I didn't like. "You are so tied up with yourself that I didn't know but you might think Mary was the colonel's grandmother. She was in here to-day, and said she didn't believe you had looked at her since she got back from ' Philamadelphy,' as old Sol, the negro, calls it."

"She's very much mistaken," I answered with some heat.

"Don't get mad with the poor child. She wasn't crying when she said it, I'll tell you that."

"I can well believe that," said I. "Why should she care whether I cast my eyes towards her or not?"

"She doesn't," remarked sister Jane, with an emphasis I did not relish. "But it's the honest truth, William, you don't treat Mary with common politeness. She never comes in the house

but you jump up and scramble about until you
get your legs under you and then shuffle off to
your den as if you were afraid the child would bite
you. Why, if she had tushes and the will to do
it, she could n't gnaw through your hide in a
week."

There was enough truth in what sister Jane
said to make it both disagreeable and embarrass-
ing, and I felt myself growing red in the face.

"I don't say you ought to follow her up and
dawdle around her," sister Jane went on, repenting a little; "you 're too old for that; but you 've
been knowing her ever since she was a little bit
of a gal, and what 's the use of running away
every time she darkens the door? 'T ain't been
a week since she asked me what was the matter
with you. I wanted to know what she meant,
and she said you had changed so since she went
off to school that she did n't know what to make
of it."

"Why, don't you see what the trouble is?" I
cried. "The change is in her. She was a young
girl when she went away, and when she came
back she was a grown young woman."

"That sort of talk is like lighting a candle in
a dark room and then snuffing it out again. She 's
changed from a girl to a likely young woman, but
that 's no reason why you should act as if you was
afeared she 'd eat you up the first chance she got.
I declare if you was n't my own blood kin, the
way you do when that child comes in would be

comical. I always have to think up some cock-and-bull story to account for it, because — reely — I don't want Mary to see how ridiculous you are."

I turned and stalked out of the room with a show of indignation that was partly feigned and partly real, and I determined then and there to conduct myself with more dignity when Mary Bullard happened to find me in sister Jane's room, or in that part of the house.

One day, in reflecting over what sister Jane had said, it suddenly occurred to me that, by changing the subject in such a manner as to take me off my feet, she had neatly avoided expressing her opinion as to the truth or falsity of Mrs. Beshears's innuendoes in regard to Colonel Bullard. But fortune (as I thought) seemed to favor my inquisitiveness in this matter, for it was not long before Mrs. Beshears, paying us one of her regular evening visits, happened to mention the name of Colonel Bullard. Whereupon I was prompt to remind her of the remarks she had made about him some months before. She laughed somewhat harshly, exchanged glances with sister Jane, which struck me as somewhat singular, and then looked into the flame of the candle. There was silence for a while, and then sister Jane spoke.

"If all fools were fiddlers, Sally, we 'd know 'em by the bag they 'd carry," she remarked.

"That 's a true word, Jane," assented Mrs. Beshears. Then they both laughed, but, for my part, I was totally in the dark as to the cause of their merriment, and am to this day.

"I'll tell you, William," said Mrs. Beshears, turning to me in a kindly way that was almost motherly, "you mustn't remember every word that the old woman lets drop. Sometimes she's fretted, but that's because she has a heap more on her mind than you've any idee of. As you see Colonel Bullard now, so he's been for many a long year. My advice, William, is for you to take folks as you find 'em, an' if they don't pester you, don't you pester them."

"But you said something about his brother," I ventured to suggest.

"Did I, reely?" asked Mrs. Beshears. "Well, I might 'a' done it, because the colonel had a brother. You know, William, the colonel's folks moved here from the Goosepond settlement down yander in Wilkes, an' that's where my folks come from. The colonel had a brother, there ain't no manner o' doubt about that. What did I tell you his name was, Jane? Oh, yes, Clarence — Clarence Bullard. He'd be somewhere's about fifty year old if he'd 'a' kept straight, but his daddy named him a book name."

"A book name!" cried Mandy Satterlee, who was sitting near the candle-stand doing some mending. "Well, the lawsy massy! What kind of a name is that?"

"A name took out of a book," replied Mrs. Beshears. "I've heard all my life that a name took out of a book is mighty apt to stunt a child, if it don't make him go wrong when he grows up. Well, when the colonel's brother was born, his daddy wanted a nice name for him, so he read and read in books, and bimeby he come across this name of Clarence, and he slapt it onto the poor little baby without knowin' or a-keerin' whether it fit or not."

"Why, what is the matter with that name?" I asked in some surprise.

"Matter!" exclaimed Mrs. Beshears. "Everything's the matter with it. Did you ever hear of anybody named Clarence a-doin' a day's work in all your whole lifetime? If you've ever heard of it, jest let me know an' I'll up an' make a black mark on the chimney-jam there."

Mrs. Beshears looked at me so seriously that I was obliged to smile, seeing which, she resumed her argument, and in a way not very comfortable to me.

"Take your own name," she said. "If Jane here had called you Bill, you would 'a' grow'd up to be a tall stout man, but she called you William, an' that stunted you in heft an' height. Don't tell me there ain't nothin' in a name. I'm lots too old to be fooled that a-way. Why, supposin' they'd 'a' called me Sarah, stidder Sal: what under the blue canopy would I 'a' looked like?"

Truth to tell, I was both vexed and amused, but I was quick to remember that the wisest of men is no match for a shrewd woman's tongue. Moreover, I was fortunate enough to perceive that my anxiety to defend Colonel Bullard was ridiculous in the extreme. It came to me in a flash, when Mrs. Beshears inquired in a tone more solemn than usual: —

"William, has the colonel got you hired in a law-case, or somethin' of that sort?"

"No, ma'am!" I replied emphatically, realizing the awkwardness of my position. "What put that queer idea into your head?"

"I did n't know," she answered.

"What became of the colonel's brother?" I asked, more to hide my own confusion than to get the information I asked for. The brother was nothing to me.

"Now that 's what pesters me," said Mrs. Beshears reflectively. "The colonel was his guardeen, but as soon as Clarence come of age, he took his name an' what little of his belongings that he had left and packed 'em all up in a carpet-sack, an' jest made a teetotal disappearance. But I most always say to myself, when I think about it, that nobody, not even the colonel, don't want any brother, when he 's got as handsome a gal as Mary Bullard. How is Mary, Jane? She ain't been out my way not sence the apples was in blossom."

Then the conversation drifted to matters in which I had no interest, and I took myself off to my room, to sit in the dark and have strange thoughts, and, when drowsiness overcame me, to go to bed and dream strange dreams. For, small as the room was, it was the door of the world to me, especially when the dark had fallen and the lights in the village had been put out one by one. I had but to enter it and set my fancy free, as a wild bird is loosed from a cage, and, lo! the stars became lanthorns to guide my imagination on her way. The dull world, where, of necessity, I had my board and lodging, went reeling and plunging through its shadow, leaving me far behind, or found me, when black midnight peered around the corner, journeying far ahead. It gave me pure joy to know and feel that I was not the awkward, commonplace mortal that my acquaintances knew; to feel that I could lift my thoughts as high as the heavens and claim an ownership in the whirling orbs of fire that I found there.

But the earth is the earth, after all, and it was not without a feeling of satisfaction that I found my feet there after my nightly routs among the constellations. On this particular night, when I went to my room, after talking with sister Jane and Mrs. Beshears, my thoughts did not lift themselves to the abiding-place of the serene stars. I had a vague idea that I had been made the victim of chaff. And then it suddenly occurred to me that Colonel Bullard had not passed through the garden on his way to and from his business since the day of the big snow. This struck me as a curious circumstance, for he had been in the

habit of coming and going that way at least twice
a day, especially of mornings, when he would
look in and say a pleasant word to sister Jane
(while Tommy Tinkins, the cat, hid under the
house) or remark to me in a cheery tone: —

"How's business in the legal world, William?
Not good, I hope, for when lawyers lack for
clients it is a sign that neighbors are at peace."

And then, without waiting for an answer, he
would begin to hum a religious tune, and go on
his way, dignified and benignant. Being in the
habit of picking my own thoughts to pieces, as
the negroes not very long ago picked the lint from
the cotton-seed, I wondered why I had not missed
the colonel's large presence from the garden some
time before. Winter had become spring, and
summer was putting on her robes, and yet, until
now, I had not observed that Colonel Bullard no
longer passed through the garden. If a shrub
had been taken from the flourishing expanse, I
should have missed it; if one of the little wrens
nesting above the door had lost a feather from
a wing, I should have known it; and how my
observation had failed in the case of Colonel Bullard, I could not understand. If it had been
Mary — but that was different, entirely different;
there is a certain atmosphere a beautiful girl carries with her that makes her presence felt.

For weeks after this, I watched for the colonel
to come through the garden, but he never came.
Once I saw him, through force of habit, come

part of the way, but he turned suddenly, as though he had forgotten something, went back, and finally came along the sidewalk. I made it a point to be at our little gate when he passed by and gave him a good-morning as heartily as I could. He bowed coldly and formally, and failed to hum a tune, so far as I could hear. It was plain to the dullest eye that Colonel Bullard was worried about something, and I could not help pitying him.

Whatever his troubles were, they must have been serious. He did not hold his head erect as formerly, and he grew so absent-minded that he frequently went home on the sidewalk opposite his house, a proceeding that was so at variance with his usual methodical habits that the circumstance, though trifling, was remarked by others less observant than myself. Others remarked also the gradual change in his manner. In this way these things were so borne in upon me, that I at length felt justified in mentioning the matter to sister Jane. I had intended to refer to them in sequence, but I got no farther than the fact that Colonel Bullard had ceased to pass to and fro through the garden. At this point sister Jane lifted up her voice.

"Mandy! Mandy Satterlee!" she called at the top of her voice. Mandy, who was in the cook-room, came running in, brushing the flour from her bare arms. "Mandy, I wish you'd take a quarter of an hour off, and go round the house and see if any of the walls has caved in, or if the underpinning has give way anywhere."

A startled expression sprang into Mandy's face. "Why, Miss Jane! what under the canopies is the matter?"

"Why, William here says that Colonel Bullard actually don't come through the garden for to tell us howdy any more. If that's so, I know there must have been a cave-in somewhere."

Mandy Satterlee usually laughed at my sister's sallies, but this time surprise and expectation faded out of her face without giving place to amusement. She merely said, "We'll hunt for it to-morrow," and went back to her cooking. As for me, I went out of the room with as much dignity as I could command under the circumstances.

But there came a time, and that shortly, when we all pitied Colonel Bullard and his family. Speaking for myself, I am free to say that I was both shocked and grieved, for the circumstances, so far as I know, were without parallel or precedent in our section of the Union.

VII.

THE PICTURES ON THE WALL.

As may well be supposed, the observations that have been recorded here in regard to the peculiar conduct of Colonel Bullard covered not a week, nor a month, but a period embracing a part of spring and the whole of the summer following the big snow. Nor was I the only one who noted and commented on the change that had taken place in his manner. It had attracted the attention of almost everybody in the community. Some suggested that he was suffering from liver troubles, while others said that the bank failures had worried him. In the entire village, I knew of but three people who were willing to admit that they could see no change in the colonel — sister Jane, Mrs. Beshears, and Mandy Satterlee — and two of them, I knew, had eyes as sharp as it is ever given to mortals to have.

On one occasion, when the matter had become common to the gossip and chatter of the village, I heard Mrs. Sue Flewellen, who had come to see sister Jane for the express purpose, making such inquiries as would lead, ordinarily, to a discussion of the colonel's mental, physical, and pecuniary condition.

“Er Jane, how is er Colonel Bullard now?” asked Mrs. Flewellen.

“Well as common, Sue, I reckon. If he's sick, it ain't come to my ears,” replied sister Jane.

“Er well, that is real funny, now. Why, er Jane, they say he's going er off into a decline.”

“He may be for all I know,” was the unsatisfactory response. “Nobody ain't too good to go into a decline when the time comes. It's what everybody has to expect some time or other.”

“Oh, but, er Jane, you must er have noticed the change in er Colonel Bullard — it's er such a change! I declare! I er feel real sorry for his er wife and family. Why, er Jane, he's not the same man; he's er no more like Colonel er Bullard used to be than er I am.”

“Well, I'll take a good look at the colonel next time I see him,” said sister Jane, “and see what's the matter with him. If he looks like he needs any physic, I'll tell him to go and see old Free Betsey. If she can't cure him, she can conjure him.”

“Oh, it's er awful, Jane — and you've never er noticed it!”

“Sue,” remarked sister Jane, with solemn emphasis, “a man's no more to me than a jaybird. I hear a flutter in the chaney-berry tree, and look up and see a jaybird. I hear somebody stepping along as big as if he owned the town, and I look up and see a man. The bird hops off

and the man walks on. Out of sight, out of
mind. If Colonel Bullard was to come and set
in that cheer there, I might notice that he wasn't
looking well, but that's about all. Why, I
wouldn't know whether William was well or not
(and he's here in the house) if he wasn't so helpless and good for nothing that I have to take pity
on him."

Now, I would have taken it for granted that
sister Jane was merely playing with Mrs. Flewellen if she hadn't made a like reply to my own
questions — a reply not in the same terms, but to
the same purport. Mrs. Beshears had seen nothing queer about the colonel, nor had Mandy
Satterlee, who, indeed, was not expected to note
any change, having been born and bred some dis-
tance from the village.

But we soon became used to whatever change
of demeanor Colonel Bullard may have displayed.
Gradually his old dignity reasserted itself; he
began to hum religious tunes again; and if he
was not as cordial to me as formerly he had been,
he was polite. But he came through the garden
no more, continuing to pass on the opposite side
of the street in going to and from his home. So
that what had been for a time the occasion of
much talk was soon forgotten, especially by those
who had made the matter the subject of aimless
gossip.

Meanwhile summer had drawn away into au-
tumn. The skies were filled with the mystic haze

that marks the season, and the gray green of the great woods stretching away on all sides deepened into more sombre tints, or blazed forth in scarlet, crimson, and yellow. The roses bloomed in their richest beauty, and the crisp cool nights and the dewy mornings were a sufficient compensation for the heat of the days.

It was on one of these fine mornings that my attention was called to a group of men and children — white and black — standing in front of the dead wall of an old building on the opposite side of the street. During the night the wall had been covered with flaming pictures, and it was these that had caught the eye of the crowd. I could hear the negroes and the children making many exclamations of wonder, while the white men seemed to be absorbed in studying the gaudy pictures. To satisfy my own curiosity, I crossed the street, and saw that these immense bills were intended to inform the public at large that Robinson & Eldred's circus and menagerie would pitch its tent and display its wonders on the date set forth, which, as I have good reason to remember, was the third day of the first week in November, the bills having been posted sufficiently in advance of that time for all the country-side to have notice served on it that the wonderful show was coming.

A great many people in the village had heard of circuses, but not more than half a dozen had ever seen one — merchants who traveled once a

year to Augusta, Charleston, or New York to lay
in supplies of goods. These favored ones brought
back wonderful reports of the sights they had
seen at the show, and the flaming bills now spread
forth on the walls seemed to be a confirmation of
their reports. I sympathized somewhat with the
natural curiosity of the community, strange as it
may seem, and presently found myself as deeply
absorbed in studying the pictures as the most
enthusiastic urchin in the crowd — so absorbed,
indeed, that sister Jane was obliged to send for
me, her messenger being the negro boy whose
business it was to wait on the table.

"Marse Willyum," said that grinning imp,
"Miss Jane say mus' she sen' yo' brekkus out
yer, er mus' she put it back in de oven? Kaze
de bell done ringded en' dem ar yuther white
folks eatin' hard ez dey kin."

Seeing that the boy enjoyed my embarrassment,
I slipped away from the crowd, and went to breakfast. To forestall the sarcastic remarks that I
thought would be directed at me by sister Jane,
I gave Mandy Satterlee a full description of the
wonders pictured forth on the gaudy bills.

"Well, the lawsy massy!" cried Mandy, gen-
uinely amazed. "What 'll folks do next? Mr.
William, you reckon them folks reely ride a-stan-
in' on the'r heads, an' you reckon the gals reely
skip the rope an' jump through the hoop while
the hosses is a-gallopin'? I lay they jest put that
in the picturs to git you in the show an' git your

money. I 'll go right over after I clean up the things an' take a look at 'em for myself."

To my surprise, sister Jane displayed considerable enthusiasm about the circus.

"I 'll go if I have to sell my Sunday bonnet," she declared with emphasis. "I have n't been on a frolic since I went to a picnic in the Glades before William there was born — and you can tell by looking at him that that 's been a mighty long time ago."

Mandy Satterlee applauded sister Jane's purpose very heartily, and when she had washed the dishes and put the kitchen to rights, she took her baby on her arm — he was now a bouncing youngster, able to walk about the house — and went across the street to get a closer view of the show bills. By this time the curiosity of the small boys had been satiated, or they had gone to other quarters of the town where other pictures had been posted, as I noticed later. At any rate, Mandy and her baby were not disturbed by other spectators. While they were standing there, Colonel Bullard came out of his house, crossed over, as was his habit, and walked down the street. He would be compelled to pass within a few feet of the flaring pictures.

I determined to watch him narrowly and observe whether his troubles, whatever they might be, had washed curiosity out of his nature. He came down the street, turning his head neither to the right nor the left. Mandy's baby had demanded a closer acquaintance with one of the big red horses, and to satisfy him, she had gone near the picture to allow the youngster to slap it with his hand, and make various ineffectual efforts to secure it. She was standing thus when Colonel Bullard passed by. He turned his head in a stately manner, looked hard at the pictures (as it seemed) and then hurried on. He went a few steps, paused, turned back, and then, catching a glimpse of me, whirled on his heel, and went down town, going a little more rapidly than usual.

I saw it all at a glance. Here was the colonel passing by the pictures. He read in a moment the big letters that explained them, but considered that it would be beneath his dignity and standing to pause and satisfy his curiosity. Then, when he passed on, the temptation to give them a clear examination was so strong that he turned again, saw me, and, rather than compromise his dignity, beat a retreat. This was the explanation I made of the event to sister Jane, who, to my surprise, seemed to be more interested in Colonel Bullard's actions than in the show bills, for she was particular to have me describe every motion he made and every step he took. Mandy Satterlee heard a part of the description.

"How nigh was I to him when he passed?" she asked in a low voice.

"You might have put forth your hand and touched him," I replied.

"Ugh!" she exclaimed with a shudder. "I

reckon it's a mighty good thing I did n't see him."

"Why, you need n't be afraid of him," said I; "though he is dignified and serious, he is not severe."

Sister Jane laughed aloud, and Mandy smiled faintly.

"I declare, William Wornum! for a grown man you're as big a goose as ever nibbed green grass. You've pored and pored over them books in yander till you can't make head nor tail out of anything that ain't to be found betwixt their leds. Why, you've got so you talk like 'em. 'Don't be afeared,'" she went on, mimicking my tone and air; "'though he's dignified and serious, he ain't severe.' Now, who on top of the globe (or on the bottom of it, either, for that matter), ever heard of anybody talking that way outside the leds of a book too big to tote?"

"Well, in the books that I read I can find out everything I want to know — everything that is worth knowing," I replied.

"What books?" asked my sister.

"The Bible, Shakespeare, Montaigne, and Sir Thomas Browne."

"As for the Bible, well and good," commented sister Jane. "But if I've ever caught you reading it more 'n twice, I hope I may never see the back of my neck. As for the balance, one was a play-actor, and nobody could n't expect any better of him; and the t'others nobody ever heard of till you fished 'em out of some trash pile. Now, I want to ask you," she continued — "when will Mandy here have gray hair?"

"Nobody knows," I answered.

"You mean you can't find out in your books," she said; "but I can tell you when her hair will turn gray."

"When?"

"When she's afeared of Colonel Bullard," exclaimed sister Jane, somewhat snappishly.

Of course it was beyond my power to carry on an argument in behalf of my favorite books with any hope of silencing sister Jane, so I did as many a wiser man has done before me — sought comfort in the books themselves, and found it there; becoming for the moment as oblivious to the joys, sufferings, vainglories, and hard trials of this world as the writers were themselves, who long ago had been taken to the restful bosom of our old mother, the earth.

And I had another means of diversion that had gradually come to me unawares, and that I could turn to when my mind grew too dull to find enjoyment in my books — Mandy Satterlee's baby. This rosy urchin grew in strength, if not in grace, and had somehow taken a great fancy to me. Before he could walk, he began to wriggle to my door on hands and knees, and made his presence known by bumping his head against the panels — becoming, in this way, a sort of baby battering-ram. I was under no necessity of standing on ceremony with this visitor. If his coming was not ill-timed, I opened the door; if it was, I had but to remain silent, and presently he would wriggle himself away, perfectly content.

In the turmoil and confusion that Mandy Satterlee became the centre of, after the child found its way into this vain world, she had neglected or forgotten to give it a name. She called it Mother's Precious, and that was all; but sister Jane, more versatile if less felicitous, had bestowed on the youngster a handful of names, all supposed to bear some relation to one another. She called him Klubs, Klibs, Klubbins, Klibbins, and Keezes, indifferently, and he, as indifferently, answered to any or all. Out of this quaint collection I chose two for my own use — Klibs and Keezes; so that in one humor I called him Klibs, and in another Keezes.

Now, there were occasions when Klibs came knocking at my door that I was glad to open to him. Especially was this the case when I had spent an hour or two in court, fiddling over the trifling details of a petty lawsuit, or when my own thoughts wearied me and books had temporarily lost their flavor. For I had no reason to be on my dignity with Keezes. I could speak to him gravely on matters that concerned me most, or I could be as nonsensical as I chose. I could even go off into a rhapsody, or impart to him secrets that I should have blushed to whisper to other ears. It was all one to Klibs. There was a perfect understanding between us. He would sit for long minutes staring at me with owl-like wisdom while I talked to him, and when I was compelled to pause for want of breath, he would give me to understand, with some show of impatience, that he longed for more of the attic eloquence for which (within these four walls) I was famous.

In this way, and with such intermissions as the nature of the case called for, Keezes and I used to spend hours together — hours that were most pleasantly and profitably spent, so far as I was concerned. Sometimes his mother would interrupt us, fearing that the baby was troublesome. If Klibs was ready to go, he would permit himself to be carried off without a murmur; otherwise he would crawl behind my chair and squall lustily if any attempt were made to remove him. I grew very fond of the child in consequence, for even a baby can flatter our vanity. We love those who love us, or, if we do not love them, we give them cause to think we do, which (until we come to the end of all things, and our manifold hypocrisies confront and overwhelm us), amounts to pretty much the same thing.

Whether Keezes was wiser than any other baby is not for me to say. My experience in such matters was circumscribed. But he had traits and predispositions that I found profitable to study. Long before he could talk, he seemed to understand the high-flown statements which, with an affectation of solemnity, I was in the habit of

making to him. If he reached forth a dirty hand
to touch a book, I had but to say: "Nay, nay,
Keezes! touch not, taste not, handle not. Go
cleanse the disreputable member." Whereupon
he would look hard at his hand and presently fall
to picking the ravelings in the frayed edge of the
rag carpet, listening patiently all the while to
whatever discourse I might choose to pour into his
unprotected ear. He had the gift of patience, a
quality that, admirable in man, amounts to genius
in a child. I can say now, even at this writing,
that Klibs was the only genius I ever was on
familiar terms with. He had taste, too, for he
was exceedingly fond of Mary Bullard; and discretion: I have seen him carry a rose in his hand
for an hour and never destroy one of its petals.
It was thus an easy matter for a man, enamored
of solitude and impatient of needless interruptions,
to tolerate — nay, to enjoy — the companionship
of this quaint baby, whose very name had been
blotted out by the bar sinister.

As the time for the circus drew near, the expectation, that was on tiptoe, had the ground cut
from under its feet by the protests that were
made from the pulpit. These protests might have
been anticipated, but they were not; and they
caused as much of a splutter as the pouring of a
gourd full of cold water in a hot oven. The very
name of the village — Hallyton — might have
been a warning to those who knew its origin.
When the settlement was founded by pioneer

emigrants from Wilkes County, the church that was built gave its name to the place. It was called Bethel. Travelers passing through, later, on their way to and from the Indian trading-posts, always found the people of Bethel carrying on a religious revival. Among these travelers were to be found many ungodly men, who scoffingly gave Bethel the name of Hallyloo — by way of indicating the extreme piety of the people. The name stuck so fast that when the settlement grew into a village and became the county site, the people met together and compromised the matter by giving to the place the name of Hallyton.

Now, the lapse of years, if it had not intensified, had by no means dimmed the piety that provoked the ridicule of the scoffers. Consequently, the pillars of the church, as such men as Colonel Bullard were called, began a crusade against the sin of circus-going (which, indeed, owing to the absence of active temptation, was not very prevalent amongst us) much to the disgust of the younger generation. What real effect the crusade had is beyond conjecture. It caused some hard feelings in the different congregations, but it gave everybody something to talk about. Mrs. Sue Flewellen came all the way across the village (and it was a pretty step, too) to tell sister Jane that she heard Mrs. Lucindy Winslett say that Mrs. Cosby had declared that she heard Mrs. Printup say that if she had known all this fuss was to be made over one poor little show (and it must be a mighty poor show to come to such a town as this) she would never have joined the church until the last of November; and she did n't care who knew it or who heard her say it.

"What sort of religion do you call that?" inquired sister Jane, sarcastically.

"Oh, er don't ask *me*, Jane, er ask most anybody er but me. Er between you and me, er Jane, I 'd give *any*thing to go to er that circus. Pony Harvey er has been to see it, and he says it 's er just grand; er the finest music he ever er listened at, and er bangles and er spangles till you er want to quit er lookin' at 'em."

"If you want to go, why don't you go?" sister Jane asked sharply. "You are white and free, and mighty nigh twice twenty-one if not more. What 's to hender you from going?"

"Er well, you know how they er talk. Why, I 'd er never hear the last of it. Er when folks move in the er first circles, Jane, er like you and me, the very least er thing they do is er picked up and er turned over, and er looked at, and so er we 've got to toe the er line. We 've made it and er we 've got to toe it, Jane; you know that er yourself."

"In the first circles?" cried sister Jane, with unmixed amazement.

"Why, of er course, Jane."

Sister Jane laughed heartily. "Well, Sue," she said, "you know I used to tell you at school that you wa'n't right bright. I can tell you now that you ain't improved a bit. You 've hit off a joke and you don't laugh at it. What in the world is the matter with you? Why don't you laugh at your own fun. First circles! and in Ashbank deestrict! Why, I 'll get William to put it down and send it to old Billy Grier to put in his almanac."

"I declare, er Jane! You turn everything into er fun. No matter about the er place; somebody is er bound to be on top."

Sister Jane suddenly grew serious. "Sue Flewellen, what can out-float trash?"

Mrs. Flewellen gave up the contest by changing the subject. Fortunately for my peace of mind, none of sister Jane's acquaintances took her sharp comments seriously. The older ones were inured to their twang and flavor, and the younger ones enjoyed the humor that inspired them. When wit and tenderness go into partnership in the same mind, the product is humor.

Meanwhile, it is to be observed that as the day for the circus approached, sister Jane became more and more undecided as to whether she should go or stay away, and she remained undecided to the last moment.

VIII.

THE CIRCUS COMES TO TOWN.

THE day set for the circus dawned clear and warm. There had been a frost the night before, but the first rays of the morning sun drove it out of sight and out of mind. One of the summer's brood of mocking-birds that had been reared in the garden was trying his pipes in the big cedar. He sang so low that, to the unpracticed ear, he would have seemed to be far away; but I knew that he was not ten feet from my little porch. He paused every now and then to listen, and well he might, for, early as it was, there was a great stir in the village. The white boys and negroes and even some of the white men were running about in great excitement, for the circus had arrived during the night, or in the early hours of dawn. Indeed, even then I could hear the lumbering sound of heavy wagons in the road behind the tavern, and when I opened my door I could catch the whinnying sound of hungry horses. Sallying forth after breakfast I could see, from the corner of the public square, dozens of men currying and rubbing down piebald horses and ponies — an operation that was watched with both interest and awe by all the urchins in the village, white and black, that were able to get away from home at that hour. In the big vacant lot behind the tavern I could see the tops of the centre-pole and the smaller poles, suggesting the illusion that a big ship had sailed up in the night and cast anchor there.

Later, when I returned home, I found a stranger leaning by the gate in an expectant attitude. He was a stranger, but I thought I had seen him before, and so I bowed pleasantly as I paused before entering. There was a sullen expression on his face, and I thought I could catch the odor of rum about him, but he bowed politely, and said: —

"Ef this is Mr. Wornum, I wish you 'd tell Mandy Satterlee that her brother would like mighty well to see her."

"Did you knock at the door?" I asked.

"Yes, I did," he replied, "an' I heard a shuf-flin' of feet in thar, but nobody ain't come to the door. Jest tell Mandy that Bud wants to see her an' tell her good-by. She 'll know. She allers useter call me Bud before " — he paused, cleared his throat, and then stood staring at the ground and pulling nervously at the lappels of his shabby coat.

"Wait one moment," I said. "I 'll send her at once."

But when I opened the door, and went in search of Mandy, I found both her and sister Jane labor-

ing under a strange excitement. Mandy, white
as a sheet and trembling, was clinging to sister
Jane and begging her not to go to the door.
Sister Jane, armed with the fire-stick (a heavy
piece of metal weighing four or five pounds), and
as red in the face as Mandy was white, was waving her weapon in the air, and making an effort
to get to the door.

"Get out of my way, Mandy Satterlee!" she
was saying. "If you are afraid of the vagabond,
I ain't. Get out of the way, and let me brain
him where he stands."

"Tut-tut!" I cried; "what does all this mean?
What is the trouble?"

Sister Jane quieted down at once. I think she
felt that I was laughing in my sleeve, for she then
and there told me that the man at her door was
the very rascal and vagabond (I use her own de-
scriptive epithets) who had brought Mandy away
from home and to town that bitter cold night, and
left her to freeze to death at our door.

"He ast me to do somethin', and I said I'd do
it," said Mandy, thinking the explanation would
stand for an excuse, "but when I got to town I
jest couldn't do it, not ef I'd 'a' died for it."

"Are you afraid of him?" I asked.

"Afeard of Bud!" she exclaimed. "Why,
no more 'n I am of ol' Tommy Tinkins."

"Then go to the door," I said. "He's waiting
for you."

"Go and stand close by," sister Jane commanded, "and if the vagabond says a word out of the way, run out and brain him."

To ease my sister's mind, I went as far as the inner door of my room and stood there. I thus became an eavesdropper without intending it. The outer door being open, every word that passed between Mandy and her brother was conveyed to my ears as distinctly as if I had been standing between the two.

"Howdy, Bud? How 's ever'body? They don't miss me much, I reckon." Neither interest nor concern could be detected in Mandy's tone, and yet I knew that her mind was controlled by both.

There was a pause. The brother, as I judged, though I could not see him, was looking at the sister carefully, examining her clothes and every feature of her face.

"You look like you 're doin' mighty well," he remarked presently. "You ain't never comin' back to the settlement, I reckon?"

"No, I reckon not. They hain't nobody out there that 'd want to see me, an' they 's a whole passel of folks not so mighty fur from there that I don't want to see." There was a touch of sadness in Mandy's voice, as she said this.

"Well, there 'll be one left out thar when I 'm gone that 'd like to see you mightily," remarked her brother.

"I 'd like to know who," said Mandy.

"Jincy."

“Jincy Meadows? Well, the laws ’a’ massy! what under the canopy does he want to see me for — *now?*”

“Well,” said the brother, slowly, “you know how Jincy is. Folks useter call him quare, an’ some say now he’s a half-wit — one o’ these here moon-calves — but Jincy’s been mighty good to me lately. He don’t run into any of his whimsies when he talks to me. I know right p’int-blank that he’s got more sense than half the people in the county. He may n’t come to see you, but ef he does, don’t give him the back of your hand.”

“Does he know?” asked Mandy, sadly.

“Who? Jincy? He knows ever’thing, but you ’d never find it out by his common ever’day talk.”

There was a pause — a longer pause than usual. Then the brother said : —

“ I jest drapped in to say good-by. I hope you ain’t got nothin’ agin’ me, sis.”

This was too much for Mandy. She broke down. “Anything agin’ you, Bud? Oh, me! Oh, me!” she sobbed, “the shoe’s on t’other foot. It’s you that oughter have ever’thing ag’in me. Oh, me! Bud, I’m lots sorrier for you an’ for mammy an’ pap than I am for myself. They’re dead an’ gone, but, oh, me! I could n’t bear to look at the’r graves. It’d kill me.”

“Don’t cry, sis,” said the brother. “The folks in the house ’ll hear you, an’ think I’m doggin’ at you. Hush, honey! Don’t you be afeard but what I 'll make that man pay for it!" There was a ring of genuine passion in his voice. "I wanted to kill him, an' I oughter 'a' done it, but I 'll do wuss 'n that. I 'll let him live an' eat the bread he 's made you an' me eat. You won't see me no more for a mighty long time, but you 'll know when that man has been paid back. Great God, sis! when I think of mammy an' pap a-lyin' out thar in the woods"—

"But they 're not lyin' there on account o' *that*, Bud — not on account o' *that!*" cried Mandy, wildly.

"No, honey, not on that account. But when I think of 'em — sis, jest say the word, an' I 'll go an' kill 'im right now an' come back an' show you his damned blood! It won't take me ten minutes."

"Oh, for the Lord's sake, Bud, don't make matters wuss. They 're bad enough now. One more tetch, an' I 'd topple over. Don't do nothin' wrong, Bud. Don't put yourself where you'll be hunted down like a wild crectur. I'll git down on my knees to you, Bud, ef you 'll only promise."

After a pause, the brother said: "Well, good-bye, sis; ef I live, you 'll see me ag'in; ef I don't, it don't make no difference. I ain't no good nohow."

"Oh, don't say that, Bud! please don't! Ef you ain't no good it 's because of me. Oh, don't leave that hard sayin' a-ringin' in my ears!"

All the answer that Mandy Satterlee got was a

short harsh laugh. I heard the gate slammed to, and knew that the queer interview was over. I turned to go away, but came near running over sister Jane, who was standing at my elbow listening with all her ears.

"What is the matter?" she cried. Having cooled off, she was as practical as ever. "There is no need to break your neck or to cripple me. The man is not after you."

There was, indeed, no need for haste in the matter, for Mandy Satterlee, instead of coming into the house, had gone to the gate, where she stood and watched her brother until he was out of sight. I was so puzzled by some of the remarks I had heard, that I wanted to ask sister Jane about them, but the matter was an extremely delicate one, and, besides, she gave me no fitting opportunity. By the time Mandy came into the house we were sitting in sister Jane's room — I 'll not say quietly, for my sister, whose temper had already been ruffled, was giving me a lecture about the precipitate way in which I had run against her.

"Where 's Mother's Precious?" said Mandy. Lifting the baby in her arms, she held it against her breast as she rocked to and fro, and had what sister Jane called "a good cry." Klibs appeared to appreciate the situation, for he patted his mother's face gently, and held his soft and rosy cheek against hers as long as she showed any signs of grief.

"I declare!" she exclaimed, when her tears had spent themselves; "Bud has got a heart as tender as any human bein' that ever lived — a good heart an' a bad temper."

"You 'd 'a' better let me gone out there and brained him," remarked sister Jane, snappishly. "'Bud,' as you call him, will do you some big damage yet. You mark my words."

"Oh, no — no! I 'm the one that ought to be brained. I 'm the one that 's done the damage — to myself an' to ever'body else that 's kin to me."

Mandy's tears were beginning to flow afresh, when sister Jane put an end to the scene. "Put that child down or give him to me, and go and see about dinner. The tavern bell will be ringing directly, and we won't have ours in the pot, much less on the table."

She spoke in a peremptory tone, but I knew that she did it to take Mandy's mind off her troubles. It was effectual, too, for in less than a quarter of an hour Mandy could be heard, above the rattling of the pots and pans, singing an old folk song. But the song had a peculiarly plaintive air, so that it must have rhymed with her thoughts.

I sat listening to the song, my mind wandering back to the days of my youth, when, suddenly, a blare of trumpets and a clash of cymbals in the street drowned both song and memories, and I knew the parade of the circus was going by. It was a brave sight for the children and negroes and for those grown people who are not accustomed to look below the surface of things; but to me the tawdriness of the affair was most manifest and pitiful. The men and women strove in vain to look gay. The toggery they wore was faded and tarnished; the horses were lean and jaded; the red paint on the wagons had been sobered by wind and rain; the very plumes that waved so proudly in the headstalls of the horses were dirty and bedraggled. There was nothing entrancing about the affair but the music; nothing gay but the painted clown who rode a diminutive mule, and even his gayety was a matter of paint and grimace.

And so the cheap procession passed, carrying with it a surging crowd that had gathered in the village from all parts of the county. I turned away from it with a feeling akin to melancholy, perceiving in a dim way that the tawdry emptiness of the thing bore some relation to the social parade which, however great or small, passes before the eyes of every observant person. This idea led me into a reverie from which I was aroused by the laughing voice of Mary Bullard in conversation with sister Jane. Presently I heard them coming, and before I could escape by the outer door of my room, they were upon me.

"Don't run, William; we are not ready to eat you yet; we 'd need a sack of salt and a week of preparation for that," said sister Jane.

"Yes; do come back, Mr. William, and hear us for our cause, as one of your dear friends said in Rome," laughed Mary Bullard. "Tell him what it is, please," she went on, turning to sister Jane.

"Oh, no, Mary, that would never do. Tell him yourself. He always makes a wry face when I want him to do anything."

"Please don't look so solemn, Mr. William," cried Mary Bullard, opening her beautiful eyes, and folding her white hands with a pretty air. "It isn't much we want him to do, is it?" She turned to sister Jane to confirm her statement.

"It ain't anything at all," placidly remarked her ally.

"Shall I tell him?" she asked again in a hesitating way that but enhanced her loveliness. Receiving an encouraging nod from sister Jane, Mary went on: "It's this, Mr. William — mamma says that I may go to the circus if you and Miss Jane will go with me."

"But" — I began.

"Please say yes, Mr. William!" she cried, coming closer and laying her hand on my arm. Light as the touch was, it sent the blood mounting to my face, seeing which, she blushed also, and turned and leaned against sister Jane.

"I was about to observe," I stammered, "that it is very curious" —

"Take a chair, Mary, and make yourself comfortable," said sister Jane, sarcastically. "Lawyer Wornum is about to make one of his celebrated speeches before the Jestice court. I wish to goodness old Judge Bowden was here!"

"Now, I don't think that's right," cried Mary, protesting, but laughing, too. "I know Mr. William will say the right word at the right time. He always does."

I swallowed my embarrassment with a gulp. "Why, of course, we will go with you, Miss Mary. What need to ask? We were going anyhow." This last statement, I could see, rather took the edge off. There was a change in the young lady's countenance too subtle to describe.

"He's fibbing," said sister Jane. "He never had no more idea of going to that circus than he had of flying to the moon. I wanted to go myself, but I didn't dast to. I 'm mighty glad you come running at me with a ready-made excuse."

"Well, it's such a little fib, we 'll forgive it," remarked Mary. "Mamma kept putting me off, but finally said I could go if Mr. William and you would take me. She never had the slightest idea you were going."

"We had no such intention," said I, boldly going back to the truth. "But now I wouldn't miss it for anything."

Sister Jane regarded me curiously. "Why, William!" she exclaimed, "you are coming out. I didn't know you had it in you."

"But I knew it all the while," Mary declared, with such an air of sincerity that I felt the blood mounting to my face again, and saw it rising in hers.

"Mamma didn't know I was such a politician,"

she remarked. "When I go back, she'll look frightened and whisper, 'what will your father say?' and I'll laugh and promise to tell papa about it myself after it is all over."

So it was settled that Mary Bullard, sister Jane, and myself were to go to the circus to hear what was to be heard and see what was to be seen. We were both ready when Mary Bullard came tripping down the garden walk. I do not know what changes she had made in her apparel, or how the trick was done — perhaps it was my foolish imagination — but it seemed possible that she had just stepped out of fairyland; a woman of flesh and blood, and yet so radiantly beautiful as to suggest some turn of magic.

I was afraid that I would carry my awkwardness with me, but Mary disposed of it in a moment. When we started, she placed her hand on my arm, not lightly, but confidingly, and from that moment I was a new man, and have never been quite the same since.

The circus was all a dream to me. I remember that there was a dingy weather-beaten tent, a crowd of people standing outside, and inside a sea of faces, with its waves piled above one another, row on row; I remember that I had to give a firm hand to Mary as we climbed upward to be lost in this sea; I remember a confusion of music, a whirling panorama of horses and riders, a painted clown who danced about and caused the people to shout themselves hoarse; I even remember sister

Jane's awful frown when a woman in skirts that hardly reached her knees came tripping forth and was lifted to a horse's back. I remember these things, and I remember that Mary always leaned a little closer to me when some daring or dangerous feat was in course of performance; but beyond this everything was vague. There was Mary Bullard sitting next me, leaning against me. That was all I knew or felt, but that was enough. If the whole affair, tent, audience, horses — everything — had been lifted in the air, leaving me sitting there with Mary Bullard, I should have been none the wiser until Mary herself had called my attention to it.

But it was over all too soon for me. It seemed but a few moments, before the people began to crowd towards the entrance of the tent.

"Is this all? Is the show at an end?" I cried.

"Why, yes," replied Mary. "Did n't you hear what the man said — that 'the afternoon's performance is now over, ladies and gentlemen,' and that there would be an entire change of programme to-night? "

"No, I did not," I replied truthfully, "I neither saw the man nor heard him."

"I know you did n't enjoy it," remarked Mary, with a little sigh, "and I 'm sorry."

"Enjoy it!" I exclaimed. "I have n't enjoyed an afternoon so much since — since you were a little girl."

She fixed upon me a look that I could not

fathom. I knew not whether it had doubt or curiosity behind it. Presently the color deepened on her face, and she turned her head away to watch the crowd, which was clambering and clattering down the rattle-trap seats, and surging toward the door. We remained in our places until the people on the rows below us had made it safe to descend.

"Did I hear you say you enjoyed it, William?" asked sister Jane. She waited for no reply. "Well, if you look that glum when you 're enjoying yourself, I 'd like to see how you 'd act if you had to go to the gallows." At which observation Mary Bullard laughed until the tears came into her eyes.

"I did n't go so far as to say that I enjoyed the circus," I explained, "and yet I have had more real enjoyment to-day than I have had since one day in May ten years ago."

"Well, if you 're as full of joy as your famine has been long, I wonder that something or other don't give way," remarked sister Jane, bluntly.

Mary laughed at this so heartily that I was not surprised to see her face grow red. As we were descending the rows of seats, she asked if there was n't a picnic on that day in May ten years ago, and when I answered that there was, the expression of her face grew so serious that I was truly sorry I had mentioned the matter at all. For on that May day ten years ago, she was a little girl, and she went to the picnic under my care and

protection. Yet her seriousness was only a passing humor. In five minutes it had disappeared,
and was succeeded by a fit of gayety that was
delightful to witness; and surprising, too, for
I had never seen her quite so buoyant since she
was a romping girl. She made believe she would
pirouette in the public street; she chaffed sister
Jane; she chaffed me; and carried herself so
merrily withal, and so discreetly, too, that I, who
knew she was the loveliest woman in the world,
had never seen her so lovely before. Her laughter was a delight to the ear, as her every movement was a delight to the eye; her eyes shone
with an unwonted brilliance, and the tenderest
rose-flush played on her cheeks.

Once in the house, she began to play all sorts
of kittenish pranks. She pulled sister Jane's ears
and then kissed her. She tossed Keezes, much
to that youngster's delight, and then cuddled him
in her arms and cōoed over him; she seized
Tommy Tinkins by the forelegs, and made believe
he was her partner in a dance; she did a hundred
things I had never seen her do since she was
a child, each performance more charming than the
last. Suddenly, while standing in the middle of
the room, with her white hand raised in a pretty
gesture, she became serious. The change was so
unexpected that I involuntarily glanced through
the windows, thinking that she had seen some
one. But no one was in sight.

"I'm too happy!" she cried. "It's a bad

sign. When I am happy like this something is sure to happen."

"Well, child, if something or other don't happen, we 'll have a mighty quiet time of it the few years we 've got to live," remarked Sister Jane.

But, though she was still smiling, and her eyes still shining with the joy she felt, she shook her beautiful head wisely. "It 's a bad sign," she repeated; "I 've heard Free Betsey say so; and I remember that when I was coming home from Philadelphia, I was just as happy as I am now. But after I came home I was miserable."

"Why, what in the world was the matter?" asked sister Jane.

"Oh, everything was changed."

"I don't see how that could be, child," persisted sister Jane. "What happened?"

"Something," replied Mary, demurely, almost sadly: "but what it was, I would n't tell for the world."

Down I came tumbling to the earth. I saw in an instant, as by a revelation, that she had been disappointed in some childish love affair. I felt myself shrunken and ugly, and older than ever. But I said nothing. I had intended to accompany her home, dusk having fallen, but now I held my peace. Something in my face must have told her that the lights had been blown out in my house of cards, for she came nearer.

"You have given me a happy day," she said, — "both of you. You have put yourselves out for me; but I 'm not going to say 'thanky,' I 'll just let you imagine how grateful I am. As for you, sir," she cried, with mock dignity, "having escorted me to the circus, you must now patch out your gallantry, as Miss Jane would say, and escort me as far as my gate, if no farther."

"I expect I 'll have to go with you," sister Jane remarked before I could answer a word. "When William once settles down for his nap, it 's a hard matter to get him to stir."

This grim satire would have amused me at another time, but I did not relish it now. I made haste to place myself at Mary's disposal, surprised at so unusual a request, but happy to grant it. I took pains, however, not to rekindle the flaring lights that had illuminated my poor little house of cards all the afternoon.

So we went together through the garden, Mary leaning on my arm as confidently as a child might lean on its father's. The pinks distilled their spices and the roses shed their perfume for my especial benefit that night, and the constellations sparkled with unwonted lustre. We said little, for there was nothing to say. At the gate she said good-night and went tripping up the steps.

I had noticed that there was an unusual stir in the house. The servants were running from room to room with lighted candles, and as I walked toward home, there were loud cries of alarm. I stopped still in my tracks, the better to hear, when I saw Mary come running down the walk.

I knew her movements, though I could not distinguish her features.

She saw me, and gave one frightened sob as she clutched me by the arm.

"Oh, what shall I do?" she cried, though her voice was scarcely above a whisper.

Trembling from a hundred vague fears, I drew her into my arms and held her so. I tried to speak, but my tongue refused its office. I could only hold her in my arms, and, with a shaking hand, stroke her hair as I used to do when she was a child.

"Freddy is lost! my poor little brother is lost! He can be found nowhere. The whole town has been searched. Oh, to think that he is out in the dark alone, and crying for me! What shall I do? Where shall I go? Oh, my poor little brother!"

Thus she moaned, with her head on my shoulder, clinging to me and shivering. My first thought was of sister Jane, and to her we went, Mary seeming to have a revival of energy. I ran fast, but she ran faster, and by the time I reached the door, my sister had the poor girl pressed to her tender heart, and was getting such small information as she could obtain.

With sister Jane, to think was to act. Her bonnet lay on the bed where she had thrown it. She seized it, dashed it on her head recklessly, and, saying to Mary "come!" sped out of the house and along the garden walk. As for me, I was too much shocked to think, though all the trifles I have mentioned seized hold of my mind and stuck fast in my memory. I fell rather than sat on a chair, and remained there supinely.

Mandy Satterlee had seized her baby, and held it tightly to her breast, as if by that means she would save it from the misfortune that had overtaken Mary's little brother. She now sat crying and sobbing as if her heart would break.

"What is the matter, Mandy? Why excite yourself in that manner?" I inquired with some severity. Her grief seemed so entirely out of proportion to her interest in Freddy Bullard that it irritated me.

"Oh, that child!" she sobbed. "That little boy!"

"You make yourself ridiculous," I said. "Of course the child will be found. It is impossible that he should be lost."

Mandy, turning her streaming eyes upon me, raised her right hand in a gesture that her earnestness made tragic.

"That poor little boy will never be found in the round world!" she cried. "It 's proned into me." Her arm fell to her side, and she betook herself again to her grief.

IX.

A CHILD IS LOST.

THERE was not much sleeping in the village that night. Each family seemed to take the loss home to itself. The men — old and young — organized themselves into searching parties, while the women flitted about the streets, going from house to house, seeking information, and finding new opportunities and occasions for gossip. The news seemed to spread over the community as by magic. The negroes were as active as anybody. Old Sol, Colonel Bullard's carriage driver, had stirred them up and was leading them. No nine o'clock bell rang for them that night. They went running hither and yonder and whither they pleased. The tramping of feet and the sound of men running and of women calling to each other in the dark came to my ears from the street, as I sat in the shadow of the honeysuckle. Though the air was chill, and the long wisps of clouds combed out by the wind gave token of dampness, the signs went unheeded so far as I was concerned.

What struck me as most peculiar — ominous, indeed — was the tone in which the people passing by, especially the women, spoke of the lost child. "He was such a bright little boy." "So full of life and fun." "He would have been five years old next August." "It was so sudden — like a clap of thunder out of a clear sky." I remembered with a shiver that many and many a time I had heard people talk so of the dead. And then the prophecy of Mandy Satterlee crept back into my mind (from which I had ousted it), and remained there.

After a while I heard sister Jane coming along the garden walk, and I joined her in the house, where Mandy Satterlee was still sitting, having now recovered from her hysterical burst of grief. There was no information in sister Jane's eyes, and so I forbore to question her. She called Mandy to a consultation in the kitchen as soon as Klibs could be tucked under cover, and they remained there some minutes. As they came back I heard sister Jane say solemnly : —

"It 's the Providence of God, Mandy," and this terse remark struck deeper into my mind than many a sermon has done. Truly, it was the Providence of God. Whether the little fellow was dead or alive, or safe, to be returned to his friends, or fated to be lost to them until doomsday, he was in the hands of the Almighty.

In a measure quieted by these reflections, I seized my hat and walked along the street toward Colonel Bullard's home. A large crowd had assembled in the pillared portico, all friends and all sympathetic. Midway down the flight of steps that led from the street to the door, I saw Mary Bullard standing. She held a lighted lanthorn in her hand, and seemed to be expecting some one to join her.

"I was waiting for you," she said, as I went forward. She ran down the steps and for the fourth time that day laid her hand on my arm.

"Waiting for me?" I asked, taking the lanthorn. There was no surprise in either my voice or my mind. I made the inquiry to make sure that my ears had not deceived me.

"Yes," she replied simply, and I was satisfied. It seemed the most natural thing in the world that she should be standing there waiting for me with the lanthorn in her hand. By some strange conceit or delusion of the mind, the incident was as old and as familiar to my experience the moment it happened as if it had occurred at the very threshold and beginning of my life, and found a thousand repetitions since.

I turned to the impulse of her movements, and we went towards the public square. In a few moments I found that we were going in the direction of the circus. For an instant — a bare instant — the idea that Mary was distraught by reason of her grief took possession of me; took possession of me and shook me as no thought ever did before or ever will again. Some symptom of it must have been conveyed to her, for she leaned more heavily on my arm.

"What is the matter?" she asked.

For answer I lifted the lanthorn and looked into her face. She smiled ever so faintly and turned her head away. Her face was pale, indeed, but, thank God, reason and intelligence shone above grief in her sad eyes.

"Don't," she said. "I'll not bear inspection to-night."

I made no reply, not even by way of apology, but the consternation that had seized me passed away as a noxious vapor before the morning sun.

The night was not yet old, and the show under the dingy tent was still in full blast. The music of the band flung sweetly over the uproar made now and then by the motley crowd; and, as we drew near, the hundreds of lights that were set in a circle around the centre pole gave a brilliant effect that could be seen from the outside, where groups of whites and negroes stood, — the unfortunates who were too poor or too economical to pay the admission fee. Through these groups we went, inquiring if they had seen anything of the child.

Business was over for the man who stood at the entrance of the tent, and he was now taking his ease in a chair, his feet flung over one of the ropes. He rose as we approached, and regarded us with a stare in which there was more amazement than respect. I was for paying the fee, but Mary stopped me by a gesture.

"I am hunting for my little brother," she said. "He has been missing since this afternoon."

"Mercy! that's bad!" said the man, taking off his hat. He raised his hand, and some one who was lounging near came running forward. "Tell Dorkins to come here."

The messenger darted away, and in half a minute Dorkins came running. "What is it, sir?" he asked.

"Show this lady and gentleman through the tent. A child has been lost. What is the name, ma'am? Bullard! Not Colonel Bullard? Well, bless my stars! Wait, Dorkins. You stay here. Come with me, ma'am."

We went inside, and it seemed to me that the eyes of the whole multitude were fastened on us — Mary, with her beautiful hair falling about her shoulders, and I with the lanthorn, which looked dim indeed in all the glaring light. Major Fambrough, who was a prominent politician and who was therefore always looking for an opportunity to make himself conspicuous, saw us at once, and was quick to jump to the conclusion that something serious had occurred.

"Unless you are out hunting for an honest man, Wornum, something is wrong," he said, touching me on the shoulder, and taking his hat off to Mary. "What is it?"

"My little brother is lost," replied Mary.

"Lost! Why, you amaze me!" cried the major. He tried hard to wear a look of concern, but the man's eyes fairly sparkled, and I soon saw the reason why. "We'll see what can be done," he said, and, walking into the middle of the ring, which was vacant just then, he raised his hand to command attention.

"Ladies and gentlemen," he began, " a great calamity has befallen our little community." ("Take him out!" some one cried. "Bring in the muel, and let him ride!" yelled some one else.) "If my political opponents desire to ridicule me," the major went on, "they should wait for the proper time and opportunity. At present I desire to announce that the family of our respected fellow-townsman, Colonel Cephas Bullard, have suffered a severe affliction. Little Freddy Bullard is lost and cannot be found. If my opponents desire to make capital out of that, they are welcome to do so."

There were sympathetic exclamations from the crowd, and a great many people began to leave their seats, but I felt that Major Fambrough had made a miserable spectacle of himself. My cheeks burned with the shame that he was a stranger to.

The man who had constituted himself our guide laughed softly. "If we had that chap in the side-show," he said, "he 'd draw the crowds."

He led us through the big tent into the dressing-room. The painted clown was sitting on a coil of rope reading a letter by the light of a candle he held in one hand. Other men were leaning about with heavy overcoats flung over their thin costumes. A woman, in short and fluffy skirts, was trying to pin a rent in her bespangled waist, and she was the first to see us. She drew back with an exclamation, snatched a cloak from a stool, and held it before her. Through the hideous rouge on her face I could see her blushes. To her Mary went straight.

"My little brother is lost," she said. "We are trying to find him."

"Ah!" the rouged woman exclaimed, turning to the rest, "her little brother is lost."

If I ever saw sympathy and pity depicted on the human countenance, I saw it on that woman's face — and on the faces of the others. Somehow they all seemed to remember that they had homes, and when we turned away, I noticed that the woman was crying, and that the clown, who, on a near view, had an old and a wizened look, had clenched his hand and crumpled his letter until it bore small semblance to a written page.

Meanwhile the man who had come with us through the tent sent his men in every direction with orders to search for the child; but they all returned with the same story. Mary thanked them all, placed her hand on my arm again, and we went home, the man going a part of the way with us, and giving us the comfort of such hope as experience and self-possession can impart. At the last he promised that if he found the child the next day, or heard any tidings of it, he would mount a messenger on one of his best horses, and send us word. I joined my thanks to Mary's.

“Don’t thank me,” he said to Mary. “I have a special reason for doing whatever I can — a very special reason.” With that he laughed softly to himself, bowed, and was gone. At another time I would have regarded this as a very neat compliment to Mary, but now I felt that the stranger was under some obligation to Colonel Bullard. I suggested this to Mary, who replied with a sigh: “I shouldn’t wonder. Father is always helping somebody, or doing good somewhere.”

So we went back home unsuccessful, but Mary was better satisfied. She had done something that nobody else had thought of, and her mind was more at ease. I would have carried her to see sister Jane, but she insisted on going straight home.

“Good-night,” she said at the steps — the portico above was still crowded with people who were as heavily charged with curiosity as with sympathy — “good-night. This has been the happiest and most miserable day of my life; and you have been so kind and thoughtful through it all.”

I murmured something in reply, watched her as she went slowly up the wide steps, and then turned and went home. There I found Mrs. Beshears, who, on account of the excitement in the village, had remained longer than usual. Sister Jane was sitting where she always sat, Mrs. Beshears was in her corner, Mandy Satterlee was rocking her baby, and Tommy Tinkins was stretched out on the hearth-rug; everything was in its usual place; and yet I felt that there had been a change — a tremendous change. The idea was so strong in my mind that I paused on entering the room and looked around; and it was not until months afterwards that I discovered the change was in me and not in my surroundings.

"For mercy's sake, William, what is the matter?" said sister Jane. "You look as if you 've been bewitched." I suppose something queer in my attitude or in my countenance must have attracted her attention, for she had a quick eye for such things. "Where 've you been gallantin' to?"

I related as briefly as possible what has been set down here, not omitting a description of Major Fambrough's oration at the circus. This last seemed to be most interesting of all, for both sister Jane and Mrs. Beshears laughed until the tears came in their eyes.

"It 's a livin' wonder," remarked Mrs. Beshears, "that that man ain't been elected to some big office too long ago to talk about."

"Why, yes," said sister Jane. "He 's a big enough fool to go to the legislature. The lunatic asylum ain't so mighty far from the state house. They tell me you can stand on the roof of one and fling a rock on top of t'other."

Then they fell to discussing the sensation of the day, which was the disappearance of little Freddy Bullard. My theory was that he would be found to-morrow, and it was a theory that lasted through many long days. For if the child had been taken up into the clouds, or if the earth had opened and swallowed him, his disappearance could not have been more complete or more mysterious.

The search was continued for weeks, and was extended to the neighboring counties. All the wells were examined, all the ponds and streams for miles around were dragged, and the circus was followed and watched by two or three young men who had been paying Mary Bullard some attention. But all to no purpose. The child was not to be found; and so, in the course of time, the village went about its business in the usual way, and the disappearance of Freddy Bullard became a story to frighten children with.

Even the fortitude with which Colonel Bullard bore the burden of his grief ceased to be the subject of remark. He seemed to accept it as his share of the misfortunes which come to the sons of men, and continued to go up and down as usual, winning the sympathy of the thoughtful and retaining the respect of all his fellow-citizens.

The event wrought a change in Mary, though I knew not whether it was visible to any eyes but mine. I can only vaguely describe it by saying that she grew more womanly, more gracious, and more charming. To me she had always been charming and gracious, but now these qualities took (or seemed to take) new lustre from her grief. And when her grief had subsided into sorrow, as it must do in the most faithful hearts as time goes on, her pensiveness, whether it shone through her smiles or took the shape of gentle melancholy, was as sweet and as touching as the notes of some old melody fluttering through the dusk from a far-off flute.

I saw with much satisfaction that the half dozen young men who had striven hard to make themselves agreeable to Mary gradually ceased their visits. They withdrew by degrees, and sullenly (or so it seemed to me), as if they were loath to acknowledge that they had failed to make an impression. My satisfaction at their evident discomposure did not spring from envy. God knows, I never had that feeling. I should have been gratified if Mary's innocent heart had found refuge in the love of some man, standing high above his fellows — a man among men in gifts and position — a man entirely worthy of her. But where was such a man to be found?

The young men I have mentioned were clever enough, as cleverness goes. They were blessed with this world's goods; they belonged to the first families; and they were regarded as "good catches" by the mothers of marriageable daughters in all the counties round about. So much so that I often shuddered at the thought that Mary (a mere child from my point of view) might be thoughtless enough to have her head turned by the flattery of their attentions. But I did her rank injustice in my thoughts. She was ever

above the small vanities that belong to youth and
her sex, and the larger ones she never so much
as dreamed of. Her motives were open as the
day. She was the embodiment of truth and innocence, and neither vanity nor the pride that
consumes had any part in her nature. She was
as gracious to the humblest as she was to the
highest. Her consideration could skim the surface of the earth as easily as it could soar above
the heights.

As I have said, life in the village soon dropped
into the old uneventful channels. It seemed that
nothing could reach the stature of an event after
the episode I have tried to describe. All things
dwindled and shrunk by comparison. And yet
the doubt besets me that I have failed to picture
forth the shock that was given to the whole community. Looking back over these pages the affair
seems tame and spiritless.

Let me say here, while the opportunity is ripe,
that this and other episodes to be told of are not
to be judged by the narrative alone. There are
gaps and lapses the reader must fill out for himself. The knack of narration belongs to the
gifted few, who need neither art nor practice to
fit them for the work. With me, all is lacking.
When the impressive moment arrives the apt and
trenchant word eludes me. The sparkling phrase,
the vivid grouping, and the illumination that
flashes the whole scene upon the mind, are want-

ing. I have tried to give the crude outline only, leaving the imagination of the reader to inject into it the elements necessary to impart a pleasure and a satisfaction that my poor gifts could never convey.

X.

FREE BETSEY RUNS THE CARDS.

THE name of Free Betsey has been mentioned somewhere in the preceding pages. I was better acquainted with her reputation than with her personality, but I knew her when I saw her, as, indeed, everybody in this section did. She struck me as a queer mixture of humility, audacity, and cunning. She told fortunes by cards, carrying a greasy pack with her for that purpose, and she sold ginger-cakes on public days and during court-week, eking out in this way a living that served her purposes well enough.

Free Betsey and I came to a closer acquaintance in a very curious way. During the early winter it was my habit to take long walks in the woods, frequently going far beyond the town branch — a small stream that was a mile from the court-house. Happily, I never found it necessary to walk in the public highway. Through the big woods and fields in all directions numerous by-paths ran — paths that had been made first by the Indians and wild beasts and were afterwards frequented by the negroes and cattle. They wound about, crossing one another, and frequently formed a labyrinth interesting to work out.

On one occasion, while following one of these paths that led me in a direction I had never traveled before, I suddenly saw Free Betsey walking ahead of me. The woods were not thick, and the path was straight and open, so much so, that the sudden appearance of Free Betsey where I had seen no one a moment before set me to wondering. Cover and hide as we will, our learning and culture have not struck deep enough to remove the dregs of superstition. These seem to have settled at the very bottom of our natures, as it were, and resist all the processes of enlightenment; so that whatever comes upon us refusing to submit to plausible explanation is like to send a cold chill along the marrow of the spine.

I had some such feeling as that when Free Betsey took shape in the path before me, congealing (as it seemed) out of the vapors of the forest. I knew it was Free Betsey by her antics. She bowed and curtsied to imaginary people as she went along, such was her seeming humility. It was "Howdy, mars'er," — "howdy, missis," — howdy, trees, — howdy, ground, — howdy, sky, — howdy, everybody that lives, — and howdy everything that creeps, or crawls or exists — bowing here, bowing there, to the left and to the right, and dropping low curtsies to all. A more uncanny figure it would have been hard to find. I could hear her talking to herself as she bowed and waved her hands, for though I had slackened my pace to avoid overtaking her, and she seemed to be going as rapidly as ever, I drew nearer and nearer. Not content with her bowing and curtsying, she broke into a song with this queer refrain: —

> " Man come to my house — it's howdy, oh, howdy !
> Man come to my house — oh, it's howdy, howdy do ! "

This over, she shook her head and laughed shrilly, and then suddenly sat squat on the ground, and fell to making marks in the path with her forefinger.

"Ah-yi! I been waitin' fer you, Mars'er Willyum — waitin' long time. Squinch-owl say ' he comin' '—he no come. Whip'will say ' he comin' ' — he no come. Blue jay say, ' day! day! ' — he come."

"Waiting for me!" I exclaimed, looking at her in some astonishment. Age had taken the plumpness from her face, but her eyes shone like those of some wild animal.

"Yasser — yasser!" she cried, rising nimbly to her feet. "Waitin' long time, an' you come. Waitin' in de woods, an' you come. My house yander — on de hill dere." She walked along the path and I followed. "What you done wid my young mistis?" she inquired.

"Your young mistress?"

"Eh-heh! De gal what you pull fum de snow. Whar she been gone dis long time? I look fer see her — I no see her."

"Do you mean Mandy Satterlee?" I inquired.

"Eh-heh! Yasser! Dat ve'y gal. She my

young mistiss. Hit come like dis: I b'long'ded to her ma's pa, an' he sot me free: yasser, he gi' me my papers. I ain't no Myrick nigger; no, suh! My ole man, he's a Myrick nigger, but dat ain't no bindin' reason fer me ter be a Myrick nigger. No, suh! My mars'er ain't set back an hire his niggers out to Tom, Dick, an' Harry. He got up fo' day wid um, an' worked um. Dey had ter arn der livin', but dey got it atter dey arned it. I'm a Bowden nigger, myse'f. Ole Gabe Bowden wuz my mars'er, an' ole Gabe Bowden sot me free, an ole Gabe Bowden wuz de grandaddy er Mandy Satterlee, an' I bless God *eve'y* day an' *eve'y* night dat ole Gabe Bowden done dead an' gone ter heav'm whar he b'longded at. Dead — dead! Yasser — dead!"

While she was pouring forth this volume of speech, she was walking along in the path ahead of me, waving her arms and shaking her head, and occasionally looking around to see whether I was following. I remembered, of course, that Gabe Bowden — the name was spelt Bowdoin on the records of the court — was Mandy Satterlee's grandfather, that his daughter had eloped with Satterlee, and that her disobedience in this matter gave him a blow from which he never fully recovered. He died not more than a year after his disappointment, and his daughter died the year following, having in the meantime given birth to a son and daughter. The family seemed to be pursued by a storm of disasters.

In a few moments we came to Free Betsey's house, which was built on land owned by Mrs. Beshears and her sisters. The woman asked me in, and placed a chair for me. It was a stout log cabin, of one room, and everything about it was neat as a pin. Even the hearth, which would otherwise have presented an unseemly appearance (being made of rough stones) was glossed and veneered by a coat of red clay, smoothly laid on. The cooking-things were clean, and the tin cups and pans shone as if they had been freshly burnished. A white counterpane was spread over the bed, and the valances were frilled and fluted quite in the style. I wondered at this, for there was nothing in Free Betsey's appearance to indicate a love of order and neatness. She must have followed my thoughts, for she said, as she seated herself on the door-sill: —

"Don't git skeer'd 'bout ole Betsey, suh. I wuz raise in de white folks' house. Dat ar counterpane dar older dan what you is — dat ar skillet older dan Sally Beshears — dat ar trivet was brung fum Ferginny 'fo' de white folks an' de tories fell out an' fit. Ne'r min' 'bout dat. Whar Mandy Satterlee? Whar my young mistiss at?"

"At our house," I replied.

"What she doin' dar?"

"Well, she is doing what she wants to do — cooking and helping around."

"Ah-hah!" cried Free Betsey. "I know'd it.

She's dar playin' de nigger! Oh, dey can't fool me — dey des can't do it! She's dar playin' de nigger! Why n't she go 'way fum dar? What she want ter stay dar playin' de nigger fer?"

Age and the pretense of humility gave Free Betsey privileges which she was in the habit of pushing to their utmost limit. So I replied by asking a question: —

"Where should she go?"

"She kin come yer — right yer in dis ve'y house!" exclaimed Free Betsey, striking the floor with her clenched fist. "What gwine ter hender her? Oh, you nee'n'ter to be lookin' 'roun'," she went on, catching the glance of my eye. "Dat ar bed dar ain't never been slep' on by no white folks, much less a nigger. Dat ar counterpin', an' dat quilt, an' dem ar sheets ain' never kiver'd no livin' human 'ceptin' ole Gabe Bowden. Look at dis!" She rose, went to the bed, lifted a side of the valance, and exposed to view a trundle bed. "Dat whar I sleep at. What I keep dis house clean fer? Fer me? Naw! What I keep dat bed fer? Fer me? Naw! What I keep fire on de ha'th fer? Fer me? Bless God, naw! What I want wid um? What I gwine do wid um?"

Gradually, as her meaning, which had been doubtful at first, dawned on me slowly, and yet surely, admiration for the negro crept into my mind and remained there.

"Tell me dat," she went on, growing more earnest. "What I gwine do wid all dis? What

I gwine do wid it? How come Mandy Satterlee
don't stop playin' nigger at yo' house, an' come
ter dis house, whar dey 's a nigger waitin' fer her
—a nigger, an' a monstus good un, ef I does say
it myse'f? Now tell me dat! 'Ain't I gone an'
nuss'd her when she wuz a baby, an' hilt her in
my arms, an' sot dar huggin' her whiles ol' Satterlee wuz cussin' an' 'busin' me 'cause I wuz a
free nigger? *Ef dey ever wuz a hellian he wuz
one!*" she cried in a burst of passion. "Ef
you 'll put yo' pillow over yo' head at night des'
fo' you go ter sleep an' when eve'ything is still,
you kin hear 'im holler in Torment. I does dat
away eve'y night, an' it makes me laugh when I
hear ole Satterlee holler in Torment."

Free Betsey paused to take breath, tore a frag-
ment of bark from one of the pine logs and began
to pick it to pieces. Presently, with a cry of disgust and hatred, she flung it from her.

"Satterlee!" she breathed the name with a
hiss. "Dey 's pizen in de blood! Look at Mandy
Satterlee! Look what de pizen has brung her to!
Playin' nigger! Ef dey 's any salvation in dis worl'
fer her, de Bowden blood 'll save her. I dunner
how it gwine ter be when she die. Ef she 's got
one drap mo' er de Satterlee blood dan what she 's
got er de Bowden blood, de angels can't save her."

Free Betsey paused again, and regarded me so
earnestly that I felt uncomfortable.

"How do she do? Do she cry an' take on?
Do she do like her sperret done broke?"

"Yes, she is very unhappy," I replied.

"Well, I thank my God fer dat much!" cried Free Betsey, lifting her hands high over her head. "Dat 's de Bowden blood. Oh, tell her ter cry — cry — cry! An' den, when cryin' don't do her no good, tell her dat her ol' nigger is waitin' fer her out yer in de woods."

"Why don't you come to see her?" I suggested, struck by her devotion. "No doubt she would be glad to see you."

"Me come dar?" She lowered her voice, and a pleased expression crept into her face. "God knows, I been layin' off ter come, suh, but I 'm skeer'd. I ain't nothin' 't all but a ole no-count free nigger, an' I been skeer'd dat ef I come dar an' ax fer my young mistiss 't would make you all mo' 'spicious er de gal dan what you is."

I followed Free Betsey's thought rather than her words, and my admiration for her grew steadily.

"I use ter know Miss Jane," she went on, "an' she 'll fly up an' flew at you at de drappin' uv a hat an' drap it herse'f. Ef I come I 'm comin' kaze you ax me, an' not kaze Mandy Satterlee want ter see me. She may not want ter see me, an' I don't speck she do, but dat ain't needer yer ner dar; ef I know'd Miss Jane want gwine ter fly up an' flew'd at me, I 'd come. I sho would — not in de day time, but in de dark er de moon."

"You may come any time," said I.

Free Betsey laughed gleefully. "Well, suh,

I 'm mos' tickled ter death ter hear you talk dat away. An' ef dat's de case, I 'll hatter tell yo' fortune." She rose from the door sill, went to a shelf on which was perched a small, square mirror, and picked up a pack of playing cards.

"Nonsense!" I protested. "You don't think I believe in that sort of stuff?"

"Eh-eh!" cried Free Betsey. "Don't make no diffunce 'bout b'lievin' er not b'lievin'. Dat don't hurt de trufe. It mostly in giner'lly hurt dem what don't b'lieve de trufe." Crude as it was, this was sound reasoning, but it bore no relation to fortune-telling, and so I informed Free Betsey.

"Ef dat's de case," she replied, "'t ain't gwine ter hurt you no how; an' ef 't is de trufe maybe it 's lots purtier dan what you specktin' it ter be." With that she sat on the door-sill again, smoothed her lap out, and began to shuffle the cards, showing a dexterity in the performance that I have never seen surpassed. Suddenly she dropped the pack in her lap, and turned to me.

"Who dat you had wid you at de circus dat time?" she asked.

The question was so unexpected, and was put so plumply that I was taken aback. I suppose I must have blushed, for Free Betsey threw herself on the floor in a paroxysm of laughter, whether real or feigned I had no means of knowing.

"Oh, you ain't done forgot de name," she cried. "I know by my nose an' my two big toes."

"I was with my sister and Miss Mary Bullard," I remarked after a while with a dignity befitting the occasion.

"De reason I ast," Free Betsey explained, "was dat I run de kyards 'bout you de day de circus wuz a callywhoopin' aroun', an' dey runded mighty quare. Dey make me open my eyes — *wide!* I say 'Heyo, how come dis?' an' 'Heyo, how come dat?' But dey wuz all mixt up wid sump'n er nudder, I dunner what. But wait! I 'll see how dey talk now."

She shuffled the cards again, then divided them into four equal parts, placing each part to itself, until she came to the fourth. This she retained in her hands, running the cards rapidly through her fingers, and studying the combinations that presented themselves. This she did a half dozen times. At last she laughed aloud, and ex-claimed: —

"Man, dis beats all! 'T ain't much better dan 't wuz de day er de circus. Yer de gal — dark complected — same gal — trouble all roun' 'er, but not de big trouble dat dey wuz — yer she is, gwine up an' down — an' dar's de trouble."

She laid the cards in her lap and took the next division, passing the pieces of painted pasteboard so nimbly between her fingers, one by one, that they seemed to move of their own will and voli-tion.

"Name er de Lord!" she muttered. "What de matter wid deze kyards? De trouble ain't no big trouble — dey ain't no sickness — dey ain't no journeys — dey ain't nobody makin' no trouble — what de matter?" She put the cards down and picked up the next division. "Folks all gwine 'long 'tendin' ter der own business — no ups an' downs — no nothin'." She took the fourth and last division in her hands and went through the same formality of skimming them through her fingers. "Ah-yi!" she exclaimed. "Yer de light complected man! what he doin' 'way off yer by his own lone se'f? Mo' trouble — all er he own makin'. What de matter wid 'im?" She took the first division and added it to the one she held in her hands. "Look at um! De dark-complected gal gwine up an' down makin' trouble fer 'er own se'f — de light-complected man settin' still makin' trouble fer he own se'f. Dat what de kyards say," she went on, looking hard at me, "an' de kyards know what dey talkin' 'bout. Dat 's your fortune, Mars'er Willyum Wornum, an' I 'm mighty glad 't ain't no wuss; I 'm glad fum de bottom er my heart."

"It 's not much of a fortune," I remarked, dryly. "But since you are so apt at such things, why don't you tell of the little boy that was lost — Freddy Bullard?"

"Don't you know 'dout any tellin'?" she asked, with some eagerness.

"I know he is lost, certainly," I replied; "we all know that."

"Is dat all?"

"It is all anybody knows," I said.

"Ain't Miss Jane done tol' you?"

"She knows no more than I do."

"Well, ef dat don't beat all! Ain't Miss Jane tol' you, sho nuff?"

I was nettled more by the tone of Free Betsey than by her words, which had no meaning for me. "Of course she has n't told me anything more than everybody knows," I replied, with some heat.

"Well den, ef she ain't done tol' you, I ain't gwine tell you, kaze she got some good reason. 'T ain't kaze she dunno. Man, suh! dey can't fool Sally Beshears an' dey can't fool Free Betsey."

"Why, you must be crazy," I exclaimed, petulantly.

"Dat des what de matter," she said, in a whisper. "Ol' Free Betsey ain't only gone crazy; she 'uz bornded crazy. Dat 's it — dat 's it!"

Of course Free Betsey, with characteristic cunning, was trying to find out what I knew (though, indeed, I knew nothing) of the fate of Freddy Bullard, so as to weave it into a rigmarole of her own when she came to "run" the cards.

"If you can tell fortunes with your cards," said I, "you can surely tell me something of Freddy Bullard."

"Not wid de kyards," she replied. "I got sump'n better 'n kyards."

With that she went to a chest that stood in one

corner of the room — a very substantial looking chest it was, too — and drew from its depths a crystal of peculiar formation, such as are sometimes found on the hills of middle Georgia. It was a very large and beautiful stone, weighing, perhaps, a pound. The surface was clear, but in its depths were flecks and splotches of white, having the appearance of a milky vapor. I took it in my hands and examined it curiously, turning it about, and weighing it in my palm. It was as fine a specimen of the kind as I ever saw, and I wondered to what use Free Betsey would put it. My curiosity was soon satisfied. She took the stone and closed both hands over it, and held it to her face, and breathed on it her warm breath. Then she rubbed it briskly on her apron and held it to the light. It may have been my imagination, or it may have been the angle at which my eyes fell on the stone, but it seemed to me that the vaporous white flecks were both thinner and fewer in number. But the appearance of the stone did not seem to satisfy Free Betsey. She warmed it again by breathing upon it, and rubbed it briskly with her apron.

"It mighty cloudy in dar," she exclaimed.

She breathed on it, and rubbed it the third time, and held it up to the light. This time I was sure that some change had taken place. The stone seemed to be dazzlingly clear, not transparent, but teeming with pale sparks of light. This, after all, may have been due to a trick of handling, but, if so, the trick was cleverly done. Free Betsey gazed steadfastly into the clear depths of the stone, mumbling something in an undertone. Presently she said: —

"A long road an' a mighty rough un. Man got de chil' by de han'. Sometimes dey er ridin' an' sometimes dey er walkin'. Sometimes de man tote de chil', sometimes he make 'im walk. Sometimes dey set down on de side de road to res'."

Free Betsey spoke slowly and hesitatingly as if she found difficulty in making head or tail of the tangle she found in the mysterious depths of the stone.

"Now dey er walkin' — walk, walk, walk, — dodgin' in de woods when somebody come by. Trudge, trudge; chil' a-cryin', man a-cussin'. Miles 'pon top er miles — cross big rivers an' little uns — up hill an' down hill — 'cross mountains yit — way off yander de Lord knows whar. Bimeby dey come to er place whar some waggoners campin'. I see smoke, I see fire, I see de tops er de wagons — one, two — dozen wagons. Man an' chil' set down. Chil' mighty nigh dead he so hungry an' tired. Man slap de chil' fer to 'im hol' up he head. So den! Man jine wid de wagons. Travel an' travel wid um. Bimeby set de chil' down in de road an' go off an' lef' 'im. Man gone! — he done gone! Man wid black beard come 'long take de chil' in he arms an' much 'im, an' den he gi' 'im sump'n t' eat. Man" — she paused, turned the stone over in her hands. "Done gone," she said, with a sigh. "De clouds done come back."

I took the stone in my hand again, but the white vaporous flecks (if they had ever disappeared) had now come back, thicker, it seemed to me, than ever. Turn the stone as I would, it refused to show the lustre that it gave forth in Free Betsey's hand. This fact struck me, but it gave me no reason to place any confidence in her power to read the future. Yet it gave me a strong sense of the impression that her apparent earnestness and sincerity might make on weaker minds. I gave her a sevenpence piece, and left her; but before I had got out of hearing, she hollered at me this prophecy: —

"You 'll see what I tol' you, an' you 'll know mo'n dat 'fo' you git many year older."

XI.

TWO OLD FRIENDS AND ANOTHER.

It has been said that time moves more slowly
in a village than elsewhere; but when a man is
nearing his climacteric (and mine I reckoned to be
the age of forty) it moves all too fast for him, no
matter where Providence has stationed him.
There were moments when I could have wished to
stop the hands on the dial, or to do with the seasons what Joshua did with the sun — bid them to
stand still. But even if the age of miracles was
not past, as many claim and believe, it were a
vain and an idle thought for an obscure country
lawyer to hope to grow younger as the years went
by or to stay the hands of time. Nor did I repine
that this was so. Providence has given us the
knack of accommodating ourselves to circumstances, and this gift is in the nature of a fortune.
I was a part of the vast procession, and, while I
had my fancies, I was not averse from growing old
with the rest. In this business I knew that I had
the world, the planets, and the myriad stars for my
companions, and, we were all journeying along
together fulfilling the same divine order.

I felt that the burden of age, rightly carried, was far more precious than the vapors of youth. The happiness of youth is according to nature; the rarer happiness of age is according to philosophy. Youth has no other knowledge than to seek its pleasure; but where experience can extract content and happiness from life, that is a gift above nature. And I felt that I had it.

Yet I could have my fancies, too, and they did me no harm. I could fancy, when I saw Mary Bullard (and I saw her every day), how it might be if I were younger; and if I dropped a sigh at such times, my discontent was as fleeting and as momentary as a gust of summer wind. I had but to turn in my chair to find diversion. I had but to pass into the street to find an ample supply of the humor that life provides for those who have eyes to see and ears to hear.

It was on one of these occasions when I had gone into the street to rid myself of fancies, which, though entirely harmless, were unprofitable, that I chanced to meet with two old friends and acquaintances (Grandsir Johnny Roach and Uncle Jimmy Cosby), men who had known my father and who had been his warm friends. Grandsir Roach and Uncle Jimmy Cosby lived together a few miles from the village, and had been neighbors of the Satterlees. They were sitting on the steps of the court-house, talking together, and I walked across the public square to shake hands with them for the sake of old times.

The two old men were well-to-do. They owned
land and negroes, horses and carriages; but back
of their prosperity were the experience of the
pioneer and the spirit of true democracy. As
they were, so were their neighbors, for in this
section the aristocracy of caste could hardly find
a spot of ground on which to plant its dainty feet.
The essence of manhood is character, and the sub-
stance of character is integrity; and integrity
went farther than wealth among this people. The
two old men had the independence that cares little
for appearances, and the spirit of economy that
adapts itself to circumstances. I could see that
they had taken their feet in their hands (as the
saying is) and walked to the village, as they had
done many times before. They seemed to have
some joke between them, for they were chuckling
and nudging each other at a great rate. They
were as glad to see me as I was to see them, and
I was very soon let into the matter of the joke
that had convulsed them.

Grandsir Johnny Roach had started to the village with the understanding that his comrade and
neighbor, Uncle Jimmy Cosby, would follow in
a few moments and overtake him. Once under
way, Grandsir Johnny Roach, with the harmless
conceit of age, made up his mind to surprise Uncle
Jimmy Cosby by pushing forward brother idly as
his legs would allow him. He w me it's a leetle
all his seventy-odd years, and thomore 'n a quarter
tism had left him with what he

knee," he could manage to move with considerable celerity. The result was that Uncle Jimmy Cosby failed to overtake him until he had reached the public square. Though both were fagged out with the unusual exertion, they regarded it as a good joke, and seemed to enjoy it immensely.

"He cotch up wi' me, William, right in the aidge of town, an' I lay he hain't strained hisself, nother. Well, well! It's nothin' to boast on, Brother Cosby. I reckon I frittered away my wind a-cuttin' up capers in my young days, an' now I'm a-payin' of the fiddler. Ther's a turrible crick in my knee-jint, an' a tremblin' in my hams if I but overdo my gait."

"Oh, yes! I cotch up wi' 'im, William," remarked Uncle Jimmy Cosby, complacently, "but I laid off to overtake 'im at the Baptizin' Creek. I've had to walk — yes, sir! — I've had to walk as I hain't walked these many long years. I put out ten minnits arter you left, Brother Roach, an' I pulled right along wi'out lookin' uther to the right or uther to the left. I allowed maybe you was in some big hurry er 'nother."

Grandsir Johnny Roach smiled pleasantly over this neighborly tribute to his powers of endurance.

"No, no, Brother Cosby!" he protested; "I'm lots too old to be in any hurry; I thess taken my time — a-githerin' 'long an' a-studyin', an' a-studysitting on the ste'n' 'long — thinkin' eve'y blessed gether, and I wa'd walk up behin' me an' slap me shake hands with

"I allowed you had somethin' er 'nother on your min', Brother Roach," Uncle Jimmy Cosby assented, "bekaze I holla'd at you from the top of yan hill, but you kep' a-polin'."

"I 'm like a steer, Brother Cosby. When he begins to git warm in the flanks he draps his head an' makes fer shade an' water."

"Well, we 're both here, Brother Roach," said Uncle Jimmy Cosby. "We 're both here, an' likewise William Wornum — an' what more can you ax than that?"

"Nothin'," replied Grandsir Johnny Roach, with something like a sigh — "nothin' but a rockin'-cheer an' a jug of fresh buttermilk. Yit I lay we 'll be obleege to put up wi' a stump an' a tussock."

The two old men sat silent for a while, apparently lost in thought. It was evident that my old friends had grave affairs to deal with. Finally Uncle Jimmy Cosby spoke: —

"The days is shortenin' up. We 've come from home an' it hain't taken us long, but before we 've been an' gone an' transacter'd a speck o' what little business we had, here 't is mighty nigh twelve o'clock."

Grandsir Johnny Roach cast a glance upward at the sun. It was swift and casual, but it was the glance of an expert. "No, Brother Cosby, you 're wrong. My two eyes tell me it 's a leetle better 'n half arter ten. It ain't more 'n a quarter to eleven, if it 's as much."

"Maybe so, Brother Roach; maybe so; I 'll not dispute you. One hour more or less hain't wuth wranglin' over, speshually on a Sat'day. One hour or three, we 've got the balance of the day before us."

"That 's so, Brother Cosby; that 's so. If we was on a frolic now, an' the fiddle was a-gwine, we 'd find two hours ample time for to git happy in — ample time."

At that moment I heard some one singing on the other side of the public square. The two old men also heard it, and paused in their aimless conversation to listen. The singer appeared to be coming in the direction of the court-house, but was out of sight on the other side.

"Can you make him out, Brother Cosby?" Grandsir Roach asked.

"That I can, Brother Roach; that I can. It 's that half-wit, Jincy Meadows. It 's a God-send that he hain't got sense enough to be as mean as his daddy. Larkin loved money better 'n he did his childern, an' now here 's his son a-trollopin' about from post to pillar, an' no manner account. I laugh at 'im sometimes, but it makes me sorry for to see sech a fool."

"Don't laugh at 'im, Brother Cosby; don't. You know what the sayin' is — ' Don't squeal at a sow; don't blate at a cow; don't kick at a mule; don't laugh at a fool.'"

"Why, you laugh at 'im yourself, Brother Roach."

"Not me, Brother Cosby, not me! I laugh wi'
'im, but that 's bekaze I can't he'p myse'f, he 's
so nimble wi' his tongue. Lord 'a' mercy!
I 've seed lots bigger fools in my day an' time
than that same Jincy Meadows."

Jincy Meadows came around the corner of the
court-house singing blithely. He was a lightly-
built young fellow, apparently about twenty-five,
quick in his movements and rather prepossessing
in his appearance — indeed, not far from handsome. I had frequently had occasion to laugh at
his flippancies, for they often went deeper than the
common apprehension cared to follow. Though
he bore the reputation of a half-wit, which is a
genteel name for a harmless lunatic, he struck me
as a young man of uncommon parts. As he came
around the corner of the court-house, he sang : —

> " 'Oh,' said the peckerwood, settin' on the fence,
> 'Once I courted a comely wench,
> But she proved fickle and from me fled,
> And ever sence my head 's been red.' "

He paused as he came upon our little group,
bowed swiftly to me, and then turned to the two
old men, his arms akimbo, and a comical expression of astonishment on his face.

"Why, the great Jiminy Craminy!" he cried,
"What is this? The state legislater in session,
and nobody to do the wind work! This fetches
my dream true. I dreampt last night I was
elected, an' 'stead of callin' on me to speak, they
called on me to treat."

"We'll not ax you that, Jincy," Grandsir Roach responded with as much gravity as was his to command.

"Well, that spiles the dream, then," remarked Jincy, "because I up'd and told the boys that a member of the legislatur, and likewise a Son of Temperance, had to be mighty keerful about the platform he stood on. But we're all here, now, and what a team we make! Johncy, Jimpsy, and Jincy — wisdom, experience, and prudence! I name these names because no kind of weather will sp'ile 'em."

Uncle Jimmy Cosby nudged Grandsir Roach with his elbow. "Jest lis'n how that boy runs on!"

"Wait! hold on!" exclaimed Jincy, holding up his forefinger warningly. "Be right still! Let's jine hands and stand in a ring. Catch hold of hands, Johncy and Jimpsy; now take Jincy's. That's it; that's the idee. Steady now! Johncy, you must blink; Jimpsy, you must wink; and Jincy'll stand here and think. Now, then, all make a wish — one, two, three! — and there you are!"

Jincy dropped the hands of the two old men, who had unhesitatingly placed theirs in his, stepped back, leaped into the air, and cut what is called "the pigeon wing" with indescribable ease and grace.

"Go 'way, Jincy; go 'way! You're a plum sight; go 'way!" cried Grandsir Roach, giving the young man a playful punch with his cane.

Jincy Meadows made a comical gesture of despair. "There now!" he exclaimed. "You can't get your wish; you teched me whilst the spell was on me. But I know what your wish was, Johncy — and yours, Jimpsy."

The old men chuckled, but appeared to have no desire to challenge Jincy's occult powers.

"What are you doin' for a livin', Jincy?" asked Uncle Jimmy Cosby.

"Bridging the Oconee, Jimpsy. Have n't you heard about it? Why, it 's the talk of the whole county. I had the bridge finished last Saturday, but it had to be tore down."

"Tore down!" exclaimed Uncle Jimmy Cosby. "What for, I 'd like to know?" There was genuine interest in the tone of his voice.

Jincy looked around carefully, as if to see that no one outside our little group would overhear him. "Don't tell anybody," he said, in a loud whisper. "I found a knot hole in one of the stringers."

Grandsir Roach shook his head and sighed. Uncle Jimmy Cosby's countenance fell. "Well, well, well!" said one, and "Well, well, well!" echoed the other.

I was so charmed with this unique method of throwing an insurmountable barrier across the path of inquisitiveness, that I resolved to test the young man's ability farther.

"Jincy," said I, "what were our two friends wishing just now?" In an instant I regretted the question, but it was too late. Jincy Meadows whirled on his boot-heel and, quick as a flash, replied: —

"They were wishing they knew where Mandy Satterlee is, and how she is getting on. Now, Johncy and Jimpsy! fair and square!" His face was flushed a little, and there was an eager gleam in his eye that I had missed before.

"Well, sir," replied Grandsir Roach, speaking slowly and with emphasis, "uther you hyearn me a-thinkin' or you're a witch for guessin'. Them thoughts was in my min'."

"An' likewise in mine," assented Uncle Jimmy.

"Now that is queer," said I. "Mandy Satterlee is at our house, and has been there for many months."

"At your house?" inquired Grandsir Roach, as if he had suddenly become hard of hearing.

"Yes," I replied.

"She's at his house," remarked Grandsir Roach, nudging Uncle Jimmy Cosby.

"Who? Mandy?" Uncle Jimmy asked as innocently as if he had heard not a word of the conversation.

"Yes, Mandy Satterlee," I reiterated.

Grandsir Roach stroked his beard, cleared his throat, and moved uneasily. "Well, sir," he said, after a pause, "I reckon she's well, an' doin' well; not overcome, as you may say, by — er — by — the — er — by whatsomever hard trials that may or may not have been her lot, an' not only her 'n, but of hunderds an' thousan's, fer the way is liter'lly strowd wi' traps an' pitfalls."

While Grandsir Roach's embarrassment showed painfully in his voice and manner, and while he was speaking, Jincy Meadows was walking about in a quick, restless way.

"Yes, Mandy is well," I responded.

"Well, sir," said Grandsir Roach with a display of feeling that rarely comes to the surface in age, "when next you see Mandy Satterlee, tell her that Grandsir Roach axed arter her perticular, an' said God bless her!"

"An' tell her that her Uncle Jimmy Cosby said Amen! to that," remarked that individual with unction.

"Johney an' Jimpsy, what word shall I send her?" cried Jincy Meadows. "I can crack jokes with you all day, but when it comes to Mandy, my head's in a whirl. My mind flutters like a rag in the wind."

Grandsir Roach came to the rescue. "Tell Mandy," said he, with the simple dignity that only age can easily and unconsciously assume, "that you met three of her old-time friends who ain't fergot her. Call out the'r names plump an' plain, an' tell her that they axed arter her an' said God bless her!"

"Why not come with me and see her?" I asked before Jincy Meadows could say a word. "Surely she would be glad to see her old friends who still take an interest in her. Come!"

Grandsir Roach stroked his beard thoughtfully. "Now, maybe she hain't prepar'd to see us. She may n't be strong. It mought do harm. Wimmen is mighty quare; you don't know one minnit what they 're a-gwine to do the next. An' no wonder — bekaze they don't know their self what they 're a-gwine to do."

Uncle Jimmy Cosby nodded an assent to this that would have been vigorous if it had not been so solemn.

"An' yit," Grandsir Roach went on, "if you think Mandy 'll be one half as glad to see us as we 'll be to see her, we 'll go right along an' say narry 'nother word." To which Uncle Jimmy again nodded his solemn assent.

"Come!" I exclaimed, with as much enthusiasm as I could now muster, for I had suddenly bethought me of sister Jane, and I was doubtful as to the light in which she would view the visitation. But Grandsir Roach and Uncle Jimmy Cosby were even more anxious to see Mandy than I had suspected, and when the invitation was repeated, they accepted it with alacrity.

Jincy Meadows, it seemed, was of another mind. "I 'll go as close as the corner," said he, "an' wait there. Johncy and Jimpsy, when they come out, can tell me more than I could find out for myself. I 'm a mighty poor hand with wimmen folks. Them that don't think I 'm crazy don't keer whether I am or not, and so it goes."

He broke into a lilting song: —

> "The chickadee married the old blue dart,
> And like to have broke the gos-hawk's heart.
> The wedding took place in the finest weather,
> And nothing was left of the bride but a feather.

"Well, Jincy, you know your own notions better 'n we do," remarked Grandsir Roach, in a kindly, soothing way. "We 'll tell Mandy we seed you, but what else to say I don't know."

"Jest tell her I 'm the same old Jincy, good-for-nothin' and no account. That 'll please her jest as well as anything."

The young man's tone was so peculiar that I looked at him narrowly, and saw that his countenance had lost the happy-go-lucky expression it usually wore. Instead, he was frowning as if his thoughts were anything but pleasant. At the corner we left him, and as we entered the gate that opened on the little porch in front of my room, I looked back and saw him whittling away with his pocket knife on the tree-box, against which he was leaning. He was not the gay figure I had laughed at a quarter of an hour earlier.

It was with some misgivings that I introduced Grandsir Roach and Uncle Jimmy Cosby under our roof on their present mission; but their coming was at my invitation, and their age, their standing in the county, and their interest in Mandy Satterlee all pleaded mightily in their behalf. What I dreaded was the reception that sister Jane might accord them. If it occurred to her mind that they had come out of mere curios-

ity, or for the purpose of placing upon Mandy a
burden of perfunctory and therefore useless advice,
she would not hesitate to send them about their
business with their ears tingling. In view of such
an emergency, I determined to leave the two old
men in my room and send Mandy to them. Accordingly I placed chairs for them, begged them
to make themselves entirely at home, and excused
myself while I went to inform Mandy of their
presence.

XII

THE MANTLE OF CHARITY.

I HOPED to find Mandy Satterlee in the kitchen, but she was sitting in sister Jane's room.

"Mandy," said I, "two of your old friends have called to see you."

She looked at sister Jane with a startled expression on her face. "I wonder what they want wi' me!" she exclaimed. "I ain't got no friends that 'd take the trouble to call on me — not that I know of."

"Who are they, William?" inquired sister Jane, in a severe tone.

"Grandsir Roach and Uncle Jimmy Cosby," I replied. The startled expression went out of Mandy's face, but a contraction of her eyebrows showed she was puzzled.

"Old Johnny Roach!" exclaimed sister Jane. "Why, I thought he 'd been translated and transmogrified too long ago to talk about. What do they want with Mandy?"

"Merely to see her," I explained. "They are old friends, and they seem to take an interest in her."

"Well, I hope we ain't to have the Georgy

militia trooping in here the next time there's a general muster; that's what I hope. Where'-bouts did you leave 'em? In your room; well, tell 'em to shake the mud off their huffs and come in here. If they're so keen to see Mandy, here's the place to see her."

I went back and invited Grandsir Roach and Uncle Jimmy Cosby into sister Jane's room. They had both known us from childhood, but of late years they had seen my sister only at rare intervals.

Grandsir Roach entered the room and looked around. Mandy had withdrawn to primp a little, as women will do, no matter how their minds may be racked with trouble.

"Where's Jane?" Grandsir Roach asked, bow-ing formally to my sister, and then turning to me.

"You must be losing your eyesight, Grandsir Roach, if you don't know me," said sister Jane.

"Why, is that reely you, Jane?" he cried, taking her hand and shaking it heartily. "Well, well, well! Why, I'd never 'a' know'd you in the roun' worl'. No; my sight is good — better'n it was ten year gone; but how was I to know you? I says to myself, as I come along, says I, ' I reckon Jane must be agein' some, because she hain't no chicken.' That's what I said. But never did I hope to fin' you lookin' so well an' so young. Why, you hain't changed a mite in twenty year!"

It was a neat compliment deftly delivered, and

its deftness lay in its unexpectedness. It was so clearly the inspiration of the moment, that sister Jane was mightily pleased, as I could see.

"This here 's Jimmy Cosby, Jane; shorely you ain't gone an' forgot Jimmy," Grandsir Roach went on. "Me an' Brother Cosby has been close neighbors for now gwine on fifty year."

"Why, of course I have n't forgotten Uncle Jimmy," said sister Jane, shaking his hand. "How could I? I used to ride his horse to water court-week."

"That 's a fact — that 's a fact, Jane," Uncle Jimmy assented. "Many an' many 's the time you use to ride my hoss to water when you was a little bit of a gal. I was mighty much obleege to you, an' yit many 's the time I 've been afeared you 'd fall off an' hurt yourse'f."

"Yes, an' she 'd 'a' rid my hoss to water if it had n't but 'a' been a mule," remarked Grandsir Roach with a chuckle. "She was a right smart of a tomboy, Jane was, but she draw'd the line at mules."

"An' I don't blame her a bit," Uncle Jimmy put in, "not narry single bit. They hain't nobody under the sun can git the bulge on a mule 'ceptin' it 's a nigger. They know one another 'crost a fifty acre lot."

"An' don't you mind, Brother Cosby," said Grandsir Roach, chuckling more than ever, "that Jane was so little that when she taken your hoss to water, she rid straddle?"

"Yes, sir — she did!" exclaimed Uncle Jimmy Cosby, "she certainly did. It had e'en about drapped out 'n my min'. If I had n't saw it, an' had to be told of it, I never would believe it. No, sir, never!"

Whereupon the two old men laughed heartily, and, although sister Jane laughed heartily, too, I noticed she was very red in the face as she placed chairs for our guests and begged them to be seated.

"We 're glad to see you, Jane, mighty glad," said Grandsir Roach, "but we called more speshually for to see Mandy Satterlee. I fully expected to see her settin' here."

Promptly upon the mention of her name Mandy appeared in the doorway and stood there. Her face was pale, and I noticed a hard, almost defiant expression in her eyes.

Sister Jane must have noticed it, too, for when she said, "There 's Mandy," her voice was pitched in a more subdued tone than usual.

"Why, Mandy, honey! Howdy, howdy!" exclaimed Grandsir Roach, rising from his chair, and going toward her. "I 'm monstus glad to see you. Me an' your Uncle Jimmy thar come speshually for to see you, an' to see how you was gittin' 'long. Did n't we, Brother Cosby? That 's the reason we come, honey, an' for nothin' else in the worl'."

I thought Mandy would have fallen to the floor. She swayed back and forth, but caught the side

of the doorway with her hand, and then, with the
cry of a frightened child, threw her arms around
Grandsir Roach's neck. When she raised her
head the color had returned to her cheeks, and
she was weeping. Still weeping, she ran from
Grandsir Roach to Uncle Jimmy Cosby, and by
the time she had so far recovered herself as to be
able to talk, the two old men were wiping their
eyes and snuffling as if they had suddenly been
overtaken by acute summer colds.

It is the privilege of age and of womanhood to
think no shame of the display of those intimate
emotions that are the spring of human love and
duty, and these old men and this young woman
made no effort whatsoever to conceal their feelings. Sister Jane went about the room pretending to arrange things, the better to hide her agita-
tion. She even went so far as to knock over the
candlestick, which was no easy thing to do. The
clatter made by this accident (for the candlestick
fell from the mantel to the hearth, and the dent
made in it is there to this day) acted somewhat as
a restorative.

"I declar' I hain't been kotch a-blubberin' like
this sence — well, not sence I dunno when," said
Grandsir Roach, "I reckon maybe we're gittin'
ol' an' fibble-minded, Brother Cosby."

"Maybe so, Brother Roach," replied Uncle
Jimmy Cosby, "but I allowed it was bekaze we
hain't saw Mandy in sech a long time, an' we use
to see her off an' on forty times a day. She was

in an' out, out an' in, constantly," Uncle Jimmy
went on, seating himself once more — an example
that was followed by all. "If she wa'n't a-comin'
she wuz a-gwine; an' not a bit er trouble, not the
least bit. She could tease an' yit not pester."

"That's the fact truth," remarked Grandsir
Roach — "it shorely is. It's the way of some
gals," he went on, turning to me. "They can
be allers in the way apperiently an' yit not pester
you. An' now she has been gone gwine on a year
or sech a matter."

, I was in the habit of noticing trifles, and it
struck me as curious that although Mandy was
present in the flesh, the old men talked about her
as if she were absent.

" She's lookin' well, oncommon well," suggested Uncle Jimmy.

"Quite so, quite so," assented Grandsir Roach
in a judicial tone. "She hain't sufferin' for lack
of provender."

"How's Aunt Sally an' Aunt Prue?" Mandy
inquired.

Grandsir Roach nodded toward Uncle Jimmy
Cosby and Uncle Jimmy Cosby nodded toward
Grandsir Roach. "I know'd it!" said one; "I
told you so!" echoed the other. And they were
even more emphatic in giving quaint advertise-
ment of their foreknowledge.

"I know'd that the minnit I laid eyes on
Mandy, she'd up an' ax about her Aunt Sally.
I know'd it'd be e'en about the fust word she'd

say. An' I says to Brother Cosby, says I, 'Brother Cosby, you watch Mandy — watch her right close, — an' see if she don't up an' ax arter her Aunt Sally the minnit she lays eyes on me.' I leave it to Brother Cosby if I did n't."

"He said them very identical words," responded Uncle Jimmy, as solemnly as if the matter was of the gravest possible moment. "An' I says to him, says I, as plain as ever I spoke in my life, ' Brother Roach,' says I, ' keep your two eyes on Mandy an' see if she don't make quick inquirements arter her aunt Prue,' says I. Did n't I say them words, Brother Roach?"

"Identically — word for word," Grandsir Roach promptly assented. "Sally's my wife," he turned to me to explain, "an' Prue 's his'n. They hain't no manner er kin to Mandy, but they 're lots closer kin on that account."

"Aig-zackly so!" said Uncle Jimmy Cosby; he spoke deliberately and slowly so as to give the proper emphasis.

Mandy laughed shyly, with a blush of pleasure on her cheeks, and no wonder. It had been long since such kindly words had fallen on her ears. "You hain't told me how they are yit," Mandy protested.

"Well as common — well as common," replied Grandsir Roach, with a sigh. "Ol' age is a-creepin' on. Not that they 're cripple; no, oh no! They git about same as ever, but they ain't nigh as soople as they was; not nigh. But they 're constantly a-complainin'. Your Aunt Sally can't have a ache but what your Aunt Prue can match it wi' a pain; an' your Aunt Prue can't have a tetch er pneumony but what your Aunt Sally'll have a tetch er plooisy. I leave it to Brother Cosby there, if it hain't so. He's settin' whar he can cont'adict me."

"That's them!" exclaimed Uncle Jimmy Cosby.

"Oh, I can see 'em now!" cried Mandy, clasping her hands together tightly. "Aunt Sally a-weavin' an' quar'lin' when the thread broke, or when the sleys would n't work; an' Aunt Prue shooin' the chickens out 'n the gyarden an' siccin' the dogs on the pigs, an' Aunt Sally a-hollerin' at Nancy, the house gal; an' Aunt Prue a-hollerin' fer the little niggers to come an' git some fresh buttermilk — I see 'em now."

"Aig-zackly so!" remarked Uncle Jimmy Cosby in his deliberate way, while Grandsir Roach, with his chin in the hand that held his cane and a pleased smile on his face, watched the young woman.

"An' Aunt Sally an' Aunt Prue settin' in the same pew at church on the fust Sunday in the month — Aunt Sally fat an' Aunt Prue lean — an' a-taking in ev'ry word the preacher says. An' Aunt Sally a-dishin' out the chicken pie at her house, an' Aunt Prue the apple dumplin' at her 'n."

"*She* knows a thing or two," remarked Uncle Jimmy Cosby, turning to me.

"It hain't been so mighty long ago, honey," said Grandsir Roach, "when your Aunt Prue an' Brother Cosby picked up an' come over to our house — le' me see: wa'n't it last Sunday night, Brother Cosby? Yes — last Sunday night. Your Aunt Sally an' your Aunt Prue is constant a-gwine an' a-comin', but it hain't so mighty often that Brother Cosby, thar, an' me picks up an' goes wi' 'em. But your Aunt Prue come last Sunday night, an' Brother Cosby, thar, come wi' 'er. Now when me an' Brother Cosby strike up wi' one another, an' hain't got nothin' better for to do than to smoke our pipes, we most allers in giner'lly gits tangled up on politics an' sech matters. Brother Cosby's a dimercrat an' I 'm a whig. He wants to run the country one way an' I want to run it another, an' so we argy, an' argy as hot as pepper, an' uther he gits mad or I fly up like a fool — an' that, too, when they hain't no more chance of uther one a-runnin' the country than they is of his jumpin' to the moon. If politics wa'n't hatched for to kick up a flurry betwixt neighbors, I dunno what they was hatched for, danged if I do!

"But last Sunday night, as luck would have it," Grandsir Roach went on, "politics wa'n't brung up betwixt us. We sot an' smoked an' listened at the wimmin a-gwine on. Your Aunt Prue had saw some new-fangled bonnet some'rs er nother, an' she sot right flat-footed in her cheer thar an' pictur'd out to your Aunt Sally ev'ry

flower an' folderol an' all the conflutements that
the consarn had on it. I winked at Brother Cosby
an' he winked at me, as we sot a-smokin' an'
a-lis'nin'. Then, not to be outdone, your Aunt
Sally, she up 'd an' tol' your Aunt Prue about
a new frock she seed some 'oman er nother have
on, an' thar they had it up an' down. Seeh a
frock I ain't hyearn tell on in many a long day
before. It had purty, flowin' sleeves, an' the
waist was cut bias, so your Aunt Sally said, an
there was a streak er ribbin here an' a stripe of
yaller trimmin' thar, an' the skyirt was gethered
so, an' braid run down the sides. An' 'whar-
bouts was the placket?' says your Aunt Prue,
an' ' 'T was teetotally hid out 'n sight,' says your
Aunt Sally. That's the way they run on with
their rigamarole.

"Bimeby I sez to Brother Cosby, says I, ' Brother Cosby, how's craps?' says I. Did n't I,
Brother Cosby? I leave it to you."

"You said them very words, Brother Roach,"
replied Uncle Jimmy Cosby, "an' I ups an' says,
says I, ' Well, Brother Roach,' says I, 'they're
lots better 'n we desarve, but not as good as I
hoped for,' says I."

"He said them identical words," continued
Grandsir Roach, looking proudly around to see
what effect had been produced on his small audience. "An' then I hitched my cheer back an'
says, says I, ' I wonder whar 'bouts in this wide
worl' Mandy Satterlee is this night?' At that,

the wimmen squared aroun' an' looked at me an' then looked in the fireplace. You mind that cheer you use to set in, don't you, honey? The one what was so high that I had to saw the legs off so you could make your feet tech the floor?"

"That was when I was a little gal," remarked Mandy.

"That's so, honey," Grandsir Roach went on, "but you never sot in no other cheer, not in my house, less'n you was a-settin' at the dinner-table. Well, thar sot your cheer in the cornder whar it allers sets at. Your Aunt Sally looked at it an' sorter draw'd a long breath, an' says, says she, ' Thar sets her cheer. It looks like it's a-waitin' for her to come back,' says she."

"Oh, did she say that?" cried Mandy. "Tell her I love her more an' more the older I git."

"Them was her words," said Uncle Jimmy Cosby, with more gravity than ever.

" Jes' so!" Grandsir Roach went on — "jes' so! It's like I tell you. But that ain't all. Your Aunt Prue she looks over at the cheer, an' ups an' says, says she, ' I ain't got no cheer fer Mandy in pertickler, but they're all her'n ef she'll come an' set in 'em. They're all her'n,' says she, 'an' the Lord knows my heart jest natchully yearns arter that gal. Day or night,' says she, 'no matter how she comes, no matter when she comes, no matter whichaway she comes, my arms is open for her,' says she."

" Word for word that was what she said," remarked Uncle Jimmy Cosby.

“Oh, I love ’em both,” said Mandy, almost in a whisper. Her voice was husky, and to hide her tears she turned sidewise, threw her arms on the back of her chair and hid her face in her hands.

“Yessum an’ yes, sir!” exclaimed Grandsir Roach, nodding first to sister Jane and then to me; “that’s the way it happened. An’ then we all sot right still an’ looked in the fire, an’ all a-thinkin’ an’ a-thinkin’ ’bout Mandy Satterlee. Terreckly, your Aunt Sally ups an’ says, says she, ‘The settlement hain’t what it use to be when Mandy was aroun’. She’d come a-runnin’,’ says she, ‘an’ grab me ’roun’ the neck an’ gi’ me a good hug most ’fore I know’d who under the blue canopies it was,’ says she, ‘an’ when it come to fillin’ the sleys, her fingers was nimble as a gray spider’s legs,’ says she.

“‘Yes, yes,’ says your Aunt Prue, says she; ‘whatsomever was to be done she’d do an’ sing all the time she was a-doin’ of it,’ says she, ‘an’ many a time when it looked like she was lonesome, she’d come an’ cuddle down on the floor,’ says she, ‘an’ lay her face agin my knee an’ set cuddled up that a-way for ever so long. If a day passed that she did n’t come, I ’d begin for to feel oneasy,’ says she. I ’ll leave it to Brother Cosby here, honey, if that wa’ n’t about the upshot of what your Aunt Prue said.”

“Even so, even so, Brother Roach,” remarked Uncle Jimmy Cosby. “An’ more than that, when me an’ your Aunt Prue went home that night —

it 's but a step; little better 'n a quarter of a mile — the fire had kinder died out on the h'ath, an' so, jest as natchual as you please, I sot to work to kindle a light. I got me a light-'ud knot whar I allers keep 'em, an' then I got down on my knees an' blow'd, an' blow'd tell it looked like I could n't blow no more, an' all that time I did n't hear your Aunt Prue make a sign of fuss. I come mighty nigh a-losin' both my mind an' my temper, the fire was so hard for to kindle; an' bimeby I says to your Aunt Prue, says I, 'Ma!' — I allers call her ma sence we had childun an' lost 'em — I holla'd out, I did, 'Ma, what in the Nation do you reckon has got into the fire?' says I. Yit not a sign of a soun' did she make, so I allowed she had gone into the next room, or maybe in the kitchen. Then I took my ol' wool hat an' fetched the h'ath a swipe or two, an' the blaze sprung up so sudden that I most fanned it out ag'in before I could ketch my han'. I looked up an' there was your Aunt Prue a-standin' right at me, an' she had her hankcher out a-cryin'.

" ' Why, ma,' says I, ' what on the roun' earth 's the matter?' bekaze it hain't so mighty often you see your Aunt Prue a-cryin' that a-way. I says, says I, ' You 're nervious, ma, an' you better go to bed.' An' then," — Uncle Jimmy Cosby paused here to chuckle — "an' then she flew up like wimmen will. 'I hain't no more nervious than you,' says she, ' an' I 'll go to bed when I git good an' ready. It 's come to a mighty purty pass when I

can't cry when I want to,' says she. I know'd
right then she was a-cryin' 'bout Mandy, an' when
she had sorter cooled off she up 'd an' tol' me so."

Mandy raised her head and exclaimed, "Oh,
don't let 'em cry for me. Oh, please don't. I
hain't wuth a thought from narry one of them good
wimmen. I love 'em — I love 'em lots better 'n
if they was any kin to me ; but I ain't fitten to be
loved by nobody."

" Why, honey ! " said Grandsir Roach gently.
" You 're fergittin' all about the Bible."

" I ain't fitten to think about the Bible," protested Mandy.

By a lift of her eyebrows and a slight motion of
her head sister Jane gave the two old men to
understand that it would be well to let Mandy
fight with her troubles in her own way. Grandsir
Roach lifted his hat from the floor beside his chair
where he had dropped it, and Uncle Jimmy Cosby
did the same.

" I thank you kindly, Jane, for permittin' of us
to come an' see Mandy. I thank you from the
bottom of my heart. It 'll do us a sight of good
if it don't do her none. An' we 'll go back home
an' tell her Aunt Sally an' her Aunt Prue how
comf'tubly she 's fixed, an' they 'll be might'ly holp
up — might'ly holp up."

He turned to Mandy. "Good-by, honey.
We 'll drap in an' see you once in a way when we
come to town if we hain't wore our welcome out
wi' Jane here."

"You can't wear your welcome out in this house," said my sister with more earnestness than I had seen her display toward people with whom she was not intimate.

"I thank you kindly, Jane; I do from the bottom of my heart," Grandsir Roach responded. He turned again to Mandy. "Honey, when you git w'ary an' tired, you know whar to come. When you git homesick "—

"Oh, I'm allers homesick!" cried Mandy. "Day an' night, night an' day."

"That's a great compliment to me," said sister Jane, trying to give a lighter turn to the conversation.

For answer, Mandy ran and seized sister Jane in her strong arms. "I love you as well as I ever did anybody," she sobbed. "Nobody in the world has done more for me than what you've done. Oh, please don't talk that away."

Sister Jane petted and consoled the poor girl much as if she had been a child, and as effectually.

"We left Jincy Meadows out thar," remarked Uncle Jimmy Cosby, "an' we've got to be agwine."

"How is Jincy?" asked Mandy.

"Well as common — e'en about the same ol' Jincy — full of queer notions. If you want to see him "— Uncle Jimmy paused, and stood waiting.

"Not now," said Mandy, "not now; maybe never — I dunno."

“ That ’ll be a mighty hard tale to tell Jincy, honey,” suggested Grandsir Roach.

“ I ’ll think — I can’t tell,” cried Mandy, standing irresolute. “ Some time — but not now. Oh, I hain’t fitten for Jincy to be a pesterin’ hisse’f ’long of.”

“ Bless your heart, honey,” said Grandsir Roach with a chuckle, “ it don’t pester Jincy the least bit in the worl’. I ’ll tell ’im for to come see you some day when you ’re feelin’ well.”

Then the two old men took their leave of Mandy and sister Jane. As I went with them to the outer door I remarked to Grandsir Roach : —

“ You and Uncle Jimmy Cosby certainly know how to deal out charity.”

“ Charity ! ” exclaimed Grandsir Roach. “ Why, William, what does Paul say? Look it up in the Bible ! Why, take charity out ’n religion an’ what in the name of common sense would be left? Nothin’ but the dry peelin’s. It ’d be like takin’ corn out ’n the shuck. Shucks ’ll maybe do for steers an’ dry cattle, an’ they ’re mighty poor ruffage e’en for them ; but you give shucks to creeturs what ’s got any sense an’ they ’ll snort at ’em an’ walk away from the trough. Why, William, a man that reely knows he ’s got a soul for to save is bound by his own sins to be charitable when it comes to t’ other folks’s sins.”

I shook hands with my two old friends and made haste to write down Grandsir Roach’s sermon on charity.

XIII.

JINCY MEADOWS COMES A—CALLING.

AFTER that, I noticed that Mandy went about
the business she had taken on herself much more
cheerfully. She had a knack of singing from the
first, but I had found out long ago that it was the
result of habit rather than of mental exaltation.
I had remarked on her singing one day when she
looked at me with surprise.

"La! was I singin'?" she asked. "I did n't
know it, an' I 'm mighty certain I don't feel much
like singin'. I reckon you an' Miss Jane take me
to be a mighty quare creetur."

But in a short while I heard her singing again,
and then I knew it was a habit that afforded some
relief from her distracted thoughts, such as I was
sure she had. I had seen the evidence of it too
often to doubt it. Yet her songs were a shade
blither, it seemed to me, after the visit of Grandsir
Roach and Uncle Jimmy Cosby; and I thought
there was a brightness about her that had been
lacking before. But I could not be sure, for sister
Jane had charged such wild extravagance to my
imagination that I was sometimes inclined to doubt
the evidence of my own eyes. But in this matter

I had Klibs as a witness, for that stout toddler was staring at me one day, not long after the visit of Mandy's two old friends, when he suddenly remarked : —

"Mammy ting now. Fwen me git feepy, she don't ky no mo. Her ting." The solemnity of this remark was shattered when Klibs followed it almost immediately with a dire threat and prophesied its results. "Me dine ter tut off Tommy tat's tail. Den Nanny Dane will tut off my wears." Which, being interpreted fairly and fully, was as much as to say that Klibs intended to cut off Tommy Tinkins's tail, a crime that would be punished by the loss of Klibs's ears.

So I said to him as solemnly as I could that it would be well to save his ears by allowing the cat to carry his tail in comfort and peace.

"Oo tut off Tommy tat's tail," suggested Klibs, by way of a compromise. "Me dit de tizzers."

"No, I thank you, Klibs," I replied. "Aunty Jane would cut off my ears, too."

"Oo tan byake de 'ookin-dass, den."

"No, no, Klibs ; go and break it yourself."

"Uh-uh!" said the toddler. "Nanny Dane tut off my finners."

I was much struck by the fact that the change in Mandy had been observed by the child, who was now about two years old. It is gratifying to have our notions confirmed, no matter from what source, and I have often observed that the most ordinary person becomes important in our estimation in proportion to his ability to flatter us by confirming our views or agreeing with our opinions.

It is not to be supposed that Klibs, the baby, was as viciously disposed as his conversation would lead one to suspect. He had been told not to worry the cat, not to play with the scissors, and not to break the looking-glass; and, like our first parents in the garden, his mind dwelt on that which he was forbidden to do. In fact, the interdiction he regarded as a suggestion, and, young as he was, his " finners " (as he called them) ached and itched to go about getting the scissors to cut the cat's tail off : and when that was impossible he wanted to see the mirror broken by some other hand. Here was the old Adam over again; and so plain a case that it confirmed the suspicion in my mind that the original Adam, not being willing to assume the responsibility, begged mother Eve to pluck the apple and taste it on the sly.

As may be supposed, the baby had thrived wonderfully. Without a special nurse, it grew to be an independent youngster, and having no other children to play with, it took on older ways than most youngsters have, and came to be very precocious. Nevertheless it may be said of Klibs that he never knew what real life and enjoyment was until Free Betsey came to see her young mistress, which she did shortly after the episode that has already been described. Mandy Satterlee, knowing Free Betsey of old, had all confidence in her trustworthiness.   Indeed, when the negro woman took the child in her arms and was gone for half a day, as sometimes happened, Mandy betrayed less uneasiness than did sister Jane, who was constantly running to the little gate and looking up and down the street.   More than once I could see that sister Jane was irritated with Mandy for not sharing her anxiety about the child.

Once I heard her say, "I 'll be bound, if I had a child I would n't trust it to no old nigger trollop and let her tote it off, you don't know where, and keep it half the day."

To which Mandy replied: "Well, if you know 'd Mammy Betsey as well as I do you would n't let it pester your mind a minnit — not a blessed minnit."

" I may not know Free Betsey so mighty well," retorted sister Jane, " but I know the nigger tribe, an' I would n't trust one of 'em out of sight with anything that I set store by."

On one occasion it happened that sister Jane, by reason of an unforeseen accident that befell Klibs, was able to shake her head and cry, " I told you so." Free Betsey was in the habit of carrying the baby to see Mrs. Beshears in the mornings or during the afternoons. She was always welcome there, for Mrs. Beshears had taken a great fancy to the baby. It chanced that there was an old gray goose brooding on a nestful of eggs in the narrow space that separated two negro cabins. Whether Klibs saw the old gray goose and desired to introduce himself, or whether he was merely exploring the nook because it presented new possibilities of mischief, it is impossible to say. All that is clearly known is that there was a tremendous noise of squalling, and flapping, and fluttering. Free Betsey was on hand before the old gray goose could do any serious damage with her strong beak and wings, but the incident exercised a wholesome influence over Klibs that lasted many months. As sister Jane dryly remarked, when she came to appreciate the humor of the affair, " Klibs came home sober for the first time in many weeks."

. We laughed heartily when Free Betsey gave her version of the event, remarking among other things that the baby was too badly frightened or too much astonished to cry. Klibs listened to the narration with a solemn air that was too funny to admit of description. When Free Betsey paused, he toddled to the middle of the floor and stood there a moment gravely regarding us. When he spoke it was to the point.

" Doose say sh-h-h ! " then he waved his chubby hands up and down and ran about with his mouth open to show how demon-like the attack had been. He concluded the pantomime by flopping down on the floor and rolling over and over to show by what shrewd antics he had escaped annihilation. Then he sat up and gave us the owl-like stare that always preceded his efforts to engage in conversation.

" Nanny Dane dine tut ol' doose's finners off," he remarked, adding: " Me byake ol' doose's 'ookin-dass; me tut 'im tail off wif de tizzers."

Whereupon sister Jane swooped down upon him, lifted him in her arms, and proceeded to " hug him to death," a threat she often made. "You precious child!" she exclaimed. "That old gray goose shan't treat you so — Nanny Dane will cut off the old goose's fingers, and you shall cut off her tail with the scissors," with much more to the same effect, some of it untranslatable.

Klibs's adventure with the old gray goose was very fortunate in many respects. It was a strong source of discipline, as we shortly found out. If he started to go where he had been told not to go, or to do anything he had been told not to do, we had but to mention the old gray goose. He had deep thoughts about the goose. He pondered over the problem she presented. He would sit for long minutes apparently studying his chubby hands, and suddenly remark: " Me ol' doose!" Then he would shake his arms up and down as the goose shook her wings. I often thought Klibs must have had a keen eye to see so much in such a short space of time, for those who have disturbed old mother goose when she is brooding have good reason to know that she never pauses to count her steps when making an attack.

One morning several weeks after the visit of Grandsir Roach and Uncle Jimmy Cosby, I heard a light knocking on my door. Opening it, I found

Jincy Meadows standing on the little porch. He
was better dressed than usual, but his face wore an
expression of extreme embarrassment.

"Sh-h-h!" he whispered. "Don't holla my
name out loud. I knocked and then I got ready
to run, but before I could jump off the porch you
opened the door. Why, you must 'a' been standin'
right there ready and waitin'."

"Come in — come in," I said, with as much
hospitality as I could muster at the moment.
"What is the matter?"

"Don't holla so loud," Jincy protested. "Why,
they can hear you on the fur side of town, much
less in the house."

"I'm not talking above a breath," I explained.

"Maybe not," remarked Jincy with a comical
air of trepidation, "but to a skeer'd man it sounds
like thunder."

"Come in," I insisted.

"Well, don't shet the door too tight," said
Jincy. "I'm two minds whether to stay or
whether to cut and run. Leave the door on the
crack, for if I was to hear a bug hit agin the wall
I'd make a break."

"Well, there is nothing here to hurt you,
Jincy," I remarked, determined to humor his
whims.

"That's the trouble," he explained, "I don't
mind knockin' and bein' knocked; I'm allers the
skeerdest when there's nothin' to be skeer'd at."

"Very well," said I, "if you want to be frightened at nothing, there 's no harm done, and if you want to run, I 'll clap my hands and cry ' Well done!' "

" Now that 's right," replied Jincy. " I feel lots more at home when I know you don't mind if I break and run. If anybody had 'a' told me ten minnits ago that I 'd be a-settin' up in here, I 'd 'a' said they was the biggest liars on the face of the earth. And yit I laid off for to come here when I loped out from home."

" Well, you are all dressed up," I suggested. " If I had met you on the street, I should have said to myself, ' There goes a young buck intent on paying a call.' "

" Would you now?" inquired Jincy, a broad grin spreading over his face. " Well, I 'll be dang! You 'd 'a' saw me and 'a' know'd it! But that 's jest the trouble," he went on, hitching his chair a little closer to mine. " I don't know what fool notion made me fling on this Sunday rig. It makes me feel like pitchin' out and 'tendin' some church or other. I ain't met a man in the road but what I expected him to pop his whip and drap me a scriptur' text. It 's the cloze; nothin' but the cloze. I says to myself, when I put 'em on, ' I 'll go call on Mandy Satterlee.' Then, when I got to the town branch, I watered my hoss and says, ' No, I 'll not call on her; I 'll jest go and ax how she 's a-gittin' on.' When I got to town, I says, ' No, I 'll jest make like I 'm axin' about her; I 'll go to the door and knock on it, light as a feather,

and then walk off as big as anybody.' Did you
recly hear me knock, or was you comin' out on
your own hook?" he asked.

"Of course I heard you knock," said I. "It
sounded as though some one were trying to batter
the door down."

He doubled his fist and looked at it apparently
with great curiosity. Then he spread out his hand
on his knee and viewed it critically. It was not
an ugly hand by any means, having known very
little hard work.

"That hand's lots too heavy," he remarked;
"lots too heavy for the rest of my body. I hit
that door as light as I could to save my life.
But, shucks! my luck's on the wrong side of the
fence, and it's a fence I can't climb, jump, nor
creep through."

"You wanted to come without being seen, and
knock without being heard," I suggested.

"That's it; you 've hit the nail plum' on the
head. I jest wanted to make like I 'd been and
called on Mandy. You know how the boys play.
They straddle a cornstalk, or a broom-handle, and
it 's every bit and grain as good as a horse to them.
I wanted to play like I 'd come and axed after
Mandy, and I 've gone and made it too natchal.
I 'd 'a' done jest as well, and I 'd 'a' felt a dang
sight better, if I 'd 'a' stopped at the corner and
sent my thoughts in 'stead of me."

Now, strange as it may appear, the humor of
the lad jumped queerly with mine. I had lived

his experience over a thousand times, but had
never carried it to the point of knocking at the
door. I had sat in my snug room and sent my
thoughts out — my thoughts that were so swift of
foot that they could travel across the garden in an
instant, and so light of hand that they could knock
at a window I knew and make no more noise than
a flake of thistle down. I knew that if the lad
before me had the whimsies, the same trouble had
seized me, the difference being that I was more
secretive, or more diplomatic, to use a pleasanter
phrase. All this passed through my mind while
Jincy Meadows was talking.

"Well, we all play at the game of make-believe
more or less," I said. "I know of nothing more
comforting."

"Is that so?" inquired Jincy. "All the folks
say I 'm a fool except a passel of old wimmen that
don't know no better. I reckon a fool gits to be a
wise man when he larns how to keep his mouth
shet."

"That is about the way of it," I answered.

"I 'm a leetle worse 'n the balance of 'em,"
Jincy persisted, "'cause they play make-belief
where nobody can't see 'em except them that
knows 'em. But look at me! When I start the
game, I run everything in the ground and break it
off. Look where I am now!"

"You 're in good company," said I, "though I
dare say you think you might be in better."

He shook his head, thought a moment, glanced

at his watch, which was a very fine one, and rose hurriedly. "I must go," he said; "it's a quarter of an hour later than it was a while ago, and I 've got a special appointment with myself on the other side of town."

"I think Mandy would be glad to see you," I suggested; "but if you are obliged to go, why that is another matter. What message shall I give to her?"

But I had no need to carry a message, nor Jincy time to invent one, for, as I spoke, the inner door opened, and Mandy herself came into the room. The surprise was mutual. Jincy backed and bowed, and made as awkward appearance as possible. Mandy blushed furiously, whether with pleasure or with sheer embarrassment it was impossible to say. Being a woman, however, she was the first to recover her self-possession.

"Why, howdy, Jincy?" she said cordially, and yet somewhat coolly, seeing that Jincy and she had known each other all their lives. Jincy took her extended hand, and shook it with formal politeness.

"I was jest a-talkin' with the squire, here," Jincy stammered.

"How 's ever'body an' ever'thing?" Mandy asked, instinctively looking at her reflection in the glass door of one of the book-cases.

"Well, speakin' one way," replied Jincy, "ever'-body an' ever'thing is gittin' on tollable well; an' speakin' another way, they ain't gittin' on so well."

" How 's that ? " Mandy inquired, giving him a quick glance.

" Easy enough," answered Jincy, recovering his equanimity somewhat. " Some 's rambled, some 's ambled, some 's took to their bed, an' some 's dead."

I wondered if Mandy, perhaps with a keener apprehension in this matter than mine, could understand what the lad was driving at. She laughed, and was about to say something, when sister Jane walked in.

" Well, the Lord 'a' mercy ! " she cried, " what 's all this ? And Jincy Meadows, too ! Why, Jincy, I ain't seen you in a coon's age — not since the day you sassed me in the street and I made your daddy spank you for it. That 's what you got for telling the truth on me. I 've been sorry for it a thousand times, Jincy. Them that have got a glib tongue, man or woman, have the right to use it. I hope you don't bear no grudges, Jincy."

" Why, not the least bit in the world, Miss Jane," answered Jincy, laughing. " It made me think about you, and if them that you think about is worth thinkin' about you 're more than apt to like 'em. That 's the way I 've worked it out; but I reckon it 's a fool way. That 's what they all say."

" No, no, Jincy ! not all, nor yet half of 'em," said sister Jane. " When you hear me say you 're a fool, Jincy, you may know it 's time to go to the asylum. I ain't said it yet. But this ain't fair — two grown men against one lone woman. Come in my room, Mandy, and if William and Jincy like hunting us up, why, they can do so — especially Jincy."

"Well 'm, I 've got some business on t' other side of town," explained Jincy, "and I reckon I 'd better go and 'tend to it."

"Business, Jincy?" exclaimed sister Jane, with good-humored scorn. "Why, you never had a scrimption of business in all your born days. Come in my room and tell me all the news."

Sister Jane was a constant surprise to me, as all women are to those who try to please them, but nothing she ever did (except on a later occasion) was more surprising to me than her attitude toward Jincy Meadows. I traced it to her goodness of heart, for Jincy had the reputation of a ne'er-do-well, and was in fact leading a roving and aimless existence, though, as I have said, his father, Larkin Meadows, was well to do, owning a fine plantation and many negroes. The majority of people thought Jincy was a half-wit and a vagabond, and only a few suspected that the lad had a mind gifted above the common.

With an embarrassment that was almost painful to witness, Jincy followed sister Jane and Mandy. He tried to relieve his feelings by turning and winking at me in the most solemn manner as I followed the three down the hallway. But I could see that this attempt at comic by-play was futile. It was far from relieving his feelings. He had evidently stumbled into a predicament (if it could

be called such) where his drollery had lost its
flavor. Yet with all his embarrassment, which I
could appreciate to the fullest extent, he managed
to put a good face on his inward misery.

Pausing at the door of sister Jane's room, he
turned to me and said: "I reckon you ain't never
accidently fell in the creek on a cold mornin', have
you, squire?" Before I had time to answer, he
went into the room and I followed.

"I did n't have any hopes of seein' the ladies,"
remarked Jincy in self-defense, as he seated himself. "I jest come to talk to the squire here about
a little p'int of law, and I did n't have time to git
around to it before you ladies come a-rushin' in."

"Maybe I can tell you more about it than
William," said sister Jane. "William has his
shingle hung out, but the whole neighborhood
knows that I 'm the lawyer of the family."

"Well 'm, it 's this," replied Jincy, winking at
me: "I called on the squire for to ax him if it 's
lawful for a country chap to jine in with these
town play-actors that call themselves 'The Philologians.' It 's a mighty big word for to git jined
on to and I did n't know but there was some sort
of a trap set in it for to catch greenies."

"La! I would n't jine it, Jincy, wi' sech a name
as that," said Mandy. "They might want to do
you some bodily harm or somethin'."

"The what?" asked sister Jane.

"The Philologians. Ain't it so, squire?"

Now there was really a company of the young

men in the village who were trying to arrange for amateur theatricals, and they had formed a club which, without regard for the proper meaning of the term (or a great deal, according to the way you viewed it), was called "The Philologians." Therefore I promptly and heartily corroborated Jincy's statement.

"Then there was another question I wanted to ax the squire," said Jincy, who was now beginning to feel more at ease.

"Out with it," exclaimed sister Jane. "I 'm as good a lawyer as William any day in the week, and Sunday too."

"You ain't answered the first p'int," replied Jincy, with a lift of his eyebrows that changed the usual vacant expression of his face to one of extreme shrewdness.

"Good!" I cried, laughing to see the effect of Jincy's reply on sister Jane.

"Maybe she can tell better when she gits the two p'ints together and jines 'em," suggested Jincy.

"That 's so, Jincy," said sister Jane with an air of relief. "You 're a better lawyer right now than William."

"Well, the next p'int is this," Jincy went on; "they want me to be a lady. I 've got to have a husband named Fazio, and I 've got to put on frocks and things, and strut around right smart. Now, what I want to know, ain't it a plum' breakin' of the law for me to put on frocks and make out I 've got a ol' man ?"

Sister Jane laughed heartily and then grew solemn. "So they say you 're a fool, do they, Jincy? Well, I wish all the people I know had as much sense as you 've got. I 'd like 'em lots better 'n I do."

"Well 'm, it 's so easy to have what folks call sense, that I ease my mind by playin' the fool."

Mandy laughed at this remark, but there was a touch of uneasiness in her manner, for at that moment Klibs marched in, accompanied by Tommy Tinkins. The baby stationed himself by sister Jane's knee and stared solemnly at Jincy. "Oo dat, Nanny Dane?" he asked.

"Old Zip Coon!" replied Jincy so suddenly that Klibs retreated behind sister Jane's chair, and from that coign of vantage smiled serenely at the young man. Tommy Tinkins, however, had no share in Klibs's alarm or bashfulness. He insisted on jumping to Jincy's knee, and was not satisfied even with that demonstration of confidence, for he reared himself to the lad's shoulder, and rubbed against his chin and neck.

"He 's not that friendly with everybody that comes along, Jincy," explained sister Jane. "That cat knows a thing or two."

"Well 'm, they 're all mighty friendly wi' me," remarked Jincy; "cats, dogs, cattle, hosses, and all the wild creeturs, specially the birds."

"What about that mocking-bird swinging on the cedar out there?" I asked.

Jincy rose and glanced at him. "Why, he 's

the same to me as if he was in a cage," he replied. "I can walk right out and call him to my hand."

"He can so!" protested Mandy, seeing me laugh as if the lad had made an idle jest.

"The proof of the pudding is chewing the bag," remarked sister Jane.

"That's so," said Jincy, "and I'll show you. Come out and see, but don't git too close."

So we adjourned to the garden. Jincy went near the tree and gave a whistling chirrup. The bird was so startled by the unexpectedness of the call that it flew to the top of the cedar, swung there a moment, giving forth the "*chuh*" cry that stands for anger, alarm and surprise, and then flew wildly to the top of the big china tree on the sidewalk. Again Jincy gave his whistling call, and the bird came fluttering back, this time making as if it would light on his hat, but flying away again. Once more the whistling call sounded, and the bird fluttered around and over Jincy's head in the most peculiar way.

"What's the matter with you?" cried Jincy impatiently. Then his eyes fell on Tommy Tinkins, who was crouching at his feet and watching every motion of the bird with eager eyes and trembling jaws. "Shucks! it's the cat!" Jincy said. "I know'd somethin' was wrong."

I enjoyed the spectacle immensely and treasured the incident in my mind. It gave me a new and higher opinion of Jincy. He begged to be excused

from returning into the house, on the ground that
he did n't want to wear his welcome out. So we
begged him to call again whenever he felt in the
humor, and he went away after formally shaking
hands with each one, even the baby.

XIV.

As I gradually learned the story of Mandy Satterlee's girlhood and young womanhood, gathering
it from her own remarks and from occasional con-
versations with sister Jane, the more deeply I
sympathized with her. No reparation that she
could make so far as the world was concerned
would place her on the level from which she had
fallen. Though this was a heavy penalty to pay,
my impression is that she never questioned the
justice of the social verdict that imposes such a
penalty. I sometimes reflected on the seeming
paradox that repentance could restore such a sinner to the favor of heaven, but not to the forgiveness of society and the world. The gates of heaven
stand ready to fly open before the most abject, the
most miserable, the most woeful of those who vio-
late the laws that were thundered from the heights
of Sinai if they come repenting; but the laws of
the world are more inflexible where a weak woman
is concerned. To protest against this were worse
than foolish; what these laws are they have been,
and so they will remain. Whether they have become a part of the social order as the result of in-

stinct or reason, 't were bootless to inquire. As
they stand now, so they would stand at the end of
all discussion. The most that can be done — perhaps all that should be done — by those whose
humanity is inclined to resent the sweeping and
implacable verdict that society renders against erring womankind, is to mitigate as far as possible, in
special cases, the anguish of those who (as it were)
have taken so wild and desperate leap in the dark,
and who have turned again toward the light, bearing the heavy burden of repentance.

That Mandy Satterlee felt and understood the
source and nature of my sympathy (as she did
that of sister Jane's) I was sure. I was sure, too,
that she gathered strength from the fact — strength
that she stood sorely in need of. In a thousand
ways, none of them obtrusive, she showed her ap-
preciation and gratitude. It is curious, too, how
one small spark of sympathy will kindle into a
flame of charity. If we had shut our door on
Mandy Satterlee and left her to perish in the cold,
our conduct would have met the approval of many
Christians who mistake their emotions for piety.
If we had taken her in, cared for her until the
storm was over, and then set her adrift on the
world, after discovering the source of her despair,
the whole community would have applauded and
magnified the righteousness of our judgment. Instead of this, sister Jane, with my hearty approval,
and with full knowledge of the step she was taking, had made Mandy Satterlee an inmate of our

small household. This naturally excited some gossip, and perhaps severer criticism than ever came to our ears. But, strange to say, in course of time the community came to share in some degree the sympathy which we felt and manifested toward Mandy Satterlee. This was due to the fact that Mandy, in her daily walk, in her comings and her goings, more than justified the humane impulse that made our little home her harbor. It was repentance that won from the Lord of all the forgiveness that made the life of Mary of Magdala beautiful, and the repentance of Mandy Satterlee was no less sincere. That much we knew, and in time the village knew it.

I hope that this was due to our example, and yet it may have been partly due to the attitude of Mrs. Bullard, Mary's mother, whose seclusion was regarded by a majority of the women in the community as exclusiveness. They criticised her for it, attributing it to pride, but secretly looked up to her as a social model, her family being of the best and her fortune an unusually comfortable one. Now it happened that Mrs. Bullard ("Mrs. Colonel Bullard," the village called her) had apparently taken a great fancy to Mandy Satterlee, and never came slipping through the garden to see sister Jane (arrayed as if she were going to a party) but she asked after our charge, and sometimes hunted through the house until she found her. I observed that Mandy always disappeared when the Colonel's wife whisked in at the door.

Whether she stood in awe of the lady's fine jewels, or of the fact that she was very rich, or that she belonged to what the common people called the aristocracy, or whether she doubted Mrs. Bullard's sympathy, or was overwhelmed by her individuality, I never knew nor had occasion to inquire. But it is certain that the young woman always met the lady with extreme embarrassment. Avoiding her whenever possible, Mandy always maintained in Mrs. Bullard's presence a reserve that bordered on sullenness, and was dumb but for the few awkward monosyllables that could be wrung from her. But this made no difference in Mrs. Bullard's attitude. If she noticed Mandy's embarrassment at all she no doubt interpreted it as a tribute to her position in the small world of the village.

If the lady was familiar with Mandy's history, she got no inkling of it from sister Jane. Yet she must have heard or suspected the truth, for I often noticed that she was more gracious and condescending to the young woman than to many who were more nearly her equals in family and fortune. Delicate as she was, the Colonel's wife had dignity, and to spare. She was accomplished, too, and could make herself agreeable. There were moments, indeed, when she was a most charming woman, and at such times she reminded me of Mary.

On one occasion, Colonel Cephas Bullard being away, I found it necessary to consult her about some business for a client of mine. I found her cold, barely polite, cautious, calculating, and shrewd. When the business was concluded, — or, rather, when the talk about it came to an end, for she would or could do nothing to satisfy my client — she offered me a glass of wine, sang a little song for me at the harp (which I had heard Mary do better), and made herself so thoroughly agreeable that I carried away a better impression of her than I had entertained before. And yet somehow I felt that I had been played with. Either she had betrayed her true character in discussing a business question, with which she showed unexpected familiarity, or she had assumed it for the purpose of baffling me. The incident gave me, indeed, a respect for her ability that I had never had, but it also gave me fresh reasons for doubting her sincerity. It was nothing to me whether or no she was sincere, but the less reason we have for mistrusting people, the more comfortable we feel in their presence.

But, as I have said, Mrs. Bullard was singularly gracious to Mandy Satterlee. When twilight began to deepen into dusk, it was nothing unusual to hear a rustle in the hall, and to see the Colonel's wife whisk in at the door, always pale, always composed, and yet as nimble and as light in her movements as a child. And she always had some excuse for her appearance. She wanted to see sister Jane about this, that, or the other, but always about something that was of no importance whatever. If Mary chanced to be talking with sister

Jane, then Mrs. Bullard had come for Mary.   If
Mary was at home, then her mother had come because of that fact; or she had slipped away to take
a little airing, or because the Colonel had company.
It is enough to make one dizzy to recall the changes
she rung in order to impress us with the idea that
her visits were either urgent or accidental.   On
one occasion I heard sister Jane say to her somewhat sarcastically : —

"Well, Fanny, some day when you have n't got
anything to trouble you, just pick up and come
because you 've a mind to.   It would look a heap
better, and you 'd feel lots more comfortable.   I
would, I know."

"Oh, I would dearly love to come, Jane," replied the Colonel's wife, "but with such a large
house to look after, and some one always calling
for the keys to get something out or to put something away, it is impossible.   The strain is terrible, Jane."

"It must be," rejoined sister Jane, "'specially
when you ain't got more than six dozen fat and
good-for-nothing niggers to look after your premises for you."

"Well, you know how Colonel Bullard is, Jane,"
said the lady.   "He will have a yardful of servants, three or four in the house, and more on the
lot.   He thinks they will be a help to me, but
they are hardly any help at all.   I only have so
many more to look after.   But if I complain he
will be sure to imagine that I don't appreciate his

thoughtfulness, though I am just as grateful as I can be. You know how men are, Jane."

"No, I don't, and I 'm glad I don't," sister Jane responded with emphasis. "I know jest enough about 'em not to want to know any more."

"Why, here 's Mr. William," said the Colonel's wife, waving her white and jeweled hand in my direction. "I 'm sure he ought to give you a favorable opinion of the lords of creation." She made a queer, coquettish little gesture, as she spoke.

"I don't count William among 'em," remarked sister Jane. "More than that, I 've had the raising of him. William and the cat know mighty well when to get out of the way of my broomhandle."

While she was talking, the Colonel's wife stood close to sister Jane in an attitude almost affectionate, touching her lightly on the arm with one hand, the other being free to gesture, or to play with a corner of the wide lace that the Colonel's wife always wore over her bosom. Such would have been her attitude with Mandy Satterlee, but Mandy invariably managed to remain out of reach of the lady's hand.

The Colonel's wife was always beautifully, even daintily, dressed, reminding me of pictures I had seen. Her hair was very fine, having the yellow gleam of amber about it, and she wore it in curls that were caught behind her ears and hung on the back of her neck and shoulders with fine effect.

On her head she wore a square of rich lace that was wide enough to resemble a matron's cap, but was caught up at one corner with a bow of pink or pale blue ribbon, which gave it a jaunty and picturesque effect. Pink and pale blue were the colors of the frocks she wore, and though I knew not the names of the stuffs they were fashioned from, I judged by their lustre and by their silken rustle that they were rich and costly fabrics.

It was said when her little boy disappeared so mysteriously, that the Colonel's wife was on the border of distraction. I never doubted this, and for that reason it was something of a shock to me when she came whisking through the garden some time afterwards, her pink frock gleaming in the dusk and her blue ribbons fluttering in the air. It was something of a shock, but common sense prevented me from rendering a harsh judgment against her. The sombre habiliments that grief chooses to employ as its signal were never much to my taste, making (as it were) too much of an outward show. But as these are matters to be settled by individual taste or preference, I felt 't would ill become me to criticise the one extreme or the other. Every heart knoweth its own sorrow, and what one may desire to parade another may strive to conceal.

There were lines of trouble and suffering in the lady's face which all her vivacity, natural or assumed, could not hide; and these added to her seclusion ought to have told the whole story. But there were moments when I doubted all these evidences, and when my sympathy was somewhat repelled. I had vague suspicions that refused to frame themselves in intelligible thoughts. I felt, in some mysterious way, that the Colonel's wife regarded me with contempt; and I was almost sure she knew I doubted her sincerity. Yet with all this, I admitted to myself that possibly I was unjust to her. As for her dress, I could understand how that might be a passion with her, her one source of recreation and enjoyment.

It was certain that she did not wear her rich fabrics for the sake of display, for she went nowhere. I knew from the gossip of the negroes that she would spend an entire afternoon before her mirror, lighting a candle to enable her to see how to give herself the last touches that tell of perfection. This done she would whisk through the garden, spend half an hour with sister Jane, whisk back again, retire to her room, and have her evening meal sent to her.

Her daughter Mary resembled her in nothing except daintiness of dress. But where the mother chose colors, the daughter preferred contrasts, whereby no single color was left as a mark for the eye, but harmonized with its surroundings, as in a fine painting. The Colonel's wife was fond of finery and of the frills and furbelows that the feminine hand knows so well how to arrange. They were all in good taste, too, — all possessing the quality of daintiness. But the effect was not so

fresh and wholesome, and not nearly so harmonious,
as her daughter's refined simplicity of dress.

The contrast between them must have been
apparent to the most casual observer who chanced
to see them together. It was not by any means
confined to the choice and arrangement of the apparel they wore, but was to be seen in their manner and attitude. The mother was airy, almost
frisky, and had some curious tricks of face and
hand such as belong to play-acting women who are
showing how cleverly they can assume a part. Her
eyes evaded yours, however constantly they might
rest on your face, and she insisted on conversing
on the most frivolous topics, though I knew she
was a woman of uncommon ability. Mary, on the
other hand, except on rare occasions, was repose itself. Her lustrous eyes were steady as twin stars
when they looked at you, and sincerity and innocence shone in them. Whenever she lifted her
hand in gesture (the most beautiful hand I have
ever seen) it seemed to illuminate and make more
effective whatever she was saying. She was viva-
cious — sometimes even prankish ; but behind it
all was sincerity, the touchstone. You knew she
was not playing a part, or taking your measure, or
trying to deceive you ; but that she was true to her
own innocent nature and disposition.

By some means, I knew not how, I conceived the
idea that there was a measure of secret antagonism
on the part of the mother toward the daughter. The
idea could not have grown out of the differences of

character and temperament that lay between them, for I knew well that opposite natures are almost invariably attracted to one another. No; it was some sign or symptom that the mother manifested — a sudden, an unexpected and a momentary lifting of the veil (if I may say so), that surprised me into the suspicion that this fine lady was playing the part of a mother, as she seemed to be playing other parts. Perhaps the suggestion forced itself upon me in too downright a fashion, but I was ever awkward at splitting hairs, even in an argument in the court-house. I cannot recall, even to my own mind, save in a blurred and indistinct way, the sign or symptom that stirred my suspicions to activity; but, whatever it was, it made on me a deep and a lasting impression.

I said a while ago that it was nothing to me whether or no the Colonel's wife was sincere. Perhaps that is too flat a statement. There were, indeed, many reasons why I was interested in studying her character and in trying to get at the heart of the mystery that she presented to my imagination. For one thing, it was ever my habit to study human nature in the persons of my acquaintances to measure their motives by their actions and to weigh them against what they were, what they pretended to be, and what they ought to have been. Rightly pursued, this is no mean diversion. Through knowing others I sought to know myself — to separate my outward self from my true self. I found that the more I studied

human nature in others the more likely I was to
recognize it in myself. For another thing (to return
to the Colonel's wife), the lady was Mary's mother,
and it pleased me to try to discern in the mother
some mark on which I could lay my finger and say,
" Heredity has transmitted this to the daughter."
But there were few such marks, and no wonder.
Mary was so truly her own true self — as original
in her mind as she was unique in her beauty —
that my studies in this direction came to naught.
But I never wholly gave them up while opportunity
for comparison remained.

Colonel Bullard had not married early in life.
He was next to the youngest of several sons, who
as they reached their majority drifted away from
the parental roof and went west, some to Alabama,
and some to the rich Mississippi bottoms, each carrying with him (in the shape of negroes, horses,
mules, and wagons) a portion of the family estate,
which was a large one. But when the Colonel came
of age, he elected to remain on the big plantation,
that stretched up and down the Oconee River to
the extent of several thousand acres. He had two
good reasons for this, as I have heard said : his
father was growing old and feeble (his mother
being already dead), and his younger brother was
too young to take charge of the business of the
estate. This younger brother was but fifteen, and
away at college, according to Mrs. Beshears (who
kindly furnished me all the facts that lay beyond
my memory and experience), when Cephas Bullard

reached the years of manhood. So that the latter had no choice but to remain on the plantation and take control of affairs, which, as may be supposed, he already had well in hand.

By the time Clarence Bullard, the youngest brother, had reached the age of seventeen, the father died, and Cephas Bullard applied in due form for letters of administration on the estate, and was appointed guardian of the minor brother. After the usual course, the business of the estate was finally wound up; the elder brothers came forward again and expressed their satisfaction at the way matters had been managed; each received his fair portion, if any portion was still due; and Cephas Bullard was relieved of the duties and responsibilities of administrator. He retained the home place and a large part of the plantation, and was still the guardian of Clarence Bullard.

Now, when Clarence returned home from college to attend his father's funeral, he remained for several weeks, and it soon became bruited about that he had learned more about drinking, gambling, and cock-fighting than was usually to be imbibed from a course in the classics. Public opinion, hearing of some of his frolics and other escapades, came promptly to the conclusion that Clarence was as reckless a blade as the county had ever harbored. There was also a great deal of wonderment expressed, for the boy was handsome and clever, and seemed to be well disposed. Mrs. Beshears's memory was to the effect that he was as pretty as

a picture, with black, curling hair, fine eyes, a
beautifully. shaped mouth and chin. Many young
ladies were enamored of him in spite of his reck-
lessness.

He returned to college, but the taste of freedom
he had had was too much for him. He grew rebel-
lious, and the authorities expelled him in sheer self-
defense. He came home again, caring (it is said)
as little for his disgrace as possible. For a period
of several months he kept the old people groaning
and the young ladies blushing over the reports of
his deviltry. And evil is an element of such vigorous constitution, that rumors of his wild exploits
still remained current after the man himself had
disappeared and was all but forgotten. It was
only necessary to set the old people's tongues to
wagging, and Clarence Bullard and his gray mare
went tearing through the country again. Time's
perspective has such a softening influence on cold
facts, that he lived in my mind as the most romantic rascal I had ever heard of outside the lids of
my books.

But he finally disappeared and was seen no
more, — whereupon gossip, that must needs have
many dainty giblets of scandal to stimulate its
digestion, began to announce in an authoritative
way that there had been a stormy scene betwixt
Clarence and Cephas, and that the elder brother
had driven the other from beneath his father's roof
without a penny. A great many other things were
said (as I have been told), some sensational and

all scandalous. But these things are not at all to
the purpose of this narrative.

Cephas Bullard remained on his plantation,
looked carefully after his interests, and thrived.
He devoted himself so closely to his business that
his wealth grew apace. By the time he was thirty,
he had made as much money as his father had
been able to make after years of hard labor. By
that time, too, he came to be known as the bachelor planter, and he showed no more disposition to
marry at that age than he had shown at twenty.
He set up a grist-mill on his place, and invested in
a wool-carding machine. He raised his own mules
and horses, and they were fine ones. He made his
own corn, meat, and all his plantation supplies except the clothing necessary for his negroes. He
bought shoes, cloth, hats, and blankets from the
wholesale houses. By the time he was thirty-five
he had formed the habit of going north every year,
for the purpose of laying in these supplies.

It was on one of these trips (and while the stage-
coach was journeying through Virginia) that he
met the lady who became his wife, and she herself
is the authority for the facts concerning that episode. I heard her tell them to sister Jane with
many dainty gestures, and in a manner not without suggestions of humor. Her voice was soft,
low, and well modulated, and she made it more
effective by the air of vivacity I have tried to describe.

She was the daughter of Cecil Brandon of Brandon-on-the-James (she pronounced it Brondon-on-the-Jeems), and must have been a very lively young lady according to her own account, — fond of horses, dogs, and of going to the play when the players strolled to Richmond.

"I was nothing but a child, Jane — only seventeen. Just think of that, — positively a mere child. I can see it all now, but then I thought I was a grown lady. That was my father's fault. You have heard of Cecil Brandon, of Brandon-on-the-Jeems. The family is older than the history of England. He was the best man that ever lived, Jane — a perfect gentleman. But he was like all gentlemen. For months — yes, months, Jane — he 'd allow me to have my own way, never crossing me in anything, and then all of a sudden — *p-r-r-t,*" — she made a sharp chirping sound with her lips — " his temper would be gone, and peace would take wings and fly from the place. At such times he forbade my most innocent amusements. He was a man, Jane, and you know a man does n't know when to be rough and when to be tender. Why, if I were a man, I 'd be mean and cruel sometimes, but always at the right time."

The Colonel's wife laughed as she said this, and her eyes sparkled almost as brightly as the jewels that flashed on her fingers.

The upshot of it was that once, when Cecil Brandon, of Brandon-on-the-James, was in one of his tantrums, Fanny Brandon mounted her horse, rode to Richmond to the house of a kinsman, and sat out the play that night in borrowed finery. Her father concluded that this prank was part of a disposition that should be tamed, whereupon he had his daughter's trunk packed, bundled her in the carriage, got in himself, and set out on a journey to Washington, intending to take Fanny to a convent school in Baltimore.

"Think of that, Jane!" exclaimed the Colonel's wife in telling of the episode. "Think of a convent for a young girl who had been used to having her own way except at odd times!"

The second day the carriage broke down, and the break was so serious that it could be mended neither by Cecil Brandon nor his negro driver. Still overwhelmed in the tantrums, Mr. Brandon determined to wait for the stage-coach, which they had passed on the road an hour or two before. He bade the negro driver to take the horses home, paid a farmer not far from the roadside to haul the wreck of the carriage away and hold it until sent for, hailed the stage-coach when it came along, and with little or no palaver, found a place for Fanny Brandon inside, while he rode on top. Evidently he was a man who did even small things in a large way, and before such men all difficulties are apt to disappear.

An accommodating passenger surrendered his seat inside to pretty Fanny Brandon, and when she had fairly settled herself, the first man on whom her eyes fell was Colonel Cephas Bullard, the man who was to be her husband.

" I never dreamed of such a thing, Jane.   Why, he was old enough to be my father ; but you see how it is ; we never know what Providence has in store for us."

Cecil Brandon, swinging his legs from the top of the coach, was not long in finding congenial company, and was soon telling jokes and laughing heartily.   He found, too, some gentlemen of the green cloth, and as few things suited him better than a long toddy and a brisk game of cards (the statement is his daughter's word for word), he made arrangements for a tussle with chance when Washington was reached.

Now, Fanny Brandon, though she was doubtless looking very pretty, was far from happy, and when she heard her father's jolly laugh nothing would do but she must fall to crying softly.   This being so, it was natural that Colonel Cephas Bullard, sitting opposite, should extend his sympathies, and offer his services, and make all effort to console her.   He was so successful that Fanny Brandon was soon able to smile shyly at him.   At the next stopping-place, which was a tavern where they had dinner, Colonel Bullard made bold to introduce himself to Cecil Brandon, and it turned out — these Virginians having a great knack of knowing in person or by repute everybody that is worth knowing — that Mr. Brandon knew of the Bullards and had a good part of their family history at his tongue's end.   Indeed, he hinted that there was kinship somewhere in the background.

When the travelers reached Washington, Cecil Brandon placed his daughter in charge of Colonel Cephas Bullard, begging him to see her safe to Baltimore and to the conventual school, and betook himself to the card-table. This was providential. Fanny Brandon had no more idea of entering the convent school than she had of flying, and when they arrived in Baltimore she turned to Colonel Bullard and said (I can imagine with what a charming air) : —

"I 'll not go on, and I can't go back ; so what shall I do ? "

Colonel Cephas was taken by surprise. He was helpless. He could not command, and he would not desert. While he was considering what was proper to do under these unparalleled circumstances, Fanny Brandon threw her head back defiantly, crying out: "I wish some respectable gentleman would ask me to marry him ! "

Colonel Cephas strode up and down a few moments, paused in front of the young lady and said simply: " Would you marry me ? "

" Would I ? " exclaimed Fanny Brandon, and placed her hand in his.

" Don't you think that was a queer courtship, Jane ? " the Colonel's wife paused to inquire when narrating these circumstances. And sister Jane replied : " There 's nothing quare, Fanny, after you get used to it."

They married, and Colonel Bullard, instead of going on to New York, went back to Washington

with his wife, sought out Cecil Brandon, of Brandon - on - the - James, and informed him that his
daughter Fanny Brandon had now become Mrs.
Bullard. Mr. Brandon was paralyzed for a moment, and it was the fall of an eyelash whether he
would seize Colonel Cephas by the throat and cane
him. But Brandon's humor came to the rescue.
He burst into a roaring laugh.

"Damn it, sir, give me your hand! I like you!
I'll lay you five to one, sir, that Fan popped the
question. Come, Fan! Did n't you?" And
when Fan demurely admitted it, Brandon of Brandon-on-the-James roared so loudly that the windows of the room rattled.

That was the way Fanny Brandon became Mrs.
Cephas Bullard. The Colonel brought her to his
plantation home — a very fine place, not far from
the Oconee. But after a time she grew tired of
the quiet life ; whereupon the Colonel bought the
Clopton mansion in the village, furnished it in
grand style, and brought his young bride there.
The society she found here was probably different
from that she had been used to in Virginia ; it may
have lacked refinement, as it certainly wanted gayety ; but for one reason or the other, or for all together, young Mrs. Bullard gradually secluded
herself.

XV.

JINCY IN THE NEW GROUND.

SUCH was the account the Colonel's wife gave of her courtship and marriage. For a long time I suspected that, following the impulse of some whimsical notion, such as frequently takes control of the feminine mind, she had exaggerated the affair by foreshortening some of the details that otherwise might have given it a perspective more satisfying to those who stickle over proprieties. I suspected that she desired to draw a strong contrast between her headstrong and wayward youth and the soberness and discretion that marked her career as a matron ; or that she intended to magnify her temper and courage when a girl, in order to impress us with her ability to carry herself boldly, though she might now be delicate and dainty in her ways and desires. But gradually I came to believe that she had given the facts simply and with no other desire than to relieve her mind and to place herself on a semi-confidential footing with sister Jane ; for after that, and at various odd times, she told us more of her history, which need not be repeated here at any length, since the part she played in the small history I have set out to chronicle was unimportant up to almost the last moment, when Fanny Brandon herself stepped out of the past (as it were) and gave us cause for special wonder. But that is a matter to be told of in its proper place.

Meanwhile, nature went forward in her resistless course as severely as ever. The days came and the nights fell — the beautiful nights with their glittering millions of stars trooping westward in orderly constellations — and the days and nights became weeks, and the weeks became months, and the months brought the seasons and the seasons the years. I could but compare the feeble and fluttering troubles of humanity, its spites and disputes, its wild struggles, its deepest griefs and its most woeful miseries, with the solemn majesty of nature. I could but feel that the solitude of the great woods and the infinite spaces of the sky, though dumb, were charged with the power and presence of the Ever-Living One. So that when reflection sat with me at odd times, I was seized with the deepest pity for all the human atoms (myself among the rest) that were surging and struggling, grabbing and grasping, and jostling against one another, less orderly and purposeful than the procession of tiny black ants that was marching day and night from the garden to sister Jane's cupboard.

Of all that I knew there was but one that seemed to employ life and the days thereof in a way that might be acceptable in the sight of heaven, and that one was Mary Bullard. Yet she made no pretensions to piety ; she simply went about among those who were poor and unhappy on missions of charity and benevolence, comforting those who were under the ban of public opinion, and carrying succor to the shabby homes of the poverty-stricken, always helping them without asking why they failed to help themselves, and carrying with her everywhere the blessings of all she met.

She had a great admirer in Jincy Meadows, who met her once when he came to see Mandy Satterlee. I introduced him to Mary simply to enjoy his embarrassment, but, to my surprise, he betrayed no shyness whatever. His self-consciousness, which was sometimes almost painfully apparent, disappeared entirely, and he conversed with an ease and fluency quite remarkable. Mary was very much amused at his drolleries and drew him out in the deftest way, taking pains to put him at his ease.

When she went away, Jincy watched her moving through the garden and then turned to me.

"Shucks, squire !" he exclaimed, "if I had n't 'a' taken a good look at Miss Mary I 'd 'a' never believed that the world held the like of her — now that 's honest !"

"How is that, Jincy ?" I asked.

"I 'll tell you, squire — if Miss Mary 'd go out in the woods and sorter git use to things out there, she 'd soon have the birds a-flyin' after her, and all the wil' creeturs a-follerin' her. She 's got the ways, and she 'd soon git the knack."

"I noticed, Jiney, that you did n't blush and stammer as I 've seen you do," I remarked.

"I did n't have time, squire — that 's a fact. I looked in her eyes, and I know'd right then and there that she was somebody that would n't make fun of me, and go off thinkin' I 'm a bigger fool 'n I reely am. So I jest braced up and felt at home. Squire, did you hear her laugh — once in particular when I told her about the crooked tree? It sounded jest like a soft note on a fiddle."

Did I remember it? Aye, and a hundred little graces that escaped Jiney's eyes. Yet I was struck, as well as gratified, by the fact that Jiney had heard and noticed the rippling music of her laughter. In the midst of his drolleries, he was telling of an experience he had in clearing up a new ground, and why he never intended to engage in that kind of work again.

"I hope you 'll believe me, ma'am," he said, "when I say that I went at this cle'rin' of the new groun' with as good a heart and disposition to take hold of it and git it out of the way as anybody could. I taken my axe and went into the timber, and started to begin on a saplin'. But I looked at the axe and then I looked at the saplin', and I says to myse'f, says I, 'Jiney, what in the world is the use of tryin' your hand on a baby tree? If you want to begin right, why n't you pick out a tree that 's got age and size on its side?'

"So I swung the axe over my shoulder and went through the timber till I found a big fine tree. I tell you what, she was a whopper. It looked like a squirrel would have to take a runnin' start and climb a quarter of a mile before he got to the top, because there wa'n't narry a limb half way where he could rest. 'T was all body from root to branch, and no branch till you got to the top.

"I went up and laid my hand on it, and then I stepped back and raised the axe, but before I let the lick fall, a thought struck me. I lowered the axe and walked round the pine. Says I to myse'f, says I, 'Jincy, here's a tree what is a tree. Maybe it's upwards of a thousand years old, and ain't grown yit; and if 't ain't, what a pity to cut it down in the bloom of youth,' says I. So I walked around the pine ag'in — it was a whopper, ma'am — and I says, says I, 'Jincy, here's a pine and a big one. It would n't make enough lumber to build a court-house, nor enough timber to build a bridge,' says I, 'and yit, if all the people of all the United States was to meet in one big convention and pass resolutions, and throw in more money than seve'm hunder'd steers could pull, they could n't have this pine put back after it's cut down. The harrycanes ain't hurt it and the thunder ain't teched it, and now here's poor little Jincy Meadows, more 'n half a fool, and yit not half a man, a-standing round and flourishing his axe and gittin' ready to cut it down,' says I.

"I drapped my axe and shuck my head, ma'am, and went on through the timber s'arching for another place to begin cleanin' up the new groun'.

I had n't gone so mighty fur when I come to a clean lookin' hickory; so I ups and I says, 'Jincy, here 's your chance. If you ever speck to make any big name for cleanin' up new groun's, you 've got to make a beginnin' some'rs, and right now 's the time, and this here 's the place. This hickory is tough, and by the time you git it down you 'll be warm enough for to go right ahead and cut 'em down as you come to 'em.' I swung my axe aroun' my head a time or two to feel of the heft, and I was jest about to make a start, when I heard a fuss up in the tree, and here come a little gray squirrel with a hickory nut in his mouth. He was comin' right down the body of the tree, but when he seen me he stopped and give his bushy tail a flirt or two as much as to say, 'Hello, Jincy! what 's up now ?' Then he got on a limb and sot up and looked at me as cunnin' as you please. I taken my hat off to Little Gray, and says, says I, ' Excuse me, mister, if you please! I was jest about to up and knock down your hickory nut orchard, and I 'm mighty glad you spoke when you did. I would n't trespass on your premises, not for the world! ' says I.

"So I ups and shoulders my axe and goes on through the timber a-huntin' for a place where I could begin the job of cleanin' up the new groun', for it jest had to be cleaned up. I come to a big poplar, and when I tapped it with the eye of the axe, I found it was holler. So I says, says I, ' Jincy, here 's a big tree that 's outlived its innerds and 't ain't no manner account. I 'll jest up an' take it down,' says I. But, bless gracious, when I tapped on the poplar 't was the same as knockin' at a door. I heard a scratchin' and a clawin' fuss, and then I seen the lady of the house stick her head out of the window. 'T wa'n't nobody in the world but old Miss Coon, and I know 'd by the way she looked that she had a whole passel of children in there. So I bowed politely, and says, says I, ' I ast your pardon, ma'am. I thought you lived furder up the creek. I hope your family 's well,' says I. Old Miss Coon shuck her head like she did n't half believe me, or it might 'a' been a blue-bottle fly a-buzzin' too close to her ears.

" But I let her house alone, and went along through the timber, a-huntin' for a place where I might begin for to clean up the new groun', because it jest had to be cleaned up. I went along till I come to a young pine, an' I says, says I, ' Jincy, here 's the very identical place I 've been lookin' for and this here 's the tree. It ain't too big, it ain't too tall, it ain't too young, and it ain't too old,' says I. But before I could make my arrangements for to cut it down, I heard a squallin' in the top, and I looked up and seen a jay-bird's nest. The old jay got on a limb right at me, his topnot a bristlin', and he give me the worst cussin' out I 've had since my hoss run away and broke old Jonce Ashfield's jug of liquor. Says I, ' Hey, hey, Mr. Jay! Is this where you stay? Then I 'll go 'way.' "

In repeating these rhymes, Jincy fitted his voice
to the notes of the jay with remarkable effect.
Mary laughed at this, but she took his story as
seriously as he did, and saw deeper into it, perhaps,
than he suspected or intended.

" I picked up my axe," he continued, " and went
through the timber a-huntin' for a place where I
could begin to clean up the new groun', for it jest
had to be cleaned up. After a while I come to a
tree that was dead from top to bottom. It was so
dead that there wa'n't a limb on it, and all the
bark had drapped off. So I says to myself, says
I, ' Now, Jincy, here you are! Now 's your time!
You can't do no damage here. The new groun' 's
got to be cleaned up, and here 's the place to begin,' says I. I shucked my coat, for the walkin'
had sorter warmed me up, and grabbed my axe,
but before I hit the lick, I thought maybe I 'd save
elbow grease and jest push the old tree down. I
give it a right smart shake and it sorter swayed
and tottered, but jest about that time, I heard a
big flutteration at the top, and out come a pair of
wood-peckers. I drapped my axe and bowed.
' You must reely excuse me, Mister Flicker,' says
I, ' because I thought you 'd have a better house
than this at your time of life,' says I.

" I picked up my coat and my axe and went
a-huntin' through the timber for a place where I
could start to cleanin' up the new groun', because
it had to be cleaned up — there wa'n't no two ways
about that. I went along, keepin' a sharp eye out,

and after a while I come across the identical tree
I had been a-lookin' for. It was a stunted black-
jack. It had started to grow up, and then it had
started down ag'in. Then it went back and grow'd
out to'rds the east, and then it grow'd back to'ards
the west — this-away, that-away and ever' whichaway. It had as many elbows as the Baptizin'
creek, and as many twists as a gin screw. So I
says, says I, ' Howdy, black-jack! I 'll jest start
with you.' And I did. I drapped my coat on the
groun', and had n't hit a dozen licks with the axe
before down came the black-jack. And no sooner
had I saw what I done than I was sorry."

"Sorry!" exclaimed sister Jane. "What for,
Jincy ?"

"Well 'm," replied Jincy, with just the faintest
shadow of a smile showing in the corner of his
mouth, "that black-jack was so crooked that it
could n't lay still. By the time it got fairly settled
one way, it 'd wobble and turn over. It wobbled
sideways an roun' and roun'; it wobbled a piece
of the way up hill, and then turned and wobbled
down. It got a kind of a runnin' start when it
headed down hill, and could n't stop itself. Old
Molly Cotton-Tail was a-settin' under a bush nigh
the edge of the thicket, jest as comfortable as you
please. She heard the black-jack a-coming in the
nick of time, and if she had n't made a break when
she did, she 'd 'a' been run over and crippled. She
was a skeered rabbit, certain and shore — and the
worst of it is, she got the idee that Jincy was after

her, and 'twas the longest after that before she 'd
set still and le' me scratch her behind her ears.

"The black-jack tried to wobble back where it
lived, but the slope was too steep, and it went on
wobbling down the branch. A passel of hogs
feedin' down there seen it a-comin' and went
through the woods a-humpin' and a-snortin.' The
hogs skeer'd a drove of cattle, and the cattle broke
and run down a lane, and skeer'd old Miss Favers's
yoke of steers, and the steers skeer'd a plough
mule, and the plough mule broke loose and run
home and skeer'd the old speckled hen off her nest."

"What became of the black-jack?" I inquired.

"You are too much for me, squire," replied
Jincy. "I reckon it 's a wobbling yit if 't ain't
got caught in a crack of the fence. I left them
diggin's. I says to myself, says I, 'Jincy, you ain't
got much sense, but you 've got sense enough to
know that you ain't much of a hand to clean up
new groun',' says I; and then I lit out and went
home."

"That 's Jincy all over," remarked Mandy smiling.

I could see that Mary enjoyed Jincy's narrative
of his adventures very much, and that she appre-
ciated the humane motive that ran through it like
a thread of gold. Jincy saw it, too, and that is why
he made the remark that has been quoted already:

"Shucks, squire ! if I had n't 'a' taken a good
look at Miss Mary, I 'd 'a' never believed that the
world held the like of her — now that 's honest."

XVI.

A PERIOD OF CALM.

THERE are periods of quiet that are difficult to describe, especially in a simple chronicle that makes no claim to go beyond the surface of events. For three, four, — yes, five — years the village, the people, and especially our little household saw few changes worth noting. So far as events are concerned we were becalmed. It would be an easy matter, if what is here written were a mere piece of fiction, to invent a succession of episodes to add interest to the narrative. I have in my mind now a half dozen scenes that are admirably fitted to do duty here. Or I might employ some such formula as I have met with in the lighter books — "Several years have now elapsed." Nevertheless, I know that during this period of calm the strangest events were slowly taking shape and growing gradually toward culmination. The years of quiet that are so flippantly disposed of in light pieces of fiction are frequently the most important of all in real life. Out of such periods Fortune comes with its favors, or Fate (as some say) with its sword.

It was so now. Colonel Bullard grew visibly

older, Mary more beautiful, and the Colonel's wife
more restless, as it seemed to me, whisking through
the dark garden between sunset and dark like a
pink and white moth. Mrs. Beshears remained
vigorous enough to continue her visits, and her
two sisters Miss Polly and Miss Becky seemed to
be no feebler in mind and body than they had been
in some years. Sister Jane appeared as young as
ever to my eyes, but my mirror told me that a man
is not as young at forty-odd as he is at thirty-five.
Mandy Satterlee was cheerful, but not gay — and
I often thought that her cheerfulness sprang from
her mother-love for her boy, who had grown to be
a fat and saucy rascal of nearly six years. Jincy
Meadows came to see Mandy regularly every
Saturday, and it was plain to all eyes, except
Mandy's, that he was desperately in love with her.
As for Mandy, she said over and often that love
was not for such as she, and though she laughed
when she said it, her voice was charged with mel-
ancholy.

It has been said that Mrs. Beshears remained
vigorous. Yet she was growing older and she felt
it and knew it, for one day she came into the
village and asked me to write her will. Its terms
were in keeping with her peculiarities. First and
foremost, her share of the property, land and
negroes, was to go to her two sisters to be held
for their use and benefit, should she die first —
with this exception, that the home place, which was
hers, was to go to Mandy Satterlee, her heirs and

assigns, provided Mandy would agree to take charge of the two sisters and administer faithfully to their wants. At the death of the two sisters, the home place and one hundred acres of land were to be Mandy Satterlee's portion. In the course of the will Mrs. Beshears expressed a desire that, at the death of her two sisters, the negroes should be given their freedom, and that the portion of real estate not otherwise devised should be sold for the purpose of transporting them to a free state. I saw a great many complications in this, should any claimants to the estate turn up, and so advised Mrs. Beshears; but her blunt reply was that if I was n't lawyer enough to draw her own will the way she wanted it, she 'd " go to somebody else and maybe have the job done better." So I drew the will the best I could, and had it witnessed by men of property and standing. Mrs. Beshears was as impatient of these formalities as she was of the legal terms, technicalities, and circumlocutions, which indeed are whimsical enough even to those who employ them. But she was satisfied when the matter had been concluded, and seemed to feel better.

I was surprised that she should leave so substantial an evidence of her regard for Mandy Satterlee, having never made any special manifestation of it so far as her actions were concerned; and I took occasion to make a remark to that effect.

" Well, you know, William, folks is selfish to the last. If I could take wi' me when I die what little

I've got, I reckon I'd hold onto it, though the Lord knows it's been enough trouble to me in this world, — let 'lone the next. But I can't take it wi' me, an' so I jest give it to Mandy Satterlee to git her to take keer of them two ol' babies of mine. Somebody's got to do it, an' I reckon Mandy'll treat 'em jest as good as anybody else, maybe better, specially when she's paid well to do it."

"But suppose they die first?" I suggested. "It is to be expected. In the course of nature you ought to outlive Miss Polly and Miss Becky many years."

"It's all guess-work, William. Natur' has its course as you say; but I've know'd it to take short-cuts, an' maybe that's the way it'll do now. Anyhow, I've made up my mind to pick up an' go to church next Sunday. I hope I won't skeer the natives."

Mrs. Beshears was not in the habit of going to church, and her statement caused me to open my eyes a little wider. She must have seen this, for she laughed and said : —

"Don't git skeer'd, William. If I go I'll try to behave myself, an' you nee'n't cut your eye at me if you see me there. Jimmy Dannielly's goin' to preach, they say, an' I want to hear him. I use to know Jimmy when he was a rip-roarin' sinner. Why, he use to go 'roun' the country a-cussin' like a sailor, an' a-bellerin' like a brindle bull; but now they tell me that he preaches jest as hard as

he use to cuss, an' if that's so, I want to hear him.
So when you hear me a-thumpin' up the aisle,
don't turn 'roun', bekaze I won't be much to look
at. If Jimmy's in the pulpit when I go in, I
hope he won't think I 'm mockin' him, because my
stick makes as much fuss as his wooden leg."

Uncle Jimmy Dannielly was the most noted
preacher we had in middle Georgia. He was a
revivalist, and although he was a Methodist, his
preaching was acceptable to the members of all
denominations — the Baptists and Presbyterians
— that had found a foothold among the people.
The reason of this was that Uncle Jimmy was
never known to preach what is called a doctrinal
sermon. He did not concern himself with creeds,
but preached the religion that he found in the
New Testament. He was a very earnest man, and
his fervor gave rise to a great many eccentricities.
Sprung from the common people, he used the language of the common people, and I never knew
how fluent, flexible, and picturesque every-day
English was until I heard Uncle Jimmy preach.
Perhaps his manner — his earnestness — had something to do with it; but there was more in the
matter, for a mere attitude of the mind cannot
give potency to language, nor can fervor, nor exaltation, nor even a great thought, always sum-
mon the apt and illuminating word, as I have long
ago found out to my sorrow.

It was said that, on one occasion, when Uncle
Jimmy Dannielly was preaching in a neighboring

town, a dandified young fellow rose in the midst of the sermon and went down the aisle toward the door, twirling a light cane in his hand. The preacher paused in his sermon and cried out, "Stop, young man! Stop where you are and think! There are no dandies in heaven with rattan canes and broadcloth breeches." The story goes that the young man waved his hand lightly and replied that there were as many dandies with canes in heaven as there were wooden-legged preachers. The truth of this last I doubted. Such a remark as that credited to the young man would have outraged public opinion, and no young man can afford to do that. The whole story is doubtless an invention, but the words attributed to Uncle Jimmy Dannielly were characteristic of his bluntness. Though in all probability he did not utter them, they nevertheless had the flavor of his style and his uncompromising methods.

Large crowds always went to hear Uncle Jimmy preach, some to renew their religious faith and fervor, some to discover the source of his reputation, and some (the great majority, it is to be feared) to be amused at his eccentricities. As it was in other communities, so it was in ours. On the Sunday morning when Uncle Jimmy was to preach in the old Union church, Sister Jane and myself found a large crowd present, though we had come early. Usually the men sat on one side and the women on the other, but on this particular occasion the custom vanished before the anxiety of the people to see and hear the preacher. I found myself, therefore, with a good many other men, sitting in the pews usually reserved for the women. I was one pew behind that in which sister Jane sat — on the very seat, as I suddenly discovered, that I had sometimes occupied when a boy, not willingly, but in deference to the commands of sister Jane, who, in those days long gone, made it a part of her duty to take me prisoner every Sunday morning and carry me to church whether or no.

There, on the side of the pew, were the letters W. W., which many years ago I had carved with my barlow knife. They were as distinct as if they had been made but yesterday, and I passed my fingers over them as one might do in a dream. It all came back to me — the beautiful singing, the droning prayer, the long sermon, the doxology, the solemn benediction. I was too tall now to lean my head against the back of the pew, and gradually become oblivious to all sights and sounds; but in the old days, keenly alive to my imprisonment, I used to sit and wish for the end until the oblivion of sleep lifted me beyond the four walls and out into the freedom of the woods and fields. Sometimes the preacher, anxious to impress some argument upon the minds of his hearers, would bring his fist down on the closed Bible with a bang that startled me out of dreamland. I remembered how I used to sit and watch the beautiful rays of sunshine streaming through the half-closed blinds of the high windows, and how I used to envy the

birds that sang and chirped in the shrubbery of
the old graveyard hard by. At such times a sense
of loneliness crept over me, especially if I could
hear the voices of children at play in the pleasant
sunshine ; and I smiled to remember what a sense
of isolation it gave me if a cow lowed in the green
pastures behind the church.

Over my head now was the same high ceiling
that had attracted my attention, if not my admiration, in the days of my childhood. It had been
painted to represent the sky, but the hand that
held the brush was not the hand of an artist. Yet
it was no doubt an ambitious piece of work. Long
waving blurs of white represented the rims of the
clouds, and in the blue spaces a few white splotches
stood for the stars. The ceiling was lifted high
above the tall pulpit and above the gallery, which
ran around the church on the sides and on the
end opposite the pulpit, and was supported by
a row of tall and stately white pillars that lent a
solemn dignity to the interior perspective, no matter in what part of the building the observer sat.
The height of the ceiling was effective in another
way. However bright the sun might shine outside, there was always a mysterious twilight haze
overhead — not dark, nor even dusky, but dim.
No matter how bright a light poured into the
church from the windows beneath the gallery, it
was mellowed and subdued ere it reached the ceiling.

Looking up now I could see a bat circling over-

head, and, as I watched, it was joined by another.
I remembered that in the days of my youth I used
to sit on the hard and uncomfortable seat and watch
the bats whirling in giddy circles, sometimes close
to the ceiling, and sometimes darting as low as the
gallery. I used to wonder where they went when
the church was closed and the windows shut. Sometimes they would disappear for a moment in the
dark space that hung grim and awful (as my childish mind had pictured it) between the gallery and
the recess behind the belfry. Then, as if they had
merely gone to carry a message, they would reap-
pear almost immediately, and begin their gyra-
tions anew, flitting about ceaselessly until slumber
closed my eyes to their movements, or a sudden
twitch or pinch from sister Jane's ready fingers
caused me to turn my head, but not my mind,
in the direction of the preacher's voice.

Thus it came about that I rarely entered the old
church that I did not live over again some part of
my childish experience, and the more so now, since
I was confronted by the crooked and unsymmetrical
W. W., that I had managed to carve on the back
of the pew in spite of sister Jane's watchful eye.

While these various thoughts and reminiscences
were tumbling over one another in my mind, the
people continued to assemble. I saw Mary Bullard come in the door, pause on the threshold, as
if waiting for some one, and then go down the aisle
with modest grace, followed by her mother. Then
came Colonel Bullard, marching along with meas-

ured and dignified tread. Their pew was to the right of the pulpit and very near it, so that it might be said of the Colonel, as it was said of another, that he had placed himself under the drippings of the sanctuary.

From my place I could just see the top of the preacher's head as he sat behind the pulpit desk, engaged either in reading the Bible or in silent prayer. He was evidently waiting for all the congregation to gather, so that there would be no noise or disturbance after services began. My eyes moved over the congregation, and finally rested on sister Jane, who sat bolt upright in her seat. There was an air of grim defiance about the set of her bonnet. One arm rested on the end of the pew, and I noticed that her turkey-tail fan, which she always carried with her on occasions of moment, was swinging in the adjoining pew. I could see the bow of the modest ribbon by which the fan was attached to her wrist. I observed, too, that in this pew sat a little boy apparently eight or ten years of age. He sat very still, but I noticed that there was a look of interest and expectation in his eyes as he turned his head from side to side. His face was brown with the sun, but was not the less attractive for that. I tried to remember if I had ever seen him before, having no other matter to interest me. Failing in this, I tried to place him by tracing his family resemblance in his features. I failed here also.

While I was idly studying the lad's face, his

eye fell on sister Jane's turkey-tail fan. With a quick glance he looked from the fan to its owner. What he saw there must have satisfied him, for he reached forth his hand and began to examine the morocco shield which held the ends of the feathers together. Sister Jane felt the movements of the fan, saw that the boy was touching it, and drew it away with an impatient gesture. I regretted it in a moment, for the lad regarded her with some amazement, and then slowly moved as far away from her as he could get, and leaned against the back of the pew. Instantly a hand was laid tenderly on the lad's shoulder, and he rested his cheek against it, appearing to take great comfort from its support. One of the huge pillars intervened between the owner of the hand and my eyes. I could not see him no matter how I shifted my position or craned my neck.

But the hand was strong and firm, and browner by far than the boy's face. On the third finger was a ring that I judged by its color and lack of finish to be of virgin gold. Sister Jane noticed the surprised expression in the lad's face and saw his movement away from her neighborhood. There was nothing petulant in the movement, nor any expression of sullenness in the child's countenance. He seemed to be grieved as well as surprised, that he had been repulsed. Perceiving all this, sister Jane relented, as I knew she would. Her attitude became less rigidly uncompromising. She leaned against the end of her pew and allowed her turkey-tail fan to fall into the position from which she had drawn it when she felt the touch of the child's hand. She even went so far as to push the fan a little closer to the boy than it had been before. He saw the movement, of course, but evidently did not understand it, for he sat perfectly still, his hands resting in his lap, and his head leaning with confidence on the firm brown hand that lay gently on his shoulder.

For my part I heartily regretted the episode. It was a small thing after all, but I knew it would rankle in sister Jane's tender heart for many a long day. I have heard her say time and again that but for the small worries of life a great many people, especially women, would be happy, and I now felt, with a sort of pang, that she would carry with her the thought that she had wounded the feelings of this lad thoughtlessly and unnecessarily. The child would forget it in a jiffy, — perhaps he had already forgotten it, — but sister Jane would remember it, though she might never refer to it.

But my thoughts were soon diverted from this trifling episode. Suddenly, as though moved by a common impulse, the congregation, led by Colonel Bullard, began to sing the beautiful melody to which some inspired hand has set the poem beginning —

" How tedious and tasteless the hours."

The volume of the song filled the church from floor to ceiling. When it was finished, the Baptist minister, who sat in the pulpit with Uncle

Jimmy Dannielly, rose and asked the people to join him in prayer. Some stood with bowed heads, others knelt on the floor, while still others sat in their seats and leaned their heads on the backs of the pews in front of them. When the prayer was finished, the Methodist minister, who also sat in the pulpit, rose and read a hymn and then gave it out, two lines at a time. A silence that seemed to be full of expectation fell on the congregation when the last note of the song had died away. Uncle Jimmy Dannielly rose slowly from the cushioned seat behind the desk, stepped forward with a limp, leaned both hands on the pulpit, and allowed his eyes to wander over the assembly.

XVII.

THE PREACHER AND THE SERMON.

As he stood thus, the revivalist presented a very striking figure. His long iron-gray hair was combed straight back from a high forehead. His eyes, though sunken, were full of fire. His face was lean, but full of strength; the nose was long and slightly curved in the middle; the mouth was large and the lips thin, but not too thin to shut out generosity; and the chin was massive. His dress was of the plainest. His coat of linsey-woolsey was even shabby. His waistcoat was cotton stuff dyed with copperas. His shirt, though white, was of homespun; the collar was wide and loose; and there was no sign of stock or neckerchief. When he began to speak, his voice was not lifted above a conversational tone, but it penetrated to every nook and corner of the church and reached every ear in the congregation.

"When I last stood in this pulpit," he said, "Brother Collingsworth sat in that seat there." He pointed a long finger toward one of the front pews. "Right behind him was the most beautiful young woman these old eyes ever looked on." The congregation knew that he was referring to Elizabeth Allen, who had been dead half a dozen years. "Over there" — pointing to the right — "was a man in the prime of life. Over there" — pointing to the left — "was a woman who was blessed with the loveliest fruits of motherhood. In the back of the church, against the wall, I saw a young man who had just reached the year of his majority. I saw all these and many more. I look for them to-day, and I fail to find them. Will some of you people who live here in town tell me something about them? Can you give me any news of them? They were all my friends. More than my friends," he went on, his voice rising a little, — "more than my friends. I loved them every one. They are not here to-day, and my heart tells me something has happened. What is it? Why are they not here to-day? Why do I miss them?"

He paused and turned to Mr. Ransom, an old white-haired man who sat in a chair near the pulpit.

"Brother Ransom, you were well acquainted with Brother Collingsworth. Where is he to-day?"

The reply of Mr. Ransom was in so low a tone that the greater part of the congregation failed to hear it. But the preacher left no doubts on their minds.

"In heaven!" he cried; "in heaven! a place he had worked more than half of a long life to reach. Pray with me, brothers, sisters, high and low, rich and poor, that every man, woman, and child that

has ever sat in this church or ever shall, — pray that
they may be found in heaven with Brother Collingsworth at the last day."

The preacher paused again and wiped his face
with his big red pocket-handkerchief.

"I see more changes than that," he went on.
"I see silks and satins, and I hear them a-rustling.
I see finger-rings and breastpins a-flashing and
a-shining. Let the women move their heads ever
so little, and I see their ear-bobs a-trembling.
What is it all for? To help you to worship God?
To help you to humble yourselves before our Lord,
the Saviour? Oh, you women! look at me! Here
you are bedecked with your finery, while I have
scarcely a shirt to my back. Why, if I thought that
silks and satins, and finger-rings, and ear-bobs, and
frills and finery would help me to worship my Lord
and make me humbler by so much as a single grain,
I'd go into the pulpit loaded down with them. If I
couldn't buy them, I'd beg and borry them — I'd
do anything but steal them — but what I'd have
them. Why, if it'd help me in the sight of God, I'd
put bracelets on my arms, and shiny rings on my
ankles, and bells on my toes, and feathers in my
hair, and when I walked into a church, the children
would scream and cry and the gals faint because
they'd think I was a Hottentot or a wild Injun.
But their blessed mothers would console them and
hush them, and say, 'Don't be afraid. He's dressed
up so because it helps him to praise and worship
God.'"

Pausing again, the preacher with a swoop of his hand threw open the big Bible that lay on the pulpit desk, and read (apparently) the first verse that fell under his eye : —

" ' They which are the children of the flesh, these are not the children of God ; but the children of the promise are counted for the seed.' Don't make any mistake, good friends," he went on, " I 'm not taking any text. I don't have to hunt texts to preach God's word. They swarm and flutter in my mind. Every face before me is a living, breathing text, and there 's a text in every minute that passes, every day that closes.

" Paul was writing to the Romans, and quoting from the Old Testament. Before the atonement, the children of the flesh were not the children of God. But when our Lord gave himself up for the sake of sinners, and was nailed to the tree, He pointed the way by which every child of the flesh may become a child of God. He showed the world the road of repentance, and suffered on the cross that the road might be clear. We are all children of the flesh ; we are all little children of the world ; we are all children of God through the Lord our Saviour. What is there hard about a saying that carries a message of life to a repentant sinner? You 'll hear it said on every hand that love begets love, that our very nature tells us to love them that love us. Are we dumb brutes, that when the Child of Bethlehem comes to us with love and mercy in his eyes, and words of love and mercy on his lips,

we must harden our hearts and turn our heads
away?

"We are all little children of the world. All
of us are sinful, but only a few of us are sorrow-
ful. Why? Plough, and you'll have corns on
your hands; sin, and continue to sin, and your
hearts will be covered over with callousness
— case-hardened. Little children of the world!
And it needs but a lifting of the mind, and a bending of the knee to make us the children of God.
Children! But what is a child without innocence.
A monster, a deformity in the sight of God and
man. But the world swarms with them; the towns
are full of them; and they wander up and down all
over the land. They are right here in the sound
of my voice! They are looking in my face, and
a-wondering what I 'm going to say next.

"Well, I 'll tell you what I 'm going to say next,
and I 'll say it so loud that the very walls 'll hear
it and repeat it to the roof, and the roof to the
world above. There are men and women in this
church to-day (and I could go and put my hand
on them) that are so deep in sin, so double-dyed
in all manner of iniquity, that they are afraid to
get down on their knees and tell God about it.
They have hid it from men and they think they
are hiding it from the Almighty. They hold
their heads high, but how many weeks, how many
days, before they will be brought low? If they
can't fool a poor old man like me, how can they
fool the Lord of Hosts?

"Little children of the world! *They* are not children; they are ravening wolves, pursuing the innocent and devouring them. And yet what a simple thing stands between them and a clear conscience! Oh, you men and women that know I 'm a-talking about you, why not try repentance? When remorse pulls you out of sleep at the dead hours of night, why not mix repentance with your misery? Remorse ain't repentance. Remorse is nothing but fear — fear that your sins will find you at the wrong place and at the wrong time. Don't trust to remorse. But when it seizes hold of you — when it is tearing and gnawing your very vitals — drop on your knees and beg the Saviour to take you into the arms of his mercy and forgiveness. And where you can make restitution, make it. And where you can make confession, make it. But repentance first, repentance last, and repentance all the time!

"And, oh, believe me! hard and heavy as its burthens are, it is not too high a price to pay for a clean heart and a contented mind, even if these were all. But they are not all — they are not half — they are not the thousandth part of the blessing that repentance will bring. It will be as a dazzling light to show to you the unspeakable beauties of our Saviour's love and mercy.

"Don't think I 'm a-talking about your neighbor. Don't think I 'm a-talking to stir up the feelings of the weak-minded or the tender-hearted. Much as the cause of Christ may need reviving in this town, I've not come here to revive it. I ought to be miles from here to-day, but I met a human wreck in the public road a fortnight ago — oh, a wretched and a miserable wreck ! — that the Lord must have sent there that my eyes might see and my ears hear him. My promise called me away, but my heart brought me here. And here I am — not to publish, not to condemn (for who am I that I should sit in judgment?), but to warn, and, may-be, bring a few hearts to repentance."

The preacher paused, and when he spoke again his voice was low and tremulous with emotion.

"Oh, unhappy world ! where sin has power to smite and wound the innocent ! Oh, unhappy men and women that must drag their children into the mire of sin and disgrace ! Look at your feet ! You are standing by an open keg of powder. Soon the pitch a-dripping from passion's torch will kindle it, the explosion will come, and then ? Oh, the pity of it ! The innocent and the helpless will be blackened and burned by it."

In this strain the sermon, if it could be called a sermon, went on. I have selected only a few paragraphs from rough notes made while the matter was fresh in my mind. But these can give no idea of the manner of the preacher. He had the gift of oratory — the magnetism that holds the attention and electrifies. By a movement of his hand or a sweep of his arm he threw a new and thrilling meaning into the most commonplace re-marks. But his magnetism was not necessary on this occasion to hold the minds of his hearers. The mysterious allusions he made to meeting a wretched man in the public road, and the pointed — almost personal — appeals he made to members of the congregation who were evidently known to him, were enough to arouse curiosity to the highest pitch and hold it there.

Some of those who went to hear the sermon expected to be surprised or amused, while others hoped to be edified; but the effect went far beyond surprise or amusement, and, on the vital point, fell far short of edification. When the congregation was dismissed and we came out, I noticed that the women, who had a habit of lingering before the church door to exchange words of greeting and frequently of gossip, talked in lower tones than usual, and some of them wore a scared look. Colonel Bullard and his wife entered their shining carriage, and were whirled away, but Mary joined sister Jane and myself, and together we walked home. Behind us I could hear the voices of Mrs. Roby and Mrs. Flewellen, rising in volume the farther they got from the church.

"I declare er, Sister Roby!" exclaimed Mrs. Flewellen, "I'm er all but pairlized. Er did you ever hear er such talk in all your er born days? It's a scandal and I er don't care who hears me er say it. Who er was he a-hittin' at, do you er reckon? And er what is at the er bottom of it?"

It was impossible to catch the reply that Mrs. Roby made, but Mrs. Flewellen kept on talking.

"Why, the er bare idee that anything can er happen in this town and er me not know nothin' 't all about it! Er Brother Dannielly is a good man — there er ain't no manner of er doubt about that ; er he 's a godly man ; but er somebody has played on er his mind. But er would n't it be er the wonder of the world if er there was something or other er brewing ? "

I could but reflect on the whimsical and insubstantial mind that doubted in one breath and believed in the next. As for Mary she never mentioned the sermon except to comment on the earnestness of the preacher and the remarkable effect of his unstudied gestures. Sister Jane had nothing to say whatever, either about the sermon or the preacher. As we went along I saw just ahead of us the lad who had attracted my attention in church. He was clinging to the hand of a tall, strong-looking man who was a stranger to me — clinging to the man's hand and talking as seriously as a grown person. The man was walking slowly, but with a free and swinging stride that betokened great strength and vitality. Presently I heard the child say : —

"Well, you know mighty well, Dan, that I would n't have hurt the fan — if it was a fan."

I looked at sister Jane and saw that she was regarding the lad with a curious expression.

"Why, of course, Cap, I know you would n't have hurt the fan ; but think of the lady — she did n't know you would n't hurt the fan," replied the man in a soothing tone. "I'll see her before long and ask her about it, and I'll bet you a thrip against a shirt button that she'll say she thought you were one of those little town boys that are always up to some mischief."

"Will she say that, Dan?" the lad asked, a pleasant smile hovering around his mouth, but not settling there.

"Why, of course she will. I looked at her once when she turned her head, and she's got a good face. Did n't you see her put the fan back and push it towards you?"

"Yes, I did," replied the boy, "but I did n't know what she meant. I thought she knew I would n't touch it after she jerked it away."

"I'm sorry you did n't," said the man.

"Well, why did n't you punch me with your thumb, Dan?"

"Ah! it was in church, you know," the man suggested.

"That's so," assented the lad. "Did you see the bats, Dan? Did you see the big dark place they kept flying into? Ugh!" he exclaimed with a shiver, "I would n't go into that place, not for — not for" —

"Not for what?" the man asked.

"Not for the little girl that was on the ship."

"She said she was going to write to you," remarked the man.

"I hope she will," said the lad.

When we came to the end of the grove of big

oaks in which the church nestled, Mary Bullard, sister Jane, and myself crossed the street, while the stranger and the lad turned to the right and went along on the opposite side.

"Do you know 'em, William?" sister Jane inquired.

"I never saw them before," I replied. "They probably came on the stagecoach yesterday afternoon."

"As likely as not," sister Jane assented, and relapsed into silence.

"The boy is a bright and manly-looking little fellow," remarked Mary with a sigh. I knew she was thinking of her brother.

"Yes; I noticed he called his father 'Dan,'" I said.

"His father!" exclaimed sister Jane. "Why, not a minnit ago you said you 'd never seen 'em before, and now here you are telling a part of their family history."

"It is reasonable to suppose the man is the boy's father," I explained.

"Now he 's supposing," said sister Jane. "Mary, keep your eye on these men."

"Oh, I do, Miss Jane. Did you never notice it?" was Mary's laughing response. Sister Jane laughed, too, and the talk turned to matters in which I was not interested. I indulged in a habit formed long ago, of listening to Mary's voice (when she was talking to some one else) without paying particular attention to the words her lips formed.

During the afternoon, sister Jane was honored by a friendly call from Mrs. Roby and Mrs. Flewellen. Mandy Satterlee had gone to visit Mrs. Beshears, as she sometimes did on Sunday afternoons.

"Don't git noways scared, Jane," said Mrs. Roby, as she and Mrs. Flewellen came in. "We ain't come to take the place, because I just saw Sister Flewellen walkin' about in her yard, a-doin' nothin' and a-lookin' lonesome, and so I hollas and says, says I, 'Sister Flewellen, supposin' we fling on our things and go around and see Jane,' says I, 'because it 'll give her the all-overs,' says I, 'but we ain't been there in the longest, and maybe she can put up with us the little time we 've got to stay,' says I."

"Yes, er Jane," Mrs. Flewellen assented, "she ·said them er very words; and I says, says I, 'Don't you er reckon it 'll worry Jane?' says I, and she er hollas back and er says, says she, 'I er reckon it will, but er she 'll git over it before er Christmas,' says she. And er so we flung on our er things and come, and er here we are, and as the er twin calves said er to the old cow, 'Er what are you going to er do with us?'"

"I hope you don't fit the whole tale," remarked sister Jane, as she shook hands with the two ladies.

"Er how is that, Jane?" inquired Mrs. Flewellen.

"Why, the twin calves turned out to be bull yearlings," said sister Jane dryly.

"Now er that's Jane all over!" exclaimed Mrs.
Flewellen, laughing behind her fan to hide her
teeth. "Er did you hear that, er Sister Roby? I
er declare, Jane! You always er give as good as
anybody sends — er don't she, Sister Roby?"

But Mrs. Roby had other fish to fry. She had
seated herself, but instead of paying any attention
to Mrs. Flewellen's commonplace remarks, she
craned her neck, first on one side and then on the
other, trying to look behind her. Then she said : —

"I don't see Mandy Satterlee, Jane. Where's
she gone? She ain't here, is she?"

"Mandy's gone out to take the air," replied
sister Jane. "If you've got any message for her,
I'll tell her about it if I can recall it."

"Was she at church to-day, Jane?"

"If she was, she run out somewhere betwixt the
sermon and the doxology," sister Jane answered,
"for I found dinner ready and a-waiting for me ;
and there was nobody to cook it but Mandy."

"Well, I do hope she didn't go, Jane," said
Mrs. Roby, with well-affected solicitude, "because
I know in reason you must have heard what the
preacher said about her?"

"Which preacher?" inquired sister Jane with
amazement.

"Why, Uncle Jimmy Dannielly," replied Mrs.
Roby in a tone less confident than before.

Sister Jane regarded Mrs. Roby with a stare
in which amazement, pity, and curiosity were all
mingled.

" Well, for the Lord's sake!" she said after a while, raising her hands and allowing them to fall helplessly in her lap.

" Why, you must 'a' heard him, Jane, because I saw you there with my own eyes, and you could n't 'a' helped but hear him." Mrs. Roby's voice had grown weak.

" Now, Maria!" cried sister Jane, in a tone in which scorn and contempt played a large part, " do you mean to set flat-footed in that cheer there and tell me that such a man as Jimmy Dannielly would leave bigger game and fly at that poor gal — and he not a-knowing her from a side of sole-leather?"

" Well, you heard what he said, Jane," Mrs. Roby explained, " because your ears is as good as mine any day, if not better, because I ain't never intirely got over that risin' that busted in my head before I had my first baby, and I know you could n't 'a' kept from hearin' every word, and if he did n't mean Mandy Satterlee who in the round world could he 'a' meant, because when anybody talks that plain, specially in the pulpit, they 're jest obliged to mean somebody; now who did he mean? I wish you 'd tell me that."

Sister Jane settled her high back-comb a little more firmly on her head — a favorite gesture of hers when patience was giving way to irritation. " Maria, age don't improve you one single bit," she said. " You ought to know mighty well from what you 've heard of Jimmy Dannielly that he

ain't the man to stumble over names.   If he did n't
call 'em out, it was n't because he was afeard, but
because he did n't want to.   He 'd just as soon 'a'
called the name as not, every bit and grain.   My
hearing ain't as keen as it used to be, but if I 've
got any ears at all, Jimmy Dannielly said the people he was talking about was right there in the
house; he said he could go and put his hand on
'em ; he said they held their heads high, and that
they would soon be brought low.   That 's what he
said.   Does Mandy Satterlee hold her head high?
Did you ever see her strutting around these
streets ? "

Sister Jane closed her lips firmly, as though she
had no more to say.   Mrs. Roby looked at Mrs.
Flewellen, as if inviting assistance, but that lady
shook her head slowly and solemnly.

" Er he said them er very words, Sister Roby —
er them very identical er words.   I says to myself
er at the time, says I, ' I er wonder who it is er in
this house er that the cap fits,' er says I."

" I believe he did say that, Jane, but the whole
thing took me back so, that I pledge you my naked
word that I forgot everything about what he said
excepting that he was a-scoring somebody, I did n't
know who, and I thought it was mighty quare if
Mandy Satterlee was a-settin' in the back of the
church and he was a-hittin' at her, poor thing,
'stead of trying to lift her up, and I 'd 'a' looked
back to see if I could see Mandy, but I know some
of the men would 'a' thought right straight that I
was a-lookin' at them, because you know how con-

ceited they are, Jane, — all except William, here, who I look on more as a member of my own family than anything else, — and I says to myself, says I, ' I 'll go over and see Jane, and find out if Mandy Satterlee was at church, because I know if she was Jane 'll be a-b'ilin' over, and no wonder,' says I, because what right has a preacher or anybody else got to attack anybody that 's a-tryin' their best to get along and do right, for I reely do believe that Mandy Satterlee is tryin' to do what 's right, because she could mighty easy do wrong if she wanted to ; and there 's another thing, Jane ; who was that fine-lookin' man a-settin' behind the pew right next to yours ; you could n't 'a' helped seein' him because he had his hand on a boy's shoulder in the pew right next to yours, and you could 'a' retched out and tetched him with the end of your fingers, — not the man, but the boy, — and I saw the man lookin' at you, and I says to myself, says I, ' Honey, if Jane could turn and see you a-starin' at her in that fashion she 'd make you feel like sinkin' through the floor,' says I."

Mrs. Roby paused from sheer lack of breath.

" I saw the child, but I did n't see the man until we came out of church, and then I saw only his back," replied sister Jane. " I don't know him from Adam's cat."

And so the conversation ran on — a great many words about nothing in particular — a singular mixture of friendliness, hypocrisy, cant, and insincerity. The ladies went away after a while, and a restful silence filled the house.

XVIII.

THE next morning, shortly after breakfast, there came a knock to which I responded. I was somewhat surprised, on opening the door, to see the stranger whom I had noticed the day before as we came away from church; and with him was the lad of whom mention has been made.

"I beg pardon," said the stranger with a bow that stamped him at once as a man of some refinement: "I believe you take boarders here?"

"After a fashion," I replied, hesitating a moment.

"I am told it is a very pleasant fashion," he remarked with a smile.

"But you will have to see my sister," I suggested, "that is, if you " —

"Naturally — of course," said the stranger, interrupting me with the most genial laugh imaginable; "here as everywhere the word is, 'Make way for the ladies!' May I see your sister?"

I invited the gentleman in, — I was sure he was both a gentleman and a reader of books, — placed a chair for him and one for the lad, and went in search of sister Jane. I found her somewhat flur-

ried over some trifling detail of housekeeping, and
not in the best humor in the world. I stood expectant a moment waiting for her irritation to subside.
Whereupon she exclaimed : —

"Good Lord, William ! don't be standing there
like you was deaf, dumb, blind, and cripple. Say
what you 've got to say and then go and let me
have a minnit's peace. If I ever undertake to
make any more jelly out of dried apples I hope I
may be forgiven beforehand for the sins I 'll com-
mit. You 've got something on your mind,
William ; spit it out."

I told her there was a gentleman in the parlor
who wanted to see her about engaging board.

" Well, you can jest go right back and tell him
to take himself off. I 've got more boarders now
than I can stomach. They are all like lambs when
they first come ; butter would n't melt in their
mouths ; but by the time they 've swallowed one
meal they are ready to strut around and spit on
the floor, and do like they owned the whole house
with the trash-barrel throw'd in for good measure.
No ; go and tell the man, whoever he is, that
enough of a good thing is enough, and too much is
the greatest plenty."

Seeing that I stood my ground, sister Jane
paused and stared at me. "The gentleman that
wants to see you," I said, "is the stranger who
walked before us from church yesterday. I have
already told him that you will see him in a moment."

" Well, you 're taking a good deal on yourself, William, I must say," sister Jane snapped.   Then in the same breath, but in a far different tone, " I look like a fright, I reckon. How 's my hair behind there? I 've jest got to change this cape. It smells like somebody 'd rubbed it with bacon rind. Go back and tell him I 'll be in directly, and if he looks like anybody, try to make yourself polite, and don't look all draw'd up like you was afeard somebody was going to say ' boo ' at you."

I hardly had time to deliver my message before sister Jane followed me. With easy address and a genial smile the gentleman bowed. " This is Miss Wornum, I believe?"   Sister Jane nodded her head. " My name is Cowardin."

" Did n't I see that child at church yesterday?" asked sister Jane.

" What about it, Cap?" Mr. Cowardin inquired with a broad smile.

The lad hung his head and fell to picking at the side of the chair on which he sat. Presently he half raised his head, with a smile and a blush, very much as a girl would do. " Yes, ma'am, you saw me," he said.

" Well, my feelings have been hurt about you ever sence," sister Jane confessed. " Wait a minnit."

She whipt out of the room, and presently came back with her turkey-tail fan.

" There, honey," she said handing it to the lad. " Take it and look at it to your heart's content, and you may tear it up for what I care. I've been feeling mean ever sence I jerked it away from you yesterday."

"It wasn't anything to feel bad about," the lad protested stoutly, but I could see that his eyes shone, and that the blush on his tanned face deepened.

"You make too much of it, Miss Wornum," said Mr. Cowardin. "The biggest things soon pass out of a child's mind."

"Yes, but they remember the little things — the things that have a taste of meanness in 'em," remarked sister Jane positively.

"That is so," Mr. Cowardin assented. "It is so in my case anyhow." He paused, allowed his eyes to rest on the floor, and seemed to be lost in thought. "I beg your pardon," he said. "I wanted to get nice quarters for that boy of mine. I believe you take boarders only by the day; but I hope you'll take Cap there and give him a bed as well as board. You'll find him the least trouble in the world. I'll not bother you myself. The tavern is good enough for me."

Sister Jane looked at the boy, and then looked at Mr. Cowardin.

The latter evidently understood what was in her mind. He fumbled about in his pockets, and drew forth a small key.

"Cap, go to the tavern and bring the lady a handful of shells from your trunk."

The lad took the key and was about to rush

away. Suddenly he bethought himself, took the
fan from the chair where he had laid it, and handed
it to sister Jane.

"It is a nice fan, and I'm very much obliged to
you," he said.

"Why, you're a thousand times welcome, honey,
and more too!" exclaimed sister Jane heartily.

"I sent him away," said Mr. Cowardin, when
the child was gone, "because you were ready to
ask me some questions about him. It worries him
very much to hear people talking about him."

"Is his mother dead?" sister Jane asked.

"I don't know whether she's dead or alive."

"Is he your son?"

"Except through Adam, he's no relation of
mine that I know of."

"Well," said sister Jane bluntly, "I hope you
ain't trying to pack him off on me and then run
away and leave him."

Mr. Cowardin threw his head back and indulged
in a laugh genuine enough to dispel sister Jane's
suspicions.

"Run away and leave Cap!" he cried. "Why,
I've carried him on my back hundreds of miles;
I've gone hungry to feed him; and I've suffered
from cold to keep him warm."

"Then who is he and what is he?" asked sister
Jane with genuine curiosity.

Mr. Cowardin stroked his iron-gray beard
thoughtfully. "The most that I know — the most
that I can say — is that he is one of the Little

Children of the World." He smiled as he said this, and I knew he had in his mind the sermon we had heard the day before. " In 1850, a party of us started from St. Louis to go to California. The gold fever was at its height then, and as soon as the news got abroad that a few of us were going, hundreds asked to join us. We were glad enough of their company. We asked no questions. We just told everybody that came that they were welcome to go with us. It made no difference whether a man was a thief, or a vagabond, or an honest man. I was pretty much of a vagabond myself about that time."

" Well, you don't look like it," said sister Jane.

Mr. Cowardin laughed. " Looks don't amount to much, Miss Wornum. I used to think they did when I was young. Why, the worst man I ever saw was fixed up just like a preacher one Sunday, and I saw him hanged the next Friday." He paused as if the incident swarmed with unpleasant memories. With a quick gesture he went on. " Well, hundreds wanted to go, and we told them to be ready on a certain day, the only conditions being that they should carry along provisions enough to last four months. We did n't know what might happen. When the day came we found that there were forty wagons. We thought there would be more, but these were enough. Before starting, my partners and myself saw that there would have to be some sort of organization, somebody to manage and control. So we called

the men together (there was a pretty big crowd of
them), and I told them that there must be some
one to take charge of matters whenever it became
necessary.   I explained the matter as well as I
could, and then some one asked me my name, and
before I knew it they had made me Captain.

"This pleased the men better than it did me,
but no matter; the choice had been made.   I
sent twenty wagons twelve hours ahead, in charge
of one of my partners, and followed with the rest.
We kept up this order for many days.   The fifth
day out from St. Louis, as I was riding ahead of
the wagons (I had my saddle-horse) I saw a child
sitting on the edge of the trail.   It was crying,
and was so badly scared that its limbs jerked as
if it were afflicted with some queer kind of disease.
I jumped from the saddle and took the little fellow
in my arms, and soon had him quieted.   When I
asked him his name, he shook his head and said,
'Fraley,' or something that sounded like it.   He
could talk plainly for a child so young, and I supposed of course that 'Fraley' was his name.

"Naturally, I thought he had been accidentally
left by the wagons ahead of us.   There were several families along, and perhaps twenty children
not larger than this child.   I judged that he was
asleep in the rear wagon, and had in some way
fallen out — just how I could not imagine.   I
thought that as soon as he was missed some one
would come rushing back along the trail, searching
for him.   So I made no bother about the matter.

I let the little chap ride on the saddle in front of me until he fell asleep, and then put him in charge of one of the women in my train, telling her to feed him and take care of him until his people called for him.

"In this way I made my mind easy about the child, and for some hours forgot him altogether. When I did go to the woman's wagon to inquire about him, he was wide awake and lively, but as soon as he saw me he held out his little hands to come to me, and refused to be comforted when I started to ride off without him. The upshot of it was that I took him on my saddle, and after that, as no one came to claim him, he used to ride in front of me for hours at a time, and I became so accustomed to his company that he was n't in my way at all. The woman took care of him and tidied him up when he was n't riding with me, but after a while I took him in my own wagon at night."

"Well, for the Lord's sake! did n't you never inquire about his folks?" sister Jane asked.

"To tell you the truth, Miss Wornum, I had bigger things than babies on my mind just then. I had to think for all those people, and we were going through a dangerous part of the country. I had to put a stop to gambling; I had to settle all disputes and put down all quarrels. The men were not members of any Sunday-school at that time; they had knives, pistols, bad tempers, and a good deal of mean whiskey along, and you know

what that means. I might have done many things
that I did n't do. But I found out afterwards
that the child was really a waif. There was no
one to lay claim to it. The woman I was telling
you of pointed out a man — a slouching, ugly fellow — who scared the boy nearly to death every
time he came near ; but I thought little of that
until one day when we were eating dinner the
child screamed and ran to me, and I saw the man
going by. I called him back and asked why the
youngster was afraid of him. His explanation
was that on one occasion, in a spirit of mischief,
he had made a face at the little chap. This was a
likely story, for the man was as ugly as sin when
he screwed his face up to show me how the boy
had been scared.

"I had no time to think it over then, but I have
thought since that the man knew all about the
child. Anyhow I let the matter pass. The youngster stayed with me, and nearly half the time he
was in the saddle in front of me. The men got
to calling him Young Cap, and I began to call
him Cap myself, and have kept it up ever since.
We 've seen hard times and good times together.
We 've lived like wild beasts in the woods, and
we 've lived like princes, and through it all we 've
stuck together, and I would n't like it much if
somebody was to jump up some day and say, 'That
boy is mine and not yours,' and prove it."

"Colonel Bullard's little boy was stolen several
years ago," I remarked. "Maybe" —

"So I have been told," replied Mr. Cowardin.

"It would be queer, now " —

"Goodness, William!" exclaimed sister Jane. "How could Freddy Bullard be found a-settin' by the road the other side of nowhere?"

"It would be very queer, indeed," said Mr. Cowardin; "in fact, next to impossible in my opinion. Yet the thought that it might be so was what brought me here."

"You knew the circumstance, then?" I suggested.

"I chanced to be in this town the day it happened," Mr. Cowardin said. "I remember you very well. That night you went to the show with a young lady — Miss Bullard — hunting for the lost child. The man at the entrance of the tent took you through, and walked part of the way home with you. He has changed greatly, has n't he?"

"Well, upon my word!" I cried. "And you were that man! You were very kind to us, but your voice was sharper — severer — than it is now."

"Ah, I was on duty then," he explained with a laugh. "Moreover, five years of such experiences as I have had are calculated to take the rough edges off a man — particularly when he has seen some of his plans turn out to be successful."

"And you think this child may possibly be little Freddy Bullard?" I ventured to remark.

"As I said, I think it is next to impossible if

we take all the facts into consideration. And yet where there is one chance in a million, it does no good to doubt or to hesitate. I remember an incident in California that will fit this case. I had worked in the ditches and gulches for months, and had hardly found enough gold to buy a pound of flour. Times were squally, I can tell you. I had worked new claims, and dug over old ones, and at last I just naturally gave up. I had no hope, and did n't care for anything except the boy. I could have picked up a fair living in the gambling-saloons; but there was Cap. I took him with me one day, and began to work over an old claim that had once been the richest in the camp. At last I paused. I was hot, tired, and disgusted. I looked at Cap. He was sitting on the bank nodding in the shade of a pine. I woke him and asked him, half in fun and half in earnest, where I must dig to find gold? 'Right under me,' he said. I told him to get from under the swing of the pick. He rolled away, and was sound asleep before you could snap your fingers. Now the spot where he was sitting was a rock, and it jutted out from the bank considerably, showing that it had been partially dug around already.

"I swung the pick over my head and tried to drive it through the rock. But it sank into the ground up to the eye. When I pried against it, the rock fell forward at my feet splashing mud and water in my eyes, and when I opened them again" —

The lad came running in at this moment. He had the shells in a beautiful little basket.

"Oh, Dan!" he cried, and then stopped still and waited.

"What did I see, Cap, that day in the gulch, when I got my eyes full of mud and water? — the last day we worked in the ditches together?"

"Goodness, Dan! You saw gold. You said that if I had n't been asleep you 'd have yelled so that everybody in the camp would have come running."

"I believe you!" exclaimed Mr. Cowardin. "I had struck a pocket, and in that pocket I found as much gold as I wanted."

Sister Jane shook her head incredulously. "Well! you are the first human being in this world that ever found as much gold as he wanted."

"I have told you the simple truth," was Mr. Cowardin's reply. "I found as much as I wanted; but I took all I found. I had been working harder than any negro ever worked for three years, but the nuggets I found in that pocket were enough to make a dozen men rich."

"You know the old saying," remarked sister Jane, "'Easy come, easy go.'"

"But for that boy," said Mr. Cowardin, "the saying would have been partly true in my case." He turned to the boy. "Well, Cap, how about the shells? Did you find them?"

"Oh, Dan! the pretty pink one that I wanted to give the lady is lost. I can't find it anywhere."

"No; it is somewhere in my trunk. I saw it the other day. We'll get it when we go back to the tavern."

The shells were exquisitely beautiful — the most peculiar I had ever seen before or have ever seen since. Mr. Cowardin explained that they were found on the coast of an island in the South Seas. Sister Jane was in ecstasies over them. She had two old conchs that she had treasured for years on account of the wonderfully delicate pink color that marked them. She looked at every shell, — there were dozens of fine ones, — and then reluctantly handed them back to the child.

"They are for you," he said, putting his hands behind him with a gesture that was both graceful and gentle.

"For me!" cried sister Jane. "Well, I declare, honey, nobody in the world could 'a' given me anything that I'd prize more. I'll empty 'em out directly, so you can get your basket."

"The basket goes along with them," the lad explained.

"If you'll notice, Miss Wornum, it's a very pretty piece of workmanship. It is made of the scales of a fish they catch in the South Seas."

Sister Jane's delight shone in her face, and well it might. The scales had been polished until they wore the lustre of pearls. They shimmered and gleamed in the light.

"Honey, how can I thank you? I don't know what I've done to have such good luck. I hope I

won't wake up in the morning and find that I 've
been dreaming. If this is what I get by being
mean to a nice boy, I 'll be mean to the next one
I see. But I don't know where in the world I 'll
find another as nice and as clever as you are."

The child blushed with pleasure, and I listened
with some degree of astonishment, for I had never
before heard sister Jane pay such a compliment to
any one, especially to one of the male sex.

"You may run out in the garden and pick some
roses," she said.

"Oh, may I?" cried the lad. He waited for
no confirmation, but darted from the room.

There was silence for a while, and then Mr.
Cowardin spoke.

"If you can take Cap, Miss Wornum, it would
relieve me of a great deal of anxiety and not add
to yours. He is a manly little fellow, but gentle
and thoughtful. He will not be here long before
he can discover from your countenance whether
you are pleased or displeased, and he will do what
he can to please you. He has seen rough times,
rough countries, and rough people, but he has been
with me so long that he has old ways about him.
He 's the best child I ever saw to be full of health
and fun."

"Well, I 'll talk with William," said sister
Jane. "I 'll find out how he feels about it. I
think we can fix up for the child— that is, if you
think the place will suit him."

Mr. Cowardin laughed. "Don't allow that idea

to trouble you. He will be delighted. I shall feel
lonely without Cap at night, for he has been my
only companion for many a long day, but he can
come and sit with me sometimes at the tavern
until I find better quarters.”

“ Or you can come and sit here with us after
tea,” I suggested.

“ Yes ; I had intended to ask permission to do
that,” he said.

“ Or you can take your meals here if the fare
suits you,” remarked sister Jane. “ Not that I
want any more boarders. The Lord knows them
that I ’ve got are enough to make a sinner out of
a saint.”

“ That would be better — a great deal better.
I could be with Cap oftener,” said Mr. Cowardin
eagerly. “ I am not trying to get rid of the boy.
He is a pleasure to me every hour of the day.
But he must go to school — that is certain — it
can’t be helped.” He spoke as if he were repeating an old argument that he had had with himself.
“ I have skimmed through some books with him,
and he can read, write, and cipher ; but he must
go to school ; he must get with other boys, good or
bad. And then I want him to have a place that
will be like home to him. He has never known
what a home is — and here he can find out about
it. As to terms,” Mr. Cowardin went on after a
pause, “ make them to suit yourself. Just imagine
that we are to give you no end of trouble and fix
your price accordingly. That is the way to do busi-

ness with strangers. Fix a good round sum and make them pay in advance."

"I'll not grumble at what I get out of you," said sister Jane bluntly. "If I grumble at all it'll be at what I don't get."

And so from that time forth, and for many days, Mr. Cowardin and the lad became a part and parcel of our household.

XIX.

THE LAD'S RIDE.

It came to pass that Mr. Cowardin gave us a great deal of his company, especially in the evenings, and it was very pleasant company, too, for he was not merely a fluent talker. Travel, wide experience, and keen observation had given him something to talk about. He visited all parts of the United States, the islands of the sea, and the countries of the east that are most conveniently reached by going west. He was well educated to begin with, and this fact had served him well. When information comes to the mind of a man who has prepared himself properly it goes through a sifting process that transforms it into knowledge that is power when it is active, and culture when it is quiescent.

It may be imagined, therefore, that we found Mr. Cowardin's conversation both interesting and instructive. He thus brought us in touch with the teeming world beyond our sober horizon, the great world that we knew of mainly by report. He told us of queer peoples and of strange incidents by land and sea, and managed in this way to broaden our views and to give a wider range to our sympathies. He had so much to talk about that he rarely had occasion to refer to himself, and this was a refreshing novelty in a provincial village where people have little else to talk of.

Mrs. Beshears had a fancy of her own that she had seen Mr. Cowardin somewhere before, but when, for my own amusement, I asked her to trace her impression to its source, it was found to rest on the belief that the expression of his face reminded her of some one she had known, but, for the life of her, she couldn't say who. He "favored somebody," but who he favored, Mrs. Beshears didn't know. At any rate she liked him, for no matter how many questions she might ask (and her inquisitiveness seemed to be without bounds or limit) he was always ready to answer them — nay, more, his good nature and his sense of humor were so fused that he seemed to invite her curiosity that he might not only please her, but also enjoy her blunt comments and observations. Naturally, therefore, the heart of Mrs. Beshears warmed toward this man of the world who treated her with such patient deference. I think all our hearts warmed toward him, for he had that indefinable charm of manner that attracts the confidence of men and women alike. He had the repose that strength imparts, and the gentleness that belongs to good breeding.

As for the lad, — the boy he called Cap, — he was even more charming in his ways than the guardian Providence had sent him. He had the advantage of youth — and it is a tremendous advantage, say what we will. Each day that passed over my head (as the saying is) made me more keenly alive to that fact, and more sensitive to it, too. The child had this great advantage, and he seemed instinctively to know how to employ it. He had never associated to any extent with other children, and this fact gave him sober and thoughtful manners. He had been so long thrown upon his own resources, so far as amusement was concerned, that he had what the women-folk called "old-fashioned ways." And these gave an additional charm to his youth, for they were based on a certain manliness of character that was clearly above all the small and petty tricks of mischievousness that are common to boys. He was strong, healthy, and as full of animal spirits as a colt — and yet shy, reserved, gentle, and polite.

From the very first he took a great fancy to Mary, and she to him, and when she used to ask for her little sweetheart (as she called him) I always felt with a pang how much happiness youth could have if it only knew how to seize and appropriate it. The lad was fond of me, too, and seemed to enjoy nothing better than to sit in my room, or on the little porch outside, and read such books as I was willing to put in his hand. He had many of the girlish ways and cute methods that innocence stamps its seal on.

It was a great sensation in the village when Mr. Cowardin bought the lad a pony out of a drove of

horses, — a pony that even the traders advised him
not to buy if he was buying it for a boy. But
he bought it, nevertheless, and, when cornered
and caught, it seemed to be impatient even of
the halter. A negro hostler, after some trouble,
led the creature around to the front of the building
in which Mr. Cowardin had his lodgings. From
among his traps (as he called them) he fished
a bridle with a long heavy dragoon bit, and a
saddle that was in some respects unlike any I had
ever seen, being entirely barren of skirts. It was,
in fact, nothing but a saddle-tree. The stirrups
were of wood, and the straps in which they hung
were wide enough to protect the legs of the rider.
After a struggle, the pony was bridled and sad-
dled; but he was a vicious - appearing creature.
He had a bald face, and his ears were continually
moving in opposite directions. My heart jumped
in my throat when I found that our lad was to
ride the horse, and somehow I felt cooled toward
Mr. Cowardin. It was a feeling that I fully recovered from only after a long interval, though I
could but see that the boy was eager for the ride.

"Shall I try him first, Cap?" Mr. Cowardin
cried out.

"No, Dan; you're too heavy."

With that the lad went forward, stroked the
pony on the nose, with no perceptible soothing
effect, so far as I could see, and then stood by the
stirrup. By the side of the horse — they called
the creature a pony because he was a trifle under

size — the lad looked small and frail indeed. He placed his foot in the stirrup. As he did so the horse swerved wildly away from him, but the lad was already in the saddle. The creature tried to rear, but was held by Mr. Cowardin; it whirled and almost sat upon its haunches, and then out of the dust and confusion I heard the clear voice of our lad cry out : —

"All right, Dan ! Give him his head."

But the horse was no freer when Mr. Cowardin removed his hands from the bridle than he was before. The dragoon bit acted as a powerful lever, even in the comparatively weak hands of the lad, so that, although a terrible struggle ensued between the horse and rider, — a struggle that held my alarm up to the highest possible pitch as long as it lasted, — an expert might have seen what the end would be. But I was no expert in such matters, nor desired to be. I could only remember that the boy was a mere child and that the horse was strong and vicious. The creature made a series of terrific leaps and bounds, but somehow the lad seemed to be prepared for each successive shock. Once the horse fell, but the lad was on his feet in an instant, and in the saddle again when the animal rose. Mr. Cowardin kept as close to the horse and rider as possible, and when the horse rose from his fall, passed a keen rawhide to the lad, remarking, —

"Now give him his medicine, Cap. Make him remember you."

The rawhide descended with a swishing sound, not once, but many times, and I could hear its *swish* as far as I could see the horse and rider, for they went careering up the village street like mad. In a little while — perhaps a half an hour — they came back. The lad's face was flushed with the exercise, and the horse was going at an easy canter.

"Why, Dan, he 's as gentle as a dog. He goes as easy as a canoe."

There was considerable applause from the spectators who had been attracted by the episode, but I confess I did not share in it. I only waited to make sure that the child was not hurt, and then I turned away from the scene with more disgust than I would have cared to confess at the time. Mr. Cowardin must have discovered it from the expression of my face, for, after telling the lad to ride the horse slowly about until he had cooled off, he joined me as I walked homeward.

"You don't admire fine horsemanship," he suggested.

"Well, I confess I don't relish an exhibition where a child is pitted against a wild beast," I replied.

"But you see what has happened," he said.

"Yes; I thank Heaven the lad is unhurt," I answered. "There were a thousand chances against him where there was one in his favor. Providence is kind even to those who tempt it."

"Chance!" exclaimed Mr. Cowardin, laying his

broad hand on my shoulder in a friendly way.
"My dear sir, do you imagine that I would trust
Cap where there is even one chance against him?
Think half a second! For six, yes, nearly seven
years, until lately, that boy has never been out of
reach of my hand. Would I be likely to trust him
where there is danger and not share it with him?"

"But you must admit there was danger of an
accident," I said.

"Beyond all question. But if you will tell me
where the lad will be safe from all accident I will
gladly carry him there."

He spoke seriously, and I saw he had the better
of the argument. But the human mind teems with
its whims and prejudices, and somehow it was long
before I could think of Mr. Cowardin without a
slight feeling of revulsion. It would have been
impossible to convince me then and there that he
was not a cruel man at bottom. I may as well say
here that I did him rank injustice in this, as well
as in another matter to be spoken of later. But
the spectacle of that child mounted on the snort-
ing and plunging horse gave a shock to my mind
that it was long in recovering from.

"Cap is as much at home on a horse," Mr. Cowardin went on to say, "as you are in your rocking-
chair. When he had been with me a year he was
a fairly good rider, and he's been riding ever since.
He learned to ride unruly horses as everything
else is learned — by degrees. For months those
he mounted were held by a lariat. In course of

time, he could ride them without assistance as well as anybody, and a great deal better than many grown men who had been practicing for years. I have seen him mount horses an hour after they had been caught in the wilderness. And if he could manage them why should I be afraid to trust him with a horse that has been broken to the saddle?"

"How did you know that?" I inquired.

"By the saddle marks on his back," replied Mr. Cowardin. "Whenever the saddle chafes and scalds a horse's back the hair will grow out white and remain white."

Inside the house, we found sister Jane boiling over with indignation. She had witnessed a part of the spectacle, and she was still nervous.

"Well, good Lord!" she cried; "if he's dead or onj'inted don't fetch him in here. When there ain't no sort of excuse for a funeral I don't want none in my house."

"What do you mean?" I asked, well knowing that I would have to stand the brunt of the storm.

"William Wornum, don't you dare to stand up there like a wax figger and ask me what I mean," she exclaimed. "You know mighty well what I mean! And there you stood with your mouth wide open, a-grinning like a simpleton, your hands in your pockets a-watching that hoss a-trying to kill that child — that baby, as you may say! I declare, William Wornum! if it had n't 'a' been for the scandal of it, I 'd 'a' picked up a stick and come out there and give you a frailing. An' if I 'd 'a' come," she went on significantly, " you would n't 'a' been the only one I 'd 'a' frailed, neither. What did you do with the child after you picked him up? Don't be a-standing there grinning at me, William Wornum! I ain't no baby on no hoss. Where did you take the child? I 'll go and look at him and see that he 's fixed straight on his cooling-board, but he shan't be brought here."

" What are you talking about, sister Jane ? " I asked again. " Mr. Cowardin here does n't understand you any more than I do."

" Well, I 'll tell you what I mean, William Wornum," she said, turning upon me. " If I 'd 'a' been in the place of two men, one as big as a mule (and not much better) and the other about the size of a stunted steer (and with no more sense), I 'd 'a' cut off my right hand before I 'd 'a' let that innocent child git on that hoss. Woman as I am I 'd 'a' cut off my right hand before I 'd 'a' risked that child's life. I say it here and I 'll say it anywhere."

Mr. Cowardin laughed good-humoredly and would have said something, but just at that moment the lad came skipping along the hallway.

" Oh, Dan," he cried, " I told the hostler to walk the pony and then rub him down. I happened to think that I saw Miss Jane standing in the porch out there when the pony fell, and she looked so scared that I thought I 'd run home and tell her how nice it is to ride a pony that is n't used to riding."

He ran to sister Jane, and caught hold of her hand.

"Why, honey, you 're all in a muck of a sweat." She got a towel and wiped the lad's face, and brushed his hair back behind his ears. "Where are you hurt, honey?" she asked with motherly solicitude.

"Hurt!" the lad exclaimed. "Why, I have n't a scratch on me."

"Well, it 's the wonder of the world, and you 'd better thank the Lord that the day of meracles ain't gone by. The way that hoss flung around wi' you was enough to jolt your soul-case loose. If you 're alive and well you don't owe them two any thanks for it." She nodded her head toward Mr. Cowardin and myself.

"Pshaw! if all horses were as easy to ride as that one was I 'd like to have a new one every two hours," said the lad.

Whereupon, he proceeded to inform sister Jane how he had learned to ride and how much he enjoyed it; and he did it with more success than either Mr. Cowardin or myself could have hoped to achieve.

"Well, all I 've got to say," remarked sister Jane, "is that if you two ain't got nothing better to do than to put that child where he 's liable to have every bone in his body knocked out of j'int, I want you to take your monkey show somewhere

where I can't see it.　I 'm that weak I can hardly lift my hand to my head, and I don't know when I 'll git over it."

" Well, I 'm very sorry," said Mr. Cowardin.

" Sorry ! " cried sister Jane.　" What good does that do, I 'd like to know ?　The man that went out one night and shot his grandmother in the corn-patch, thinking she was a bear, was sorry, but that did n't help matters.　To be sorry don't mend no broken bones, neither does it call the dead back to life.　If that hoss had broke the child's neck, we 'd 'a' all been sorry, but what good would it 'a' done ? "

There was no reply to such an argument as this, and Mr. Cowardin attempted none.　The result was that sister Jane was soon in a good humor, and in the course of a few days she talked of the affair in a manner that showed she was proud of the lad's accomplishments as a rider.

Now, as I have said, I shared in a measure sister Jane's feeling of indignation at the equestrian performance, but, in my case, the feeling took the shape of disgust.　I hoped that Mary Bullard had not been a witness of the scene, for I felt sure that her sensitive nature would be shocked by it.　But, to my amazement, she came running through the garden for the express purpose of telling the lad how bold he was, and how beautifully he sat the horse.　Her enthusiasm showed in her face, too, for her eyes sparkled with pleasure, and she was lovelier than ever.

And presently — which was more wonderful still — Mary's mother came gliding along the garden walk to congratulate the child. She took his face between her hands and kissed him on his forehead. She was even more enthusiastic than Mary.

" I must thank your little boy for reminding me of my home," she said to Mr. Cowardin. " I have n't seen such a thing — oh, it has been years. Why, when the child began to use the whip and the horse went plunging by, everything faded before my eyes and I was at home again. I never thought anybody but a Brandon could manage a horse like that."

" A Brandon ! " The exclamation came from Mr. Cowardin. The Colonel's wife understood it to be put as an interrogation.

" My father's family name," she said, holding her head a trifle higher, I imagined. " I never saw any one but a Brandon ride as this child did to-day. He reminded me of my brother Fred. I was a tot of a girl, but I can remember how my brother rode when he mounted an unruly horse. My father kept a stable of racers," she explained. " Oh, and it carried me back to old times when I saw this child to-day ! " she opened and closed her delicate white hands nervously.

Mr. Cowardin made some deferential response that seemed to please Mary and her mother, for they both laughed, and Mary blushed. I have forgotten what the remark was — some pleasant

formality, — for at that moment I seemed to see
everything in a new light.   It came over me suddenly (and the thought announced itself to my
mind with a sharp pang) that, possibly, Mr. Cowardin had made a deep impression on Mary.   My
ears buzzed and the room seemed to be reeling
around me, and I was compelled to catch hold of
the back of the chair behind which I was standing
to reassure myself that the people and things
around me were substantial.

I have never been able to discover what put such
an idea in my head.   It was probably the outcome
of many incidents, all of which became more sug-
gestive than ever when illuminated by the possibility I have mentioned.   I remembered a hundred
things that had seemed to be but trifles until this
possibility shed a new light upon them.   I remembered how eagerly Mary had listened to the ac-
counts which Mr. Cowardin gave of his adventures
— with what rapt attention she had followed not
only his words, but his every gesture.   And now, it
seemed to me that her enthusiasm over the horsemanship of the lad was intended as a tribute to
Mr. Cowardin.

And why not?   Here was a man who seemed to
possess every quality necessary to make a fond woman happy.   If he was older than I, which seemed
to be probable, he was still in the prime of life.
His years sat upon him lightly.   He was evidently
a man of affairs.   I knew he was rich, and while
he was not an Apollo, he was not unhandsome.

He was a man of character and education — just such a man, in short, as would be likely to attract a woman who admired strength allied with gentleness.

And then, somehow, I felt myself relegated to the rear — carried to the infirmary (as it were), where I might speculate on the pleasures of life, but could participate in them no more. I could admire Mr. Cowardin, I thought, but I felt that my disgust over the risk he had caused the lad to run could not easily be dissipated. So thinking I made some excuse and went out into the garden, where presently I stood gazing at space until I fell into a profound reverie that was not all unpleasant, for it is so ordained that a mind not given entirely over to the small affairs of life has its own special resources that it can draw upon at pleasure.

From this reverie I woke to the fact that Mary was near.

"I 've heard of such things, but I never saw a man in the clouds before," she said laughingly.

"Where?" I asked, looking toward the zenith. My thoughts were so far afield that I took her words literally — a fact that caused me to blush and wonder at my own stupidity. This made Mary laugh all the more. Then she grew serious.

"You were disturbed when you came out a while ago," she remarked. "What was the matter?"

"Nothing — nothing at all," I replied with increasing embarrassment.

"Oh, please don't tell fibs," she insisted.

"Something was troubling you. Won't you tell me what it was?"

"Old people should never bother young folks with their troubles," I replied. "I am older than Mr. Cowardin."

"What a pity you are so old," she said, her face reddening. "You ought to get a pair of crutches. What has Mr. Cowardin to do with it?"

"Nothing. He appears to be a young man."

She smoothed a knot of ribbon, hesitated a moment as if about to speak, then sighed and turned away.

XX.

MEMORIES OF CLARENCE BULLARD.

'T WAS impossible to say whether Mary was angry or no. 'T was impossible for me to fathom her moods, but that my self-humiliation might be made more complete, I chose to torment myself with the belief that some thought of Mr. Cowardin had evoked the sigh. I did now, as I had done many a time before: I went to my room, locked the doors, seized my other self by his ears, dragged him to light, and asked him by what right of possession, hope, or expectation he had reason to feel anything but pleasure when Mary Bullard gave a friendly or even a fond smile to any human being who seemed to be worthy of it. As usual on such occasions, the miserable Ego tried to take refuge in all sorts of lame and paltry excuses, but I gave him a lesson that he would long remember, and finally tucked him under my waistcoat out of sight again. To do him justice it should be said that he went to sleep and slept comfortably for some time, not daring to intrude on me with his troubles.

When Mrs. Beshears came as usual the night following the lad's display of horsemanship, sister

Jane described it with all those little exaggerations of adjective and gesture that a woman
instinctively employs. Nor was she sparing in
criticism of the carelessness that prompted Mr.
Cowardin and myself to place the child on the
vicious horse, though she knew I had no more to do
with it than a person who had never heard of it.

"Well! that puts me more in mind of some
of the deviltries of Clarence Bullard than anything
that's come to my ears in many's the long day,"
remarked Mrs. Beshears.

Mr. Cowardin turned half around in his chair
and looked hard at Mrs. Beshears! "Did you
know Clarence Bullard?" he asked.

"What I didn't know of him I heard about
him," remarked Mrs. Beshears, nodding her head
in a self-satisfied way. "Not that I ever blamed
him for anything I know'd or heard. No, bless
you! His daddy named him a name out'n a book,
an' the poor child couldn't help that. He was
tetotally ruined before his eyes was open, as you
may say."

Mr. Cowardin laughed heartily, almost gleefully. "Did Clarence ever do any serious harm?
Did he ever rob or kill anybody? It has been
many a day since I've heard his name mentioned.
I had come to the conclusion that he had been forgotten by everybody in the land of the living."

"No, he never done any rank harm that I know
of," said Mrs. Beshears. "He was jest full of
devilment, an' he used to go ridin' aroun' from

post to pillar, whoopin' an' yellin'. Come down to the pinch, he had more harm done to him than he ever done to anybody. So I 've heard an' so I believe. If you want to know all about it jest ax Cephas Bullard. Bless your heart! *he* knows. Did you ever strike up with Clarence Bullard in his travels?"

Mr. Cowardin was looking hard at Mrs. Beshears and her question seemed to take him by surprise — so much so, that he rose from his chair, straightened himself to his fullest height, and then sat down again.

"Why, yes," he replied. "I knew Clarence Bullard very well. I was with him in California. In fact, we went there together. He was one of my partners."

"Did he get rich, too, like the rest of you?" Mrs. Beshears inquired.

"He was comfortably well off when I bade him good-by," said Mr. Cowardin.

"Well, I 'm glad of that from the bottom of my heart!" Mrs. Beshears exclaimed. "He won't miss what 's been filched from him."

"I never heard him complain of anything of that kind," said Mr. Cowardin. "If he had any such trouble he kept it to himself."

"I believe every word of that," cried sister Jane. "You need n't mind Sally. She says a heap more than she means. She talks about how wild Clarence Bullard was, and yet I 've heard her sing his praises to the skies."

"That's a fact, Jane," said Mrs. Beshears, with a smile. "I say what t' other folks said. Clarence Bullard was as handsome a young man as the Lord ever made."

"Handsome is as handsome does," suggested Mr. Cowardin.

"That's so," assented sister Jane; "but I mind how Sally and me went to camp-meetin' once on a time. She was married and I was done past the marryin' age, but we went with a crowd, and when we got there, we was like two fish out of water. We stood around with our mouths open, a-feeling like two fools that did n't know where to go nor what to do. Clarence Bullard was there, dressed up fit to kill, and he had a crowd of giggling gals around him. When his eye fell on us, he made his excuses to the gals, and come a-running with his hat off. He wa'n't nothing in the world but a boy in looks, but he know'd what to say, and 't wa'n't a minnit before we was a-feeling at home and a-having jest as much fun as the next one, and maybe more. He brought us water, and he took us to dinner. Make me believe Clarence Bullard was mean! Why, all the lawyers in Philadelphy could n't do it."

"And yet it was a very small thing to do," said Mr. Cowardin.

"You may think it 's a little thing for a young man to make two lone wimmen feel like they ain't lost, but I don't," remarked sister Jane with kindling indignation.

"No, ner I," cried Mrs. Beshears.

Mr. Cowardin rose from his chair. " Well, if Clarence Bullard knew that he was so kindly remembered for one small act of politeness he would be very grateful to you," he said, and turned to go from the room.

"Wait!" cried Mrs. Beshears; "come here and le' me look at you right close." With that she limped across the room, took Mr. Cowardin by the arm, and led him closer to the candle-stand, where she scrutinized his face closely, much to his embarrassment, as it seemed. "I jest wanted to see if my old eyes fooled me," she explained. "Now you can go." He went out laughing, followed by the lad.

"That's so about Clarence Bullard," Mrs. Beshears remarked, after she and sister Jane had exchanged glances. "I've had so many ups and downs sence then that I had clean forgot it. The Lord knows, old folks like me hear so much an' know so little that it's mighty nigh onpossible to keep from doin' harm wi' the tongue."

"I've had ups an' downs myself" —

"But not like me, Jane — not like me. Oh, no, Jane! not anyways like me. I declare, I'm so nigh fagged out that I'm right on the p'int of givin' up. That's the truth if ever I spoke it."

"I've had my ups an' downs," sister Jane went on, "but that ain't hindered me from recollecting how Clarence Bullard done that day at the camp-meetin'."

“Well, you know, Jane,” explained Mrs. Beshears, “I was married, an’ I did n’t set so much store by what Clarence Bullard done as you did. But he treated us mighty nice, an’ I ’m glad — truly glad — that he ’s got money of his own an’ ain’t beholding to none of his kinnery.”

The lad came back in a little while, told us all good-night (placing his arms around sister Jane’s neck in a way that pleased her mightily), and went to bed. Somehow the conversation lagged. Mrs. Beshears was not as lively as usual, and she started home earlier than was her habit.

“I ’m not feelin’ well, Jane,” she said, as she bade us good-night. “I ’m not well at all. I ’m right on the p’int of givin’ out. If I ain’t feelin’ no better to-morrow night than I am to-night you need n’t look for me. My room ’s better ’n my company, I reckon, an’ you won’t miss me much; but I declare! I ’ve been a-comin’ so regular that I ’ll have to git some of the niggers to watch me in the forepart of the night for fear I ’ll git up an’ try to come in my sleep.” Mrs. Beshears laughed at the thought, but the laugh was neither strong nor gay.

“Do as I do,” remarked sister Jane, almost sternly. “Don’t give up to your sick whims and fancies.”

“Lord! I ’ve been a-holdin’ of ’em at arm’s length for so long that I ’m a-gittin’ weak. The feelin’ that I ’ve got now ain’t no fancy. I wish it was. But I ’m a-gittin’ old and tired.”

And it was even so. Never again did Mrs. Beshears come limping to our gate. We thought little of the matter the next night when she failed to come, but when two nights passed without bringing her, sister Jane began to grow uneasy, and the next day she sent Mandy Satterlee to see what the matter could be. Mandy could hardly have arrived there before Mose, the negro foreman on Mrs. Beshears's place, came to inform us that his mistress was very ill indeed, and to beg that Miss Jane be so good as to go see what the trouble was.

"Has a doctor been called in?" sister Jane asked.

"No 'm, dey ain't," answered Mose, scratching his head. "Miss Sally so sot ag'in doctors an' doctor truck dat I skeered fer ter fetch one dar, kaze dey ain't no tellin' but what she'd bounce out'n bed an' lam' me an' de doctor too."

Sister Jane was truly indignant, and no wonder. "Well, the Lord 'a' mercy!" she cried; "do you mean to stand up and tell me that you've been setting at home, letting your mistress die without calling in a doctor, you trifling, good-for-nothing rascal?"

Moses seemed to be very much alarmed at sister Jane's display of anger. He moved about on his feet uneasily, and pulled at his hat, which he held in his hand, in a way that showed his embarrassment.

"Wellum, you know how Miss Sally is, yo'se'f, ma'am. She ain't make much complaints. She des lay dar an' not say much, an' we-all ain't know how sick she is twel I hear her runnin' on like she out'n her head, an' den I come atter you hard ez I kin, kaze I know'd you'd tell us what ter do."

"No," said sister Jane, "you did n't want any doctor there. You and the rest of the niggers out there have got it in your heads that if Sally Beshears pegs out you'll be free. But you'll be sold off'n the court-house block if I have to have it done myself. Go and tell Dr. Biggers to hurry out there as hard as he can. I want to see you move now!" Mose, thoroughly frightened, went off at a run.

Shortly afterwards, Free Betsey came, and the word she brought from Mandy Satterlee was that Mrs. Beshears was very low indeed, that sister Jane was to come at once, and that Free Betsey would get dinner and attend to the baby if that arrangement was satisfactory. It was the best that could be done, and when sister Jane had called in one of her lady acquaintances to superintend affairs for her, she was ready to go. For a wonder she asked me to accompany her, and I was more than willing, for I had a sincere regard for Mrs. Beshears, albeit her sharp tongue had fretted me many times.

When we arrived, the doctor, a jovial old gentleman of great experience, was already there. He was so accustomed to such scenes that he smiled as he told us that nothing could be done. An attack of influenza had caused a general breaking-down of the system. That was all, and yet it was enough. Dr. Biggers had met us at the door on his way out to his buggy, but he turned again and went with us into the sick-room. Through force of habit he again felt the pulse of Mrs. Beshears, and this seemed to fret her, for she jerked her hand away with a muttered exclamation of impatience.

"She has had a very strong constitution," remarked the doctor suavely, "but you know, Miss Jane, the strongest constitution will break down after a while." His smile was blandly cute as he spoke. "I have left something to be given from time to time. The young woman there" — pointing to Mandy — "knows what to do. She was an old friend of yours, I believe, Miss Jane?"

"She is yet," replied sister Jane tartly.

"Of course — of course," remarked the doctor in a soothing tone. "I understand. I appreciate your feelings, Miss Jane. They do you credit."

He pulled on his gloves as he spoke, smiling all the while, and then bade us good-day, still smiling. As he went out, he slammed the door, quite by accident. The noise seemed to arouse Mrs. Beshears from her stupor, and she began to talk.

"Howdy, Jane? — You well? — Weather don't bother me, does it? I jest come anyhow, if I have to paddle through mud and wade through water." There was a pause, for Mrs. Beshears's breath came short and quick. "Where's the baby?" She reached forth her arm and felt around until her

hand rested on a pillow. This she patted gently.
"Don't wake the child up. Keep the cover on it.
Where's Phyllis? Tell her to look after Polly
and Becky. Give 'em their coffee an' put plenty
sugar in it. — Heigh-ho! I'm that tired I don't
know what to do. There ought to be a man to
look after this place. Oh, Lord!"

I chanced to look toward the fireplace where
Miss Polly and Miss Becky sat. Miss Polly
reached across and touched Miss Becky on the
knee.

"You hear her, Becky?"

"I hear her, Polly," replied Miss Becky, shaking her head as solemnly as her palsied condition
would permit.

"Arter a man!" said Miss Polly grimly.

"Yes," replied Miss Becky, "allers arter a man.
She'll git none of our money."

"Not a thrip!" responded Miss Polly.

"They've been a-gwine on that a-way ever sence
I put my foot in the house," said Mandy to sister
Jane in an awed tone.

"And before, too," remarked sister Jane. "Let
'em alone."

"I must git up," said Mrs. Beshears. "Where's
my shoes? Somebody's kicked 'em under the bed,
I reckon. Git 'em out! I've laid here long
enough. I must go and see Jane. I'm obleege
to go. Why, if I was to miss goin' she'd think
somethin' terrible had happened."

Miss Polly nudged Miss Becky again. "Jest

listen at her," said Miss Polly. "Wants to git out'n bed an' go gaddin' up-town."

"I 'm a-list'nin'," replied Miss Becky.

"Wants to go gaddin' arter a man," remarked Miss Polly.

"Allers a-gaddin' up-town," echoed Miss Becky. "She shan't have none of our money."

"Not a thrip!" Miss Polly declared.

While these two decrepit old women were nodding their heads together like two muscovy ducks, Mrs. Beshears was growing more and more talkative. Her mind wandered far afield, but it always came back to thoughts of sister Jane, and it seemed to me that she was less restless, when she was talking about her long-time friend.

Sister Jane tried to talk to her and to soothe her, for she had a deft way with sick people, but Mrs. Beshears was always impatient at these attempts to call her back to consciousness.

"Don't pester me!" she railed out. "Somebody 's all the time a-pesterin' me when I 'm goin' to see Jane, or when I 'm tryin' to have a confab with her. Oh, go 'way! Don't pester me. You thought I wa'n't comin', did n't you, Jane? But here I am, as the flea said to the sick kitten. How 've you been since I saw you? And where 's that great Mr. Somebody I saw t' other night?"

Again Miss Polly nudged Miss Becky.

"You hear that, don't you?" she asked.

"Don't I?" said Miss Becky. "Arter a man. She shan't have none of our money."

“Not a thrip,” Miss Polly assented. “She could n’t find it to save her life.”

In this way, Mrs. Beshears rambled in her delirium, her sisters tracing everything she said to a desire to gad about in order to find another husband. She sank very rapidly. Her remarkable energy and the manifold cares she bore on her shoulders had worn out her nature, and now she had come to the end of it. When her thoughts flew away from sister Jane, they went back to the days of her youth, and in this way it pleased Heaven to lighten her last moments by permitting her to live over again in the brief space of a few hours the happiest years of her life.

Sister Jane sat by the bed, and held one of her old friend’s hands, weeping softly all the while. At the last, Mrs. Beshears opened her eyes, half raised herself in the bed, and cried out : —

“Jane, yonder ’s Sarah Ann! Wait, honey, an’ tell me the news! ”

Her head sank back on the pillow, and in a moment all was over. Mrs. Beshears had joined her sister Sarah Ann, who had died fifty years before.

By the terms of Mrs. Beshears’s will, Mandy Satterlee was to take charge of Miss Polly and Miss Becky and administer to their wants, but, to my surprise, Mandy refused to have anything to do with them.

“ Why, I would n’t live there an’ listen at them two poor ol’ creeturs a-talkin’ about the’r money an’ about somebody a-marryin’ — I would n’t stay there an' have all that kind of talk ding-dong'd into my head eve'y day, not fer all the land in the country, nor fer all the money that could be scraped together betwixt this an' Kingdom Come."

And nothing could change her. Sister Jane tried to convince her that it was to her interest to go, but Mandy disposed of all arguments by falling into a fit of weeping, saying that if she was n't wanted where she was, she could go somewhere else, but never would she go where " them poor ol' creeturs was," unless somebody tied her and toted her there, and even then she would n't stay. I think sister Jane was secretly pleased with Mandy's decision.

Under the circumstances, there was but one thing to be done. The Judge of the Inferior Court had appointed me administrator of the estate, and I felt it my duty to send Miss Polly and Miss Becky to the asylum at Milledgeville, where, as pay boarders, they would receive the best of care and attention. This, in fact, was the suggestion of the Court, and I lost no time in carrying it out. I imagined that the most difficult part of my duty would be to get the two old women to consent to make the journey. But the way was smoothed by Free Betsey, who, under pretense of telling their fortunes, informed them that they would shortly go on a journey. For this, strange to say, they were eager, and gladly allowed Free Betsey to get out their faded finery, shabby and long out of date, and brush it up.

So completely had the idea of the journey been

impressed on their minds by Free Betsey that they were for getting ready every time they heard the wheels of a buggy or carriage rolling by.

Free Betsey prepared them for the day, and they were ready and waiting when Mr. Cowardin and myself went for them in a carriage hired for the occasion. It was thought best that I should go with them, and Mr. Cowardin had volunteered to go with me, and proposed to make himself useful by driving the carriage. I gladly accepted his offer, and found that the journey, short as it was, would have been lonely indeed but for his genial and interesting conversation. But sometimes a silence fell between us, and then it was pitiful in the extreme to hear the worse than childish talk of Miss Polly and Miss Becky.

"If Sally had n't been so sot on gaddin' about she might 'a' come wi' us," said Miss Becky.

"We 're gittin' 'long mighty well wi'out her, I think," Miss Polly declared.

"Lawsy, yes!" Miss Becky assented, and then began to chuckle. "She 'll come back an' find us gone, an' then what 'll she do? Won't she be took back when they tell her we 've gone a-travelin'? I would n't be as jealous as Sally is, not for the world. Oh, she 'll be sorry she went a-gaddin'!"

"She won't do a thing when she finds out we 're outer sight an' hearin' but go a-huntin' aroun' for our money," Miss Becky declared.

"She 'll dig under the house, an' under the trees, an' maybe under the bushes in the yard."

"But she won't git it. It's hid wher' she won't never look," said Miss Polly.

"Maybe we ought to a-brung it wi' us," suggested Miss Becky, taking alarm at her own demented fancies.

"Don't you fret, Becky," said Miss Polly. "It's hid wher' she'll never git it."

Poor Mrs. Beshears! She had devoted herself to her sisters, and now they did n't even know she was dead. They had been told so, but they imagined it was part of a scheme to deceive them.

"She thought she was mighty cunnin'," remarked Miss Becky. "She told the folks that come to see us that she was dead, an' they did n't have no better sense than to b'lieve her. She did n't fool us, did she?"

"Fool who?" cried Miss Polly, with a fine assumption of scorn. "I went an' looked at her, an' thar she was, all laid out. I looked at her right close, an' she wa'n't no more dead than I am. If you'd 'a' said man or money to her, she'd 'a' opened her eyes an' 'a' jumped up. She thought she was mighty sharp, but she did n't fool me!"

I was truly glad when the journey was over, and the two demented old women were safely placed in the state asylum. We gave the horses and ourselves a good night's rest, and started back home, which we reached in due time, though an incident occurred that seemed to puzzle and worry Mr. Cowardin.

XXI.

As we were nearing home, being not above four miles from the village (Mr. Cowardin driving, and I sitting on the seat beside him for company), we heard the rattle of wheels behind us. Turning, I saw a light two-horse top-buggy, — a vehicle that was rare enough in these parts to attract attention, — drawn by a pair of fine bays. Two men were seated in the buggy. One was large and handsome, having the color of health in his face, while the other was smaller and had a sallow complexion. The large man wore a mustache and a tuft of beard on his chin. The face of the other had not known the touch of a razor for months, perhaps for years. It was covered with a dark yellow beard. They overtook and drove around us at a convenient place in the road, and I saw a bottle between them. When they had passed us a little way, the large man, who was driving, pulled his horse up, turned his face toward us, and asked how far it was to Hallyton. I informed him to the best of my ability. The smaller man seemed to be very impatient.

" 'T ain't fur," he said. " Not more 'n four mile. Did n't I tell you so?"

I saw then that the face of the large handsome man was flushed not with the color of health, but with liquor, and I judged from the tone of the other that he, too, had been free with the bottle.

The buggy went forward more rapidly than our lumbering old carriage, and it was soon lost to view.

"I'll be worried until I go to sleep," said Mr. Cowardin, when the travelers were out of sight and hearing. "I've seen that sandy-haired man somewhere before."

"Why, so have I," was my reply. "He's some countryman hereabouts that the gentleman is accommodating with a ride."

"No," Mr. Cowardin insisted; "I have seen him somewhere in my travels. But where? Were you ever bothered about such things? They give me no end of worry."

"Why, not at all," I remarked. "If I see people once and can't remember their names when I see them again, it is well and good with me. I go on about my business and think of them no more. Now, I'm certain I have seen the sandy-haired man somewhere, but when and where I neither know nor care."

"Well, it is different with me," said Mr. Cowardin. "If that man's face was n't impressed on my mind I should never remember it. I'll bother with it until I go to bed, and then to-morrow, when I'm not thinking about it, the name, place, and all the circumstances will pop into my head, and that will be the end of the matter."

He allowed the horses to jog along, and for some time seemed to be lost in thought. Suddenly he turned to me.

"What is your opinion of Mary Bullard's mother?" he asked.

"My dear sir," I replied, "that is a very peculiar question."

"It is, indeed," said he, with a smile. "But it was not intended to be a question. I simply happened to speak my thoughts aloud. We have queer thoughts sometimes. I was just thinking that Mrs. Bullard is out of her element here. She seems to try hard to fit herself to circumstances, but they are so different from those she was brought up in that they refuse to be fitted. Were you ever in Virginia, Mr. Wornum?"

"I never was."

"Then, of course, you can't understand the difference between — between — well, the right word is lacking; but let us say roughly, between the society there and the society here. If I could get hold of some word that meant social hospitality and all its results, that would be the word to use. But you can see what I mean. Now, in Virginia, where Mrs. Bullard came from, society means a great deal more than the word conveys. To put it broadly, the home life of the people has expanded until it takes in all who are congenial. Now there is not the smallest symptom of that sort in your little community here. There is a touch of it to the east of us — in Wilkes County and that region. I am as sorry for Mrs. Bullard as I ever was for anybody in my life. I should imagine she was a very high-spirited woman."

I could appreciate to some extent the justice of his remarks, but I was surprised to find that he was such a close observer.

"I have no need to ask your opinion of the daughter," he went on with a smile, whereupon I felt my face reddening — "nor anybody else's opinion for that matter," he hastened to say, as if by that means to cover my blushes. "I have sometimes wondered that she has never married, considering at what an early age the girls marry nowadays. I have had the same thoughts about you, and it is as impertinent in the one case as in the other." He laughed good-humoredly and chirruped to the horses.

"As for me, I have passed the limit by a dozen years," I remarked.

"And pray what is that limit?"

"Thirty years."

"So! Then I am a quarter of a century beyond it. If I were you, I should lift the limit to suit the circumstances. What is a dozen years this side of fifty?"

"As to your case," I suggested.

"Why, bless you! a quarter of a century is something substantial. It stands fiery off, like the poet's star. Besides, where the inclination is lacking the will is dead. Tut, tut, boy! look at me! I wanted but a half dozen years of twenty-one

when you were born. I was rambling about the
world as full of sedition as Aaron Burr before you
had shed your milk teeth. You 're a mere child ! "

Mr. Cowardin's good humor ran high — higher
than I had known it to do before. His talk
rambled in all directions, but almost invariably
came back to the Bullards or to our own little
household.

" If you were not so ready to blush," he said as
we drove through the public square of the village,
" I could give you some good advice and tell you
some good news. But 't would all be in vain;
you 'd blush violently, refuse to take the advice,
brand the news as a piece of fiction, and say in
your heart, ' The man is a spy.' Some day when
you 've nothing on your mind but pleasant thoughts,
remind me of the advice and of the news and I 'll
give you a dose of both. No, no ! not now, not to-
day ! " he protested when I showed a disposition
to seek the advice and the information. " Any
other day would be better than this. What we
need now is a good dinner and some hours of rest."

But I noticed with some surprise that Mr.
Cowardin ate but a bite of dinner when we reached
home, and took no rest at all, for I saw him soon
after walking about the village with the gentleman
we had seen driving the buggy. He finally came
with the gentleman as far as our gate, showed him
Colonel Bullard's house, and then came into my
room.

" I 'm still puzzled over the chap we saw this

morning," he said as he seated himself. "The man who was driving the buggy is a Mr. Moreland of Richmond. He used to know Mrs. Bullard in Virginia when she was a girl. He has just gone to pay her his respects. No doubt she'll be glad to see anybody she knew when she was a girl. But this man seems to be a pretty tough customer. They tell me at the tavern that he had the whole town searched until a handful of mint was found, and then he seemed to be as happy as a lord. He smells as if some one had poured a bottle of bergamot oil over his clothes. Faugh!" exclaimed Mr. Cowardin, "wherever he goes, people will imagine he is a typical Virginia gentleman. Outwardly he's the poorest kind of a counterfeit, whatever he may be inwardly."

"What is he doing so far from home?" I inquired, striking involuntarily the usual note of provinciality.

"Traveling — traveling as he thinks all Virginia gentlemen should," said Mr. Cowardin. "But think of a Virginia gentleman talking about nothing but racing events, cock mains, and driving all over the country to see them! Nonsense! If you could search under the seat of his buggy you'd find all the tools of a blackleg, including a dozen bottles of liquor."

Mr. Cowardin seemed to be very much disgusted with the handsome Mr. Moreland. And the man was handsome, despite the somewhat puffy appearance of his face. He had curly black hair, a strong

profile, and he walked with a swagger that was by
no means unbecoming.

"As to the other fellow," Mr. Cowardin was
going to say, when I interrupted him —

"But if this Mr. Moreland disgusts you, why
bother about the other fellow, who may be worse."

"That's the point. I want to see whether he's
worse or better. He may be the real gentleman,
you know. But this Moreland pretends to know
as little about him as I do. It seems he picked
him up somewhere several weeks ago, and has
been carrying him along for company. Moreland
is n't even sure of the man's name. He calls him
Satellite, but thinks his name is Simpson or Samp-
son. The name is nothing to me. I know the
man's face; it puzzles me, and I want to find out
where I saw him last."

"Well, I see nothing in him to puzzle or to interest anybody," I said. "I too have seen the man
somewhere, but I would n't give a copper to know
when or where."

"Oh, you have other matters to think about,"
remarked Mr. Cowardin, with a twinkle in his eye,
— "interesting matters, too, if I 'm any judge;
while I have little else to occupy my mind at the
present moment. I 've already found out that my
man has gone out of town into the country, and that
he rode 'shank's mare,' as the saying is."

"What did I tell you?" I cried. "I was certain he belonged hereabouts. The next time you
see him, he 'll be driving a yoke of steers, hitched

to a big wagon, and in the wagon he 'll have three pounds of frothy white butter, two dozen eggs, and a half dozen sickly chickens. He 'll exchange these for eight yards of calico, a hank of yarn, a plug of tobacco, and a bottle of Maccaboy snuff."

Mr. Cowardin laughed, and, calling for Cap, — the day being Saturday and a school holiday, — went out into the street, and a little while after I saw them go by on horseback, the lad on the pony, which, instead of being vicious, was now merely full of spirit. As they rode away, I noticed (and not for the first time) a striking resemblance between the two — a resemblance that was not confined to their pose and gestures, but was carried out in the profiles of their faces; and I wondered whether this man was playing a part, whether the story he had told us about the child was not a fabrication. It was an idle thought, and I did not pursue it far, keeping my eye on the door of Colonel Bullard's house. I desired to see how long the stranger would remain, yet I knew that such curiosity was vulgar and unworthy. It remained ungratified, too, for the stranger failed to issue forth from the house while I sat in my room. I judged from this that he had found a warm welcome there, which was, indeed, the fact, as we found out from Mary, who declared with a laugh that her mother was entertaining one of her old beaux.

"You should see her," Mary said to sister Jane. "You can't realize the change. I went into the parlor to entertain him while mamma was primping, and I thought I was succeeding pretty well. But when mamma came sweeping in, looking like a girl, she cast poor me into the shade. 'Why, Fanny!' said the gentleman, 'you look hardly a day older than you did the day I last saw you,' and in the midst of their compliments I slipped out. And — just think of it! — they never missed me! Don't you think it is too bad, Mr. William," she went on turning to me, " that a poor girl should have a mamma as young as she is ? "

" No, indeed ! " I replied stoutly ; " not when the mamma is as beautiful and as charming as the daughter."

Sister Jane paused in her work, whatever it was (for she was never idle a moment save when she was sound asleep), and looked hard at me, and Mary opened her eyes wide.

" William is coming out," said sister Jane. " He's been to the asylum in a carriage, and he's got charge of a tumble-down plantation, where the buzzards are setting on the fence, waiting for the mules and cows to die of starvation. Why, a month ago he'd no more 'a' spoke a piece like that, jest dry so without any provocation, than he'd 'a' jumped in the Oconee River with his clothes on."

" No, I don't think he's coming out at all," re-marked Mary, laughing at sister Jane's good-na-tured sarcasm. " It does n't seem natural to hear him paying compliments. Yet it was such a neat. and pretty one I think we should forgive him this time. Mamma would, I know."

"For one of my age" — I tried to speak as blandly as I knew how, but I could feel my voice shake a little — "it should have been a compliment to the mamma, but it was n't."

Sister Jane pretended to heave a sigh of relief. "I declare, William! when you said 'one of my age,' I thought you were going ahead and speak that piece about 'appearing in public on the stage,' and I says to myself, 'Laws have mercy! Maybe we 've gone and left the wrong folks at the asylum.'"

I sometimes thought that sister Jane pushed her humorous comments too far, and this was one of the occasions; but Mary neither laughed nor paid any attention to the remark.

"You are indeed venerable, Mr. William," she said lightly. "After a while I shall have to lend you a crutch. We have a pair somewhere about the house."

I felt grateful to her for passing off so serious a matter as a joke, and I looked my thanks, if I did not speak them.

"William's age is like the moonshine," remarked sister Jane; "bright enough to blind, but not hot enough to burn. It 's a disease with him. He 'll be old long before his time."

"What I mean," said I, "is that I am old as compared with Mary."

"Oh, is that it?" cried Mary. "Then I am old and decrepit as compared with Mr. Cowardin's little boy. It is dreadful to be so old. I 'll limp

home and see whether our famous company has
gone, or whether he is to stay to tea." She limped
from the room, but, the moment she was outside,
ran along the garden walk as nimbly and as grace-
fully as a fawn.

The gentleman stayed to tea, and for some time
afterwards, and we heard that night what was new
to our ears — the rippling, musical laughter of
Mrs. Bullard come floating across the garden.

"Fanny Brandon's come to life again," remarked sister Jane grimly, when she heard it.

The next day or the day after, Grandsir Roach
and Uncle Jimmy Cosby came knocking at our
door, as they had done many times since Mandy
Satterlee took up her abode with us, and I was
glad of it, for they always had something both sen-
sible and cheerful to say. Their visits seemed to
make Mandy brighter, being the strongest evidence
that she still had a hold on the hearts of those who
had known her in her happier days. These old
friends came now, bearing gifts. There were some
dozens of fresh eggs and a few pounds of butter
for sister Jane, some yards of checked cloth for
Mandy, and some socks, a knit jacket, a pair of
mittens, and a cloth hat for Klibs, Mandy's baby.
Grandsir Roach explained the matter: —

"When I seed what Sally and Prue was a-doin'
— or as you may say, what they had done gone
an' done, for I never know'd what 'pon top of the
green globe they was a-doin' ontil it was done done
— when I seed how big it looked to bring, an' how

little it 'd look arter it was brung, I says to 'em,
says I, ' What in the name of sense are you two
wimmen a-doin' ? Don't you know in reason that
this little bunch of eggs an' this here little dab of
butter will look mighty poor an' small by the side
of the store what Jane has already got laid in ?'
says I. I leave it to Brother Cosby here."

" He said them very words," remarked this willing witness. " ' They 'll look poor an' small,' says
he, ' by the side of the store what Jane has already
got laid in,' says he."

Grandsir Roach looked relieved. " An' Sally
— it mought 'a' been Prue, but I think 't was Sally
— says, says she, ' Well, I don't keer how they
look ; the eggs is new laid an' the butter is fresh
made, an' we 'll send 'em anyhow, let 'em look
ever so small by the side of what Jane 's got,' says
she."

" Well, goodness knows," sister Jane began, but
Grandsir Roach closed his eyes, pressed his lips
together, shook his head, and lifted his hand. He
would not be interrupted, and sister Jane was compelled to pause and listen.

" 'T was uther Sally or Prue, I 'll not be too
mighty certain which, an' she says, says she, ' Let
'em look small as they will by the side of what
Jane 's got, we 'll send 'em anyhow,' says she, ' bekaze it hain't the size, or the heft, or the wuth of
the things — it 's the intent,' says she." He turned
his head slowly and looked at his companion for
confirmation.

"You 've got eve'y twist and turn of the discourse, Brother Roach," said Uncle Jimmy Cosby; "you 've got it pat.   'T was uther Prue or Sally, I 'll not say which. 'It 's not the heft of what 's in the hamper,' says she, 'it 's the intent what goes wi' it for good measure,' says she.   Whichever an' whatsoever it was, she said them very words."

"Well, may the Lord bless the good old souls!" exclaimed sister Jane with real enthusiasm.   "Jest tell 'em that if there was but one egg and but one spoonful of butter, I 'd be glad to have it.   It 'd be a sign they had me in their minds, and what more do I want than that?"

"We 'll tell 'em, Jane; we shorely will.   It 'll make 'em both feel better," said Grandsir Roach.

"Yes 'm," remarked Uncle Jimmy Cosby, "we shorely tell 'em, an' they 'll be might'ly holp up — might'ly holp up."

"Mandy, honey, did Sandy tell you wharabouts he 'd been at, an' all he 'd saw sence he 's been gone?" asked Grandsir Roach.

"Who — Bud?" cried Mandy.   "Why, I hain't laid livin' eyes on Bud, not sence the day he come an' tol' me good-by."

"You hain't!" exclaimed Grandsir Roach.   He turned his eyes solemnly on Uncle Jimmy Cosby. "You hear that, Brother Cosby!   Mandy hain't seed nuther ha'r nor hide of Sandy, not sence the day she told him good-by!"

"Tooby shore! Tooby shore!" said Uncle Jimmy Cosby in sad surprise.   "You may well say 'tooby shore,' Brother Cosby," remarked Grandsir Roach.

"Yes," replied Uncle Jimmy Cosby, "bekaze we seed him no longer'n yistiddy."

"Bud? You seed Bud?" cried Mandy.

"With our four eyes," replied Grandsir Roach solemnly. "An' more 'n that, we teched him with our hands, an' talked wi' 'im by word of mouth."

"A true word! We seed 'im wi' our four eyes!" echoed Uncle Jimmy Cosby. "As true a word as ever was spoke."

"An' you reely seed Bud!" Mandy's voice was low, as though she knew not what to say. She seemed to be dazed.

"As plain as we see you a-standin' thar," said Grandsir Roach. "We not only seed him, we talked wi' 'im ; we not only talked wi' 'im, we shuck hands wi' 'im, an' passed the time of day."

"Percizely!" responded Uncle Jimmy Cosby.

"I says to him, says I, 'Sandy, your cloze is all right, but you look stove up. You look much as if you'd been drug thoo a hot sandbank feet foremost.' I said them very words. 'What in the nation is the matter wi' you?' says I."

"He says, says he, 'Grandsir, you ought to know as well as me. You know I've had fam'ly troubles,' says he. Says I, 'Sandy, the only fam'ly trouble I ever know'd you to have was Dram,' says I. 'You had it by the time you could vote, if not before, an' you've got it yit, or your breath belies you,' says I."

"Oh, don't blame Bud — blame me!" cried Mandy. "Lay all the blame on me!"

"You hear that, Jane, William, an' Brother Cosby?" said Grandsir Roach solemnly, almost reproachfully. "It's mighty few things you could ax me, honey, that I would n't run an' jump to do, but I'll be danged if I do that."

"What did I say to you, Brother Roach?" inquired Uncle Jimmy Cosby indignantly, "Did n't I say to you right before his face that Sandy Satterlee was a triflin' vagabon' from the day he put on britches? Did n't I tell him so, an' dar' him to take it up?"

"You did, Brother Cosby; I'll say that for you. You shorely did."

"If Bud's a vagabon' I'm the cause of it," said Mandy. "I know it an' feel it. Oh, me!"

She placed her hands before her face to hide her tears. At this sister Jane stepped forward, caught hold of Mandy's hands, and forcibly pulled them away from her face.

"Look at me, Mandy!" she said sternly; "that's not the truth, and you know it, and if you don't know it it's because you've got the tenderest, lovingest heart that ever beat."

"Oh, I don't want it to be the truth," cried Mandy, "but I'm afeard it is — I'm afeard it is!"

"Thank you, Jane! Thank you kindly for that," said Grandsir Roach. "Brother Cosby an' me can set an' think, an' we do a heap of it fust an' last, but not like you, Jane. You know how to say the right word. Good-by, Jane; good-by, honey, ontell you see me ag'in. Me an' Brother Cosby have got to be a-makin' our departure. We'll drap in before long — an' may God bless you all!"

Uncle Jimmy Cosby shook hands in silence until he came to Mandy. He held her hand a moment in both of his, patted it gently, and said: —

"Don't fret, honey; don't fret. We're constant a-thinkin' about you."

XXII.

MANDY seemed to be very much troubled because her brother, whom she had not seen for so many years, had ignored her on his return, and she wondered why it was so, and grieved over it as a woman will.

"He started out as a vagabond," said sister Jane in her matter-of-fact way, "and he's got worse and worse. You may thank your stars that he's done gone and forgot all about you. He ain't worth a thought."

But this explanation was not satisfactory to Mandy. "I'm to blame," she repeated over and over again. "I'm the one that's to blame. Ef it had n't but 'a' been for me, he 'd 'a' stayed here at home, an' maybe he 'd 'a' been doin' well by this time. Oh, me!"

"Was he doing well before he went away?" sister Jane inquired.

"Well, he was gittin' ready to go to work an' settle down," was Mandy's reply.

"It frets me to hear you talk so," sister Jane insisted. "He 's never done a hand's turn in his life, and he never will. He was born trifling and he 's stayed so. He ain't worth the wrappings of your little finger. He 'll never put his foot inside my gate, not if I know it."

Sin has a long arm, but Mandy gave it credit for having a longer. So she worried herself over her brother day after day. But he never came to see her, and when he did come, it seemed to be mightily against his will.

When Jincy Meadows made his visit to Mandy he brought news of her brother, and, although it was puzzling to me, it seemed to be the most satisfying that she had heard.

" I reckon maybe you ain't seen much of Sandy sence he took up his residence with the dry cattle," said Jincy.

" I hain't laid eyes on him," replied Mandy, " bekaze he hain't been a-nigh me."

" And he ain't comin' if he can help it," Jincy went on. " Why, he 's a sight to behold, Sandy is. What he 's got on his mind, I can't tell you, because I don't know, but it 's lots bigger than he 's got room for — I can tell you that."

" Oh, I know he 's troubled about me," cried Mandy.

" You would n't say so if you could see him," said Jincy. " He goes about the woods like a stray steer. If he had horns and know'd how to bellow, he 'd be the identical thing itself. His voice is as squeaky as if he 'd been callin' out the figgers at a stag dance. He 's got horns, but he gits 'em out of a bottle."

"Yes — I know," cried Mandy. "I 've drove him to drink."

"There you go!" exclaimed Jincy. "Ain't I tellin' you that Sandy 's done something he 's sorry for? You know what sort of a chap he is better 'n I do, and I know him toler'ble well. I run up on him in the woods the other day. He was settin' at the foot of a tree dozin' like, and close to his head was a bottle. Says I, 'Sandy, what 's the word?' says he, 'Jincy, if I was as happy as you it would be a good word.' Says I, 'If I was sorry, Sandy, I would n't try to drown it in the flowin' bowl, nor in the bottle neither.' Says he, 'The bowl that 's big enough to drown mine in ain't never been made, Jincy.' Says I, 'Sandy, have you been to see your sister sence you got back?' Says he, 'Jincy, I could n't bear to have Mandy look at me. I used to rail at her,' says he, 'but she 's too good to so much as look at me.'"

"Did he say that?" asked Mandy in a low voice.

"He did," said Jincy, "and more!"

I thought to myself that if it was a piece of Jincy's own invention it was done cleverly and in a good cause.

"What more?" Mandy inquired.

"He says, 'The next time you see Mandy, Jincy, tell her howdy, and tell her that if I 'd 'a' done as she wanted me to do I 'd 'a' been better off than I am right now or ever will be ag'in.'"

"Poor Bud! I never was so sorry for anybody

in my life!" Mandy sighed deeply, and no doubt would have wept if Jincy had n't been sitting close by with his Sunday clothes on. Nevertheless, it was something of a relief to her to feel that she was not directly responsible for her brother's condition of mind and body.

A day or two afterwards Mr. Cowardin called me aside. "I 've found my man," he said. "The man we saw with our friend Moreland," he explained, seeing that I did not follow him.

"Where is he?" I inquired in rather an aimless way.

"In my room," he replied. "He 's a little shaky, and needs bolstering up, but as sure as you 're born, the fellow has information in him. Why, he 's an old traveling companion of mine. He was in the wagon train that I carried to California. He 's as cold-blooded a scoundrel as I ever saw," Mr. Cowardin continued almost savagely, "and I expect to have many a pleasant hour with him."

I did n't pretend to understand this, but it was all the explanation I could get at the time. Mr. Cowardin went off in high glee, apparently, and we saw little of him, except at meal-times, for two or three days.

Meanwhile, Mr. Moreland, the Virginian gentleman, was a daily visitor at Colonel Bullard's. If he was n't there in the afternoons he was there after tea. The Colonel's wife evidently found him very agreeable company, for on more than one occasion we saw her riding out behind his handsome bays, to the great astonishment of the villagers. It could not be denied that they made a handsome couple as they whirled through the streets in the buggy drawn by the high-stepping horses. The Colonel's wife seemed to have grown very much younger. Her eyes sparkled with something of the ardor of youth, and color began to show in her face. She came to see sister Jane once after she had been riding with Mr. Moreland, and I could imagine how beautiful she had been in her youth. Indeed, she was not so old now, and only a little excitement and exercise in congenial company were necessary to make her a very handsome woman. I could see that, and I wondered if Colonel Bullard himself was so blind that he failed to perceive the necessity of providing the gentle stimulant of congenial company and outdoor exercise for his wife.

Such was my thought, and I have remembered it and smiled a hundred times over its shallow inconsequence, for, right upon its heels, I found myself the unwilling spectator of an episode so extravagant and sensational as to cause me to doubt the evidence of my own eyes and ears.

Of one episode, did I say? It never rains but it pours, and for a time I seemed to be overwhelmed with a flood of the most painful experiences that could be imagined. And yet in these, as in the ordinary affairs of life, the hand of Providence was guiding, and the fact struck me with such force as to enable me to fortify my mind and to maintain a confidence in human nature that otherwise would have been sadly shaken.

I said awhile ago that the Colonel's wife came to visit sister Jane after one of her rides with Mr. Moreland. As matters turned out, it was her last ride with that person. That night sister Jane and myself were sitting in her room, talking about poor Mrs. Beshears and the affairs of her estate, when we heard Mr. Cowardin enter the house. We knew him by the firm way in which he walked. He came along the hall, paused as if listening, and then, coming to sister Jane's room, rapped lightly on the lintel, the door being partly closed.

"Come in and tell us howdy," said sister Jane.

Mr. Cowardin came in, looked about the room, and then went to the door again and looked up and down the hallway.

"I saw a buggy standing at the door," he explained, "and I was certain you had company."

"A buggy!" cried sister Jane. "Why, what upon earth!"

"Mr. Moreland's team," said Mr. Cowardin. "I thought the gentleman had come to shake hands all around." His tone was half serious, half sarcastic.

"When I want to shake hands with a demijohn," remarked sister Jane, "I'll go over to the tavern and shake hands with a new one."

Ordinarily, Mr. Cowardin would have laughed

at this comment, but now he did not even smile.
He stood in the floor with his hands in his pockets, and stared steadily at the dim flame of the
candle that was sputtering on the stand close to
sister Jane's head as she leaned over her sewing.

"You know the fellow I was hunting for and
found," he said, turning his eyes on me. "Well,
he's an interesting person. He's a little shaky on
his feet, but he's sober now, as he says, for the
first time in several years. He's full of information, and some of it will surprise you as much as
it did me. He told me something that I thought
was a preposterous lie, but I'm afraid it's the
truth. At any rate we shall soon see."

Pat upon the word, we heard a rustle in the
hallway, the light tread of nimble feet, and the
next moment Mrs. Bullard entered. She seemed
to be arranged for a journey. She had on a dove-
colored frock, the soberest garment I had ever seen
her wear. She had entered the room apparently
in great haste, but paused as she saw Mr. Cowardin. He made way for her, lifted his hat, and,
without speaking, turned and went outside the
door into the hall. The surprise that the Colonel's
wife felt on seeing him showed plainly in her face
and manner, but she recovered herself almost immediately.

"I've just come to say good-by, Jane. I'm going back to my home and people. You know what
my life has been here, but you don't know all.
You don't know what I know. Just think of a

Brandon, Jane, leading the dog's life I have led. Go out to-morrow and look at the big kennel on the corner, and thank God that Fanny Brandon has broken the chain at last."

"Why, what on earth is the matter?" asked sister Jane. "You talk like a crazy person."

"Don't ask me, Jane — don't ask me! You'll find out soon enough. Crazy! I have never had a sane moment until this hour! Where is Mandy Satterlee? I must thank that woman for giving me an excuse for leaving the people I loathe and the life I hate!"

She had worked herself into a grand passion, and she seemed to me to be more beautiful the more furious she grew. Mandy, who was in the room across the hall, came in just then.

"Did anybody call me?" she asked. Seeing Mrs. Bullard, she blushed. "I declare, I 'm a sight to be comin' in here. I did n't know you had company."

"Never mind the company, Mandy Satterlee!" exclaimed the Colonel's wife. "I 'm going away from here, and I 've called to tell you good-by and to thank you for what you 've done for me."

"What I 've done for you!" Even by the dim light of the sputtering candle I could see Mandy's face grow white.

"*You* know what it is, Mandy Satterlee! You know well, and I want to thank you. Who could have thought that *you* would have been the one to give me freedom?"

"Oh, me! Oh, have n't I had trouble enough?" Mandy's cry was a heart-rending one. It was a note of anguish, of self-condemnation, and an appeal for mercy. I hope never to hear such a cry again either in this world or the next. She threw herself on the floor by the side of a chair, leaning heavily across it, the picture of misery and despair.

The Colonel's wife went close to Mandy and stood above her with clenched hands, breathing hard.

"Oh, to think of it!" she exclaimed, turning to sister Jane with tragic hints in her eyes. "To think that *she*" — the Colonel's wife raised her hand and pointed at Mandy with a gesture of rage and scorn — "to think that *she* should have been the one! Why, Jane," — she lowered her voice almost to a whisper, — "I loved that man! You would n't believe it, would you? I loved him — but now I hate him — oh, I loathe the very air he breathes!"

"Oh, why — *why* can't I die?" moaned Mandy.

"Die!" cried the Colonel's wife. "Why do you want to die? Who are you, and what are you? I am the one to die — and I am dead to that man. Oh, the miserable creature! Why did Satan throw him in my way?"

At that moment Mr. Cowardin appeared in the doorway and motioned me to him, whereupon I hastened out of the room, glad of any sort of an excuse to fly from a scene so paralyzing. I remember that I was glad to feel I could use my limbs at all. Once out of the room I breathed freer.

In the dark hallway, Mr. Cowardin laid his hand on my shoulder. "If she starts away," he said, "detain her. Use force if necessary. Within twenty-four hours she'll thank you for all the bruises you give her."

He turned and went swiftly out into the street. What he did there he told me within half an hour. He went to the buggy, and leaned against it, placing one hand on the framework and the other on the whip-thimble.

"The lady sends word that she can't come," he said. "She says the gentleman must go away with all possible speed."

The occupant of the vehicle was Moreland, and he seemed to be more than half drunk.

"Where's Fanny?" he cried. "I saw her go in the house there. Let her bring her own messages. Go back and tell Fanny that I'll not go till she herself tells me to."

Meanwhile, Mr. Cowardin had hardly reached the street before the Colonel's wife went to sister Jane and laid a hand on her arm as of old. "Good-by, Jane! You are a good woman. All the rest of us are devils. Where's William?"

She came out into the hallway as she asked for me, and I stepped forward and barred the way. She seemed surprised at this, and I thought the shadow of a contemptuous smile flitted across her face, but I was not certain; yet the bare thought of it rendered me less infirm of purpose than before.

"You seem to be glad to see me go, William," she said, taking the hand I held out to stay her passage. "Well, it is natural. We have long misunderstood each other: you have taken me to be a fraud, and I have judged you to be a fool. Right or wrong, we are quits. Good-by."

"No, Mrs. Bullard," I said with a firmness that was as surprising to me as it was to her, "it is not good-by. You are to remain here."

She looked hard at me as if trying to read my mind. "Then you *are* a fool," she said through her clenched teeth. With a strength for which I was totally unprepared, she wrenched her hand from mine and whisked past me in the hallway like a shadow. She was fleet, but I reached the outer door as she did, and placed both hands against it, holding it shut with all my weight and strength, knowing now that I had to deal with a desperate woman.

But even this knowledge did not prepare me for the tactics she employed. She seized me below the waist, dragged me suddenly backwards, and I fell prone upon my hands and knees. Before I could recover myself, she had wrenched the door open and was gone. But she never crossed the sidewalk. As she jumped through the door I heard Mr. Cowardin exclaim: —

"Look to yourself, sir!" and then I heard a report like a pistol. He had seized the whip and brought it down upon the backs of the horses with a blow so powerful that it sounded like an explosion. The creatures gave one leap forward, and then broke into a wild run. Fortunately they kept in the middle of the street, and in a few moments, as we three stood listening, we heard them settle down into a steady gallop, which showed that the man in the buggy, drunk as he might be, had them under control.

"I'm sorry I did n't hit the man instead of the horses," said Mr. Cowardin.

"Perhaps you'll be pleased to lay it on my back," said Mrs. Bullard with smothered rage. She rushed toward him, and tried to wrench the whip from his hand. But she made only one effort. The knowledge of her impotence suddenly overcame her, and all her strength left her. She would have fallen to the ground but for the sustaining arm of Mr. Cowardin. But, such was her versatility, if I may use the word here, that she recovered almost immediately.

"Don't touch me!" she exclaimed savagely.

"I'll not hurt you, madam," said Mr. Cowardin gently. "If I have come between you and your designs, it was not for your sake, but for the sake of one I love dearly. You'll thank me for what I've done, when I tell you the news I have for you. But we must go inside."

"I have nowhere else to go," she said simply. "I'll not go back yonder; I'll die first!" She stretched a hand toward her home, looming up cold, dark, and solemn in the darkness. " Who are you, sir, that you are bold enough to take advantage of a weak woman whom you know nothing of and who has done you no harm?" · Her rage rose again as she turned toward Mr. Cowardin.

" Madam, with the exception of your husband and your own family no one in the world has a better right to do what I have done," he answered. " I have some news for you that is of more importance than anything that has happened to you during your whole life."

" It is not true, sir," she replied. " I have lost my son, I have lost my husband, and I have given up my home. What could be more important than these things?"

" Come inside," said Mr. Cowardin.

" Yes, for the Lord's sake, Fanny, come in!" exclaimed sister Jane from the darkness of the doorway, and her voice brought us all back to the realities of every-day life. For my part, I was beginning to forget on which end I stood, so astounding were the transactions that had taken place before my eyes.

" Excuse me, Jane," said Mrs. Bullard in a more natural tone; " I had forgotten where I was."

She went in, and Mr. Cowardin and I followed. The Colonel's wife was calm enough when she got inside the door — almost too calm, it seemed to me, after the tremendous outbreak that has been described. But I could see that the fires of anger still glowed in her eyes; she was calm, but still desperate.

The noise that had been made had aroused Klibs from his innocent sleep, and Mandy was holding him close against her bosom when we returned to the room. Hearing our footsteps, and possibly suspecting that we had succeeded in detaining Mrs. Bullard, the unfortunate young mother had moved her chair to the darkest corner of the room, where, with her back hair falling over her shoulders and her child hugged to her breast, she could safely hide from human eyes whatever emotion she felt.

"Now, sir," said the Colonel's wife, turning to Mr. Cowardin, " what is the information you have for me? I hope it is important enough to excuse your unmannerly — yes, your unmanly — conduct to-night. Don't think you 'd be standing there or I here if I were a man ; or if there was a man in this miserable community to whom I might appeal for protection. Wait!" she said, as Mr. Cowardin made a movement as if to speak. Her voice was hard and cold. " Wait! Don't imagine for a moment that I will believe a word you say. After what I 've seen of your actions to-night, I know you are capable of any lie. I want to hear how you are going to excuse yourself." Her Virginian blood and grit showed to advantage here, undoubtedly, and I began to admire her.

Mr. Cowardin regarded her with kindly eyes

and his voice was very gentle when he spoke. "Madam, if you think you can afford to wait here five minutes until I can go across the street and return, I shall try to make good my promise." He paused expectantly.

"What can I do but await your pleasure and convenience?" she asked with a contemptuous smile. "Owing to you, I have nowhere to go even if I were not disposed to wait. Pray where could I go?"

Mr. Cowardin regarded her with a puzzled look. He seemed to doubt whether he had followed her meaning. At that moment neither he nor I had the key to either her words or her extraordinary actions. But he turned and walked down the hallway. Just as he reached the door we heard a hasty knocking. He opened the door almost before the knocking ceased. Then we heard the voice of Colonel Bullard.

"William! have you seen "— Here Mr. Cowardin interrupted, but we could not hear the words. "Excuse me, sir; in the dark I mistook you for William, who is an old friend of mine. Show me the way. I must see Jane and William!"

At the same moment the Colonel's wife whisked out and across the hall. I saw her enter the room that had been given up to Mandy.

XXIII.

As Colonel Bullard entered the room I saw that a great change had come over him. His gait was unsteady. A letter or paper that he held in his hand shook as though he had been seized with a rigor.

Sister Jane did not wait for him to speak. She rose and stood looking at him. "Cephas Bullard, you are the very last person in the world that I ever expected to see darken my door after knowing what I know and you knowing that I know it —the very last person in the world." But her voice had no note of surprise in it; on the contrary it was charged with indignation.

"I was compelled to come, Jane. My darling wife has left me; here is her letter. I am a ruined man, Jane. Have you seen Fanny? Has she been here, William?"

"Yes, Colonel, she has," I replied.

"She came to say good-by," remarked sister Jane.

"Where was she going, Jane? What did she say? Did she leave any word for me? Did n't she send me some message? Oh, I know her heart, Jane, and I never will believe that she went away from me without leaving me some word more satisfactory than this." He held the letter on a level with his eyes, his hand trembling so that the paper made a rattling noise.

"She said she was going away from this hateful place for good and all," explained sister Jane. "She did n't tell me her reasons, and I did n't ask her, because I know'd 'em well enough."

" Don't be too hard on me, Jane," he pleaded.

"It 's not me that 's hard on you, Cephas Bullard. It 's your own wickedness."

"Oh, it 's true, Jane! it 's all true! But if you only knew how I have suffered ; if you only knew the agony I 've endured." He paused as if seeking sympathy, but he got none. I was shocked at sister Jane's manner until she spoke again, and then the whole truth that I had been utterly blind to before burst upon me, and it brought with it a feeling of disgust for Colonel Bullard that I was long in overcoming.

"I reckon it 's so fixed that other folks can suffer some as well as you," said sister Jane.

She stretched forth her hand and pointed to Mandy Satterlee, who was bending so low above her child that she seemed to be crouching in the rocking-chair. Colonel Bullard's glance followed the direction of sister Jane's gesture, and he shrank back as his eye fell on Mandy.

"You are right, Jane, and I am wrong," he cried in a broken voice. "I 'm a terrible sinner,

Jane. That is why my dear wife has left me. That man Moreland told her about my wretched sinfulness, and I confessed it, Jane. I did n't spare myself. I ought to have told her long ago; but it is a fearful thing to confess, Jane, and I never had the courage. It is a terrible thing to do, — and yet" (the Colonel lowered his voice) "I thought — oh, I fondly hoped, Jane — that my dear wife would forgive me. And I shall always believe that she would have forgiven me if she had known how I love her. That will be my only comfort, Jane, if I ever have any peace of mind at all!"

I could but remark how, even in the midst of his penitence, he seemed to regard his own trouble and his own misery as of more importance than all other troubles and miseries put together. It is the way of the world, especially the way of man. I have seen women who could put their own troubles aside to sympathize with the miseries of others, but I have never seen one of my own sex who had the courage or the generous impulse to make the attempt.

"You say she 's been here, Jane," said Colonel Bullard, after a pause, during which he re-read the letter in his hand, holding it close to the candle. It was a very brief note, as I could see, and doubtless had the rare merit of terseness.

"She came to tell us good-by," remarked sister Jane, "but she spun it out into a good many words."

"What did she say, Jane? Did she seem to be particularly bitter against me? Oh, that I could have seen her for one moment!" he exclaimed in a despairing tone.

"It's jest as well you did n't," said sister Jane, with an abundant lack of sympathy in her voice. "You know Fanny Brandon most as well as I do, I reckon, and you can figure to yourself about what she said."

"That's the way she signed herself here — 'Fanny Brandon.'" The Colonel spoke as if he had heard nothing that sister Jane said save his wife's maiden name. He repeated it again — "Fanny Brandon" — and then slowly placed the letter in his pocket and clasped his hands behind him.

"I 'll not deny that I expected to find her here, Jane," he said after a pause. "At least I hoped to find her here. But that is not all I came for." He turned to me as a source from which he might expect more sympathy than sister Jane had shown him. "I came, William, to make what reparation I can. Surely, surely, it is not yet too late for me to do that. It ought to have been made long ago; but it is not too late — don't tell me it is too late."

Before I could make any reply — indeed, I knew not what to say — sister Jane spoke. "What do you mean by that?" she asked.

Colonel Bullard hesitated, and then drew from his pocket a roll of bank bills, and laid it on the candle-stand. Released from the pressure of confinement the bills slowly swelled out, and would have fallen to the floor had not the Colonel reached forth and placed his hand upon them.

"Here is a sum of money, William. I want you to take it and invest it for the benefit of Miss Satterlee and her child. If the sum seems too small, I am willing to double it at your suggestion."

It was curious how the voice of the Colonel assumed a business-like tone when he came to speak of a money transaction. Mechanically I reached my hand to take the money, but I drew it back quickly at a word from Mandy Satterlee. She had risen from the rocking-chair, and now stood not far from sister Jane. She had placed her sleeping child on the sofa. Both hands were held to her head as if to prevent her hair from falling about her face. With a sweeping gesture she flung her hair behind her and stretched forth her arm, pointing at the Colonel.

"Take your money away from here! Take it away! I would n't tetch it, not to save my own life — much less your'n! Take it out'n my sight! I never said a word ag'in you in my life; not by word or look have I ever laid any of my trouble at your door; and yit here you come wi' money! Miss Jane," she went on, turning to my sister, "this man 's a-takin' a mighty heap on hisself. It 's a lot more my trouble than it 's his'n. I was out there in the woods, lonesome, an' I wanted somethin' I could call mine — somethin' that 'd be my own

— somethin' that nobody on the wide earth would dast to claim. Here it is!" She stepped swiftly to the sofa and kissed her child, and as swiftly returned. "I never dreamed of the trouble an' misery it'd bring on me an' other folks, an' I've suffered, an' I'm mighty sorry, — I'll allers be sorry, — but I'm the one that's to blame. Make him put up his money, Miss Jane."

Oh, the passion of motherhood! For the first time in my life I began to realize its nature — its weakness and its strength.

"What can I do, William?" said the Colonel. "I've lost my son, my wife, and I can turn nowhere for comfort and peace."

"Oh, yes, you can," exclaimed sister Jane. "Where's your Bible, I'd like to know, and where are your prayers?"

"No, Jane; I'm the vilest hypocrite that ever breathed the breath of life."

"If you reely think that, Cephas Bullard, you're already a long ways on the road to'rds forgiveness," said sister Jane.

"It is well enough to talk that way, Jane, but my wife is gone. If you knew her as I know her you would know what that means. Jane, I love that woman. She'll never forgive me, and she has run away with a man she used to know when she was a girl; but if she were to come back to-night, to-morrow, or a year from now I'd be glad to forgive her."

"You would?" cried sister Jane.

" Most assuredly, Jane."

" Well, you 're one among a thousand."

Sister Jane had hardly spoken the words before the Colonel's wife glided into the room, and laid her hand on his arm.

" Did you say you could forgive me ? " she cried. " Oh, if you can forgive me I can forgive you ! " Her whole attitude had changed.

The Colonel stood stock-still and looked at his wife in a dazed way.

" Is it really and truly you, Fanny ? " he gasped, " or am I losing my senses ? " He passed his hand over his face.

She answered by leaning her head against his shoulder and laughing hysterically — a laugh that jarred on my nerves because of its theatrical flavor. And yet I knew that such a laugh — strained and artificial — was intended to hide emotions that led far from laughter.

" Fanny ! Fanny ! " the Colonel cried, " you don't know how you have frightened me."

" I am worse frightened than you were," she replied. She clung to him as a child might. Presently her eyes met mine. She ran to me and threw her arms about me. " Oh, William ! You don't know what you have saved me from — you and Mr. Cowardin ! "

She ran back to her husband and clung to him almost frantically. He caressed her as though she were a spoiled child.

" I thought I was a ruined man, Fanny. I

knew I deserved to be, but it was so hard to give you up. "

He clung to her and she to him, and I saw then that they had come to a clearer understanding than had, perhaps, ever existed between them. I saw, too, that my whimsical and unexplained prejudices had been severely unjust to the lady. For the first time in my life I understood to what lengths the rage and fury of jealousy will lead a woman of spirit.

" Please make him take his money," said Mandy, touching the Colonel's wife gently on the shoulder. " I would n't tech it, not to save a thousand lives."

" I 'll relieve you of it," remarked the Colonel's wife with a slight frown. She took the money, rolled it tightly, and placed it in her belt.

" I think we will go now," suggested the Colonel. " Jane, I am sorry to have disturbed you. I trust you will forgive me."

" Well, there 's been a good deal of forgiving going on around here," said sister Jane. " If you feel any better you need n't worry about me. But I 'll say this, I 've got a lots better opinion of you than I 'd 'a' had if you had n't 'a' worried me in jest the way you have. You ain't half as good as you might be, but you 're a heap better than I thought you was."

" But *I* love him, Jane," the Colonel's wife asserted, as if that disposed of the matter.

" Oh, I hope you do," said sister Jane. " I don't expect everybody's stomach to be as weak as

mine when it comes to lovin' folks. Where's
Mary all this time while you two are a-prancin' an'
a-caperin' up and down?"

"We must be going, Fanny," the Colonel insisted. "It would n't do to have that child frightened at our absence."

"Mary 's perfectly happy," replied the Colonel's
wife. "She 's deep in one of William's books.
But we ought to go. Jane, I hope you 'll not be
too hard on me. I 'm happier now than I 've been
in years."

"I 'm truly glad, Fanny," replied sister Jane.
"It takes so mighty little to make folks happy,
that I wonder there ain't more of it in the world.
If we keep a sharp lookout we 'll get our share of
it, I reckon."

The Colonel and his wife bade us good-night,
and were going away when we heard footsteps in
the hallway, and in came Mr. Cowardin, ushering
in the man I had seen riding in the Moreland
buggy. He was completely sober now, and I
knew him at once as Mandy's brother Sandy. She
knew him, too, and ran to him, crying, "Why
Bud, what 's the matter? Have they took you
prisoner?"

For answer he said: "Howdy, Mandy; you 're
lookin' monstus peart." His sister's hand was on
his shoulder, but he made no attempt to greet her
in a brotherly fashion. He stood stolidly, almost
stupidly, it seemed to me, and the bad opinion I
had of him grew rapidly worse.

Mr. Cowardin had summoned the Colonel and his wife back, and the lady remarked as she re-entered the room, "I had almost forgotten you, Mr. Cowardin, and that means I have forgiven you for what I thought was your rudeness awhile ago."

"It means, too," said Mr. Cowardin, "that you had forgotten about the interesting information I had promised to give you."

"Yes, I had forgotten it entirely," the Colonel's wife confessed. "I am so happy, you know."

"In that case, we may as well postpone the story this man has to tell. Satterlee, I'll not need you until to-morrow."

"Oh, no, squire; you can't come that game," protested Sandy. "When I go out of that door out yonder I ain't comin' back no more tell I send fer Mandy. Oh, no, squire; I don't want nobody a-doggin' arter me arter to-night."

"What is it?" asked the Colonel. "It is possible that he knows about our son, Fanny — our darling child that was lost."

"Oh, is it *that?*" cried the Colonel's wife.

Sandy paid no attention whatever to either one. "You 've done the right thing by me, squire, an' I'll do the right thing by you. But I'll tell you now, I 'm not gwine to hang on the pleasure of *that* feller — no, I'll be danged ef I do! An' I'll not be dogged arter."

"Then tell what you know, and be done with it," said Mr. Cowardin.

What Sandy told, the reader may have suspected

from the first, though the fact did not dawn on me until the man entered the room. He had stolen Freddy Bullard, made good his escape, and at last dropped him on the wagon trail in the far West, where he was found by Mr. Cowardin. Sandy Satterlee had no qualms of conscience. He was sorry for the child, but he suffered no remorse over what he had done. When he had concluded, he paused a moment, and then said : —

"Now, ef there 's anybody aroun' here that wants to know *why* I took the baby jest let 'em up an' say so, an' I 'll tell 'em why. An' ef there 's anybody here that wants to drag me up in court about it, let 'em drag."

The Colonel, holding his wife's hand in one of his, patted it gently, as he replied : " No, sir ; there is no one to make any complaint. My friends here all know why you took the child. You caused the innocent to suffer ; but that was my fault — all my fault. I have taken all the blame. I know that the Almighty has not entirely forsaken me, for He has had my boy restored to me."

Sandy seemed to be very much disappointed at this, or else I mistook the expression of his face. He rubbed his hand over his beard in a dazed way.

"Dang it all, squire ! " he exclaimed, as he turned to Mr. Cowardin. " I allowed I 'd git my head took off over here, an' I come primed to do some taking on my own hook."

" Then you 'd better take yourself off somewhere and try to l'arn to be honest," said sister Jane quick as a flash. "You ain't worth the powder an' lead it 'd take to kill you."

"Phew!" whistled Sandy under his breath. "Show me the door, squire, an' I 'll jest hop across the street an' jump in bed."

When Sandy was gone, the Colonel's wife was wild to see Freddy; she insisted that he should be roused from his sleep so that she might carry him home. But Mr. Cowardin was not to be prevailed upon. He would not permit the child (as he said) to jump out of sleep into conditions so new to his experience; and though the Colonel's wife added both tears and threats to her entreaties, Mr. Cowardin remained obdurate. For one more day, he said, the child should be his. Then Mrs. Bullard changed her ground. Might she see her child as he lay sleeping? Certainly, if she would solemnly promise not to arouse him. So the mother and father, with Mr. Cowardin, sister Jane, and myself, went on tiptoe to the lad's bedside. And he made a beautiful picture as he lay there, rosy with health, dreaming pleasant dreams that brought a faint smile to his half-parted lips. His mother crept toward him and gazed at him with clasped hands, smiling, although the tears ran down her cheeks. Then, quick as a flash, she stooped and kissed him. The child stirred, but did not open his eyes.

"Oh, I hoped he would wake!" she whispered, as she turned away.

"I thought so," said Mr. Cowardin in a warning tone.

"Oh, I think it is cruel not to allow us to take our child home!" said the Colonel's wife. She seemed to be greatly agitated.

"It may seem so," replied Mr. Cowardin. "But his mind must be prepared for the great change that has taken place in his condition. I must teach him"—he paused, looked hard at the flame of the candle, and stroked his beard—"that there are others he must care for more than he has ever cared for me."

"Might we not be depended on to do that?" The voice of the Colonel's wife was gentle, but there was something about it that jarred on my nerves.

"That is the trouble, madam," said Mr. Cowardin; "that is a part of the infliction. But you will have to excuse me." He crossed the hallway, went into the lad's room, and closed the door after him.

By one word, sister Jane covered his retreat and changed the current of our thoughts. "Which one of you had the good manners to thank the man for what he has done?" she asked bluntly.

Mrs. Bullard started impulsively into the lad's room again, but sister Jane stopped her.

"Oh, I want to get on my knees and thank him, Jane. I'll not speak above a whisper."

"No; don't go in there. There's plenty of time for thanks. Go home and dream over your good luck," said sister Jane.

Whereupon the Colonel and his wife bade us

good-night, and went home by way of the street instead of by way of the garden.

It was owing to this fact that Mary missed them when she came running through the garden. She was laughing when she entered the room, but her face wore a scared expression, and I thanked Heaven that she had not seen and heard all that had happened near where she now stood.

She had been reading, she said, and had not noticed how quiet the house was until she closed her book. The servants had all retired, and she went to her mother's room. Finding no one there she roused the house girl and searched the house. Then she came running through the garden, thinking to find her mother talking to sister Jane. She was surprised that her father had also paid us a visit, and seemed pleased, too.

"I could tell you some mighty good news," remarked sister Jane, "but I reckon I'll have to leave it to William as he takes you back home. If you stay to hear it your folks'll think you've run away."

So, as we walked through the garden, the weather being warm and fine, I told her as briefly as I could (suppressing Sandy Satterlee's motive altogether, and making him out a worse villain than he really was — for which I hope Heaven will forgive me) how her brother had been stolen, and how he had been recovered and brought back by Mr. Cowardin. Whereupon, Mary, womanlike, insisted on going back to see her brother as he lay asleep. I told her the objections to this, and protested as strongly as I could where Mary was concerned, but she pleaded so prettily and with such sweet eloquence, that I was fain to turn back with her and to be the means of gratifying her desire to see once more the brother she had long mourned as dead.

We returned, therefore, much to the surprise of sister Jane. Mr. Cowardin was very gracious in the matter. He was willing that Mary should see her brother, and I noticed that he did not lay her under the injunction of silence. She stood by the lad's bed and gazed on him with heaving bosom. Then she knelt at the bedside, burying her face in her hands. She came out smiling beautifully through her tears.

"How can I thank you?" she cried, giving Mr. Cowardin both her hands. He held them, I thought, a trifle longer than good taste demanded, regarding her all the while as if his mind were far afield. My idea of his violation of good taste, or etiquette, or whatever you may please to call it, was blown to the four winds by his next words.

"It would please me very much," he replied, "to hear you call me 'Uncle Clarence' the next time I see you."

"But if you are not Uncle Clarence?" Mary suggested in a half-frightened way.

"But if I am," he insisted.

"I don't understand," said Mary, turning away from him and going to sister Jane.

“No, it is not easy for a little girl to understand,” he remarked with something like a sigh. “But no matter. It is not absolutely necessary for you to call me ‘Uncle Clarence.’ ”

“ But I want to, if ” —

“ If he’s the genuine article, guaranteed not to rip in the seams or frazzle at the sleeves,” laughed Mr. Cowardin.

“ Wait! I ’ll tell you whether he’s your Uncle Clarence or not,” said sister Jane. “ Hold this candle, William.” She put on her “ sewing-specs,” as she called them, went forward in a business-like way, placed one hand over Mr. Cowardin’s beard and the other over his mouth, turned his face to the left and then to the right, and subjected him to the closest inspection. She saw what poor Mrs. Beshears must have seen the night she scrutinized the gentleman’s countenance.

“ If it ain’t him you may kill me dead ! ” she exclaimed, turning to Mary. “ I ought to ’a’ know’d him long ago. Clarence Bullard ! what on earth do you mean by changing your name and acting like this ? What have you done to be ashamed of your own name ? I hope to the Lord you ain’t one of Murrell’s men.”

“ I have n’t changed my name at all,” he said, laughing genially. “ I merely lopped off the Bullard when I left home.”

“ It brought you good luck, I reckon,” remarked sister Jane. “ Mary here will have to change her name before she ’s right happy.”

And Mary, innocent child, not seeing the **deep** meaning of the words, merely laughed at **the con-** ceit, **as** she said : —

" My uncle's name was Clarence Cowardin Bul- lard. **It** is written out so in all his school-books. **Oh, I** hope you are he ! " she cried still doubtfully. **" I** should be so happy ! "

" Go and be happy then, my dear. You cer- tainly deserve **to be** the happiest woman in the world. Good-night ! " She ran to him and kissed him, at which he seemed to **be** mightily pleased.

I may as **well** say here **that,** to my mind, there is nothing **so** stupid **as a mystery** that seems to be without excuse, **and I** could **not, for the life of me,** imagine **why** Clarence **Bullard should** change **his** name and go strolling about the country from **post** to pillar. I think **he saw** something of this in my face, for he seized the first opportunity, when there was no one to hear him but sister Jane and myself, to touch upon the matter.

" **A** man never has an **idea** of his own **until** he's thirty," he remarked.

" Thirty ! " exclaimed sister Jane. " You'd better say eighty ! "

" 'T would come nearer the mark," he replied. " **But I was a mere** lad, though a pretty wild one, when **I left home.** I had a tremendous quarrel with my brother, and fresh fuel was added **to my** anger by the fact that he told me some **very** un- wholesome truths about my conduct. **At** bottom, **as I know** now, I was more disgusted with myself

than with him, but I was sure then that I hated
him so vigorously and resented his authority so
keenly that I despised the very name of Bullard.
The feeling was so strong in me that it was months
before it cooled down, and by that time I had
lopped off the Bullard part of my name. Even
then I was sure I had done right, and for years I
hugged the delusion that my brother had driven
me from home with the intention of robbing me of
my share of the property. The truth is, he never
drove me from home at all, but simply refused to
supply me with funds until I had reformed."

"He did n't want to be Satan's banker," remarked sister Jane, "no matter how close he got
to the Old Boy in other ways."

"Precisely so," he assented with a smile. "It
was not until I found the child, and began to feel
that I had a responsibility on my shoulders, that
I began to realize what a fool I had been. Don't
be deceived in me," he said with a more serious
air than I had ever seen him assume. "It is only
very lately — only during the last half dozen years
— that I have played the part of a gentleman. The
rest of the time I have played the part of a vagabond. Don't imagine I was a very nice man when
you saw me at the circus, or that I had any kind
feelings for my brother. What I wanted to do
was to find his child and restore him with the words:
'That is the way I repay you for robbing me of my
own!' I was a vagabond, indeed, but a romantic
one, don't you think?"

XXIV.

THE END OF THE SKEIN.

ONCE more I walked with Mary through the garden. The September dew had moistened the air, and saturated it with the rich perfume of the roses that had now begun to renew the glory of their springtime bloom. Though I was with Mary, I had a sense of loneliness that I found troublesome to account for. Whether the sensational events of the past few hours had depressed me, or whether my own thoughts had suddenly taken on a melancholy hue and flavor I could not say.

We walked along in silence until nearly opposite the summer-house that stood in the middle of the garden. Finally Mary spoke : —

"Oh, I am so happy and thankful!" she cried. "It is just like a story in a book."

"No," said I; "in books of the lighter kind chance and accident try to play the part of Providence, but neither one is orderly enough. It was no accident that caused your Uncle Clarence to bring Freddy back."

I then told her all the circumstances, as Clarence Ballard had told them to me.

"Well, we have found what we lost," she said at last.

"No, we have not," I replied. I was not too melancholy to be contentious. "I have lost something that I cannot find again and never expect to."

"Oh!" she cried. Then, after a pause, "What was it?"

"Why, years ago I lost a little sweetheart, and I have never been able to find her since."

"Did she die?" Mary asked. She spoke in so low a tone that I barely caught the words.

"Oh, no!" I replied with a miserable attempt at levity; "she just grew up and 'from me fled,' as Jincy Meadows said in the song."

She made no response, but, somehow, we had paused under the stars in the garden walk, and the odor of the roses wrapped us round. I was never more frightened in my life, and my heart went down into my shoes as I suddenly asked myself what sister Jane would say if she could have heard what I had already said, and could see me standing there staring at Mary like a fool. The thought made me more desperate than ever, and I made another plunge.

"Yes; I lost my little sweetheart in the summerhouse yonder. She put her arms around my neck, kissed me, and said she would always be my little sweetheart. She was only twelve years old, but after that she gradually disappeared, and a young lady appeared in her place."

"Do you really remember that?" Mary asked, looking me in the face.

"Is it so easy to forget such things?"

She made no reply but looked off into the night. "Do *you* remember it?" I asked.

Still she made no reply, but the dim light of the stars showed me something in her face that was more eloquent than any words could have been. And I drew her toward me and held her in my arms, and began at that instant a new life and a new experience blissful beyond all expression.

How long we stood there I do not know. It was Mary herself who brought me back to the world and its affairs.

"Please, please tell me what you could see in me to be afraid of?"

A dozen other questions she put to me none of which I could answer. When I bade her good-night at last, and turned away, she called me back.

"Tell me truly," she said, "were n't you just a little bit jealous of Uncle Clarence when you thought he was Mr. Cowardin?"

"More than a little," I replied with such emphasis as to cause her to laugh.

There was a pause after this and I stood awkwardly waiting to be dismissed.

"Well, sir?" she suggested demurely.

"Good-night!" I said again, but still stood waiting. She came very close to me.

"Is *that* the way you say good-night?" It was the sweetest challenge that Innocence ever gave to Timidity, and though she blushed mightily, I did not allow the challenge to pass.

I returned home in a very exalted state of mind,

as may well be supposed. I seemed to be walking on the air. Unconsciously I was whistling a gay melody when I entered sister Jane's room, and the sound was so unusual, coming from me, that she, plodding away with her sewing, looked up in surprise.

"You must 'a' had a mighty tough time toting Mary home," she said as I seated myself. "I allowed she must 'a' tripped over an ant-hill and broke her neck, poor gal."

"What put that idea in your head?" I inquired.

"Why, you've been mighty nigh a half hour walking up to Cephas Bullard's and back ag'in. I can shet my eyes and go and come in less 'n five minutes, and not be bellowsed neither."

I vouchsafed no explanation, and she went on with her work. I tried to sit quietly in the chair, but the effort was beyond me. I crossed and re-crossed my legs, moved my feet about and constantly changed my position, and caught myself unconsciously snapping my thumbs and fingers.

"What did Mary have to say about her uncle?" asked sister Jane.

"Oh, Mary!" I replied, coming back to earth. My thoughts were so abstract and unusual that even the name of my dearest had a strange sound when spoken by other lips. "Well, Mary did n't have much to say."

Sister Jane looked at me again, and this time more narrowly.

"What under the sev'm stars has come over

you, William Wornum? You 're setting there acting for all the world like a jumping-jack! Have you got the fidgets? And what are you grinning at? You look like you 'd seen a monkey show out there in the garden." Then the truth seemed to dawn on her, and she burst out laughing, and laughed till the tears came in her eyes. " I 'll bet a thrip to a ginger-cake that Mary got you in a corner out there in the garden and asked you to marry her."

" She did nothing of the kind!" I cried, embarrassment lending more heat to my words than the occasion demanded.

" I know better, William Wornum. I told Mary no longer than yesterday that if she ever got you, she 'd have to pop the question herself. And now it 's happened! She 's asked you to marry her, and you 've told her you 'd have to think the matter over before you made up your mind."

" Nonsense! What do you take me for, sister Jane?" I cried.

" For a simpleton that has had his head between the leds of books so long that he don't know daylight when he sees it," she replied.

" Oh, don't I? You 'll know better shortly."

The humor that danced in her eyes faded away into a tenderer expression. She took up her work again, and spoke as if addressing it : —

" I wish I may die if I don't believe he 's had sense enough to see what everybody knows!"

" What is that?" I inquired.

"Why, that you and Mary Bullard have been head over heels in love wi' one another sence the year 1."

"Well, good-night," I said.

"Wait!" She put by her work, came to me, pushed the hair back from my forehead, and kissed me. "The Lord knows, if she loves you half as well in her way as I do in mine — and I believe in my heart she does — you'll be the happiest man in the world."

Though my dear sister has been dead for years, I can close my eyes now and feel the gentle touch of her hands, and hear the notes of love and tenderness ringing true in the tones of her voice.

The day after my memorable experience in the garden with Mary — an experience that softened and subdued all the events of my life both before and after — Jincy Meadows came to see Mandy Satterlee. He came dressed in his best, as usual, but this time he wore a different air. There was something more decisive in his manner. I chanced to be in my room when he knocked, and I opened the door and invited him in.

"Squire," he said, "did you ever ast a gal to have you?"

The question was so sudden and unexpected that it took me back as the saying is.

"That is a leading question, Jincy," I replied; "the court will have to rule it out."

"Danged if I don't believe you have, and that right lately!" he burst out after regarding me a moment. "If it's so, I hope Miss Mary is the one you ast."

"She is too good for me, Jincy," I remarked.

"Oh, I know that, squire. I know that mighty well," he assented plumply. "She's too good for anybody, when it comes right down to the plain facts. But somehow I've allers coupled you two together in my dreams. Hundreds of times in my sleep I've seen Miss Mary and you a-walkin' along, and Mandy and me a-comin' along behind. And if one half of the dream is to come true, I hope to gracious the other half will too."

"I hope so, too," I said.

"Honest, squire?" he asked eagerly.

"Why, certainly. Why not?"

"I'm mighty glad of it, squire; and I tell you now, I've come to see Mandy about them very dreams. Now, how can I git a fair chance for to see her by her own 'lone self, as it were?"

"Now is your opportunity, Jincy — as good as you'll ever have. Sister Jane has gone shopping, and Mandy is in the room back there doing some mending."

He hesitated a moment. "Squire, do I have to holla 'Hello!' in the woods, and ring a cow-bell before I go in there where she's at?"

I told him there was no need for any formality in the matter, and invited him to go right in. He shook my hand with humorous gravity.

"Good-by, squire. If you're writin' any letters to anybody soon, remember me to all kind friends

I love so dear, and over my grave shed one bright tear."

With that Jincy walked down the hallway, treading so lightly that I could hardly hear his footsteps on the floor. Presently I heard Mandy give a little scream. The hallway conveyed every sound to me through the open doors.

"Oh!" she cried; and then after a pause, "Jincy Meadows! you oughter be ashamed of yourself to come slippin' in that a-way. Where's everybody? How did you git in?"

"I crawled under the door, but don't tell anybody; they'd never believe it," Jincy replied.

"You might 'a' knocked," protested Mandy.

"I've knocked about so much that I don't want to do any more knockin'. Folks might think it was my trade."

"Oh, go off, Jincy!" cried Mandy; and then, "Have a cheer. I dunno where Miss Jane is."

"No, I'll not set down. I've jest come to tell you a dream."

"Oh, you're allers a-dreamin', Jincy."

"I don't mind it when I don't wake up hungry."

"Set down an' tell me your dream."

Whereupon Jincy told the dream he had hinted of to me, only amplifying some of the details.

"Now you reckin that dream'll ever come true, Mandy?" he asked.

"It ought n't to," she replied.

"That's mighty hard on the squire and Miss Mary," said Jincy calmly.

"Oh, I was n't talkin' about *them*," protested Mandy.

"What's the reason the other part ought n't to come true?" he insisted.

"I can't tell you, Jincy, but I can show you."

I heard her cross the hall, and stupidly wondered what reason she could show him. Then as she re-crossed the hall, the truth came to me in a flash. She had gone to fetch her child which was taking its morning nap.

"That's the reason, Jincy," she said sadly, as she returned to the room.

There was a pause, during which I judged that Jincy was subjecting the child to a critical examination.

"I 've seen bigger reasons," he remarked after a while, "but not any that was more plumper, as you may say."

I heard him walk slowly out of the room to the wide back entrance, where he stood perhaps half a minute chirruping to a mocking-bird. Then I heard him walk into the room again.

"Why, what in the world are you cryin' for, Mandy? I jest stepped out on the back porch to laugh."

"What was you laughin' at?" she cried with mingled grief and indignation.

"Why, because you said I was going to git in a dispute wi' that young un."

"I never said so," she declared.

"Why, you did, and if the squire was here I'd

prove it. You said the young un was a reason.
Now a reason is a argyment, and a argyment 's a
dispute, and on account of the dispute the most
principal part of my dream could n't come true."

" Well, I did n't mean to say all that, Jincy."

" That 's what I allowed. Now, I 'm not dis-
putin' wi' the young un, because I want to give it
the identical thing it needs."

" What 's that?" inquired Mandy.

" A daddy!" responded Jincy promptly, and,
as I thought, bluntly. " Now, I 'll ast you why
that part of my dream can't come true?"

" I ain't good enough fer you, Jincy." Mandy's
tone was full of despair.

" Well, you know I ain't much, nohow," said
Jincy.

" I don't know any sech of a thing," cried
Mandy. " You 're better 'n anybody I know."

" Then allers take the best when it 's no trouble
to git it. What about the dream? Can't it come
true?"

" Oh, I reckon."

" Don't reckon."

" Oh, go off, Jincy ; I 'll have to say Yes to git
rid of you, you pester me so !"

After a little Jincy came out, but I made it convenient to be standing on the sidewalk by the
gate.

" You need n't remember me to all kind friends
I love so dear, squire," he said, shaking my hand
again. " The dream done the business. So long !"

Mandy's announcement of the affair to sister Jane was characteristic.

"I reckon I'm the biggest fool in the world," she said by way of a beginning, and then went on with whatever work she was doing.

"What's the matter now? Have you gone and broke a piece of my blue chany?" sister Jane inquired.

"It's lots worse 'n that," replied Mandy, laughing.

"If it is you'd better be laughing on the other side of your mouth. What is it?"

"Oh, jest me an' Jincy," said Mandy, moving about the room more briskly than ever.

"Well, what about you an' Jincy?"

"Did n't I tell you I was a fool?" Mandy exclaimed with well-affected surprise. "I ain't got a grain of sense. Who is Jincy Meadows anyhow? Ever'body says he's a born loony, an' I'd a heap ruther stay here wi' you-all than to marry him — a heap ruther."

"The stars above!" cried sister Jane.

"Ain't it the truth!" said Mandy, though apropos of what I failed to discover. "We're allers a-doin' what we hain't got no more idee of doin' than the man in the moon. I declare to goodness! When I think of what a fool I reely am, it turns my stomach. But that Jincy Meadows, he come in here an' taken me so by surprise that I did n't know my own name. How he got in, I 'll never tell you, but git in he did ; an' when

I up'd an' looked, thar he stood wi' his han's in his pockets an' his mouth wide open. I dunno but what his tongue was a-hangin' out. He like to 'a' skeer'd the life out'n me."

"Then up you jumped and run to him, an' says, ' Oh, yes, Jincy! I 'll have you and thanky too,' " remarked sister Jane.

"Why, Miss Jane!" Mandy blushed red as fire. "Please 'm don't talk like that. We got to runnin' on, an' he told me about a dream he had, an' a whole lot of fool talk, an', before I know'd it, I had done up'd an' tol' him I reckon I 'd marry him. If I had n't 'a' done it, I 'd 'a' never got rid of him on the face of the earth. I never did see anybody that could pester me like Jincy Meadows can. I never had no more idee of tellin' that man that I 'd marry him than I had of flyin' — not a bit."

"Well, you might 'a' done worse," said sister Jane. "Where you 'd 'a' done better, I don't know. Jincy Meadows has got more sense than you and me and William all put together."

"You reckon!" exclaimed Mandy with a tone akin to awe in her voice.

"I know it!" sister Jane declared.

"I don't keer," Mandy protested; "his havin' sense don't hender me from bein' a fool. I know I look like one."

"It 's mighty easy to be one," was sister Jane's comment, and there, for the time, the matter dropped.

Late that afternoon Clarence Bullard came in with our lad. The two had been off in the woods, and there, in the solitude of the forest, Freddy was told the facts of his history that were already familiar to sister Jane and myself. The lad did n't seem to be very much elated over the change in his fortunes.

"Just think of me calling Dan 'Uncle Clarence'!" he said with fine scorn. "I'll bet they'll want me to call Miss Jane and Mr. William by some new name. I won't do it!"

"You don't have to, honey. Jest call us anything that pops into your mind, and if we know you're a-callin' us we'll come a-runnin'!" remarked sister Jane soothingly.

"Sure enough?" The frown on the lad's face gave place to a pleased expression.

"Try it some day," said sister Jane with great apparent earnestness.

The youngster laughed, but the puzzled expression soon came back on his face. "But if I was to call Dan 'Uncle Clarence,' he would n't come; he ain't used to it."

"Call me plain Dan just as long as you want to," said his uncle.

"Yes, but I'll know I ought not to," the lad insisted. "I don't mind saying 'sister Mary,' but all the rest of it will choke me before I get through with it — I just know it will."

But we managed to soothe him after a while, and when he had dressed himself in his best, which was as good as money could buy in our village, he went with his uncle to his father's house. Both wanted sister Jane and myself to go with them, the boy being keen for our company ; but we thought that our presence at such a time would be in the nature of an intrusion. So we sat at home and sent our kindest thoughts and best wishes along with our friends.

It was all a seven days' wonder in the village, especially among the negroes, who imagined that only a miracle could have brought the child safely home after so long a time. Old Sol, Colonel Bullard's man-of-all-work, who always pretended to be wiser than anybody else, was not behindhand now. When I saw him a day or two afterwards, cleaning up and clearing away the summer's growth in the garden, he leaned on his rake long enough to say :

"I know'd in reason, Marse William, dat dat ar chil' wa'n't no common chil'. Kaze he useter come down yander ter de stable whar I wuz at, an' he'd sorter mope 'roun' like he los' sumpin'. I say, I did, 'What de matter, honey?' He say, 'Look like ter me dey ought ter be a gray hoss in dat stall dar, an' a side-saddle hangin' on dat peg dar.' I say, 'Dey useter be dar many 's de day gone by, but how come you ter know it, honey?' He say, 'I dunno how come. I speck I des up an' dremp it.' I shuck my head, I did, an' 'low ter myse'f, 'Uh-uh! sumpin' u'er gwine ter happen 'roun' yer sho.' An' you see yo'se'f, Marse William, what done happen."

It turned out that the lad really had a vague recollection about his parents and his home, but he was ashamed to say anything about it at the time.

Not long after the episodes that have been related, another event occurred that had a sobering effect on some of our people. The day had been sultry for September, and for hours not a breath of wind stirred the leaves on the trees. About three o'clock black clouds began to roll in from the southwest. Among them, and in the centre, was a great whorl of dun-colored vapor that seemed to rise higher and reach lower than the rest.

Before I could realize it — almost before I could shut the doors — a terrific storm burst upon us with a roar so deafening and a force so violent that it seemed as if the great globe on which we stood would be shaken to its very centre, if not torn apart. It was a roar such as might be expected if the thunders of heaven should drop from the sky and run along the ground trailing their deafening chorus after them. The storm was over and gone in five minutes, being followed by a downpour of hail. Then the air grew cold as winter, and a half hour afterwards the sun was shining as brightly as ever. But the storm left with me a new knowledge of the weakness and impotence of man, and with it came a feeling of depression almost unaccountable. And yet, as I found out afterwards, the centre of the storm had passed a mile to the west of us, striking fairly across the Beshears place.

Late that afternoon, Mose, who was still the

foreman of the place, came knocking at our door
with a small sack full of gold and silver coins of
all descriptions — about five hundred dollars in all.
The wind had blown the dwelling-house to atoms,
and in the ruins of one of the chimneys the negroes
had picked up these coins.

A feeling of sorrow came over me as I handled
the money. This was the precious store that had
been hidden away by Miss Polly and Miss Becky
— the accumulation of years of pinching and sav-
ing. The hand of the Almighty had lifted the
cover from their hoard, and scattered it about with
the rest of the rubbish.

I wondered that the negroes did not appropriate
the money for their own use, and said so.

" Well, suh," explained Mose, " dat ar money
b'longed ter Miss Polly and Miss Becky. Dey
yearned it, an' dey hidden it dar. Hit's der'n.
Mo' 'n dat, dey done losted der min's, an' when anybody taken money fum folks like dat, sump'n bleeze
ter happen to um. Dat what dey tells me."

I placed the money in custody of the court, glad
to be rid of the hoard and have it off my mind.

What remains to tell has practically all been
told. Heaven was kind to us all, and especially to
me, singling me out, as it seemed, for as much
happiness as ever falls to man's lot in this world.
I saw, too, that, though the wounds that sin makes
may be deep and grievous, the sorrow that repentance brings can heal and hide every one. We saw
Mandy Satterlee frequently after she became Mrs.

Meadows, and though she was cheerful and contented, the light of penitence was always in her eyes.

As for Colonel Bullard, he gave his closing years to good deeds, and if penitence did not shine in his eyes, it manifested itself in his life and made its influence felt throughout the community.